BACKLASH

ALSO BY LYNDA LA PLANTE

Fiction

BACKLASH

An Anna Travis Novel

LYNDA LA PLANTE

BOURBON STREET BOOKS

An Imprint of HarperCollins*Publishers*
www.harpercollins.com

FIRST U.S. EDITION

Library of Congress Cataloging-in-Publication Data

La Plante, Lynda.
    Backlash : an Anna Travis novel / Lynda La Plante. — First U.S. Edition.
        pages cm.
    "Originally published in Great Britain in 2010 by Simon & Schuster UK Ltd."—t.p. verso.
        ISBN 978-0-06-213434-9 (pbk. original : alk. paper) — ISBN 978-0-06-213435-6 (electronic) 1. Travis, Anna (Fictitious character)—Fiction. 2. Murder—Investigation—England—London—Fiction. 3. Women detectives—England—London—Fiction. 4. London (England)—Fiction. I. Title.
    PR6062.A65B33 2013
    823'.914—dc23
                                                                                                2013017479

13 14 15 16 17   RRD   10 9 8 7 6 5 4 3 2 1

To the memory of George Ryan

Sometimes in life you are fortunate to meet someone who has a special energy. George was a young woman when she joined my company. She became an important part of my life at probably the most important time. I was so proud of her achievements, and to see her marry Glenn and become mother to two wonderful children – Felix and Isobella – was a joyous time. George was vibrant and loving and leaves everyone who had the fortune to know her sad and bewildered by her passing. This book is dedicated to her memory, and my admiration for her burns bright.

Acknowledgements

Special thanks and gratitude go to all my team at La Plante Productions: Liz Thorburn, Richard Dobbs-Grove, Cass Sutherland, Sara Johnson, Karol Griffiths and Ellen Steers for all their committed and valuable support.

Many thanks also go to Duncan Heath and Sue Rodgers at Independent Talent Agency and Stephen Ross, Dan Ross and Andrew Bennet-Smith at Ross, Bennet-Smith.

To the stars of the *Above Suspicion* series, Kelly Reilly and Ciarán Hinds, I give thanks for their dedication to the show and their strong portrayal of my characters.

My thanks for the constant encouragement from my literary agent, Gill Coleridge, and the team at Rogers, Coleridge & White.

The publication of this book would not have been possible without the hard work and support of Susan Opie and the team at Simon & Schuster: Ian Chapman, Suzanne Baboneau, Kerr MacRae, Nigel Stoneman and Dawn Burnett; I am very happy to be working with such a terrific and creative group of people.

Chapter One

'Quiet night so far, isn't it?'

'Yeah, an' we've still got seven hours to go before the shift finishes!'

The two uniformed officers in the night duty patrol car were chatting whilst driving past a council estate in East London, and all was quiet in the residential street, in contrast to the numerous clubs, bars, restaurants and buzzing nightlife of Shoreditch, just down the road. And so the van bearing the logo *KIDDIES PARTY DATES* stood out as it failed to give way for a pedestrian waiting at the zebra crossing.

'Is he on another planet?' said the officer driving.

'Bit late for a kiddies' party,' his colleague joked. 'Go pull him over, we've nothing better to do at the moment.'

As they drew closer the van driver began to accelerate away from them and suddenly, without indicating, took a sharp left down a side street.

'He's trying to avoid us. Turn the blues and twos on,' said the officer at the wheel as he sped after the van and turned into the side street. 'Where's he disappeared to? There's no way he could have made it to the other end of the road without us seeing him.'

As the police car moved slowly down the street they saw

the van parked up between two cars with its lights off. On their approach the driver ducked down, seemingly avoiding their headlights, and the officers could clearly see the van's logo silhouetted in the patrol car's blue flashing light: a grinning clown's face with balloons and decorations painted around it.

'My kids would run a mile if they saw that bloody clown's face,' said the officer driving as he pulled up in the middle of the road.' Gives me the creeps. I wouldn't hire them.'

He got out and walked casually towards the driver, shining his torch into the van, and tapped on the window, indicating for the man to open it. As the window was slowly lowered, the driver put up a hand to shield his face.

'Leave the keys in the ignition and step out of the vehicle, please.'

'Why?'

'Because I've asked you to and you're acting suspiciously.'

The driver suddenly grabbed the ignition keys and tried to start the van. The officer yanked open the door, pulled the man's hand away from the keys and dragged him out of the vehicle while his partner, seeing what was happening, hurried out of the patrol car to help.

'Hands where I can see them.'

'I was just having a rest. I've been working all afternoon.'

The officers quickly had the driver face down on the pavement with his hands cuffed behind his back while they patted him down, discovering a worn leather wallet, which contained a few five-pound notes and a library card in the name of Henry Oates.

'Just stay still, Mr Oates. Is that your name?'

'Yeah, Henry Oates.'

Oates didn't argue, but remained calm, as one officer pulled him up from the pavement and pressed him against the side of the van, while his partner returned to the patrol car to check on its registration plates and the identity of its driver.

'You've been working, you say?'

'Yeah.'

'Do you live round here?'

Oates straightened and half turned. The officer pushed him in the small of his back.

'Just stay where you are. This shouldn't take long.'

'Christ.'

'This your van, is it?'

'It belongs to a friend. I just help him out.'

It turned out that the van was neither insured nor registered to Oates, and the MOT was out of date. The control room radio operator informed them that there had been a number of overnight break-ins in the area, leading the two officers to suspect that Oates might be involved and could be using the vehicle to carry stolen property.

'Why were you trying to avoid us?' asked the police driver.

'I wasn't. I didn't even see you. I've parked up here cos it's near home.'

'What's in the back of the van?'

'For fuck's sake, just party gear, balloons, pumps and stuff like that,' Oates replied, becoming noticeably more agitated as he tried to turn towards the officers.

'So we won't find any nicked gear then?'

'No way,' Oates said as he suddenly started to gasp for breath and mutter something inaudible as one officer started to walk to the rear of the van.

The officer opened the back door of the van and leaned forward with his torch then suddenly jumped back startled as a helium balloon with the grotesque clown's face on it wafted almost mockingly out of the van. Composing himself he continued his search, making out a number of cardboard boxes with something large wrapped in black bin liners between them.

The officer leaned in closer so he could reach the edge of the bin liner without getting into the van. He pulled at it gently, then gave it a hard yank, at which part of the bin liner came away easily. The beam of his torch fell on what appeared to be matted blonde hair covered in wet blood. Cautiously he leaned further forward and pulled away more of the bin liner. Now he realized that what he was looking at was a body – a woman's body. Slowly he reached out and felt her neck for a pulse, but although she was still warm it was clear she was dead.

Easing himself from the van, he radioed for immediate backup, before turning back to his fellow officer and Oates.

'Well, well, Henry,' he said. 'What sort of party have you been to tonight?'

During the journey to Hackney Police Station Oates stopped muttering, even appearing to accept his situation in a resigned, offhanded manner, and on arrival was booked in just after midnight on Friday, 12 October 2012. He said that he was thirty-eight and had no permanent address because he was living rough. He was given a clean police-issue tracksuit to wear, then after his DNA sample and fingerprints were taken Oates was allowed to speak with the duty solicitor on the phone, who advised him to say nothing and informed him that an Adan Kumar would attend the station in the morning to represent him. Oates was then placed in a cell for the night. He asked for a cup of tea, but made no reference to why he had been arrested.

The next morning at 5 a.m., much to the annoyance of his wife, DCI Mike Lewis was awoken by the sound of his mobile vibrating on his bedside table.

'Mike Lewis,' he grunted into the phone.

'Sorry to disturb you, sir, this is DC Roy Hunter from the murder squad. A woman's body has been discovered in the back of a van over in Hackney and they've arrested a bloke called Henry Oates.'

Mike sat up, and his wife moaned as he threw the duvet to one side.

'What?' Mike asked, still not fully awake.

'DCS Hedges is heading up the investigation and he wants you in for a 7 a.m. handover briefing at Hackney Police Station.'

'Gimme the address . . . no, the crime scene!'

He jotted down the address and leaned over to kiss his wife and give her his apologies, but she was fast asleep. Dressed and using his battery shaver he headed across the landing and peeked in to see his twin boys, who were still asleep, before quietly heading down the stairs.

En route to the station Mike visited the scene, and was immediately taken to one side by the Crime Scene Manager, who told him that a handbag had been recovered containing documents in the name of Justine Marks.

The body was still in the back of the van as there were a lot of items around it that needed to be photographed then seized and bagged before she could be removed and taken to the mortuary. The post mortem was to take place at 2 p.m. that afternoon.

Mike decided that he would carry out a short interview with Henry Oates beforehand. Paul Barolli would assist him in doing so, while DC Barbara Maddox and DC Joan Falkland, with whom Mike had worked many times previously, set up the incident room at Hackney Police Station and obtained details of any next of kin for Justine Marks.

Mike Lewis and Paul Barolli entered the custody suite interview room. Oates was sitting on one side of the table with his legal representative, Adan Kumar, by his side. They sat down opposite Oates and Kumar. Paul informed Oates that the interview would be recorded and leaned over to the DVD equipment attached to the wall and pressed the start button, causing the recorder and two wall-mounted cameras in the room to light up. Mike introduced himself and Paul then cautioned Oates, telling him that he didn't have to answer any questions but that anything he did say might be given in evidence. Mike was about to commence his questioning when to his and Paul's surprise Oates suddenly sat upright and then leaned across the table.

'Right then, I may as well tell you what I already told my solicitor. Now where shall I start – or should I ask where you would like me to start?' Oates enquired.

Mike was about to ask a question when Oates raised his hand, indicating to Mike to be quiet.

'If you want me to tell you what happened then please don't interrupt me.'

Mike and Paul looked at each other in surprise, taken aback by Oates's willingness to speak freely and Kumar allowing him to do so. Mike decided it was best to hear what Oates had to say before putting any questions to him and allowed him to continue.

Oates told his story: he had borrowed the van off the owner James Hully, who was selling it. He had taken it out at night for a test drive only because he didn't have a driving licence or insurance and he knew there would be less traffic and fewer police about. He went on his own to the Eagle pub in Hackney just before closing time where he'd noticed a group of 'pissed-up' women. After one pint he left to go home and was driving down the road when he saw one of the women and was worried because she was drunk and on her own so he stopped to offer her a lift, but she had refused and continued to walk on. Oates had followed her and asked her again if she needed a lift. This time she had been, in his words, 'Rude, told me to leave her alone.' He had driven past her for about fifty yards and then stopped and got out to tell her he was just trying to help. Oates claimed that she told him her name was Justine and she agreed to accept his lift and got into the passenger seat. She agreed to have sex with him and he had driven to some waste ground by Hackney Marshes and they had both got into the back of the van to 'do the business'. After they had sex she suddenly turned hysterical and violent, kicking him in the balls, and he had panicked and hit her to keep her quiet. Oates explained that he had just reached out for anything close to force her to stop screaming. He thought he had struck her with a section of the pump used to blow up the balloons.

*

7

Mike was not happy with Oates's claim that Justine's death was unintentional but he knew before a further interview that he would need not only the results of the post mortem, but also to speak with Justine's friends who were at the pub and importantly with any next of kin, who should by now have been traced by Barbara. Before ending the interview Mike asked Oates where he currently lived.

'I live rough.'

'Then why did you say you left the pub to go home?' Mike asked.

'I don't have a home as such, just a squat that I use sometimes.'

'Where?' asked Mike.

'Number eight, Holcroft Road,' Oates indignantly replied.

'That's a two-minute walk from the Eagle pub where you first saw Justine, isn't it?' Barolli enquired.

Oates made no reply and Mike Lewis informed him that he would remain in police custody while 'the squat' was searched, the post mortem carried out and some further enquiries were made about him. Oates suddenly became agitated.

'I've told you what happened. It was an accident so why do you need to keep me here?'

'You don't just hit someone by accident, Mr Oates, and the post mortem will tell us if your story is a lie or not. So unless there is another version of events that you want to tell us about, this interview will be terminated.'

There was a long pause; Mike began to gather up his paperwork and Barolli was about to turn the recording equipment off when Oates said that there was something he'd like to tell them.

'Are you going to tell us what really happened to Justine?' asked Barolli.

'I've already told you.'

Mike said that he had had enough of Oates's truculent behaviour and that the interview was over.

'Justine wasn't the first. Before her was a ginger girl, exchange student from Dublin called Julia.'

'Are you saying you've committed other murders or you know who has?'

'If you let me finish I'll tell you. Julia was about a year and a half ago, but she was the second.'

'You just said that the student Julia was before Justine,' Mike said, and Oates interrupted him.

'No. You're not listening to me, are you! Julia was the second, long before her was Rebekka Jordan – she was the first.'

Mike was taken aback by Oates's sudden admissions, particularly about Rebekka Jordan. There had been extensive press surrounding her disappearance just over five years ago when she was only thirteen years old. The enquiry, which had been quickly moved up from a missing person case to a suspected child abduction and probable murder, had been headed up by none other than Detective Chief Superintendent James Langton. Mike knew that he needed detailed answers from Oates, who appeared to relish the sudden renewed attention, but with Kumar present he would have to play this by the book as he needed Oates to make a full and frank confession concerning any other murders he might have committed.

'Have you murdered other women?' Mike asked.

'You're the detective, you tell me,' Oates replied and laughed loudly.

Kumar was quick to interject, suggesting that it was a good time for a break as he would like to have a private consultation with his client before he answered any more questions. Mike told Oates that he didn't have to take Kumar's advice as this was his opportunity to say what happened to Rebekka Jordan and Julia.

'Are we playing roulette, officer?'

'Oates decides if he wants to play, Mr Kumar, not you!'

'Well I am advising him to make no further comment.'

'It's a simple yes or no, Oates. Did you kill Rebekka Jordan?'

Oates said nothing but arrogantly turned and nodded to Kumar.

'Looks like Henry wants to take my advice, DCI Lewis.'

As Mike stormed out of the room he barked at Barolli to close the interview and then meet him in the office.

Mike was still seething by the time he had climbed the two flights of stairs to the allocated murder squad office, where he found Joan and Barbara were inputting data into the HOLMES computers and preparing the incident board. It was immediately obvious to everyone present that DCI Lewis was in a foul mood.

'Joan, request a copy of the Rebekka Jordan cold case file from archives and check with the national missing persons bureau for a Dublin girl by the name of Julia. Get them to search back over the last five years.'

'A few more details would be helpful, sir. I thought we were dealing with the Justine Marks case?'

'And maybe a whole lot more by the looks of it, so just do as I ask. Where are we with next of kin?'

Joan informed him that Justine's husband was Simon Marks, a stockbroker in the City, and arrangements had been made for a detective to take him to the mortuary at 1 p.m. to formally identify the body of his wife.

Mike sat in his office, fully aware that there was a lot to do and little time in which to do it. He wondered what Oates was up to and if his tentative admissions to two other murders were even true. It didn't make sense that Oates should be lying about Rebekka and the unknown Irish girl Julia, however Mike knew both cases would have to be fully investigated and Oates's involvement proved or disproved. The burning question was when, if at all, should he inform DCS Langton, as he was currently on sick leave recovering from a knee operation and DCS Hedges was in temporary charge of the murder squads. Mike Lewis made up his mind and asked Barbara to get everyone gathered for an office meeting in thirty minutes.

With the team all there Mike gave them a rundown of the interview with Oates, unaware that Paul Barolli had already filled them in on why he was in such a bad mood. Mike had decided that the Justine Marks murder would be the initial priority and he himself would attend the mortuary for the identification by Simon Marks. He told Barbara to contact the Eagle pub and see if they had any CCTV and to arrange interviews with Justine's work colleagues. Joan informed Mike that she had asked 'Mispers' to run an enquiry on any Irish girls with the name Julia but it could be some time before they got back with any results on such limited details for a five-year span.

Joan also said that the owner of the van that Oates had borrowed was indeed a James Hully, who had a history of petty crimes and had, he insisted, been sick in bed when

Oates had borrowed his van. His wife maintained that her husband had not left their flat for two days and that on the night of the 11th of October he had had a very high temperature and was in bed very ill. Hully lived on the estate close to the pub and had access to a lockup garage where he kept his van. He claimed that it was not insured or licensed because of poor business and he was planning on selling it. Oates had told him he was interested in buying the vehicle and wanted to test drive it so he let him try it out while he was ill as long as he did a few party deliveries for him. Hully alleged that he did not know Oates very well, but had met him occasionally at a local pub. He said they had played darts together and during a game he had mentioned to Oates that he was selling his van and quitting his job as a children's entertainer. Apart from that, he knew nothing more about Oates or where he lived.

Before finishing the meeting Mike Lewis raised a couple of actions that he felt needed urgent attention.

'Joan, I need you to prepare a full file on Oates. I want to know everything about him since the day he was born. Paul, contact the Crime Scene Manager and organize a full forensic search of the squat address Oates gave us.'

Mike then thanked them all for their hard work so far but continued that as there was still a lot to do he would have to cancel all weekend leave for the team. There were a few sighs around the room as they got up from their chairs to go home.

'Hold it. I haven't finished yet,' Mike said and they all sat down again.

'The fact that we are looking at Oates for other possible murders is to stay within these four walls and there will be serious repercussions if there's any press leaks. DCS

Hedges or I will decide as and when DCS Langton should be informed of any developments concerning the Jordan case.'

Simon Marks was devastated and needed to be helped from the mortuary viewing room. He told them that Justine was twenty-seven years old and was a bank clerk at a Hackney branch of the NatWest Bank. She'd been joining some of her co-workers for a baby shower party after work on the 11th of October. She had not taken her car into work as she knew they would be drinking and the girls had ordered taxis to take them home. Justine told him not to wait up for her as she would be late, and when he discovered she had not returned the following morning he had not been that concerned as he thought she might have stayed over with one of her friends. Simon only became worried later that morning when he called her work to be told that she had not come in. He had started to ring round various friends when the police arrived to give him the terrible news.

Whilst at the mortuary Mike, anxious to know the cause of death, spoke with the pathologist, who was at the time still completing the external examination of the body, photographing, measuring and detailing all the injuries. He said that he would not be able to give an exact cause of death until he had completed a full internal examination as well, but Mike pressed him for his opinion on his initial observations. It was immediately clear that Oates had been lying about Justine's death.

When the body first arrived at the mortuary the pathologist had carefully cut open the bin liners to preserve them for fingerprints. He had noted that Justine's bra had been pulled up around her neck and twisted so tightly that the hook and eyes of the strap had left puncture marks in the nape of her neck. Her tights and knickers, although still on her, were both torn and ripped. Her leather zip-up boots had scuffmarks on both heels, which implied she might have been dragged backwards along the pavement and into the back of the van. Justine had also suffered a heavy blow to the back of her head with a blunt instrument, which had caused a depressed fracture and an indentation mark in the shape of a half-moon. The pathologist was of the opinion that the head injury probably didn't kill her but it would certainly have knocked her unconscious. From the severe bruising and scratch marks to her thighs and vagina, it appeared that she might have been raped whilst unable to struggle or defend herself.

All her clothing, swabs and toxicology samples had already been taken to the forensic lab for examination. Because of the head injury and the possibility Justine might have been strangled or suffocated to death the brain would have to be left in formaldehyde for two weeks and then sent to an expert in forensic neuropathology for examination, which would further delay the pathologist's final report and his finding on the actual cause of death.

Mike Lewis asked if a balloon pump handle could have caused the head injury but the pathologist doubted that it would be heavy enough or leave the half-moon impression. Mike put in a quick call to the lab and asked for details of items that had been recovered from the back of the van. Amongst them was a nine-inch heavy-duty spanner which the pathologist said could leave the type of head injury that Justine had suffered. Mike asked the lab to make the spanner a priority.

*

On his return to the incident room Barbara informed Mike that there was no CCTV at the pub but she and other officers had spoken with Justine's colleagues. On the evening of the 11th at about 7 p.m. eight of them had taken over a small private room in the Eagle pub, and they had ordered food and bottles of wine to be brought up from the bar. The evening was to be a baby shower for their co-worker Avril, who was expecting her first child, but as she had decided that she would not return to work after the birth, it was also a farewell party. At just after eleven the party broke up. Two of the girls' husbands had turned up to give them a lift home and Avril, who had not been drinking and had her car, had offered to give two of the girls a ride home as they lived quite close to each other. The other two got into a taxi, but Justine had said she would get her own one as she lived in the opposite direction. The last sighting of Justine was as the girls were driven off in their taxi. She had waved to them from outside the pub, standing in the car park.

All the girls were certain that Justine had been the last to leave. None of them could recall ever seeing Henry Oates and not one of them said that Justine was the type of girl to get into a stranger's car, let alone agree to have sex with someone she didn't know. Justine was a very calm, quiet woman and in a loving relationship with her husband. Avril, in particular, was inconsolable. She said that Justine was one of the nicest people she had ever known, always helpful and had bought a beautiful gift for her forthcoming baby. She wept when she said that Justine had confided that she and her husband Simon were desperate for a child and were saving for IVF treatment as Justine had some medical problem with her fallopian tubes. She was adamant that Justine would not have accepted a lift from Oates; she was by far too cautious.

Barbara said their accounts of the evening matched Oates's description of seeing the group of girls leaving the pub just after closing time, but if Justine had been going to get her own taxi home it seemed strange that she should start to walk up the road as Oates had described. Mike wondered if yet again Oates was lying and he had in fact hit her over the head and dragged her into the van whilst still in the Eagle car park.

Barolli had obtained a search warrant and gained access to Henry Oates's property. It was a basement squat in a run-down Victorian terraced house and was only three miles from the estate in Hackney. Although the present owner wanted to demolish it he was unable to do so due to a preservation order and the premises had not been lawfully occupied for six years. The owner didn't actually object to the squatters as he hoped it would encourage the council to lift the preservation order. The three rooms used by Oates were filthy and stank of stale food and urine. A team of forensic officers began the careful search for evidence.

The wardrobes were full of dirty clothes and boots and there appeared to be no clean laundry. The single bed was disgusting, with filthy sheets and blankets heaped on a bare mattress. They did find numerous items of women's clothing in a black bin liner and these were removed for further examination. The bathroom contained worn, dirty towels and a shower curtain grey with a hideous residue of grime hanging limply over a brown-stained bath. The toilet looked as if it had been out of order for some time; the bowl stank and the chain to flush it was broken. The team found numerous knives in the small kitchen annexe, plus a carpenter's bag that contained hacksaws and hammers and two large sharpened screwdrivers. These were also taken away to be tested by the forensic team. The overpowering smell in the kitchen came from fifteen beer bottles lined up by the back door; they all contained urine. Opening the back door there were even more bottles, which were smashed, and the officers could only presume that Oates had used them to piss into as his toilet was broken.

'What an absolute shithole,' Barolli told Lewis. 'Toilet full of piss and crap, not to mention the floor and—'

'For Chrissake, I don't need any more description, Paul. The guy is a pig and obviously lived like one,' Mike said, shaking his head.

'They got bags of stuff to be sifted through at the forensic lab. Poor bastards'll need to wear masks, everything stinks,' Paul further informed Mike, who walked off into his office.

As Lewis and Barolli prepared for a further interview with Oates, Joan again spoke with missing persons, hoping to identify the woman called Julia that Oates said he had killed over a year ago, but as yet they had not found a match. Mike gave instructions for Joan to continue pressing them for a result and asked what she had found out about Oates's background. She'd discovered from her enquiries with Jobseeker's that he was unemployed and living on benefits. He had worked spasmodically at various building sites as an unskilled labourer, but had been in and out of work for many years. He was divorced and his wife and their two children had returned to live in Scotland eight years ago.

*

Mike Lewis and Paul Barolli questioned Oates for the second time with Adan Kumar, his solicitor, present. Oates was delighted that they wanted to speak with him again and he seemed in an almost euphoric mood. Mike went over the Justine Marks murder first but Oates calmly and firmly maintained that her death was an accident and he had never meant to hurt her, repeating that she had come on to him for sex. When Mike informed Oates of his visit to the mortuary, the bra round Justine's neck, her head injury, torn clothing and the bruising consistent with rape, Oates accused him of lying and trying to fit him up with murder. He then started spurting out one name after another, saying they were all well-known cases where the police had 'stitched them up'. Mike had never heard of any of the names and Oates was rambling so fast that he and Barolli had difficulty in following what he was saying. Realizing that he was not going to budge on Justine's death, Mike was content that Oates's performance would show a jury he was a conniving but not a very convincing liar.

Mike now moved on to the disappearance of Rebekka Jordan. No sooner had he mentioned her name than Oates became noticeably irritated, chewing his bottom lip and repeatedly beating his right foot on the floor like a distressed animal. Mike asked him if he had abducted and killed her. Oates snapped back that what he said before was all bullshit and made up 'for a bit of a laugh' and he knew Rebekka Jordan's name because of all the news coverage the case had received. When Mike asked why he had suddenly become so upset and defensive, Oates replied it was because he knew that the police would try and fit him up with the Rebekka Jordan murder as well.

*

Mike Lewis walked away from Oates sickened, but determined to put the loathsome creature away for the murder of Justine Marks. He also intended to thoroughly investigate the other cases. The CPS gave the go-ahead to charge Oates with the murder of Justine Marks and so he appeared at the magistrates' court the next morning. Kumar made no application for bail and Oates was remanded in custody in Wandsworth Prison to await trial for murder. Mike, who had attended the hearing, took the CPS solicitor aside to tell her about Oates's admissions regarding Rebekka Jordan and the girl called Julia, and that he would be making further enquiries.

Back at the incident room, Joan informed Mike that there were a few possible hits about Julia from 'Mispers' and that Barbara had gone over to their offices to get copies of the reports. Meanwhile, the Rebekka Jordan case file and Langton's investigation report had been collected from archives overnight and were in his office.

Mike was taken aback. The thick file of documents for the Jordon case made it obvious that Langton had left no stone unturned. After nearly two years of enquiries with hundreds of statements, Langton had been unable to uncover a suspect. Rebekka Jordan had disappeared after taking a riding lesson at her local stables in Shepherd's Bush. She was last seen on CCTV footage walking from the stables towards Shepherd's Bush Tube Station, wearing a backpack believed to contain her riding hat. There were no blackmail notes, no calls and no sighting of the little girl, even after the extensive press coverage and television crime show requests for anyone with information to come forward. Thousands of photographs of Rebekka had been posted up by her family as well as the police, along with a description of what she was wearing the last time she had been seen: a yellow polo-neck sweater, jodhpurs, a riding jacket and black boots. All these items of clothing were replicated for a reconstruction using a lookalike girl to re-enact her last walk from the stables. Again, it had brought in no useful information. Rebekka had disappeared without trace.

Mike Lewis was totally drained after looking over the files that now covered his desk for nearly three hours. Was it possible that Henry Oates was telling them the truth? Had he been involved in the murder of Rebekka Jordan, or was he making up the details in some sick game that he wanted to play with them? There was a knock at his door and Paul Barolli entered.

'We were wondering what time you wanted to call it a day. A few of the team have evening arrangements, it being a Saturday, but I'm up for a pint if you fancy one.'

'Everyone can knock off at five and then tomorrow I want the case file and statements for Justine Marks put together so we can concentrate on the Jordan case from Monday.'

'You think he's bullshitting us?' Barolli asked, thumbing through a file of witness statements.

'Christ knows – he clearly lied about how Justine Marks died then says he killed Rebekka Jordan and a Julia who we don't even know exists yet. To be honest I couldn't tell you, but I can't just ignore his claims, lies or not.'

'No way you can do that, especially not with the Jordan girl. It's bloody Langton, Mike, he ran the enquiry into Rebekka Jordan's disappearance. You're going to have to run all this by him.' Barolli tapped the file in front of him.' This must have hurt; no result after this amount of work.'

'Yeah. I know he's probably hurting right now, he's just had knee surgery. I don't even know if he's out of hospital.'

Barolli grinned. 'Well that should keep him out of our hair. He'll come down on this like a ton of bricks. You know him, hates to lose and an unsolved case is always hard to stomach.'

'I've got to call Hedges first and update him as he's the boss while Langton's off sick. To be honest I'd like some guidance from Langton and if this Julia links to a "Misper" there will be mountains of work, more staff needed and it's all going to cost.'

'Fancy that pint then?'

'No thanks, I promised the wife a bottle of wine and a takeaway curry.'

Mike phoned Hedges, who seemed to be upset that his evening in front of the television was being interrupted. Mike tried to be as brief as he could, going over the salient points of the investigation so far and requesting more staff. Hedges said that more staff was not an option as Mike had no direct evidence as yet to link Oates to Rebekka Jordan's disappearance and as far as he could see the name Julia had just been plucked out of thin air by Oates.

'DCS Langton was in charge of the original investigation into the disappearance of Rebekka Jordan so I wondered if I should make contact with him about the latest development concerning Oates?' Mike asked cautiously, knowing that Hedges and Langton were not the best of friends.

'That's entirely up to you, DCI Lewis, but while he is off sick I am in charge of the murder squads so any lines of enquiry he raises will go through me for approval,' Hedges curtly replied.

'Yes, sir, and I'm sorry for bothering you when you're busy but have you considered getting Sky Plus so you can pause live TV when your viewing pleasure is interrupted?' Mike asked tongue-in-cheek but his irony was wasted on Hedges who simply put the phone down.

Mike was just switching his office light off when he saw Barbara come through the door, clutching a folder.

'I'm just off home – I thought you'd be long gone by now.'

'No, sir, I've been at "Mispers" all day looking over files.'

'The look on your face tells me I'm not going to like this.'

'Well it's only a possible, but her name's Fidelis Julia Flynn, aged twenty-one. She's originally from Dublin but was living in Kilburn, had ginger hair and has been missing for about eighteen months.'

'You said her name was Fidelis.'

'Yes but all her friends know her as Julia. Told them she preferred it to Fidelis.' Barbara handed the file over to Mike. '"Mispers" made a lot of enquiries, took a shedload of statements, but nothing, just like Rebekka she disappeared without a trace.'

Mike looked at the young woman's photograph on the front of the file. 'In some ways I hoped that Oates was lying. Not because I don't want another case to investigate, but it's the thought that another young girl has probably been beaten, raped, then murdered, leaving a whole family destroyed by one man.'

'Sorry, sir.'

'Don't be sorry, you're just doing your job. I'll look over the Flynn file at home tonight.'

Mike checked the time and decided he'd put off the call to Langton until he'd read the Flynn 'Misper' file. He also felt way out of his depth, but wouldn't want anyone to know it. The Henry Oates investigation could make or break his career. He needed a good night's sleep to determine how to approach the case because it could easily spiral out of his control. Mike knew if he was to take on the Rebekka Jordan and Fidelis Julia Flynn investigation as well as that of Justine Marks then Hedges would have to give him a very big team of officers, even more so as one of those cold cases had been headed up by DCS James Langton.

Chapter Two

DCI Anna Travis was having an enjoyable Sunday morning at her private health club. She had recently taken up a post DCS James Langton had recommended her for, as DCI in charge of Specialist Casework Investigations running a team of experienced detectives finding new lines of enquiry in unsolved murder cases. Anna was happy in her new role, particularly appreciating that the hours were not as long as in her previous position and it was rare that she had to work weekends.

After an advanced aerobics class she relaxed in the Jacuzzi and sauna and was looking forward to a light lunch at the club bar followed by a lazy afternoon in front of the television with a glass of wine and a DVD. Having showered and dressed, Anna checked her mobile, only to discover there were three missed calls from James Langton and a curt text message saying, 'Where are you, call me now!' She was surprised by this and irritated by his intrusion on her day off; she knew he had lately undergone knee surgery and she had a sinking feeling that something had gone wrong, but she nevertheless pressed the call button. He picked up immediately.

'Travis! Where the hell are you?'

'I was trying to relax at my health club. Are you all right?'

'I need you to come and see me a.s.a.p. I'm at home.'

'I thought you were in hospital?'

'No, I checked out yesterday. How long will it take you to get over to me?'

'Well unless you're dying I would like to have my lunch first. Is it really that important on a Sunday?'

'Yes it is and I'll tell you why when you get here.'

He hung up. Typically brusque without even a hint of why he suddenly needed to speak with her. Anna had not actually seen or spoken with Langton for months and although she was aware he would be on sick leave for at least eight weeks after his operation, she wondered what could be so urgent that he needed to disrupt her day off.

When Mike Lewis arrived at the station that morning he thanked the team for coming in on a Sunday and immediately put up on the incident board a picture of Fidelis Julia Flynn that had been taken when she was a bridesmaid at her sister's wedding. Joan remarked on how much Fidelis had the Celtic look with her curly auburn hair, green eyes, freckles and soft complexion. Although her innocent beauty was evident it seemed overshadowed and saddened by the thought that Henry Oates had probably murdered her.

Mike informed the team that Fidelis liked to be known as Julia and that she had come over from Dublin, in September 2010, to study at the City University. She had spent her first term in the university's halls of residence and over Christmas had answered an advert in *Time Out* to share a flat with two other female students in Kilburn. To help pay her rent she worked part-time at a nearby Texaco garage. Mike said that about eight weeks after she moved in Julia had told her parents that her flatmates were high and mighty and she had argued with them about paying equal rent as she had the smallest room. Although she seemed desperate to find another place to live her parents had encouraged her to ignore the other girls, stay put, and discuss the rent with the landlord. It was after this conversation that Julia's parents became very concerned, as they suddenly heard no more from her, which was unusual as she called home most weekends. They had repeatedly called her mobile, leaving messages and texts, but all to no avail, so after about three weeks they contacted the Dublin Garda who then informed the Kilburn missing persons unit.

Barbara said that she had spoken personally with the officers assigned the Flynn 'Misper' investigation and that they had made extensive enquiries, even travelling to Dublin to interview the family. Her two flatmates had said that she just upped and left and wanted to know if her parents would pay her outstanding rent. City University said she suddenly stopped turning up for lectures, and her boss at the garage, aware she was looking for somewhere else to live, thought she had just 'moved on'. Julia had no credit card, but her bank account was overdrawn to the limit, with no transactions just prior to or since the time she had gone missing. Her mobile phone had been 'pinged' by sending a signal to it to try and determine its location, but it was clear it was no longer in use and that the battery was long since flat. Calls and texts had been checked but nothing out of the ordinary turned up. Fidelis Julia Flynn, like Rebekka Jordan, had simply disappeared with no evidence of foul play, but the fact that it was eighteen months since she had gone missing matched the interview admission of Henry Oates.

Mike Lewis then told them he was going to call DCS

Langton and he didn't want to be interrupted. As he retired to his office the admiration and respect for Langton was immediately obvious as members of the team shouted out 'Give him my regards!' and 'Tell the old bastard to get well soon, but don't hurry back!'

Mike was on the phone for nearly an hour, but no sooner had he put the receiver down than the impatient Paul Barolli was knocking at the door, ever eager to find out what Langton had to say.

'Come in, Paul. Before you ask, yes I have spoken with him and—'

'So you talked to Langton?'

Mike tapped his right ear. 'Is it still red? He hammered away at me for an hour, firing off questions like a machine gun.'

'From hospital?'

'Nope, he discharged himself yesterday, but he's supposed to be resting up and doing physiotherapy as he can't walk without the aid of a Zimmer frame.'

Barolli smiled. The image of the energetic Langton using such a thing amused him.

'It's not funny, Paul. He went off the deep end about the Rebekka Jordan case; I knew he would. I suspected he loathed having no closure on it and I was right. He's something else, he is − it was as if it had happened last week instead of five years ago. I've always known he was obsessive, but he was barking at me like a Gatling gun, and I couldn't answer half his questions because I've not even read his entire case file yet.'

'Better get on with it then. I'll also brief the team about familiarizing themselves with it. Do we focus on Rebekka rather than the Irish girl?'

'No. Langton wants them both opened up, said we need to put the pressure on, so we'll have to go back to Henry Oates and see if we can get any more details. I can't organize a big search party until I can be sure he's not stringing us along.'

'That what he said?'

'No. You know Langton, he'd have the fucking Army out. Good news is he's going above DCS Hedges to the Commander to get clearance to beef up our team and get a bigger budget. Reopening these investigations is going to cost.'

'Joan said that her social enquiries showed that Oates had done some building work. If he killed them he had to get rid of them, maybe buried them somewhere on site.'

'Good point, Paul, ask Joan to find out where he worked but especially the dates, then we can prioritize any searches that fit the Jordan or Flynn timescale.'

'Big career move for you though,' Barolli said with a smile.

'Yeah, or a desk job for eternity if I mess up. Whether that bastard Oates is lying or not I can guarantee it won't be Langton that takes the backlash, it'll be me.'

'Sometimes, you know, it feels good to have not got my promotion – I don't think I could take the pressure.' Barolli chuckled as he headed out of the office.

Mike made no reply, but wondered if he was taking on too much. However, he put in a call to the Wandsworth Prison governor to arrange a visitation with Oates and then called Oates's solicitor. He hadn't liked the tall thin and waspish Adan Kumar when they had met previously, and now he disliked him even more.

Kumar was very well spoken, choosing his words

carefully and continually repeating himself, in a rather condescending manner.

'DCI Lewis, how can you expect my client to answer any further questions about Rebekka Jordan or a fictitious Irish girl called Julia? He has told you he read about the Jordan girl's disappearance and he simply made up the name Julia.'

'Well, Mr Kumar, let me remind you he said Rebekka was the first and Julia, a year and a half ago, was the second. He described Julia and said she came from Dublin—'

Kumar then interrupted. 'As I recall my client never actually said he murdered either of these girls. Did he?'

'No, but he intimated as much and I believe would have said more if you hadn't advised him to make no further comment.'

'You know full well that my role is to protect the legal rights of my client and give appropriate advice where I think fit during an interview.'

'I am aware of that but we are still making enquiries.' Mike was quietly seething at Kumar's arrogance.

'I am pleased you are aware, officer,' Kumar said sarcastically.

'Be aware then, Mr Kumar, that Fidelis Julia Flynn, a twenty-one-year-old from Dublin, was reported missing from Kilburn eighteen months ago. I personally did not know this until your client raised her name in interview so I want to speak to him in connection with her disappearance!'

'Mere coincidence and conjecture, DCI Lewis, not to mention a different Christian name.'

'Just make sure you are at Wandsworth tomorrow morning at 10 a.m., remand wing, interview room two. Thank you for your time, Mr Kumar.'

Mike slammed the phone down. As much as it annoyed him he knew Kumar was right as Oates had not made a full and frank admission that he had murdered a woman he knew as Julia. Mike looked at the 'Misper' poster for the young Irishwoman. You idiot, he thought to himself, realizing that in his anger with the solicitor he had made a big mistake in revealing that Fidelis had been reported missing. Kumar could now advise Oates to say he got her details from a missing persons poster.

Mike was beside himself as Langton had told him to get the bastard to talk. The DCS had made it clear that if there were an element of truth in what Oates was saying then Mike would have to draw it out of him slowly and carefully.

Mike knew he needed to recover lost ground, particularly if he wanted to escape Langton's wrath. He thumbed through the typed copy of his interview with Oates, using a highlighter pen to mark the relevant references: 'ginger girl, exchange student, Dublin, Julia, year and a half ago'. In frustration he threw the pen across the room, racking his brain about his exact words to Kumar, almost certain he'd only said Julia was a twenty-one-year-old 'Misper' from Dublin. He again looked at the 'Misper' poster, comparing the details to those in the interview, and intuitively he knew something wasn't right. Grabbing the Fidelis Julia Flynn file from his desk he hurriedly scanned the original report and her parents' statement. Suddenly everything became clear. It wasn't what was in the Flynn file, it was what was missing that was the possible link. Mike leapt out of his seat, shouting for Barbara before he had even opened his office door.

Anna parked her car almost directly outside Langton's flat in Warrington Crescent. She knew the area well as she had lived a few streets away at one time, and Langton had also lived with her in that flat when he was recovering from a brutal attack that had left him with appalling injuries. His present kneecap problems were a result of that assault. It had been so severe that for a period it was doubtful if he would recover, but to everyone's amazement, Langton had such focus and determination he had returned to work after only six months. Now her relationship with Langton was long over, though they had worked together since on numerous cases. Anna had at times found their friendship difficult to deal with, but Langton had been a strong support for her in her heartbreak after the man she was about to marry was murdered. In many ways she and Langton were very similar; Anna with immense strong will and ferocious determination had dealt with her grief by continuing to work case after case.

By the time her fiancé Ken had been killed, she had already moved away from Maida Vale to live in a top-floor modern apartment at Tower Bridge. His death had hardened Anna and she had formed a protective shell around herself. She kept her distance, allowing no one to get close, and was loath even to mention what had occurred. Langton had encouraged her to go for promotion to Detective Chief Inspector, a process that had been time-consuming, but Anna had no outside interests other than her health club. She was gaining a reputation as a very dedicated officer with her tough no-nonsense attitude and almost obsessive attention to detail, which had paid off, and she was firmly on the fast track, particularly in her new role.

Anna Travis had won respect from each of the various murder squad teams she had worked alongside, and yet it was only Langton with whom she continued to have a strong emotional bond, one she doubted she would ever break. They had been through too much on both a personal and business level. Even so, having had no contact with him for some considerable time, she felt a slight trepidation meeting him at his home. Since their break-up, Langton had married his second wife, adopting her daughter Kitty, and had a son with her, called Tommy.

Anna had only ever met Langton's wife, Laura, once many years ago, and it had been very difficult as at the time she herself had been very enamoured with Langton and very young. She subsequently became personally involved with him after he had left Laura and, when their relationship didn't work out, he had, or so she presumed, returned to be with Laura again. Attempting to discover anything further about Langton's personal life was difficult, since he was very private and most of what she did know had come via incident-room gossip, rarely from Langton himself.

She rang his doorbell and then had to wait at least five minutes before he answered the intercom and buzzed her in. Her mind raced with all their past history as she moved slowly up the stairs to the second floor, where the front door to his flat was open. She gave a polite knock and entered.

The flat was a jumble of kids' toys, tricycles and skateboards, and propped on a hook on the wall was Langton's racing bike. Anna called out, at which there was a bellow from Langton telling her he was in the bedroom. Unsure of the layout of the flat, she walked into the main living room, which was yet another jumble of children's toys, including a large doll's house, which lay on its side with miniature furniture littered around it.

'There's some coffee on in the kitchen if you want one,' he called out. Anna found the kitchen, which was in the same state as the rest of the flat. There was dirty crockery stacked in the sink, with empty containers of microwave and takeaway meals spread out on the table. She rinsed a mug clean and then looked around for the coffee percolator.

'What are you doing?' he shouted.

'Getting a coffee, do you want one?'

'No.'

Carrying the mug, Anna walked along the narrow corridor. One door was open and it was obviously Kitty's bedroom, judging from the pink duvet left on the floor alongside various clothes. She pushed open the next door with her elbow and walked into the master bedroom. It was huge with high ceilings, a massive double bed with a carved headboard and fitted wardrobes, but like the rest of the flat it was untidy.

Langton was wearing a threadbare blue dressing gown and a T-shirt. One leg was propped up on a stack of pillows and sporting a plaster cast from mid-thigh down to just above his ankle. He was unshaven, which made his face look sallow, and he had dark circles around his eyes. Littered over the bed were stacks of files, with more loose on the floor, and he had a notebook open with a pencil stuck behind his ear.

'Sit down. Chuck everything off and sit on the bed.'

'Where's Laura?'

'In the country with the children for the school holidays. Said she might pop home for the weekend, but I had to get them out of the way. They prefer it there anyway.'

'Don't you have anyone cleaning or cooking for you?'

'No. I send out for takeaway or microwave what I need.

Look, don't start ... I know the place is a tip and she'll sort it when she gets here. Half the stuff needs to be chucked out anyway; it's like a minefield out there.'

'I saw the doll's house.'

'I fell over it last night.'

She sipped her coffee; it was tepid. She noticed an array of dirty coffee mugs and bottles of pills on the bedside cabinet.

'Well I'm here. Was the operation a success? I thought maybe something had gone wrong.'

'It's excruciatingly painful and I can't – or I'm not supposed to – walk until it's all set, or the plaster has dried or whatever, but that's not why I wanted to talk to you. You seen anything of Mike Lewis?'

'No.'

'He's on a murder enquiry; woman found in the back of a van, Justine Marks, uniform patrol caught the guy red-handed with her body trussed up along with kids' entertainment gear. His name's Henry Oates, no previous record, admitted to killing her but claims it was an accident. They've not got the full post mortem report yet so no exact cause of death but from an early overview it appears that she was struck from behind, dragged off the street into the back of the van then probably raped. But that's not the reason I wanted to talk to you either.'

He hardly drew breath in his agitation, at times shifting his weight as if to relieve the pain in his knee, and moaning as he reached over for a dog-eared file at the end of the bed.

'During the first interview, this Oates character claimed that he had killed before, a girl by the name of Julia, said it was around eighteen months ago. Mike tried to get more out of him but his brief Kumar interrupted the flow, advised no comment and demanded a private consultation.'

'That's always been Kumar's tactic when his client's in a corner,' Anna remarked with a shrug of her shoulders.

'Second interview Oates said nothing more except that he had made it all up for a laugh. Anyway, he was charged with the body in the van and remanded in custody.'

'Do you think he was lying then?'

'I don't fucking know, that's Mike's problem, but since Oates was charged they found a possible "Misper". Irish girl called Fidelis Julia Flynn, been missing for eighteen months and liked to be called by her middle name.'

'Well that's something solid to work on, so what's the problem?'

'Would you stop interrupting and listen? That case isn't my main concern, this one is.'

He flipped open the file and passed a photograph to Anna.

'That is Rebekka Jordan, aged thirteen, went missing five years ago, and this prick Oates claimed that he also killed her.'

Anna looked at the photograph and in the back of her mind she did vaguely recall the case. Rebekka was exceptionally pretty, with straight blonde hair worn past her shoulders, and she was wearing a white shift dress. Langton took out more photographs, of Rebekka laughing with a pet poodle, standing by a pony, on a horse wearing jodhpurs and a velvet riding helmet and holding a large cup and a rosette. The more photographs Langton passed her, the more Anna began to remember the case, in particular that it still remained unsolved and had been headed up by Langton. Rather than interrupt she decided to act as if she was unaware and let him continue.

'Rebekka was last seen at four-thirty on March 15th 2007. She walked out of the riding stables in Shepherd's Bush and headed for the Tube station; her parents lived in Hammersmith. It was only two stops, but no one saw her on the Tube; no one had seen her since that last moment she left the stables, which was caught on CCTV footage. She never returned home.'

He opened the file and removed a stack of photocopied papers.

'I led the investigation. These are just a few samples of the thousands of statements. It was beyond belief that she seemed to have simply disappeared off the face of the earth, and after a year, one of the most frustrating years of my life, I had no suspect, nothing. Eventually I had no option but to cold-case the enquiry and keep an open-ended investigation. Since then, nothing has surfaced, not even a tip-off, no gossip, no prisoner coughing up to a cellmate ... that was, until this guy Henry Oates was picked up.'

Anna watched as he opened a pillbox and took out two tablets, which he swallowed with water before he continued.

'Henry Oates claimed that Rebekka Jordan was his first victim and Julia the second. He got the time frame right for Rebekka, and if Julia is in fact Fidelis Flynn then he was right there as well.'

'You said that in interview he told Mike Lewis he had made it all up for a laugh.'

Langton leaned back, closing his eyes. 'I think the son of a bitch said that because Kumar told him to and he also advised him to say that he knew about Rebekka Jordan because of the press coverage.'

Anna was slightly thrown by Langton's comment. 'So

are you saying Kumar is aiding and abetting Oates by telling him to lie to the police?'

He opened his eyes and leaned forwards. 'Not directly, no. Kumar's not that stupid, but Oates is a bit dense and obviously open to suggestion. Second interview he said that not only had we fitted him up with the Justine Marks murder but we would fit him up with Rebekka Jordan's as well. Now that stinks of suggestion by Kumar!'

'Yes I agree, but if that is the case then it also suggests that Kumar thinks Oates may be telling the truth or he simply doesn't want his client to drop himself further in the shit for crimes he may not have committed.'

'Whose side are you on?'

'Yours of course, but without further reliable evidence you know his admission is worthless.'

Langton sifted through a thick dossier and took out a single page. 'We had used every angle possible: TV re-enactments of her last sighting, girl dressed in the identical clothes, et cetera. But we did retain one piece of information – it's small and it could be inconsequential, but we had thousands of sickos calling up claiming they'd seen her, knew where she was. I don't have to tell you, you know what it's like, but you also know they all had to be checked out, so we never revealed the fact that Rebekka was wearing a pink Alice band on the day she disappeared. In the photographs you can see she had that long fine silky hair, but her mother always said Rebekka hated it over her face and she knew that on the day she last saw her, Rebekka wore the Alice band to the stables and would have taken it off to wear her riding hat, then replaced it to go home.'

Langton went on to say that Rebekka's riding hat was never recovered. She would have been carrying it home with her that day, a fact that was revealed to the public in the hope that it might have been found and so given some indication of where she might have been abducted or dumped. It was obvious his recall of the case was very clear, but what he had not made clear to Anna was why he had wanted to see her. He was very emotional, perhaps due to the fact that his stepdaughter Kitty was around the same age. Anna knew that with Oates as a new suspect the Jordan case should be investigated by the murder squad. She wondered if Langton had just wanted a sympathetic ear, so she remained silent.

'The name Henry Oates never came up in my investigation. If it wasn't for my bloody knee and being off sick I'd be having a real session with him right now. Christ, I don't even know what he looks like.'

'How old is he?'

'Late thirties, lives in a shithole property in Hackney that's due for demolition. Unemployed, mostly living on benefits, but has done some part-time labouring work.'

'Any history of mental illness?'

'Don't know. Police doctor who examined him said he was fit to be interviewed.'

He searched through a file and brought out a loose sheet.

'This is the Jordans' address. I've kept in touch, but not for the past six months. To be honest I found it harder every time I saw them, that look of expectant hope on their faces cut like a knife. Even after five years it never diminished. I used to feel I had failed them. It's obvious that I have, in retrospect, but for them to get some kind of closure would give me peace of mind.'

'And for the parents?'

'The guilt that on this one occasion they let their

daughter travel home by herself and she disappeared out of their lives, the "if only" syndrome, has never left them. The mother feels it the most, but if you could find the evidence to convict Oates and maybe even recover Rebekka's body that would give them some peace.'

Anna pointed out to Langton that at present, with a new suspect, it was not a review case. Langton firmly reminded her that her remit as DCI on Specialist Casework was to identify and advise on new lines of enquiry in unsolved murders. He then informed Anna that he had already got the Commander's approval for her to take on the revived investigation into Rebekka Jordan's disappearance. Langton started to gather up the files. She helped pick up the scattered photographs and papers from the floor beside his bed, handing them to him to stack and replace into the many dog-eared, well-thumbed folders.

'I'm depending on you, Anna, to see if this Henry Oates is a nutcase or the lead I've been waiting for.'

She sighed and shook her head. 'Don't put me in a position that will make Mike feel like I'm undermining him – it's not fair on him or me. This is now his investigation and I don't think bringing me on board is ethical, or not at this stage anyway.'

'Bullshit. You don't run Specialist Casework just because you're experienced in murder investigation. It's your attention to detail, lateral thinking and ability to spot new lines of enquiry that got you the post.'

'Thanks for the compliment but all the same I'd rather—'

'I don't want allegations from Kumar that Mike has been subjective and tried to make the crime fit where the Rebekka Jordan investigation is concerned. I need you to carry out an independent review and concentrate on whether or not you can discover any new evidence connecting Oates to Rebekka Jordan's disappearance and murder.'

'But if Mike is to continue with the Fidelis Julia Flynn enquiry we'll have to cross-reference. It'll be imperative we work together.'

'So get on with it. I won't take any crap about treading on anyone's toes. Life is too short, especially Rebekka Jordan's. I want you to liaise with me and keep me abreast of any new information. I know you're available and I reckon you will be diplomatic enough to make it work between you and Mike.'

She sighed and he reached out to take her hand.

'Do it for me, Anna. Forget about everything else, please? You know if I could I'd be taking over but right now it's impossible. I've got to stay put until I'm healed, I can't fucking walk straight, and I promise you I'll sort it out with Mike in the morning. He's got his hands full with the Marks and Flynn cases so there won't be any hard feelings.'

'All right. Let me familiarize myself with the files, but please make sure Mike gets to know I'm on board first. He has been a DCI longer than me, after all.'

He grinned and still held on to her hand. 'You look good, still too thin though. You eating properly?'

'Yes,' she said as she withdrew her hand.

'You're hair's got longer – I like it. Still see you are wearing the same Travis uniform: smart suit, white shirt and ...' He leaned over to look at her feet. 'How you manage to totter around on those high heels I'll never know.'

'Do you need a water or coffee before I go?'

'Nope. You get going and thank you for coming.'

*

Returning to her car, loaded up with the files in a large cardboard box, Anna felt not only put upon, but angry at herself for not having been firmer. She could have point-blank refused but with the Commander backing Langton there was little point in arguing. Then she started to feel guilty about leaving him alone in his flat and that maybe she should have sorted out something for him to eat, even cleaned up his mess in the kitchen, but she told herself to straighten up. He had a wife, let her look after him; she didn't want to get involved. She knew from old that as a patient he was a nightmare. She drove off, heading back to her flat, passing her old one on the way. A lot of time had passed since she had lived there with Langton and, she supposed, in some ways, she should feel honoured that of all the officers Langton had worked alongside, it was she whom he had wanted to oversee the Rebekka Jordan case.

Langton eased himself from the bed in a lot of pain and used the walking frame to edge himself slowly into the kitchen where he opened the fridge and took out a bottle of vodka and some ice, just managing to get a glass from the cupboard without falling over. He poured himself a large measure of vodka. Even though he felt hungry, he couldn't be bothered to call up and order something from the local Chinese or pizza parlour. Manoeuvring himself with the walking frame and his drink, he eventually made it back to the bed; he took two more painkillers and eased himself back to lie prone. Heaving his leg up to rest on the cushions, he reached for the phone and called the Commander to request more staff for DCI Lewis and report that DCI Anna Travis had said she would be happy to reinvestigate the Rebekka Jordan case.

*

Mike Lewis was not available when Langton rang the murder team office on the Monday morning, and so Barbara took the call and listened as Langton described his knee operation in detail and what agony he was in. She hung on, making all the right sounds, as he moaned and groaned about being unable to get out for weeks, before he eventually asked her to make sure Mike called him as soon as he was back in the incident room. He made no mention that DCI Travis would be joining the team, but instead he questioned Barbara about the developments to date. Barbara left a Post-it note on Mike's desk to ask if he would please call the DCS. In brackets, she suggested he didn't ask about the operation.

Mike Lewis was with Barolli and Henry Oates's solicitor Kumar at Wandsworth Prison. Whilst they waited for Oates to be brought from his cell Barolli set up the portable DVD and camera to record the interview. Kumar asked if there was anything to be disclosed to him prior to the interview. Mike said that he wanted to speak with Oates about the missing girls Rebekka Jordan and Fidelis Julia Flynn. Kumar told Mike that he didn't think his client would have anything further to add to his previous interview other than he had seen a missing persons poster for Fidelis Julia Flynn. This statement did not surprise Mike, though Paul Barolli wondered how he had come to know about Fidelis prior to the interview.

Oates was brought into the interview room by a prison officer and sat in a chair next to Kumar. He was dishevelled and unshaven, kept his head down and appeared noticeably depressed. Before the tape was started he asked in a hushed voice how long he would get for Justine

Marks' death. Paul Barolli asked him if he meant murder, which caused Oates to look up and sulk even more. Kumar told Oates that as yet he had not been found guilty and the officers wanted to speak to him regarding other matters. Barolli started the tape and cautioned Oates, who then said that he hadn't been sleeping well, was suffering from diarrhoea, unable to eat and feeling very down. Barolli sarcastically apologized for the poor living standards Oates found himself in but to Mike's surprise there was no reaction or reply from the prisoner. Kumar of course used his client's appearance and situation to reflect on how good it was of him to assist police and be interviewed.

Mike went over Oates's initial interview, concentrating on his comments about Rebekka Jordan and the girl he referred to as Julia, and asked if it was a correct account of what he had said. Oates nodded and Mike asked him if he could take that as a yes. Mike then asked him if it was still his position that he had made up admitting to the murder of the two girls and again Oates nodded. Mike pointed out for the benefit of the DVD recorder that Oates had nodded yes to his questions and asked Kumar if that was correct and Kumar agreed that his client had indicated yes.

Paul Barolli was finding the interview a deeply frustrating waste of time, especially if Mike was only going to go over what had been said before, as it was clear that Oates would say he had already seen the 'Misper' poster for Fidelis Julia Flynn. Mike produced the poster and slid it across the desk in front of the prisoner.

'This is Fidelis Julia Flynn from Dublin, aged twenty-one, and as you can see she has ginger hair. She went missing about a year and a half ago. Do you recognize her?'

'Is that the poster you saw, Henry?' Kumar interjected, and Oates nodded. 'As you can see, officer, Henry is a bit under the weather today but he would like you to be aware that he recognizes the poster and its details although not Miss Flynn personally.'

'So you only remembered the name Julia from the poster and you recited the details as part of your having a laugh whilst making up you killed her,' Mike suggested. Oates again nodded, then, encouraged by Kumar, answered yes. Barolli couldn't believe that Mike was not only asking such a question but was also giving Oates the answer as well. Thinking the interview would now end he had his finger ready to press the 'off' button when Mike raised his hand, indicating he hadn't finished.

'Can you tell me, Mr Oates, how you knew she was an exchange student?'

Oates, without looking, pointed at the 'Misper' poster and Kumar accused Mike of going round in circles.

'Mr Oates has just pointed to the poster of Fidelis Julia Flynn. Is that correct, Mr Kumar?'

'DCI Lewis, what is the point in continuing this interview? Henry, you're not denying you said she was an exchange student, are you?'

'No, it was on the poster.'

Mike deliberately paused, saying nothing. Both Barolli and Kumar were perplexed, but Mike waited until Oates looked up at him, picked up the poster and held it in front of Oates's face.

'Show me on this where it says she was an exchange student.'

Oates took hold of the poster and traced his finger along the information on it and his demeanour began to change. Kumar leaned over to look.

'Look as much as you like, the word "exchange" is not there.'

'I read it somewhere – it must have been on another poster about her.'

'No. All the posters, large or small, were the same. One of my staff confirmed it with her parents this morning. Julia was, as you rightly said, an exchange student from Dublin University.'

'Someone told me but I can't remember who.' Oates then sat upright and looked Mike in the eyes.

'You've never seen the poster until now. You knew about her because you met her, didn't you?'

'I think you said to me, DCI Lewis, that she was an exchange student.'

'How could I tell you something I didn't know, Mr Kumar?'

'I made it up,' Oates said and then asked to be taken to his cell. Kumar insisted that he needed to speak with him but Oates just stood up and walked towards the door, hurriedly followed by the solicitor.

'What a good guess, Mr Oates. I will keep digging and finding more evidence against you and each time I do I will come back and interview you again. Interview terminated 10.45 a.m.'

Mike turned on the ignition as Barolli got into the car beside him.

'That bastard Kumar schooled him about Fidelis Julia Flynn. I wondered where on earth you were going with the interview but you really fucked him with her being an exchange student.'

'Not as much as I hoped – it's circumstantial and doesn't take us much further,' Mike pointed out, shifting into gear.

'Do you think Kumar will prime him to say that he did meet Julia but didn't kill her?' asked Paul.

'Kumar makes me want to puke. He knows Oates is lying but won't encourage him to give it up. We need to find some direct evidence so we can get him out of prison and back in police custody for a few days. Then we can really put the pressure on him.'

Mike knew it was going to be hard to report the outcome of their interview with Oates to Langton as they were no farther forwards with the Rebekka Jordan case. It was clear to both officers that Oates had met Fidelis Julia Flynn but they both knew that, without a witness, that fact alone, even if Oates admitted it, would never be enough to charge him with her abduction or murder.

Chapter Three

Anna had spent most of Sunday night in bed reading the dense file on Rebekka Jordan, eventually falling asleep at around 3 a.m. A number of items were jumbled and she had carefully taken her own notes, marking down dates, times, interviews and witnesses, and read some of the hundreds of statements covering over twelve months. Langton's scrawled writing was over many of the pages; some details were underlined or highlighted. There were also lots of photographs of Rebekka, her parents and siblings, and a thick dossier of press cuttings. There were DVD recordings of the CCTV footage and the television reconstruction, plus home videos from Rebekka's family, which she had yet to watch.

After the prison visit Lewis dropped Paul Barolli off at the station and told him to write up the Henry Oates interview report while he went to the pathology lab to collect the interim post mortem report on Justine Marks and get an update from the forensic department as well. He wondered whether he should phone Langton to tell him about the interview with Oates but decided that rather than keep calling him while he was off sick he would read the post mortem report and speak with the forensic scientist first so he could give as full an update as possible. He knew however that Langton's main concern would be any developments in the Jordan case.

On arrival at the lab Mike decided to go to the forensic department first to speak to Pete Jenkins, the lead scientist who was overseeing the Justine Marks case. He had examined her high-heeled leather boots, confirming that the direction of the scuffmarks was consistent with her being dragged backwards along the pavement. Justine's silk skirt, torn blouse, tights and knickers were all stained with her blood, and they had found traces of Oates's semen on the vaginal swabs. Strands of her hair were on the larger end of the heavy-duty spanner, along with Oates's palm print on the shaft. The fact that there was no blood on that end of the spanner suggested he had only struck her once with it, but the extent of the man's depravity was revealed when, sickeningly, the scientist said that on the other end of the spanner they had found vaginal discharge, skin tissue and blood matching Justine's DNA. As Mike listened to the scientist's findings his growing contempt for Henry Oates boiled within him as it became even clearer how evil and calculating a liar he was.

After visiting the forensic lab Mike went to the pathology department and collected the interim report on Justine Mark's post mortem. He had not eaten since breakfast and decided to browse through the report while he grabbed some lunch at the lab canteen and look for any links to Pete Jenkins' forensic results. As Mike knew, Justine Marks had a severe head wound at the back of her skull and the indentation had a half-moon appearance. The pathologist had now looked at the heavy-duty spanner recovered from the back of Oates's van, and observed that Justine's head injury was indeed consistent in shape and size with the larger end of it and he confirmed that the blow would most certainly have rendered her unconscious. She had a perforated right eardrum and there was blood in her nostrils and mouth. Mike, having seen Justine's body at the mortuary and discussed the external injuries with the pathologist, flicked through the report to the internal examination details. As expected, the pathologist had found injuries consistent with Justine being violently sexually assaulted with one end of the spanner. Also of interest was that dissection of the neck had revealed that the muscle tissue around her throat was bruised and the hyoid bone fractured, indicating she had been strangled, possibly by use of her bra, which was found around her neck. The concluding paragraph gave the cause of death, pending further tests on her brain, as asphyxiation by ligature. Although they had no witnesses to Justine Marks' abduction and murder, it was clear from the pathology and forensic evidence that Oates had intentionally murdered Justine. Even to a hardened and experienced detective like Mike Lewis it was horrific to contemplate that Fidelis Julia Flynn and the thirteen-year-old Rebekka Jordan could have suffered the same terrifying death as Justine Marks had at the hands of Henry Oates.

Anna woke early, had a quick shower and then, still in her dressing gown, began to sift through the numerous DVDs and videos from Rebekka Jordan's file. She watched the CCTV footage three times before slotting in the television reconstruction, followed by the numerous interviews to the press by Rebekka's parents. Lastly, Anna watched a home video of the victim. There were various scenes that had been edited together, which showed the pretty girl from around the age of eight, at birthday parties, or on a trampoline with her blonde hair loose as she jumped up and down laughing, demonstrating her prowess as she performed a variety of tumbles and somersaults. She was magical to watch. There was extensive footage of Rebekka riding in gymkhanas, again proving her athletic ability as she flew over jumps with ease. Then came a poignant clip of the girl having her hair brushed by her mother and showing the loss of her milk teeth, giving a funny gapped smile to the camera. Next she was holding up some small figurines to the camera and calling them by various names. Finally, there she was singing, in an ivory white angel dress for a Nativity play. Then the screen went blank.

Anna was about to press rewind when another image of Rebekka dancing with her mother appeared on the screen. This was obviously where Rebekka got her looks from, as her mother was blonde, attractive and elegant as they waltzed together. It was a very touching moment when the mother twirled her around and the little girl's dress billowed out, but something else caught Anna's attention. Pausing the action, she stared at the screen, certain that the doll's house behind them was the same one she had seen in Langton's flat. Although Anna had still not read up on all the statements and enquiry results for Rebekka Jordan, she felt, having read Langton's investigation report, that she knew enough to begin her enquiry. She arrived at the station just after nine and went straight to the incident room on the second floor. Joan Falkland was carrying a coffee and buttered teacake to her desk as Anna took off her coat.

'Hello, Joan. Where can I park myself?' she asked as she put her briefcase and the large box containing the Jordan files on the floor.

Joan looked at her with surprise, and at the same time gestured over to an empty desk. 'We're short of space in here but DCI Lewis is trying to get us moved to a bigger office.'

'Is Mike in?'

'He's gone to Wandsworth Prison with Paul Barolli so he may be some time yet. I can let him know you called in.'

'That's okay, I'm not in a rush.'

Joan began to mark up notes on the incident board, assuming Anna had popped in to speak with Mike Lewis.

'You going to introduce me?' Anna asked.

'Oh sorry, ma'am, yes of course. Everyone, this is DCI Anna Travis.'

Joan introduced her to two clerical staff and three DCs attached to the case, adding that DC Barbara Maddox was having breakfast. Anna had worked with Joan, Barbara and Paul on four previous cases. With Mike heading up the investigation she wondered how the team would react to her taking over the Rebekka Jordan investigation.

'What's the canteen like?'

'Good. You want a coffee?'

'If you're having one, yes thank you.'

'Want anything with it, teacake, toast?'

'Nope, just coffee.'

In the canteen Barbara was gossiping with a colleague as Joan joined them.

'You are not going to believe it. DCI Travis is upstairs in the incident room.'

'What's she want?' Barbara said as she squirted tomato ketchup over her poached eggs and tomato.

'Come to see Mike Lewis, didn't say why.'

'Langton was on the phone earlier, kept going on and on about his knee surgery. He left a message for Mike to contact him, but didn't mention Travis. She's in charge of that specialist unit so it must have come from him, you know how friendly those two were.'

Joan nodded in agreement. 'She looks well. It was terrible what happened to her. I often think about it, you know. One minute you're congratulating her on getting engaged and then the next minute he's been murdered.'

'She's worked a couple of cases since then,' Barbara pointed out.

'I know, I know, I was just saying how it affected me, and she was straight back to work. I wouldn't have been able to cope at all. Langton had to tell her, you know, he got the call at the station. I will never forget that day. You okay for coffee? I'm taking one up to her.'

Barbara gave a sarcastic cooing sound and then leaned close to whisper, 'Bringing her in over Mike's head is going to cause problems, believe me – he's anxious enough as it is.'

'It's rare but I have worked with two DCIs on the same case before. And let's face it, we've no further details about the other two cases we've now got to work on.'

'Well I'm just saying her presence isn't going to help matters.'

'I'll get her coffee then we'd better get back up there. You know what she's like, God forbid we start off on the wrong foot with her.'

'I haven't finished my breakfast,' Barbara said.

'I'm sure that's all you're worried about, Barbara, you

just want to stir it up. I've always got along with her and I know why you haven't.'

'What?'

'You were always jealous of her relationship with Langton. How often have you run to the canteen for his chicken toastie, picking out the tomatoes because he hates them?'

Barbara refused to rise to the bait, sliding her unfinished plate to one side and walking off with a foul expression on her face. Sometimes Joan really pushed it with her.

Anna was studying the mug shots of Henry Oates. Langton had said that he had no idea what Oates looked like. The man had a very unpleasant expression. His hair was a dirty blond, very thick and wiry. He had wide-set pale blue eyes and a boxer's face; the bridge of his nose in profile was very flat and saddle-shaped, but turned up at the end with pig-like nostrils. His mouth was very narrow and turned downwards, and, like a petulant child, he glared into the camera lens.

'Unpleasant-looking, isn't he?' Anna said, as Barbara and Joan walked into the office.

'He's even nastier in the flesh; his skin's very pale – red-head's skin with freckles,' Barbara replied as Anna turned and glared at her.

'No offence, ma'am. You've got red hair, but you don't have that coloured skin.'

Anna chose to ignore Barbara's acerbic comment.

'Is he fit? You can't tell from the mug shots,' Anna asked as Joan handed over her coffee.

'Wiry, with big shovel-like hands. Barolli said he stinks like a skunk and lived in squalor like an animal,' Joan replied as she moved along the board to point out the photographs taken from Oates's basement flat.

'So you joining the team, are you?' Barbara asked.

'I don't think that's a matter that concerns you, DC Maddox.'

Barbara, having been put in her place, trudged over to her desk as Joan told Anna how well she looked.

'Thank you. How's your mother?'

Joan pulled a face. 'Same as usual, nothing is ever good enough for her. She's got me waiting on her hand and foot, but she's got meals on wheels delivering her lunches. She doesn't really go out any more, her focus in life is the TV, and I got Sky for her so she's got enough channels to keep her happy.'

Anna asked if the HOLMES computer in Mike Lewis's office was live and linked to their case, and on being informed that it was she picked up the Jordan files along with her briefcase and said that she had some work to catch up on while she waited for Mike's return from Wandsworth. She had contemplated revealing that she would now be heading up the Rebekka Jordan investigation but felt it would be rude not to speak with Mike personally before informing the team together.

Anna was looking at Henry Oates's details on the computer and noting that there was little known about him other than his age, date of birth, current address and that he was divorced with an ex-wife and two kids who now all lived in Scotland. She did not see DCI Mike Lewis enter the main office, but Barbara did, and from her desk she watched his reaction as he opened his office door.

'Travis.'

Anna looked up and smiled. 'Hi, Mike. How's it going?'

'I'm fine. How's things with you?'

'Great, thanks. I hope you don't mind me using your desk. I needed computer access to your investigation so I could get up to speed.'

Mike was wrong-footed, but made no reference to the fact he was surprised to see her, and even more surprised when she had implied she was on the team. Tight-lipped, he hung up his coat and drew the blinds down as his office window looked out into the incident room.

'What's going on?' he asked in a brusque manner.

Anna immediately realised that Langton had not, as he had promised, spoken to Lewis.

'I got a call from Langton about the Rebekka Jordan investigation.'

'Yes, and . . .?'

'He said he'd ring you.'

'About what exactly?' Mike asked as he pulled up a chair and sat opposite her. Anna could clearly see that he was upset.

'First off, Mike, let me make it clear that I've been put in an awkward situation here. Langton had already spoken to the Commander about me coming on board so my hands were tied . . .'

'Can you get to the point, please, Anna?' Mike asked.

'As you know, Langton dealt with the original investigation and in his usual obsessive way wants a result. Some closure for the Jordan family, and I agreed to reinvestigate only if you were happy about it.'

'Well this is all news to me and, to be honest, it's sort of pulled the rug from under me slightly. If he was unhappy about the way I've been conducting my investigation—'

Anna, wanting to diffuse the situation, interrupted him. 'Mike, he's not. He feels that you have too much on your plate running all three investigations together. To ease your workload he wants me to look at the Jordan case and you to deal with Fidelis Flynn and see what similarities we find that may link Oates to their disappearance and murder.'

Mike mulled Anna's comments over in his mind before replying. 'Oates thinks I will try and fit him up so independent investigations would help counter that type of allegation,' he conceded.

'Mike, you are the senior DCI and it's your team so I understand if you are uncomfortable with me being here. I want to assist you in any way I can and will do whatever is necessary so that we can work together rather than in any competitive manner.'

'As you can see my office is tiny with just the one computer terminal.'

'I know that. I'm quite happy to work in the team office.'

He shrugged, and again she waited for his response.

'Okay by me, but so far we have been unable to get any admission from Oates that what he said in his original statement about killing two other girls was the truth. He claims he made it up or we are trying to fit him up with murder. I interviewed him this morning at the prison and the reality is I'm no further forward.'

'Kumar's representing him, isn't he?'

'Yeah, and straight up I can't stand him. I think he's schooling Oates but I can't see why as he's bang to rights for the murder of Justine Marks.'

'Which he has admitted to?'

'Well he's lying, trying to say it was an accident. I went to the pathology and forensic labs after the prison visit and there's a load of evidence against him for murder.'

'Do you think Kumar might go for manslaughter on the grounds of diminished responsibility?'

'There's no medical history to show Oates is mentally unstable and Kumar hasn't asked for pre-trial psychiatric reports.'

'It's early days, Mike. If you have evidence against Oates only for Justine Marks then Kumar knows there's a good chance the CPS may accept a manslaughter plea on diminished.'

'That's Kumar and the court's problem, but if that situation arises . . .'

Anna pursed her lips and put up her hand to interrupt.

'What was he like during the interviews?' she asked.

'His moods changed. At the station he went from calm to belligerent then visibly anxious, chewing his lip and tapping his foot.'

'What about at the prison?'

'He seemed depressed and avoided eye contact until I confronted him about how he knew Fidelis Julia Flynn was an exchange student.'

'He may not have killed her. He could have met her legitimately and be frightened to say so as he thinks it would implicate him in her disappearance.'

'You really know how to brighten up my day, Anna.'

'Sorry, Mike, just being devil's advocate. If Oates did kill Rebekka and Fidelis then he had to dispose of the bodies somehow, somewhere. If it wasn't for the uniform officers stopping Oates Justine Marks could have been just another "Misper" statistic.'

'We know he's done some work on building sites but where and when is proving difficult to find out. He's been virtually unemployed for ten years and claiming benefits, so anything extra was probably cash in hand.'

'Well he can clearly drive so maybe he disposes of his victims locally.'

'I know that, Anna, but with the length of time since both girls went missing and no confirmed locations it's like looking for a needle in a haystack. I had a search unit check Hackney Marshes but they found nothing.'

'Not much to go on then?'

'You said it.'

Anna stood and picked up her empty coffee cup.

'You know what Langton always asks me, or used to ask me? He would always want to know what my gut feeling was. What's yours?'

Mike leaned back in his chair and swivelled from side to side. 'Well he's obviously lied about how Justine died. As for Rebekka and Fidelis, why confess to a crime you didn't commit?'

'Attention, notoriety maybe?'

'Then why retract the confession?'

Anna sighed and Mike raised his hands in a submissive gesture.

'So in answer to your question, my gut feeling is uncertain. If you want to know what I really think about Henry Oates then read the post mortem report and let me know your gut feelings.'

Mike handed the report to Anna as he got up from his chair and went over to the blinds to open them.

'I will let the team know that you are investigating the Rebekka Jordan case while we concentrate on Fidelis Julia Flynn.'

Mike opened the blinds and noticed that Barbara, Joan and Barolli were huddled together whispering to each other.

'Do you want to do it together?' Anna asked.

'I don't think there will be any need. These walls are

paper-thin and by the looks of it that lot have been eaves-dropping our conversation.'

'Some things never change,' Anna said with a smile.

'Bet you'll be glad of a bit of extra help from Travis,' Barolli said as Mike entered the main office.

'It's DCI Travis, or ma'am, and that goes for you all and yes she will be heading up the Jordan investigation and you will give her your full cooperation as and when she asks for it.'

As Mike Lewis briefed the team Anna went through the post mortem report and murder scene and mortuary photographs. What she saw made her stomach turn as she began to fully understand exactly how Mike felt about Henry Oates. He was a loathsome individual with no shred of humanity, who needed to be locked away for life. In wondering what drove men like Oates to such depravity she realized how little she or indeed Mike and the team actually knew about him.

Anna went into the main office, put her files and briefcase on an empty desk and asked Joan to track down Henry Oates's ex-wife in Scotland. She then turned to Barbara.

'Get as much background as you can on Oates. I want you to go back five years. Start with his social security and National Insurance records – any child support, divorce, births; he's got two children so there has to be something.'

Barbara gave a hooded look to Joan over her computer but Anna was onto it fast.

'That a problem for you, Barbara?'

'No, it's fine by me. In fact Mike had already asked for as much data as possible.'

'Good. Paul, have you got a full list of all the items removed from Oates's squat?'

'Not yet. You want me to get on to the crime scene guys?'

'Yes. Apart from it being a pigsty, from the photographs it looks to me as if he was a hoarder, maybe kept tokens from his victims, so they need to weed out women's clothing, jewellery, anything that could link him to the two new cases.'

'I'll give them a push to get cracking.'

'Is Pete Jenkins still at the lab?'

'Yeah, in fact he's dealing with our case. You want to talk to him?'

'Ask him if he could make it a priority for his staff to list and check everything that was taken in. Say I'll talk to him later today.'

Anna began sorting through the Jordan family statements, thumbing backwards and forwards. Although five years had passed they were, at the time, obviously well off; they had a large three-storey detached house with a Filipino live-in domestic helper, a gardener, and a cleaner that came in twice a week. Mrs Emily Jordan did not work, but had been an interior designer before her marriage to Stephen Jordan, a graphic designer. He had offices in Canary Wharf and often worked from home, using the loft conversion as an extended office. Rebekka, their only daughter, was a day pupil at a private school in Knightsbridge. Her two older brothers had been at boarding school and were not at home when she went missing.

As Anna was wondering how much their family life and relationships had changed since the disappearance of

Rebekka, Joan approached her, excitedly waving a piece of paper.

'I have a contact number and address for Henry Oates's ex-wife. She is working at a dry-cleaner's in Glasgow. As for his two daughters, the eldest, aged eighteen, is in drug rehab and the other, only sixteen, is six months pregnant.'

'That was fast. Good work.'

'I spoke with the Department for Work and Pensions and they put me in touch with the Glasgow housing association. Mrs Eileen Oates has a criminal record here in London for prostitution and drug abuse. It appears she's now drug-free with no arrests or convictions for nine years.'

'Thanks, Joan. Did you speak to her personally?'

'No.'

'Okay, I'll do that and in the meantime can you get me a contact number for a DCI on the Glasgow murder squad?'

'Yes, ma'am.'

Mike Lewis drew up the blinds from his office window and tapped to indicate he wanted to talk to Anna. It irritated her slightly that he couldn't walk the few steps from his office to ask her, but crooked a finger instead; it reminded her of the way Langton often did it.

'You wanted to see me,' she said, entering Mike's office without knocking.

He held up the phone, covering the mouthpiece with his hand. 'It's Langton, he wants to talk to you.'

'Oh thank you.'

Mike walked out, closing the door. She sat behind the desk and waited a moment before she spoke into the phone.

'DCI Travis.'

'Listen, I've just had a lengthy talk to Mike. My feelings are these: it's a no-brainer the fact they have Oates bang to rights for the murder of Justine Marks.

'Mike told me about his latest interview with Oates and my take on the bastard is this: the more visits he gets and the more attention we give him, the more he's going to string us along. I don't think he's mentally unstable and anyway Mike tells me Kumar hasn't raised the issue of pre-trial psychiatric reports.'

'I think it's only a matter of time, though, and it would be in his client's best interests,' Anna replied.

'This is what I want the team to concentrate on. We need hard evidence that ties Oates into the two other murders he claimed to have committed.'

'It's hard without him giving us more details.'

Langton snapped and raised his voice. 'If he killed them he's dumped the bodies, so he will have left evidence. Find it, find them, it'll surface. When you have the evidence apply for a break in police custody from the prison, bring him in and scare the living daylights out of him.'

'What about a BIA to help with the interview strategy?'

'A BI what . . .?'

'Behavioural Investigative Adviser – they provide support and advice that links the academic basis of behavioural science to the investigation of serious crime.'

'You mean a profiler. No fucking way.'

'They are now police-accredited psychologists and might help us to understand Oates's way of thinking. We often recommend them on case reviews.'

'If you need a shrink to tell you how to interview a suspect then I suggest you go back to your desk at Specialist Casework. If Oates wants to play at being crazy you find the evidence to show he's a devious bastard who knew exactly what he was doing. Remind him what happened to Peter Sutcliffe the Yorkshire Ripper – the judge rejected diminished responsibility and the expert testimonies of four psychiatrists who all thought he was a paranoid schizo.'

'That was thirty years ago, things have changed and—'

'Yeah and thirty years later he's still in Broadmoor, so if Oates or Kumar think they can pull one over on us then they're both mistaken. You been to see the Jordans yet?'

'I'm still reading the case file. I need—'

'Get it done and go and see them.'

He hung up and Anna was left infuriated with the phone in her hand. Langton's pent-up anger was fuelled by alcohol or his medication, she thought. She had just replaced the handset when Mike returned.

He cocked his head to one side. 'You look as if you got a similar tirade. If you ask me he needs a psychological assessment.'

Anna didn't mention that she too had concerns about Langton. Mike took off his jacket and started to roll up the cuffs of his shirtsleeves.

'I suggested bringing in a BIA.'

'I can guess what his reply was. He thinks they're full of crap.'

'I told him it might help us to understand Oates . . .'

'Well that's between you and Langton, but for now we should do what he suggests. See if there is any evidence we can track down, and in the meantime we let Oates stew. As we agreed, you take Rebekka Jordan and I'll concentrate on Fidelis Julia Flynn. We can compare what we uncover for any similarities or links in their disappearance as the investigation progresses.'

'Whatever you say, Mike.'

'It's not me, but Langton, and whatever I think about

him right now, he's still got more years of experience than either of us. You know what I really find unnerving . . .?'

She shook her head, nonplussed.

'He's never met Oates, right? Yet he seems to have more of an angle on him than I have.'

Mike informed the team that he and Barolli would concentrate on Fidelis Julia Flynn with the assistance of half the team while Anna concentrated on the Jordan case with the other half. Barbara and Joan were to receive all the incoming information from both teams, update the HOLMES computer, mark up the incident board and identify any similarities in the girls' disappearance or connections to Oates which could then be raised and discussed in a full team meeting.

Adan Kumar had contacted Mike to say that Henry Oates would not, at the present time, be fit for further interview. Mike immediately thought the solicitor had asked for a psychiatric assessment but it transpired that Oates was currently in the prison hospital recovering from an assault in the shower room which had left him with severe bruising and concussion. Oates, naive about prison life, was unaware that even remand sex offenders are marked men and had made the mistake of boasting to other inmates that not only was he awaiting trial for murder and rape but was also suspected of the abduction and murder of a teenage girl. Mike felt no sympathy for Oates's predicament but was inwardly pleased that the incident would give him breathing space to continue his investigation whilst keeping Kumar, who now wanted to vent his anger on the prison service, off his back.

*

Anna, like Mike, felt no sympathy for Oates. She looked again at the information about his ex-wife who had left London eight years ago. She was trying to determine whether or not it would be worth it to travel to Glasgow for an interview. She decided that she'd first have the meeting with Rebekka Jordan's family, as she wanted to find out if, by any chance, Henry Oates had worked for them, perhaps done odd jobs around their home, anything that could be a direct link to him. She knew that she would have to tell the Jordans about Oates's arrest and the possibility he might be involved in their daughter's disappearance. She was not looking forward to the visit as she knew that she would be reawakening the most terrible memories for the Jordans and the last thing she wanted to do was give them false hope that Rebekka's body might at last be found. Anna decided that she would not divulge the details of what happened to Justine Marks, but just say that Oates was awaiting trial for her murder.

Chapter Four

The Jordan family were still in the same house in Hammersmith. Anna's call had, as she knew it would, made a deep impact on Emily Jordan. Before she'd even rung the bell, the door was open wide.

'I am Detective Chief Inspector Anna Travis. Thank you for agreeing to see me.'

'Please come in. Stephen will be right down, he's working upstairs.'

Anna was led through the narrow hallway into a long, eye-catching and modern galley-style kitchen with a black-and-white tiled floor and black granite worktops. The Aga, along with all the wooden cabinets and cupboards, was white with every large kitchen appliance integrated into the design. A sizeable T-shaped dining and relaxation area had clearly been added as an extension to the original kitchen. It had a glass-domed roof which filled the room with natural light and French doors that opened out onto a small but well-maintained garden. There was a white two-seater sofa and small television in one corner and the walls were adorned with large blow-up photographs of two handsome blond boys and many of Rebekka, one of which had a string of paper daisies threaded around the frame.

Emily had coffee brewing and Anna accepted a cup of lovely fresh Brazilian. As Emily offered her a plate of home-baked biscuits, her hand shook. Stephen Jordan then walked in and directly introduced himself. He was a very handsome man, wearing a pale blue cashmere jumper and old brown cord trousers, with dark blue suede loafers and no socks. Stephen had dark hair with flecks of grey at the sides and soft brown expressive eyes. In contrast his wife had pale blue eyes with silky thick blonde hair down to her shoulders. She was wearing jeans and a chequered shirt, and was taller than Anna, at least five feet eight or nine, and very slender. They made a very elegant couple and she saw him catch his wife's hand gently as he sat on the arm of the sofa. Emily remained standing.

'I want to be totally open with you both and explain why I am here,' Anna began. 'I wish I had more information for you, as what I do have isn't much to give you any comfort and for that I am deeply sorry.'

They looked at each other, and their pain, the pain that Langton had described, was plainly still extremely raw. She could feel it.

Anna knew that she had to be careful not to mention the name of Henry Oates or his legal team could dismiss any identification the Jordans might make. So she explained to them that they might have seen in the papers or on TV that police had arrested and charged a man with the abduction and murder of Justine Marks, and that during interview this man had said that he had killed two other women: a girl he referred to as Julia and their daughter Rebekka. Anna told them that she was taking the admissions very seriously and would be making a full and thorough investigation. Neither of the Jordans spoke, but Stephen's hand gripped his wife's more tightly.

'However, he now claims that both admissions were a lie and the only reason he made them was for a laugh as he had read all the media coverage about Rebekka at the time she went missing.'

Still they remained silent.

'He has been re-interviewed but given us no further details and now still denies any involvement in your daughter's disappearance. I have a photograph that I would like you to look at to see if you recognize him or can give his face a name.'

Anna opened her briefcase as Stephen stood up, releasing his wife's hand. He delved into his pocket and took out a pair of glasses as Anna handed him the photograph of Henry Oates. They stood very close together, both looking at the picture, and then Stephen turned to Anna.

'No, I don't recall ever seeing anyone like this.'

He passed the photograph back to Anna.

'I'm afraid I don't either. It's the sort of face I think one would remember,' Emily said.

As she replaced the photograph into her file Anna asked them if the name Henry Oates was familiar to them but they both said no. She sipped her coffee and looked over to the extension. 'How long ago was your extension built?'

Stephen hesitated, and it was Emily who said that it was six years ago and completed just before Rebekka went missing.

'I designed it and brought in the builders,' she added.

'Can you recall who dealt with the planning permission at your local council?'

'We didn't need planning permission because of its size. I applied for a certificate of lawful development and the building inspector visited a few times and that was it.'

'Were you still living here while it was completed?'

'Yes. In fact we redesigned the kitchen at the same time and it was all done at once. We sort of camped out in the other rooms.'

'Do you remember the name of the building company?'

Emily turned to her husband, who said he would have the details in his office upstairs. Left alone with Emily, Anna asked about the photographs.

'I did them,' said Emily. She went over and stood by her daughter's picture. 'The boys made these daisies.'

'They are at boarding school, aren't they?'

'They are both at university now. When Rebekka went missing I became very protective and wanted to change their school so they would be at home, but Stephen felt it was better they were away – you know, kept to a routine as it was such a terrible time. They have both been trau-matized by what happened to Rebekka, she was such an adorable child and they worshipped her. She went to a school that specialized in learning difficulties, as she was dyslexic, but not badly. She was such a physical child, sports and athletics and . . .' her voice dropped '. . . horse riding.'

Stephen returned with a folder and placed it on one of the worktops.

'The building company brought in a team of men to dig out the garden as there was a stone patio and some trees directly outside the old kitchen. I'm not sure who they hired, but I have the builders' names. I gave the detectives copies of these when Rebekka disappeared.'

Anna smiled, thanking him as he passed her a neatly written note with all the contact numbers and addresses.

'Do you think this Henry Oates might have worked for them?' he asked.

'It's possible he used a false name but we'll be making new enquiries.'

Anna closed her briefcase and stood up, about to leave, just as the phone rang. Stephen answered. He spoke briefly to someone and then turned to his wife.

'Show DCI Travis her room, darling. I'm going to have to take this call upstairs. Will you put it through for me?'

'Yes of course.'

'It won't take long. Then maybe you'd like to come up and see my office, top floor, I keep all the press cuttings up there and . . .'

'Thank you,' Anna said, not really wanting to prolong her meeting, but having no real reason not to.

'How is Detective Langton?' Emily asked.

'He's well, thank you. Well, not that well actually, he's had some knee surgery which is why he is not here personally.'

'He was so good. I don't know how we would have coped without him. He was such a support and his kindness meant so much to us. We also appreciate that he has kept in touch since.'

Emily seemed to find it hard to refer to her daughter's disappearance and her slender hands constantly toyed with a delicate gold chain bracelet on her wrist.

'I know he did everything possible, I know that. Please pass on our regards to him and I hope he makes a full recovery.'

'I'll most certainly do that.'

Emily gestured for Anna to go ahead of her into the hall.

'You have a lovely home,' Anna said.

'I was a designer, and may even return to work soon.

Stephen is very encouraging about me starting again, so maybe one day.'

They headed up a winding staircase with polished pine floors and white walls that had colourful paintings on them, all of the seaside.

'These are very old. We have a cottage in Cornwall – well we used to, we sold it two years ago. We'd go there every summer.' Midway up the stairs Emily stopped and looked back at Anna. 'I wait, I just wait in case there is a call, you know that if we were away I'd miss it. Now I can't seem to get out of the habit, if you can call it that. The waiting is never over.'

They reached the landing, which was also of polished wood, with tapestry rugs, and there was a huge glass chandelier with coloured glass flowers.

Emily opened a bedroom door and stood back.

'I've kept it exactly as it was. This is Rebekka's room.'

It was bright with pale blue draped curtains tied with big floppy bows. There was a single bed with oversized dolls laid out on the pillows and a white wardrobe with one door open to show racks of dresses and shoes. Against one wall was a large mirror, ballet shoes left beside it, and a pink net tutu hung over one of the carved arms. Like the rest of the house the floor had bare wood boards, but these were painted a pale blue colour. Next to the wardrobe there were rows of worn riding boots and crops in a heap beside a long trestle table. The table was covered in bits of material and a small red sewing machine stood alongside boxes of fabric that were neatly labelled as lace, velvet and wool. One large box was open to reveal a stack of tiny naked dolls, some without limbs or heads. There were also pots of glue and a paint box with a jar beside it filled with brushes and crayons.

'She spent hours up here. She'd make the dolls for her doll's house and even the furniture. She was very inventive. She made little mirrors with tin foil for the glass, and the wigs from her own hair; she'd collect it from her hairbrush and we even found her cutting one of the boy's curls when he was sleeping.'

'The doll's house?' Anna said, recalling the one she had seen at Langton's and the Jordans' home video she had watched.

'Well, Stephen made it for her, but she had started to really want a bigger one, she said she couldn't fit in all her families. He is halfway through designing a new one; you'll see it in his office. It's very grand and exactly how she wants it, with the main wall opening up to show off the different rooms.'

Anna gave a sidelong glance to Emily as she lightly touched her daughter's hairbrush on the small kidney-shaped dressing table.

'So what happened to her old doll's house?' Anna asked as she pretended to be interested in the tiny figure of a dog; it was made out of plaster and no bigger than her thumbnail.

Emily hesitated and then gave her bracelet a twist. 'James was telling us it was his stepdaughter's birthday, he said he felt dreadful as he had meant to buy her a gift, but had been held up interviewing someone, so Stephen gave him Rebekka's.'

Anna was quite shocked on two counts. One, she presumed the woman's mention of James referred to Langton, and the other that they would part with something of their daughter's.

'She didn't want it,' said Emily, maybe sensing her reaction. 'She'd grown out of it and Stephen was so sure she'd

72

come home that he wanted to finish the one he was building as a surprise.' Again Emily twisted her bracelet round and round and her voice dropped to a whisper. 'He hasn't. I think he finds it too distressing, you know, to finish it.'

Emily covered her face as she started to weep, awful shaking sobs, and Anna instinctively went to put her arms around her. She felt terribly frail and Anna could smell a soft flowery perfume.

'I am so sorry, so sorry. I don't want Stephen to see me like this.'

She broke free and backed away from Anna.

'He's upstairs. Please go and see him. I'll be downstairs.'

Anna waited a moment and then headed up a narrow staircase to the top floor, where she found Stephen sitting at a large trestle table similar to his daughter's. The room included high-tech computers and sound equipment, but nothing much else. In one corner was, as Emily had described, a half-finished huge elaborate doll's house.

'I have really come to say that I'll be leaving now, but I will be in touch if I have any further news.'

'She'll be nineteen next month. Hard to come to terms with how she would have grown up. She'll always be thirteen, won't she? Always young, always a child.'

'It must be heartbreaking.'

'It is. Maybe if we get something that will let us bury her. We have no grave; we have just hung onto hope for five years. It's harder for Emily because she won't leave the house.'

He got up and moved closer to Anna, putting his hand on her shoulder.

'I beg you to find out where she is and what happened to her, then we can move on and sell this house, because it's like a haunting, she's still everywhere. I love my wife and I just want her to get over this terrible guilt she feels.'

Anna found the warmth of his hand on her shoulder and his closeness uncomfortable, and she stepped back.

'I'll show myself out. Thank you for your time and I promise I will do everything in my power to give you some peace.'

Anna did not return to the kitchen, but let herself out and hurried towards her parked Mini, bleeping it open and getting in as fast as she could. It all came down like a heavy weight. The pain inside the white, sparkling-clean house and the anguish of Rebekka Jordan's parents became confused with her own past. She broke down and wept for the man she had loved and for the future she had lost with his murder. The scene she had just witnessed also brought something else home to her very strongly: she had no one, no one to take care of her like Stephen Jordan, who obviously loved his wife Emily.

Pete Jenkins, an old colleague and friend, called Anna that evening. She hadn't heard from him for a long time. He explained that he had tried to contact her in the incident room at the station.

'You were out and about and didn't answer your mobile.'

'I'm sorry, I had it on silent and haven't checked it since.'

'Well it's nothing urgent, more of a moan, as I've been told you want all the crap they removed from your suspect's home sifted. I didn't get a clear indication from fatty Barolli what I'm to earmark so I thought I'd ask you.'

'Well, I need you to examine anything that may

connect Oates to the victims he claimed he murdered; female underwear especially, something he might have kept as a sick token like jewellery as well.'

'The obvious?'

'Yes, I suppose so. The young girl Rebekka was wearing a pink Alice band, no press release on it, but then her backpack and riding helmet were never recovered. Did you get details of her clothing sent to you?'

'No, and nothing for Fidelis Julia Flynn either.'

'I'll sort it out in the morning.'

'Okay. In the meantime, I'll put a mask on and start digging around. You know we have about fifteen disgusting black bin liners full of stuff. I've had a couple of assistants start to comb through it all, but I'll get on with it personally in the morning.'

'Thank you.'

'Dinner should be on the cards.'

'You got a rain check on that.'

'Maybe come to my house, meet the wife; she's lumbering around as we're expecting a baby next month.'

'Oh, I didn't know. Congratulations. Do you know what it is?'

'No, but if it is a boy, he's going to be called Harold. It's taken some time to get her to agree to it, but it's my grandfather's name.'

'Lovely. Fine, I'll wait to hear from you.'

She sensed that Pete would have liked to chat more, but she didn't feel like it. Her brief affair with him had been a long time ago.

As she hung up she felt another pang of sadness. Pete and his wife were about to start a family, and she remembered laughing and talking with Ken about raising a big family together. He'd wanted a rugby team! He had been a very good rugby player and she had watched him playing a match, along with his sister and his two boisterous nephews cheering on their uncle Ken from the sidelines. Now there were no tears, not like earlier in the afternoon; it was just the sadness that enveloped her. She didn't want to go over any of the files and instead had an early night, taking two strong sleeping tablets to make sure she slept. She liked the feeling of sinking into her pillow as they took effect and her mind went blank.

The next morning it was not her alarm that woke her, but the telephone ringing at six-thirty. Disorientated, she sat up, first catching the time on her bedside alarm clock and then anxiously reaching for the phone.

'You awake?' Langton's voice rang out.

'I am now!' She pulled the duvet around her.

'You talked to Rebekka's parents?'

'Yes.'

'I meant to tell you about the doll's house. I'd fallen over the bloody thing when I got out of the hospital.'

'Really.'

'It may appear to be unethical to you, but they insisted, so I took it home for Kitty.'

'Do you know what time it is?'

'No. Is it early? Only I sleep most of the day and I can't get comfortable. Why haven't you called me?'

She sighed. 'Because I don't really have anything to tell you, only that Mike split the team into two and I'm work-ing on—' She was interrupted.

'I know, I spoke to him last night.'

'So you have the update on what we're doing.'

'I do, but not from you. How did you find the Jordans?'

'Painful, heartbreaking and they didn't recognize the photograph or the name Henry Oates.'

'Too much to hope for, I guess.'

'Yes, but I'm checking into an extension they had built by local builders just in case they used part-time labourers when they were digging up the ground.'

'We did that, but then we didn't have a suspect.'

Anna unwound the telephone extension cord as she got out of bed and reached for her dressing gown.

'You going to interview this creep's ex-wife?'

'I'm thinking about it, but I'll have to go to Glasgow.'

She switched the phone from one hand to the other as she put on her robe.

'I'm in agony. This bloody cage round my knee is torture.'

Anna listened as he moaned and groaned about how long it was going to take before he could get out of the flat. Eventually she said that she needed to make herself a coffee and take a shower.

'You okay?'

She sighed and said that she was just fine.

'You got very upset when you left the Jordans, you were crying.'

She was stunned. Emily or Stephen must have been watching from the house.

'Yes. As I said, I found it very emotional and they are a really nice couple. It made me feel inadequate as I didn't really know what to say to them or how to help them.'

'Tell me about it. Five years, Anna, five years they've waited.'

'They said you were a great comfort.'

'Yeah, yeah, not good enough though, is it?'

She repeated that she needed to get going and eventually

he hung up. Langton was really something else, and even though she knew his frustration must be almost as agonizing as the surgery on his knee, she was irritated by his call. Not until she had made some toast and a fresh mug of coffee did she realize that in some ways he must have been concerned about her. She actually felt better and less emotional than she had the previous evening.

Before she left for the station, she looked into the Jordan files where Langton's team had questioned the builders that had built their extension. They had given the names and contacts of all the men who had worked for them, and they had all been checked out. It was, for the Langton enquiry, another dead end, but Anna would double-check and now show the photograph of Henry Oates.

At the station Anna made straight for Barolli to let him know that he had not given a clear instruction to the forensic team about what evidence to look for. He was rather petulant and explained that he had specified any items that could possibly have been kept as tokens from the two victims. She told him about the Alice band and he said that as he hadn't been informed about any pink Alice band he hadn't listed it as a priority.

Anna discovered a Post-it note from Joan on her desk informing her that a DCI Alex McBride was waiting for her to call him. When she was put through to him she had difficulty following what he was saying as he had a very thick Glaswegian accent. Anna told McBride about Oates's arrest and that she wanted to come to Glasgow to interview Eileen Oates as part of her investigation. McBride told Anna that Eileen had two daughters and lived on a council estate. Although she had a previous record for prostitution in London, they had nothing on file, but her elder daughter had been busted for drugs numerous times and was also arrested for streetwalking. The younger girl was pregnant by a sixteen-year-old Jamaican living on the same estate, and they were due to be married before the birth.

'The ex-husband Henry Oates is not known to us up here, and it appears he's not been a part of their lives for a long time. In fact Eileen Oates has been involved with a man we interviewed on suspicion of an armed robbery and murder. The reason why we're so up to date on her is due to her relationship with this man. Eileen Oates gave the suspect an alibi, stating that he was with her at the relevant time. A security guard was shot and died from his injuries and we believe she's lying to protect her boyfriend.'

Anna decided that she would make the trip to Glasgow and McBride promised he would arrange for Eileen to be brought into their station for further questioning on his case, and if she agreed, Anna could interview her there.

Anna next arranged to meet the building contractors who had worked on the Jordans' extension. Owned and run by two brothers, Bill and Norman Henderson, the company was based in Barnes, not far from Hammersmith. It took Anna over an hour to cross London from Hackney due to rush-hour traffic as it was four in the afternoon. Henderson Building Contractors operated from a small yard at the back of a row of shops on Barnes High Street. Anna parked up in the yard beside an open-backed lorry that was being stacked with wood planks. Two white vans and an old Land Rover were also in the yard.

*

Bill Henderson was waiting for Anna. He was much older than she had anticipated; white-haired and with a ruddy complexion. He introduced himself and as they headed into the office he told her the yard had once been a stable and outhouses, and they had converted the stable into their business area. As he ushered her inside she thought the office was hardly a good advert for their work, as it was cramped and untidy with an old mahogany desk and walls lined haphazardly with designs and architect plans for various builds. The filing cabinets were bulging with documents and there were stacks of files and folders left on every available surface around the desk. This had a computer, telephone, fax machine and jars of pens and pencils on it. A worn leather desk chair and two equally worn armchairs were the only other furnishings.

'Sit down, please, my brother will be here any minute, he's just making sure the truck gets out with a delivery.'

He seemed like a lovely man in his old knitted sweater and baggy trousers tucked into wellington boots. He asked if Anna would like a coffee or tea as he could rustle one up from a small annexe of a kitchen.

'No, I'm fine, thank you.'

He sat behind his desk and opened a drawer, taking out a dog-eared folder.

'I got this ready for you. It's all the team that worked on the Jordans' extension. We had the same hardcore group back then that we still use on an almost permanent basis and we hire in extra when needed.'

He placed the file down on his desk, turning it towards Anna.

'We still haven't got over that missing little soul. She was a sweetheart, made us all feel helpless. What it must have done to her parents. I've got grandchildren her age and

Norman has grandsons the same age as the Jordans' two boys.'

Anna nodded and opened the file. She had taken out her notebook to check the lists from the original enquiry.

'Do these men still work for you?'

'Yes, apart from Don, he died a couple of years ago of cancer. He was our electrician, good solid hard worker with a lot of experience.'

The door burst open and Norman Henderson walked in. He had the same thick unruly white hair as his brother, but was taller and thinner. He wore a yellow workman's jacket with their company name printed on the back and he carried a white hard hat, tossing it onto the top of the filing cabinet before shaking Anna's hand in his big gnarled fist.

Anna waited until Norman had settled, taking off his jacket and sitting on the edge of the desk.

'I have a photograph of a man I'd like you both to look at,' she began.

'I'd like to get whoever took her by the throat. She was such a lovely child and so well behaved,' Norman burst out.

Anna first passed the photograph of Oates to Bill, who put on a pair of spectacles. He studied it with his lips pursed before passing it over to his brother. Norman scrutinized the picture, then looked to Bill.

'I don't think I've ever come across him, have you?' asked Norman.

'No. Looks like a boxer with that flattened nose.'

'Does the name Henry Oates mean anything to either of you?'

Bill and Norman looked at each other and shook their heads while Anna took back the photograph.

'Stephen Jordan mentioned that there had been a considerable amount of work clearing a section of the garden and patio before the extension was built.'

'Yes, we had to dig down a few feet for the footings, move out a lot of shrubbery and a couple of deep-rooted trees. We had to remove the garden fence and come into their property from the street at the back of their house. We needed some extra hands and we brought in a mini digger.'

'Were the rest of the workers your usual team?'

Bill scratched his head and then leaned over to take back the file he had passed to Anna. He thumbed through it. There were many receipts and invoices for the extension materials along with a letter of lawful development from the council.

'It's a long while back now, well over five years ago. In fact, looking at the invoice it was June 2006 when we first started the ground clearance.'

He flicked back and forth, finding the list of the people he had used on the job.

'Do you recall using anyone not well known to you?'

Bill ran his teeth over his bottom lip and then wagged his finger. 'There was the tree surgeon, remember, Norman? We didn't know him well back then. One of the trees we needed to chop down hung over into next-door's garden and the roots went under their fence.'

'It was a wall, Bill, they got quite nasty about it, even when we explained to them that we'd rebuild the wall and to whatever specification they wanted.'

'You're right. You'd be surprised what aggravation we get. I remember having to sit and explain over and over that we were not taking any inches from their garden, just removing the roots of the blessed tree, and that the adjoining wall would be replaced and in a better condition than the one we needed to pull down.'

'Right, it was buckled and quite dangerous because of the roots – the tree must have been sixty-odd years old. I think they even got a solicitor on it, you know; it's a conservation area around there.'

'This tree surgeon?' Anna prompted.

'Right, yes, young bloke, has a small company in Kingston, he's quite posh. Upper-class type, qualified landscape gardener and tree surgeon who worked part-time at Kew Gardens, or he did,' Norman said.

'He's not on the list, is he?' Anna asked.

They both shook their heads.

'Did you tell the police about him at the time?'

'He had nothing to do with the extension, so I'm not sure. He just helped with the tree and then some of the clearance. I remember he took the old bricks away for us, probably to re-use them,' Bill said as he flicked backwards and forwards through the paperwork file.

'Ah, here we are, his invoice with a phone number and address near Cobham. He set up his own garden centre called Markham's not far from his home. Good, he is, we've used him a few times since. I'll give this number a ring for you.'

'It's okay, thanks, a copy of the invoice will be fine and I will ring him later,' Anna said.

As it was almost seven, Anna had not bothered returning to the incident room as she needed to change and get ready to go to Euston Station to catch the sleeper train to Glasgow. She put in a call to Andrew Markham's garden centre office when she got back to her flat, but was told that he was still on holiday in Thailand. She also rang

Barolli and he had given her what little update they had on Fidelis Julia Flynn, which included interviewing her old flatmates. Although they had said she had left leaving rent unpaid, she had also left two suitcases of her belongings, which had been seized by the local detectives who initially investigated her disappearance. Barolli said that he had arranged for the cases to be brought over to the incident room so he could go through them.

In was another day without a result and Anna could understand Langton's frustration. She was not too hopeful that her trip to Glasgow would be of any use, but without anything else it would at least give her more of an insight into Henry Oates's background and possibly assist a behavioural investigator, should she persuade Langton to use one.

Chapter Five

Anna had not expected to be met at Glasgow, but standing on the station platform as the train pulled in was a uniformed officer. The patrol car drove her to her hotel and the officer waited while she took a shower. It was not yet nine when she was driven to the Glasgow police station and again she was surprised to be met, by DCI Alex McBride, who had fresh coffee and oatcakes for her on a tray in his office. He was a very well built man with broad shoulders and a wide pleasant face, dotted with moles, and eyebrows so thick they were like an extension of his brown curly hair. When he shook her hand, her elbow jerked up and down, it was such a firm grip.

McBride filled her in with the details of the armed robbery case in which the security guard had died from gunshot wounds. Anna listened attentively, remembering that their main suspect was the boyfriend of Eileen Oates. As he had given Eileen as his alibi, she had been questioned and they had looked into her background. One daughter, Megan, aged sixteen, was pregnant and living at home and the other, Corinna, was a known heroin addict. Corinna had also been arrested for prostitution on two occasions, but the courts had deferred sentencing on the condition the young woman agreed to go into rehab. McBride informed Anna that he had contacted the centre this morning to check on her progress, only to discover that she had walked out after a week or so and her current whereabouts were not known. McBride suggested she was probably in a drug den somewhere and they'd no doubt find her in a gutter with a needle in her arm. But they had not had any sightings of Henry Oates or any reports of him ever visiting his ex-wife.

Their suspect for the bank robbery was a Donald McAleese. He had an extensive police record for assault, fencing stolen property and burglary. After finishing her coffee, Anna was taken to the incident room and shown McAleese's details and photograph.

'Do you suspect that Eileen is lying?'

'We do, and we know that she and McAleese were cohabiting at one time. We had numerous call-outs from neighbours a few years ago. She would always drop charges for assault, but he is a very violent man and it's possible she's too scared to admit she's lying.'

McBride took Anna through the statements taken from Eileen. She had claimed that McAleese had been with her the afternoon of the robbery and had spent the evening with her visiting a local pub and afterwards taking home fish and chips. The police were only able to verify that McAleese was with her in the pub during the evening and that they were later seen in the fish and chip shop. Eileen was his sole alibi for the afternoon of the robbery.

'The robbery went down at two-thirty in the afternoon on a security van and the whole thing was recorded on

CCTV. It was carried out by two masked men, one with a sawn-off shotgun and one with a hand gun. The man with the sawn-off pointed it at the driver's head while the other demanded the money from the guard who had just come out of the bank. The guard turned to run so he shot him twice in the back of the head with the hand gun,' McBride explained as he turned a computer screen towards Anna and played the CCTV of the robbery.

'That defies belief. A life lost for what, a few thousand pounds,' Anna said, taken aback by the gratuitous violence and the senseless death of the young security guard.

'For nothing. The scum thought he had made a collection from the bank but he'd just made a delivery so the container was empty.'

'Why do you suspect McAleese if they were both masked?' Anna enquired.

'You could see on the CCTV video that the man who did the shooting had a pronounced limp in his right leg. Well, so does McAleese, as the result of a bad motorbike accident a few years ago.'

Anna paused by the incident board to study the mug shots of Donald McAleese. He was a tough mean-looking man, with small close-set eyes and his thinning greasy hair combed back from a high forehead.

'Where is he now?'

'We've got him under surveillance, living with his mother, but without more evidence and with no identity for the second man we don't have enough to arrest and charge him.'

'How many suspects can you have with a limp?'

She smiled, but McBride was not amused. He checked his watch.

'Let me go and check if Mrs Oates has been brought in. You want me to leave you alone with her?'

Anna nodded.

'Can I get you another coffee?'

'No, thank you.'

As she waited to be called to the interview room, Anna had another look at Donald McAleese's mug shots and decided Eileen Oates didn't have great taste in men.

Eileen Oates looked younger than Anna had expected. She had blonde scruffy hair, a thin pale face with acne scars, buck teeth, and she was wearing a scruffy pink jacket with jeans and imitation Ugg boots. Stirring a beaker of tea with a plastic spoon, she glanced up at Anna as she was introduced. McBride hovered for a few moments before leaving the interview room.

'Is this sugar or salt? I've not got ma glasses.'

Anna picked up the white packet and said that it was sugar. She tore off the top and passed it to Eileen.

'Ta.'

'Thank you for agreeing to talk to me.'

'I hadda an option, did eh?'

'May I call you Eileen?'

'If ye wannae, it's ma name.'

'First off, I want you to understand that I am not here in any connection to Mr McAleese. It is concerning your ex-husband Henry, and if it's okay with you I'd like to tape our conversation so I can write up my notes when I get back to London.'

Anna placed her Dictaphone on the table.

'Nae problem, hen, but I cannae help, I've not seen him for years, not that ah would wannae see him. Day I moved back here was the best thing I've done. I shouldae done it before, but with two bairns, I was dependent on ma mother to help me out, which God bless her she did.'

Eileen sipped her tea, sucking her lips together.

'It must have been hard bringing up two girls on your own,' Anna suggested.

'Tell me about it. I had one fuckin' run off from rehab and t'other's pregnant. It's a vicious circle tryin' to keep 'em on the straight and narrow. I think Corinna's problems come from that bastard. Told her I slept about and he wasnae her real father and on top of that if he wasnae knocking me around wanting sex he was after her.'

'You mean sexually?'

'Aye. I caught him in her bedroom, she was only ten. I took a broom and belted him. After that I'd had enough so I packed a few bags and while he was out I took what I could and left with the girls.'

'Did he try to get you back?'

'Nae, I said I'd report him tae the polis. For all his fists and loud mouth, he was scared they'd arrest him. He was also, believe it or not, ashamed about trying it on with his own daughter, blubbering that he was drunk and got intae the wrong bed.'

'Was that the last time you saw him?'

'It was, aye, he did try, but I wouldnae even speak to him. Couple of years later he sent some presents one Christmas for the girls, but it was just the once. We've moved a few times so he had nae forwarding address.'

'But you must have made contact when you filed for divorce?'

She shook her head and said the solicitors had handled the papers. Eileen then tapped the table with her finger.

'Not a penny because he was unemployed and had nae income. I got sweet F-all, but at least it meant he couldnae find us. Is that why you're here, is he trying tae see us?'

'No, I'm here in connection with a murder your ex-husband has been arrested for and charged with.'

'Well, not before time. He shoulda been banged up years ago for what he did to me, never mind his own daughter. We'd not have had food on the table if I hadnae . . . it was him that put me on the game.'

Anna listened as Eileen went into a lengthy excuse as to why she had been charged with prostitution, and the more she talked the angrier she became, constantly slapping the table with the flat of her hand.

'I've worked as a shop assistant, shelf filler, cleaner, but I never did it again. Now I've got a steady job in a dry-cleaner's and part-time in a bar. Bein' brought in an' out of this place is doin' ma heid in, I could lose my jobs. So if you're finished with me, can I go?'

Anna opened her briefcase. 'This shouldn't take long, Eileen, but I need your help. You see, your husband also claimed that he had been involved in two other murders.'

'I wouldnae know about anythin' he done. Like I told you, I've not seen him for over eight years.'

Anna took a photograph of Rebekka Jordan out from her file. 'One of the possible victims is this little girl, missing for five years. When your husband was arrested for the—' Anna was interrupted.

'He killed that wee bairn? Is that what he's been arrested for?'

'No, another woman, but he claimed he had killed this child. Her name is Rebekka Jordan. But he then retracted his statement, denying that he had admitted having anything to do with her disappearance.'

'She's just a wee child.'

Eileen looked at the photograph of Rebekka, shaking her head and sucking in her lips.

Anna explained that Rebekka had last been seen leaving a stable yard in Shepherd's Bush. She asked if Oates had ever worked in that area.

'I wouldnae know. He did odd jobs, but I cannae remember if he was workin' there. I don't even know where he lives now. When I left him we had a place in Brixton, but I know the solicitors for the divorce had a hard time tracing him to sign the papers as he wasnae living there. He used to move into squats, never had any money.'

'You said previously that he had assaulted your eldest daughter. Do you know if he had ever had sexual contacts with other young girls?'

'When he was drunk he'd have sex with a dog. He was a perverted bastard, but I wouldnae know if he had other wee girls.'

'Tell me about when you went to London and met him.'

She said that she was sixteen when she left home in Glasgow due to a drunken and abusive father. Her mother had arranged for a friend's family, who lived in East London, to take her in and they had a daughter, Anne, who was the same age as her. Anne's father, who had recently died of cancer, had been an amateur boxing promoter and not long after she had arrived in London they all went to a boxing match at York Hall in Bethnal Green. This was where she first met Henry Oates, who had fought in one of the bouts that evening. Henry had invited her out for a drink and she liked him and they started a relationship shortly after they first met and he was always very protective of her. She had believed, like

Henry, that he was going to become a successful professional boxer. They'd being going out for just over a year when Eileen fell pregnant with Corinna, so they married before her birth. Eileen took out a crumpled tissue from her pocket, her eyes brimming with tears.

'His boxing career didnae take off so he tried tae get into the Army, you know, get permanent work. It seemed like he'd only just got kitted out with his uniform when they threw him out.'

'Why was that?'

'Said something about him being unsuitable. Knowing him, he probably got inta a fight.'

'Carry on, tell me more about Henry.'

'After that he took odd jobs, but we were always short of money and we moved from one dump tae another. He'd even started tae think Corinna wasn't his . . .'

'Sorry, can I ask why he thought Corinna wasn't his?'

'When she was born she had darkish skin. As she grew, her hair was matt black and tight curls, started wearing it like them Jamaicans do when she got in her teens. He was convinced she wasn't his. I told him ma grandmother's hair and skin was like that but he just wouldnae believe me. Said I'd tricked him intae marriage over Corinna and then when I was expecting Megan he thought I just wanted tae keep hold of him by getting pregnant again.'

She wiped her eyes and blew her nose.

'Just thinking about it makes me upset. It was as if he blamed me for everything that went wrong. All those wasted years, being knocked around, trying to make ends meet. I went out working the streets at night, while he was supposed to be at home looking after the girls, but I'd come home and he'd have been out drinking, leaving them on their own.'

Anna put out her hand to reach for Eileen's and she gripped it tightly.

'You did what you had to do, Eileen, and you brought them here to Glasgow away from him. I admire you. It must have taken a lot of guts; it's always hard for a woman who is abused to have the strength to get out of—'

'Vicious fucking circle, that's what it was. It's not got better.' Eileen started to cry in earnest. 'Now after all I done, I've got a heroin addict on the run from rehab and the other bairn's got herself pregnant. She's just sixteen, a boy from off the estate. And I'm nae better; I've gone from one bad'un to another. Take a look at this . . .'

Eileen pulled open her jacket and drew down the top of her sweater. She had a massive dark blue-black bruise in the centre of her chest and red marks around her throat.

'Oh Eileen, I am so sorry. Is that from McAleese?'

'You know he's got form for violence?'

Anna nodded, by now wondering if there was any point in continuing to question Eileen. As there had been no contact with Henry Oates for so long she doubted if she could gather anything more than that he'd been a despicable human being from way back. Eileen meanwhile pulled her sweater back up to her neck and then closed her pink jacket.

'You know I said I had no connection to why you have been brought here to the station for questioning, and I don't. I asked to meet you because I am trying to find out what happened to Rebekka Jordan and if your ex-husband killed her as he claims. I doubt that you can help me, but I want to help you. Eileen, you have to be strong and if you are being abused again and forced into assisting Mr McAleese, you can get protection. If necessary you can be placed in a witness protection programme that will take care of you, move you and your daughters to a safe place.'

Eileen had her hands clenched together, twisting the tissue round and round. Her voice was hardly audible.

'He'll kill me.'

'You will never be free of him if you don't accept help. Remember how you felt when you took control of your life and left London.'

'You're right. I've had enough shit shovelled over me.'

Eileen lifted her hand, opening and closing her mouth. 'I've just remembered something ... oh my God ... yes!'

Eileen touched the photograph of Rebekka Jordan still left on the table between them. She half rose from the table and then sat down again.

'That last time he called me it caught me by surprise; it was very late at night. Oh Gawd, it's got to be five years ago, more even, maybe six, but you said something about the wee girl worked at a stables?'

Anna felt her body tense. She didn't correct Eileen that Rebekka didn't work at the stables, but had been taking riding lessons.

'I've just remembered what he said to me. We hadnae said two words before we started arguing. I called him a layabout, something like that, and he ... Oh Gawd almighty ... let me get this right ...'

Anna waited as Eileen licked her buck teeth, running the tip of her tongue round her lips.

'Okay, this is how it went doon. I think he started callin' me a whore and I said to him that he was nothing but a layabout who never earned a penny, that's when he mentioned he had a job. I called him a liar again and he got really mad, screaming at me that he was working in a stables shovelling shit. I think he said stables, but that would be the only place, shit from the horses, am I right?'

She gave Anna a smile. It altered her whole drawn face.

'Have I helped ye?'

'Yes you have. One more thing, Eileen: do you know if he owned a car around this time?'

'Nae, he could never afford tae pay for one. We never had so much as a bicycle between us.'

'When he did these odd jobs did he have access to vehicles?' Anna asked.

'I dunno. I dunno if he even had a driving licence. Is there any chance I can nip out to the car park for a fag and a coffee?'

'Sure, I'll ask an officer to get you a coffee.'

While Eileen was out having a cigarette break Anna took the opportunity to go over what she had recorded on her Dictaphone. She listened intently to the last part of their conversation and in particular where Eileen had mentioned that Oates said he was working in a stables and she wondered if this could be the connection to Rebekka Jordan that she was looking for. She wrote in her notebook to make further enquiries at the stable about employees who had worked there for at least a year before Rebekka went missing.

Eileen was brought back to the interview room by a uniform officer.

'You okay to carry on? There are just a few more things I need to ask you,' Anna said.

'I've been thinking about what ye said about being free of McAleese. I don't want tae lie for him any more but I'm scared of what he'll do tae me.'

'So you lied about him being with you when the armed robbery happened?'

'Aye, but he said he'd shoot me through the heid as well if I didnae give him an alibi.'

'I understand, but you need to tell DCI McBride what happened. It's his investigation, not mine, and I have to return to London,' Anna said sympathetically.

'Can ye not stay with me, make McBride give me the protection ye said I could have, because if he doesnae I'm terrified he'll kill me or hurt ma daughters,' Eileen said as she clung to Anna's hand.

'I'll talk to McBride for you, Eileen, but you should ask for a solicitor to be present. They will provide you with one.'

Eileen sighed and then blew her nose.

'Ye know, with Henry I put up with a lot more. I did it because at the start I used tae feel sorry for him. He'd had a terrible upbringing, do ye know about it?'

'No, but I am interested and it could help me with the investigation.'

Eileen explained that Henry's mother had been a junkie on the game and Social Services had taken him from her when he was about eighteen months old. They found him left in a dump of a place; he'd not been fed and was filthy, then he was put into care. Eventually his mother got him back, not because she loved him but because she wanted the child benefit for drugs. Henry was around five years old, and she and her punters started knocking him about so they took him off her again when he was eight and he went back in a care home.

'He told me he used tae always fight with other kids but it always ended up with the staff giving him a good beat-

ing. Anyways, he run off when he was just a teenager and
got tae London, started to work for some old bloke that
was an ex-boxer and he took it up, he was like a sort of
mentor tae him.'

'Where was the boxing club?'

'Bethnal Green, near the York Hall where they have all
the fights. The old boy trained him and everythin' and he
started out as an amateur. He was good, ye know, had a lot
of potential. This old guy raised money for a club tour to
America and wanted tae take Henry, but he needed his
birth certificate tae get a passport. He tracked his mother
down tae Liverpool and went tae see her. She was still
using drugs and on the game . . .'

Eileen sniffed, wiping her nose with the back of her
hand. She told Anna that Henry never had a proper father
and when he tracked his mother down he asked her about
him and she told him that she never knew who it was and
didn't care either but it had to have been some waster as
that was the only blokes she'd ever known, wasters that she
went with to get a fix.

'Did he go to the States?'

'Nae. The rest of 'em did, though, and while they were
there the old boy snuffed it, had a massive heart attack. It
really hurt Henry, he'd become like a dad tae him, even let
him live with him, but when he died his missus kicked
him out. He carried on boxing, but I think that was
because being in the ring made him feel better about himself and the club was the only place he had any friends.
That was all just before I met him. So you see, I used tae
feel sorry for him cos he'd never really had nobody . . .
turns out he was like what his mum said, a waster. I know
I wasted years on him.'

*

McBride was taken aback when Anna joined him in the incident room and announced that she would be leaving in time to catch an earlier train back to London.

'Did you get anything out of her for your case?'

'Not much, however ...I think she will give up McAleese, but she is very frightened. She's been beaten up. I think she will talk if she gets protection. Can you arrange that?'

'It depends ...'

'He threatened to kill her. Take a look at the bruise on her chest, and she's got a pregnant teenage daughter, she's scared for her as well. Eileen Oates is an abused woman, but taking her back over her abusive past with Henry Oates I think made her aware that she was in the same old situation. She's scared McAleese will kill her. If you offer her witness protection I think she'll make a statement against him.'

'I'll get a car arranged to take you to the station.'

'Thank you.' Anna was slightly taken aback by his abruptness.

McBride cocked his head to one side and gave a small tight-lipped smile. 'Thank *you*.'

As the train sped her back to London Anna once again sifted through the file on Rebekka Jordan. All the current employees at the stables had been questioned five years ago and all their names and addresses were listed. On top of these were the part-time workers and Saturday morning stable hands and trainees. Henry Oates's name did not appear, but after her conversation with Eileen, she would now have to talk to the owners to take them back at least a year before Rebekka went missing. She sat back in her seat and closed her eyes. She thought about Eileen Oates.

She was a sad creature, like a wounded animal incapable of any self-esteem. She opened her eyes and made a note to check if they could trace any known associates of Oates from his boxing days as he might still have kept up with them.

Back in Hackney, Barbara and Joan had been busy compiling the statements gathered from people who had last seen Fidelis Julia Flynn. The flatmates had been able to give a clear picture of the evening she left, the last time they had seen her. She had given no indication that she was meeting anyone. Although all Fidelis's landline and mobile phone calls had been checked at the time she was reported missing Mike had instructed Barbara to go over them again. Her flatmates had brought in their old BT telephone bill, which they had kept because Fidelis had made a number of calls and had not paid for them. These were all highlighted in pink and indicated that she kept in touch with her parents in Dublin on a regular basis. The other numbers were for a hairdressing salon, a local cinema and the garage where she had worked. A number that had been called on several occasions from her mobile had turned out to be to an unregistered pay-as-you-go phone, which to date had not been traced. Mr and Mrs Flynn had sent more photographs of their daughter, taken in Dublin shortly before she came to London. Barolli had looked through the suitcases and a zip-up bag which contained make-up, a sponge bag, clothes, shoes, handbags and a purse that had two twenty-pound notes in and some change. There was no diary, no notebook, and searching the pockets of the handbags he had found nothing but a couple of old crumpled receipts and a used lipstick.

*

Anna had fallen asleep on the train and woke with a jolt as her mobile rang. It was Langton, impatient to know if there were any developments from Glasgow, but her phone repeatedly cut out and so he suggested she came over to his flat straight from the station. As she had already told him that Oates might have worked at the stables and that this was basically the only new information, she was loath to see him because she knew he would grill her on every part of her interview with Eileen. She received two text messages from him, the first asking her to pick up some milk, bread and eggs and the second to also buy a bottle of vodka.

By the time the train arrived back at Euston it was early evening, so Anna bought the groceries from the first shop she saw in the station and caught a taxi to Maida Vale. She stopped in Floral Street not far from Warrington Crescent where Langton lived and from an off-licence bought him his vodka. After keeping her waiting on the doorstep for five minutes, Langton buzzed her in; when she reached the front door of the flat it was ajar. Someone had obviously cleared up as the main room was tidier than when she had been there previously. Placing the groceries and vodka in the kitchen, which was also clear of dirty dishes, she called out, asking if he wanted her to make a coffee or tea.

'Just bring in the vodka and some ice,' he called back.

Anna opened the fridge, which she was pleased to see contained some bacon, lettuce, a cooked chicken and what looked like a dish of fried rice. She found where the glasses were kept, filled one with ice and went into the bedroom. He was propped up on pillows with his leg stretched out on a square cushion from the sofa, and he was unshaven, wearing the same old dressing gown with a T-shirt beneath it and pyjama bottoms with one leg cut out for the plaster cast.

'You having one?'

'No. I only had a sandwich on the train so I won't stay long as I'm tired out. I didn't sleep on the way there. The sleeper is comfortable but the rhythm of the train kept on changing and—'

'Yeah, yeah,' he interrupted, unscrewing the top from the bottle of vodka. 'So take me through it all. What is she like, for starters?'

Anna drew up a chair and opened her briefcase to take out her notebook as she described Eileen. He listened without interruption, sipping his vodka with the ice clinking in his glass. She explained how the most important information came up, the stable connection, that Oates could have worked there and met Rebekka up to a year before she went missing, but she obviously had not had time to check it out. She added that she wanted to check out the boxing background to see if Henry Oates was still friends with anyone connected to the club, and that she had asked Joan to see if Oates had ever held a driving licence or owned a vehicle.

'If he kidnapped or snatched Rebekka off the street, he must have been driving something,' Anna pointed out.

Langton drained his glass and topped it up again before replying. 'He could have stolen a vehicle . . .'

'Or if he was working odd jobs there's a possibility he might have had access to a vehicle,' Anna suggested.

'Shovelling shit,' he muttered.

She closed her notebook.

'That's it then, is it?' he asked.

'Fraid so. Do you want me to fix you a sandwich or

something? I see there are some groceries in the fridge apart from what I brought.'

'Nah, I'll get something later.'

'I don't mind.'

'I don't want a fucking sandwich, all right?'

'Fine. I'm going to take off home, it's been a long day.'

He reached out for her hand. 'Sorry. Thank you, but I'm not hungry. Why don't you make yourself something to eat?'

'No, I'll get back home, have a shower and—'

'There's a chicken.'

'No, thanks. I see the flat has been tidied up.'

'Yep, had a visit from Laura's sister. She was not happy about the mess. Gave me a headache thudding around with the hoover and her duster, repeatedly reminding me how neat and tidy Laura and the kids are.'

He paused and sighed.

'Christ, my Kitty's not much younger than Rebekka was when she disappeared. Time goes fast – not for that poor little soul though. Sometimes when I look at Kitty, the way she's growing up, I think of what it must feel like to be the Jordans; their child will never grow older, will always be exactly as she was the day they last saw her.'

'They keep her bedroom as she left it.'

'Yes, I know.'

She leaned forward and kissed his cheek.

'I'm going off home now. Are you sure I can't get you anything to eat?'

'Nope. I'm fine. My wallet's on the table over there so take whatever I owe you for the groceries and this.' He picked up the bottle of vodka and topped up his glass yet again.

'On me, and maybe ease off on the vodka if you're taking painkillers,' Anna suggested cheerfully.

'Go on, get out, you sound like my wife.'

Anna was surprised. He had never, as far as she could recall, ever called Laura his wife, which of course she was.

She put on her coat, eager to leave, and, picking up her briefcase, she couldn't resist throwing a little dig.

'Well I'm glad she's looking after you.'

'Get the money I owe you, Travis, or I won't be able to tap you for doing anything else for me.'

Anna crossed to the living-room dining table and picked up his wallet. It was well-used, worn leather. Inside on one half were credit cards and on the other side a flap with photographs of his children Kitty and Tommy. She took out a twenty-pound note and was replacing the wallet when she noticed that beneath the table was the doll's house. When she had last been at the flat it had been open; but now it was shut and she could recognize the exterior.

'Good heavens. I hadn't noticed that this is a replica of the Jordans' own house.'

'Yeah, Stephen made it. Kitty isn't interested in it any more. Laura's sister put it under there. I dunno what to do with it. I can't throw it out.'

Anna bent down, drawing the doll's house further out from beneath the table. It was exceptionally well made and beautifully painted. The front door and porch area with its two tiny pots of plastic flowers were just like those of the Jordans' house in Hammersmith. She eased it further round to see the back of the house.

'It was made before the extension,' Langton said.

Anna leaned forwards on her hands and knees. There

was some kind of a back garden attached to the house. A tiny swing was still upright, there was a mock crazy-paved patio made of small cut-out cork squares and close to the back door was a broken tree and some small squashed shrubs made of Plasticine. There were marks where there had been a fence and a hand-painted brick wall was still partly upright, the paper torn.

'What are you doing?'

'Just looking at how well constructed this is, but I can see from the kitchen that as you say it was crafted before they extended the house. There's no Aga cooker and it's now all white with painted floorboards. This must have taken hours of work. Have you seen the little stools and tables? Perfect.'

She closed the doll's house and stood up, linking the hooks to fasten it shut. Beside the house was a plastic bag containing more furniture and some tiny dolls.

'I'm going,' said Anna.

'Talk tomorrow.'

'Yes, I'll call you.'

As she left she could hear him switching on his television. She let herself out and closed the front door. Heading down the stairs, not paying attention, she almost tripped on the frayed carpet.

There was something about the doll's house that stayed in her mind, but she put it to one side because as she stepped out of the house the rain was lashing down. She ran along Warrington Crescent to Maida Vale Tube Station, and then endured an uncomfortable ride to Tower Bridge, having to switch Tube lines, and did not get home until after ten.

*

Her coat was still sodden from the rain so she hung it over the heated towel rail in her bathroom before having a shower.

Anna's own fridge was virtually empty. She sighed, knowing she should have bought some groceries for herself, never mind Langton. She made some beans on toast and a mug of tea, taking them on a tray to eat in her bedroom. Her initial nagging thoughts about the doll's house returned. Putting down the tray on the floor beside the bed, she reached for her briefcase and took out her notebook. She flicked back a few pages, but nothing triggered a response until she got to the name Andrew Markham, the tree surgeon used by the builders for the Jordans' extension. She got off her bed and turned on her computer. Andrew Markham had a very professional website describing his company, with landscaping and tree surgeon qualifications alongside pictures of gardens he had designed in the past few years. She knew he was away until the end of the week, but from the website she was sure he would have other employees she could talk to.

Still unable to stop her mind churning, she opened her bedside table and searched for a pencil. If the doll's house represented how the Jordans' property had looked before the extension, there had to have been a considerable amount of earth removed to be able to lay down the new foundations. She recalled one of the Henderson brothers saying there had been a sixty-year-old tree that needed to be removed, as well as shrubs, a fence and brick wall. It seemed to Anna that there must have been a lot of work for one landscape gardener to complete on his own. She wondered if Andrew Markham might have used cash-in-hand labour to remove the debris from the Jordans' back garden. Still unable to switch off, she sat on the edge of her bed, checking the files to see if Andrew Markham had made a statement or had even been interviewed. There was no reference to him; perhaps due to the fact the work had taken place so long before Rebekka went missing. Had Langton, unaware of the ground clearance work, missed the possibility that Andrew Markham could also be a suspect? She wrote his name in her notebook, underlining the importance of talking to him as soon as she could.

By the time she turned off her bedside light it was after midnight, but it still took her half an hour to eventually fall asleep.

Chapter Six

'Mind if I sit with you?' Anna asked Barbara the next morning. She'd decided to get to work early and have breakfast in the canteen.

'Good heavens, no.' Barbara put her *Daily Mail* to one side, eyeing up Anna's loaded tray, piled with eggs, bacon, sausages and fried bread, plus coffee, in stark contrast to her own bowl of half-eaten bran cereal. 'Not on a diet then?'

Anna smiled and shook her head.

'I've been on one for twenty years. I hate bran, it's like chewing cardboard, but I reckon my system has got used to it. I crave a big fry-up, but I get terrible indigestion. I've got packets of Rennies in all my handbags and pockets because if I'm not careful I get this heartburn after anything fried.'

Anna tucked in, not really paying any attention to Barbara's stomach condition.

'How did it go in Glasgow?' Barbara eventually asked.

Anna gave her a sketchy outline, ending with the one new possibility that Henry Oates had worked in a riding stable.

'Well, shovelling shit could mean anything, road sweeping even.'

'I know.'

Barbara sipped her green tea and pulled a disgusted grimace. 'I hate bloody green tea as well.'

'You have anything from yesterday?' asked Anna.

'Not that much. Trying to piece together a character build and last known sightings for Fidelis Flynn. We had her flatmates in, nice girls, both at art college when Fidelis answered the advert for sharing. They said she was younger than them and from what I could gather they didn't want to know that much about her. She was behind with the rent and was always very argumentative; you know the type of thing that happens with flat-sharing.'

'I don't actually.'

Barbara gave her an odd look of surprise. 'Well it's who takes the last of the butter, uses your shampoo and doesn't clear up after themselves that starts the friction. They said she was always a few quid short for the rent ...' Barbara leaned forwards. 'She didn't intend leaving – well I don't think so, because we found her make-up and a purse in one of the suitcases she left with her clothes, and in it were two twenty-pound notes and some loose change.'

'But did she take any other belongings with her?'

'They didn't really know what was missing, if anything, because they didn't know what she had in her wardrobe. All they recalled was that the evening Fidelis went missing she left their flat to go to work and didn't appear to be worried about anything. They thought she might be working late as the garage stays open until midnight, but what they did remember was that she always carried a rucksack-type bag. When she didn't return, they did nothing.'

'Doesn't quite make sense. Why did they think she'd done a runner without paying the rent she owed if she'd left her make-up behind and the wardrobe was still full of her clothes?'

'No, they were packed into the suitcases and zip-up bag that local police seized later.'

'Still sort of doesn't sit right. Also, if there was money and she was short of it, why leave it behind if she didn't intend returning?'

'A workmate at the garage was questioned when her parents reported her missing. He said that he had an on-off relationship with Fidelis and although she had started seeing a male nurse they were still friends. He had expected her to come to work the night she went missing.'

'Was this the first time she'd failed to show up for work?'

Barbara nodded and said that she and Joan had talked about it and what they came up with was that Fidelis had maybe intended leaving, perhaps was even going to meet someone to rent another room somewhere. But as she'd left her belongings and money behind, they thought she must have been planning to return, at least for that night.

'Did you get anything further from her phone calls?'

Barbara's eyes opened wide and she smiled. Anna knew that she was at last about to be told something encouraging.

'Yes, the unregistered phone. I ran a property lost or stolen check on the number and I got a hit. Reported stolen in a mugging a few days after Fidelis went missing.'

'Good work, Barbara. So who does the phone belong to?'

'A Barry Moxen, and he's coming into the station this morning, never even knew she had been reported missing. He's a nurse who works in Charing Cross Hospital. When I talked to him he said he had not seen or heard from Fidelis for almost nineteen months. He met her at a New Year's party and had been having a sexual relationship with her on a regular basis and when he didn't hear from her he just presumed she had finished with him.'

Anna moved her plate aside.

'It's unbelievable, isn't it? The girl goes missing and everyone that appeared to know her never reported it. If it wasn't for her parents we'd maybe never have even known she'd disappeared.'

Barbara returned to the incident room and repeated her conversation with Anna to Joan, who suggested they quickly update the incident board with all the data as she didn't want Anna finding fault. They had just completed it when Anna came in from the canteen, but she went straight to her desk. The first thing she did was pick up a voicemail from Pete Jenkins at the forensic lab. When she rang back he was not available as his wife had just been taken into hospital; her waters had broken and the baby was coming earlier than expected.

Anna had no other calls so she picked up her marker pen and went over to the section of the incident board that was allocated to Rebekka Jordan. She began listing all the information she had gathered from the last few days.

Barbara glanced up. 'Looks like she's writing a novel,' she whispered to Joan. But they didn't get an opportunity to read it all for themselves until Anna had gone into Mike Lewis's office.

'What's this about the doll's house?' Joan wondered. She peered closer and then pulled a face.

'She's got a suspect, Andrew Markham.' Barbara tapped his name and Joan returned to her desk.

'Do you watch *CSI*, Barbara?'

'Sometimes, why?'

'They had a long-running case, over quite a few

episodes, about a serial killer that sent in these little doll's house rooms to police just before the murder. Then after the murder he posted these tiny dolls with knives stuck in them or gunshot wounds matching how he had actually killed the victims. One even had a teeny little cup and poison . . .'

'I didn't see it.'

'My mother never misses an episode.'

Mike listened as Anna brought him up to date and finished by asking if she could put Joan or Barbara onto tracing any known associates of Henry Oates. He agreed. They had found no address book or diary in Oates's basement so they had no idea of who he knew, but they had been gathering details on his infrequent employment through his National Insurance number and Jobseeker's. It appeared that whenever the Department for Work and Pensions threatened to withdraw his Jobseeker's Allowance he managed to find work for six to eight weeks. Apart from the jobs listed it appeared he had basically worked for cash in hand. They had tracked down various building, painting and decorating businesses, but it was tedious work and questioning each employer was taking up a lot of time. The priority was to check construction work he could have been involved in eighteen months previously and if there was any site that might be linked to the disappearance of Fidelis Flynn.

There was no record of him having worked for Andrew Markham, even though they had gone back as far as seven years. Anna suggested they send someone to the stables again to see if anyone could recall him working there on a cash basis.

Mike agreed, but observed that the old stable yard had

recently been taken over and refurbished. The new stables were much larger, but still close to the Shepherd's Bush flyover.

'I'd like to go and look at this Andrew Markham's garden centre,' Anna said.

'Okay. I'll get Barolli to check out the stables for you, and go ahead with asking Barbara to trace any boxing associates of Oates.'

'Thank you.'

Mike smiled. Sometimes she forgot what a good-looking man he was; very blond and blue-eyed. He was also dressing much better since he had been made a DCI, in suits and freshly laundered shirts. In fact, he was starting to resemble Langton – not quite as flashy – but she noticed that like the 'Guvnor' he now had bags from the local dry-cleaner's in his office.

'What?' he asked, seeing her looking at them.

'Just you look different, very smart and slightly like Langton – you are prepared for an all-night session.'

'What?'

'The dry-cleaning. He always used to have half his wardrobe in his office.'

'Oh right, yes, just for convenience really, and this afternoon I've got that prick Adan Kumar coming in.'

'What's he want now?'

'Just to look at the list of forensic exhibits and the unused material in the Justine Marks case.'

'Has he said anything about a psychiatric assessment of Oates yet?'

'No, and Langton said don't raise the subject with Kumar.'

'Oates being in the prison hospital could help Kumar's argument that he's not the full ticket.'

'Right. I know that, but we've been running a check every day with the prison governor and Oates hasn't required any further medical treatment since the assault. They said he's suffering from depression and put him on suicide watch just in case.'

'Do you think he's faking it?'

'Could be. Couple of days he refused to eat, but now he's accepting food and complaining that he's hungry, so he doesn't sound to me as if he's climbing up and down the walls.'

'Anything worth re-interviewing him about yet?'

Mike shrugged. 'I'm in no hurry and he'll be in the hospital wing for a few days yet.'

Again she thought how attractive he was when he gave a lovely smile.

'I'm hoping we get more on your enquiry and the Fidelis girl. They've got a boyfriend coming in this morning.'

Anna stood up and said she'd clear her desk and then get over to Andrew Markham's garden centre.

'You got a bad feeling about this guy?'

She hesitated and then after a moment nodded.

'The thing is, as far as we can tell Oates never owned a vehicle and did not have one when Rebekka Jordan went missing. Whoever picked her up had to have access to a car or a van to snatch her off the street. All the CCTV footage on the day she disappeared from the Tube station shows no sighting of her buying a ticket or catching a Tube, so she had to have been grabbed during that short walk from the stables to the station.'

'Yeah, but in the report two cameras were out of action, so it's a possibility she did go into the station, met her killer on the train maybe.'

'But not one witness came forward, not even after the TV reconstructions or all the press handouts; she had to have been snatched not far from the stables. Well that's what I think.'

'You could be right,' Mike conceded.

'See you later then,' Anna said as she headed for the door.

'I forgot to tell you DCS Hedges rang while you were in Glasgow.'

'What's he want?'

'Well he is supposed to be in charge while Langton is off. He gave me an ear-bashing about Langton going above him. Pissed off with me as well, said that if Langton wants to run the show from his sickbed then he can get on with it. Reckoned if it all goes tits up it's not his problem.'

'So we don't need to keep updating him as well.'

'Looks like it, yeah.'

Anna returned to her desk and asked Joan to ring York Hall, the big amateur and professional boxing venue, to ask the head trainer if he remembered Henry Oates, his friends or sparring partners and to find out if they kept a library of old fight programmes or posters. Before leaving she took a quick look over Fidelis Julia Flynn's board. They now had more recent photographs of her. In one picture she was smiling, revealing her slightly crooked teeth. In another she was standing with a spaniel puppy, laughing, wearing a floral dress over black tights and Doc Martens boots. Anna sighed. There was always something from the photographs of the missing or murdered girls that haunted you. It was the light in their eyes, which you knew was now gone.

'They were sent in by her parents,' Joan said as she opened a drawer in her desk. 'There's more if you want to see them.'

'No, thank you. I'll be on my way. Be back after lunch and I'll be on my mobile anyway.'

Before she left the station she couldn't resist heading down to the interview rooms on the floor below.

Barry Moxen was sitting opposite Barbara. He had black hair, spiky and gelled, a lot of acne, and was wearing a heavy leather biker's jacket. Anna watched for a few moments via the window in the door and as she turned to leave Barbara saw her.

'You want to talk to him?' Barbara opened the door.

'I don't think so.'

Barbara closed the door and stepped out into the corridor.

'I showed him the picture of Fidelis. He says she always called herself Julia and that she was seeing the bloke from the garage before she went out with him. He was working night shift at the hospital the whole week during the period Fidelis went missing. I rang them and they confirmed it. Last time he saw her was the weekend before his night shift when they went to the cinema. Julia told him she was fed up with the girls in the flat she shared and she was going to see some other rooms for rent and that she'd call him when she got a new address. She never did. Like he told me on the phone, he reckoned she'd ditched him.'

'Did he try her old flat?'

'Yeah, he was told she'd moved out.'

'Okay. Just ask if he knew the address or location of any of the new places Fidelis was going to view. Did she use a letting agent, look in the papers or online, *Time Out*, *Gumtree* or whatever, then you'll have to check back and see if she contacted any of them.'

'Oh right, will do.'

*

Andrew Markham's garden centre was hard to find. It was not far from Cobham in Surrey, but the entrance was on a curve in the road, so easily missed. It had a barred gate with a notice to please make sure the gate was always closed. Only a small sign indicated that it was also a garden design company. Anna opened the gate and drove a few feet before she returned and heaved it shut. She found herself on a dirt track with big cart ruts and deep puddles. On one side was an open field; the other had a large barn with private property notices fixed to the side. The lane went on for about a quarter of a mile before a green-painted sign read *MARKHAM'S GARDEN DESIGNS*.

A big red arrow pointed to a high barred gate, which was standing open enough for Anna to drive in.

The garden centre had about an acre of land. Scattered around were modern greenhouses and there was another large barn, full of tractors, vans with the company logo, and a Range Rover. There was a trailer-cum-caravan with 'Office' printed on a card on the door. Anna knocked and waited, but there was no answer. She tried the door, but it was locked.

Now she wished she'd put her wellington boots in the car as it was very muddy, forcing her to hop over two deep puddles as she headed for the first greenhouse. Plants grew in profusion, every shelf creaking with different varieties of flora. It was very well heated and irrigated, but it was also empty.

'Hello? Anyone here?' she called out.

There was no reply so she made her way towards the second greenhouse. Outside were hundreds of clay pots of every size and a few stone statues. Anna could see more plants and inside this greenhouse the sprinklers were turned on. They gave a fine spray, making the windows steam up.

Anna looked around the yard. The last building was the barn, and she plodded through the mud to get to it. The old wooden door was ajar and through it she could hear the sound of a tinny radio playing Bruce Springsteen.

'Hello? Is anyone here?'

She peered inside: it was huge. Both sides were stacked with sacks of peat and soil reaching the ceiling. Then her gaze fell on a mass of gardening equipment – rakes and brushes and shovels – all piled in a square wooden pen. Wheelbarrows were propped against each other in a row and beyond them was a stable. A horse's head stuck out, chewing straw, and the closer Anna got the more she could smell the overpowering stench of manure. A large second pen held bales of straw and sacks of horse feed. Propped above an old carpenter's bench were saddles and riding equipment, and hard hats balanced on pegs.

The second stall was empty but Anna was drawn by the sound of water and clanging buckets.

'Hello?' she called.

There was a girl wearing jodhpurs, a green padded jacket and a cloth cap. She had rubber riding boots on and was using a hose to wash down the walls.

'Excuse me. Hello,' Anna tried again.

The girl turned and gasped with shock as Anna had surprised her. She pulled out an earphone.

'Christ, you scared the hell out of me.'

'I'm so sorry. I've been calling out for ages.'

'What do you want?'

Anna showed her ID and the girl pulled off a thick padded leather glove.

'Shit, this isn't that bloody farmer having a go at us again, is it?'

'No, but if you could spare me a few minutes I'd like to talk to you. I am Detective Anna Travis.'

'I'm Mari. Here, take the keys and go into the caravan and I'll finish in here. Only the other horse will be back any minute and I want it clean before he's here.'

Anna opened up the caravan and got into the warmth. An old Calor gas heater made it feel like an oven. There was a decrepit floral sofa with the stuffing hanging out, two equally old armchairs, a large desk, and filing cabinets that were new and covered one wall. There was also a small kitchen with rows of chipped mugs and instant coffee jars and boxes of tea bags with names taped to them.

It was about fifteen minutes before Mari banged into the caravan, making it shake.

'That man is making our lives a nightmare. We are not allowed to put up a decent sign on the road, so we don't get any passing customers – not that we really need them – but it's a constant battle. I hope to Christ you shut the gate when you came in.'

'Yes.'

'Good, because God forbid it's left open. That bastard comes down the lane like something out of a Gothic nightmare. Trouble is, Andrew was left this patch of land by his father and he, the so-called farmer, wants him to sell up, which Andy refuses to do unless he's paid a good price. He just wants his bloody cows to use our path.'

Mari took off her cloth cap and a cascade of wild golden ringlets came loose. She was an exceedingly pretty woman. Devoid of any make-up, her skin was like a young child's with ruddy cheeks and she had freckles dotted over her small neat nose.

'So what's this all about then?'

She plonked herself down on one of the worn arm-chairs, indicating for Anna to sit in the other.

'Well my full title is DCI Anna Travis from the Met murder team.'

'Wow. Well my full name, believe it or not, is Marigold Summers – bane of my life. My sisters are also named after flowers; theirs are Daisy and Violet. Hippy parents, obviously, but everyone calls me Mari.'

Anna smiled. Mari was a character, albeit it a very attractive one, with her skinny frame beneath an old man's shirt, jodhpurs and rubber riding boots. She also had tiny slender hands.

'Do you smoke?'

'No I don't.'

'Mind if I make a roll-up?'

'No.'

'So why are you here? I think Daisy said she took a call from some detective about contacting Andy, but he's in Thailand, due back this weekend.'

Anna watched as Mari fished in her pockets and took out a small square tin, pinched some tobacco out of it and very professionally rolled a thin cigarette. Licking the paper and twisting the end tightly, Mari then got up and fetched a lighter from the desk.

'So what is this all about then?'

She sucked at the thin roll-up and flicked the lighter on a couple of times before the tobacco caught.

'It's about a missing teenager; a girl called Rebekka Jordan.'

Mari gave no reaction to the name as she leaned forwards to listen.

'Mr Markham did some work on a property in Hammersmith for a Mr and Mrs Jordan. It'd be over five years ago.'

There was still no reaction from Mari as she puffed at her roll-up.

'Do you have documents here that could give me a list of the people Mr Markham employed on that specific job?'

'I can have a look. I wasn't around then. His filing system is a bit of a mess, his accountant goes mad, he's always behind, but half the time it's not his fault. You'd be surprised how late people pay their bills. The posher and richer they are, the worse they are. He's forever sending off invoice after invoice.'

Mari began to pull open drawers in one of the filing cabinets and turned to Anna.

'Sorry, I've forgotten what I'm looking for?'

'Mr and Mrs Jordan from Hammersmith.'

Mari banged open one drawer after another.

'It'd be a help if he put them in alphabetical order.'

'Tell me about Mr Markham?'

Mari turned and grinned.

'He's fabulous. I adore him. I was in love with him from the age of seven as he knows my parents. I was always obsessed with horses and he used to be part of the local hunt. In fact the two hunters we've got are sort of a charity case as they're ancient, but he won't let them be sent off to the glue factory. We give the local kids riding lessons and—'

'Is he married?'

Mari was now sitting on the floor with a stack of folders, skimming them and putting them to one side.

'He has been twice, but with him working all hours here they didn't last. He lives in his mother's house now, but you'll often find him kipping on that old sofa. Ah! Hang on . . .'

Mari had a thick file filled with papers and drawings and pictures of greenhouses cut from magazines. She carried it to her chair and sat balancing it on her knee.

'I think this is it. Gosh, it was quite a big job. There's loads of invoices. What do you want to see?'

'Did he use regular workers? Can you see if there is a list of people he employed to do the job?'

Mari skipped through the pages and then passed the file over to Anna.

'I can't really tell you. It was quite a long time ago. He used to work part-time at Kew until he got this place up and running.'

Anna smiled as she tried to sort through the mess of documents.

'How many people work for him on a permanent basis?'

'Well there's me, my sister Daisy, two old blokes that he uses for the heavy lifting, and William who does the deliveries and buys any plants we don't grow here.'

'Have you ever seen this man before?'

Anna passed Henry Oates's photograph to her. She looked and wrinkled her nose.

'No, don't know him.'

'When Mr Markham does a big job, say like the Jordans', does he bring in extra help?'

'Yeah, if he needs to. I mean the two old guys live locally and they don't go out on jobs as they've got their work cut out here. William sometimes helps out, and me and Daisy, but the commissioned work is always handled by Andy. If he needs muscle he'll get self-employed casual labour.'

'Cash in hand, would that be?'

'Yes, always is for part-timers. I think he's got a group of guys he uses on a regular basis when they are needed.'

'Do you have their names?'

Mari chewed her lip and then picked up the lighter, sticking her roll-up in the corner of her mouth.

'Now, they may be in his address book. He's mind-blowing cos he uses a big old leather thing from years ago. We buy him new ones, but he likes to keep the old moth-eaten one cos he can't be bothered to transfer all the names and addresses.'

Mari was now looking over the desk, moving stuff aside and opening drawers.

'What about a computer?'

'He uses a laptop all the time, carries it with him. It will probably be at his house.'

'Would he have a record of employees on his computer?'

'Yeah, he might have.'

Anna was getting frustrated. The Jordans' file contained invoices, a list of plants, costings for the removal of a small fishpond and plans for a new garden layout and large new pond. There were photographs of the back of the Jordans' house, showing the trees and shrubs that required removal. Amongst the papers were more diagrams of the brick wall that was to be replaced, the fences and then many samples of materials for the extension and proposed garden changes. It was almost impossible to find anything about how many people would be required to do the job, but it confirmed her belief that it would have been impossible for one man to do the clearance. She knew from the builders that Markham had excavated areas of the garden so the footings and foundations could be laid for the extension. From the dates on the invoices she calculated that Markham started the clearance work at the end of June 2006 and it probably took about two weeks to complete.

Mari dumped a thick leather-bound diary onto the desk. Page after page was covered with Post-it notes, stuck with Sellotape to some pages, and at the back were names and addresses, hundreds of them. There were so many scribbled notes and crossings-out, it was difficult to decipher anything, but Anna began to sift through it anyway.

'When did this girl go missing?'

Anna looked up as Mari began rolling another cigarette.

'Five years ago.'

'Oh wow, long time. How come you are asking questions about it now?'

'We have a suspect.'

'Wow, that's interesting. And you think he might have worked for Andy?'

Anna looked up, surprised that Mari had worked it out.

'Yes, it's possible, but I really need to talk to Mr Markham.'

The sounds of a horse's hooves clattering on the cobbled stones outside made Mari yank open the caravan door.

'Daisy, I'm in here! I washed down the stall so you can give him his feed!' she yelled, then shut the door and pointed to a black-and-white photograph pinned on a noticeboard.

'That's him, he's such a dozy lovable nag. He's seventeen hands and twenty years old now.'

Anna smiled as she glanced at the photograph. Mari lit her second roll-up.

'Is that Mr Markham riding?'

'No, that was his father. Do you want a coffee?'

'Yes, please.'

DS Paul Barolli had a fear of horses – in fact it was almost a phobia. He'd been given one lesson, aged seven, and the horse had trodden on him and injured his foot. He hated the smell of the manure, his stomach churned and he wanted to pinch his nose. The stables were very busy with young children having lessons in the manège area, the horses' hooves throwing up sand as the instructor shouted for her pupils to sit up straight and gather in the reins for a trot. There were youngsters and adults mucking out stables, grooming horses and buffing up leather saddles. Barolli, not paying attention to where he was going, found himself stepping in a fresh mound of horse muck.

The stable manager's assistant, Kelly, a young girl in jodhpurs and thick polo-neck sweater, was removing her boots when Barolli was ushered into the reception office. He attempted to explain the reason for his visit, but was constantly interrupted as another girl answered the telephone, arranging rides and lessons and asking Kelly for timetables. It was hard for him to concentrate as he was sweating profusely, but he began to ease up when Kelly suggested they use an adjoining small office where they wouldn't be disturbed.

Barolli showed Kelly the photograph of their suspect.

'We are interested to know if there is anyone working here who recalls seeing this man. He may have worked part-time and used the name Henry Oates.'

'Five or six years ago?' Kelly said, looking at the photograph.

'Yes.'

'I've heard about the girl that went missing, but you do know the whole stables have moved as it's a much bigger organization now and we also have an equestrian training ring and large indoor—'

He interrupted her. 'Yes, yes, we are aware of that, but would you know if there are any employees still working here from the old stables?'

'It's likely, though I wouldn't know, to be honest, I've only been here eighteen months, but I can get someone to find out for you.'

'Thank you.'

Kelly returned to the larger office and Barolli could hear her asking if it was possible to run a check on the computer for a Henry Oates. She came back in and explained that they had a big turnover of people at weekends and that they also had a lot of trainers and owners coming through as they stabled privately owned horses.

'It's more likely this person worked mucking out. I doubt if he would have owned or ridden a horse, just been part-time labour,' Paul told her.

'What happened to the girl?'

'Her name was Rebekka Jordan. It has been an ongoing investigation, but we've had a couple of new leads so they have to be looked into.'

'But you don't know what happened to her?'

'No we don't.'

Kelly glanced at her wristwatch and apologized, saying she only had another few minutes before she was due to teach a lesson in the indoor arena.

'I can walk you round the stables if you like. I presume you'll want to show everyone this photograph.'

'I'd like to wait to see if there is anyone from five years

ago and then talk to them in here. I'm allergic to hay, I get hay fever.'

It took Anna over an hour to read through the whole of Markham's diary and finish checking the files for the job at the Jordans'. Mari had returned now and again to top up her mug of coffee. By the time Anna left she felt it had been a lot of time wasted and she still had no connection between Andrew Markham and Henry Oates. She had found some memos listing cash payments for part-time labour, but no names had been mentioned. She had made a copy of the dates and times Markham had worked for the Jordans, but his payments for the clearance had been settled by the builders. The fee for his work on the redesign of their garden, after the extension had been completed, was paid directly to his company account. Markham had finished working at the Jordans almost six months before Rebekka went missing.

It turned out that the head groom and one of the riding instructors had been employed as young stable hands at the old yard when Rebekka went missing, but neither of them were able to identify Henry Oates. They remembered Rebekka, particularly as both had been questioned by Langton's team. They did recall that often part-time labour would be used when the stables were being repaired. The previous owners used to hire from a job centre, but they were often youngsters. Barolli had heard enough, and couldn't wait to get back to the station.

Barolli and Anna arrived back at the incident room at the same time.

'Got nothing new from the stables,' he said. 'There were

two blokes who'd worked there for over five years and they'd also been questioned by Langton's team and cleared, but they didn't recognize Oates as ever being seen around there.'

'I didn't get much luck either.' Anna wrote up her section of the board, underlining that Andrew Markham was still to be questioned on his return from Thailand.

'What's he doing there?' Barolli asked.

'Holiday.'

'Ah, likes the young girls there, I bet. That's why most blokes go there. They throw themselves at you.'

'Really? Well, we'll see what he says, but according to this girl Marigold Summers, he buys up a lot of artefacts there and gets them shipped here for his garden displays.'

'Excuse me, ma'am.' Anna turned to see Joan standing there. 'I've had some luck on the boxing front. I've sent out one of the guys to York Hall to bring in old posters and programmes that they had in storage and I've got a couple of names and possible addresses for boxers that trained there in the nineties and were friends with Henry Oates.'

'Good. Put the details on my desk, Joan.'

Realizing it was getting late, Anna went to the Ladies for a wash and brush-up and then rushed to the canteen. By the time she returned to her desk it was after six, and Barbara and Joan had already left.

Anna seriously considered packing up and doing the same. Beside her desk was a large brown carrier bag with a lot of rolled-up posters and old boxing programmes, all with that distinctive musty smell as if they had been stashed in a damp cupboard somewhere.

The two ex-boxers identified as friends of Henry Oates were a Timmy Bradford and Ira Zacks. There was an address and home number for Bradford and a mobile number for Zacks. Anna sighed – she really didn't feel fresh enough to contact them and arrange interviews so marked it up as a priority for the morning. She decided she wouldn't even look over the posters and programmes, but make her escape and have an early night.

As she headed to the car park, Anna's phone rang. Langton. She didn't answer, but it immediately rang again. She swore under her breath, certain it would be Langton, but it turned out to be Pete Jenkins from the forensic lab. Feeling guilty about not calling him about his baby, she answered.

'Pete. I was just about to call you.'

'I've been at the maternity hospital. Baby came early. She's doing all right, but it's been touch and go; she was just three pounds and has got some infection, so she's still in the intensive care unit. Her breathing's getting better, though, she's a real little fighter.'

'I'm so sorry, but a baby girl, congratulations!'

'She going to be called Matilda, Maddy, and she's got thick black curly hair. It's scary; she nearly fits into the palm of my hand.'

'I love the name. How is your wife?'

'She's very tearful and it's hard to go back onto the ward with all the other mothers as they have their babies with them, so she's coming home. In fact I'm going to pick her up now.'

'Fingers crossed then, and thanks for calling.'

'I just wanted to say I'll be back at the lab tomorrow. My assistants have done a lot of dirty work sorting stuff if you want to come in. I'll be there around twelve.'

'See you then.'

'Okay, bye now.'

Anna sighed and started up the ignition, just as her mobile rang yet again. It was Langton this time, of course, but she was eager to get home.

No sooner had she got through her front door than her landline rang. This time she decided to pick up.

'Travis?'

'Yes. How you doing?'

'Don't you answer your effing mobile?'

'Been out interviewing.'

'Any chance of you dropping in?'

'Not tonight. I've only just walked in.'

'On your way in tomorrow then, we can have breakfast. Bring some fresh bagels and smoked salmon. I also need some coffee.'

She scrawled his requests on a notepad by the phone.

'See you in the morning about eight.' She cut off the call, not wanting to talk further. He was starting to really grate on her nerves and she'd tell him so in the morning.

Lying in bed after a long hot shower, she mulled over the day's progress. She didn't have a lot. There were no further developments in the Rebekka Jordan enquiry. She thought about Pete with his beloved little Matilda in an incubator and it made her wonder about what it would be like, God forbid, to lose a child. Ken had wanted a family – his rugby team – and she had wanted it too. An awful sadness swamped her. She had hoped for so much and had been left with nothing.

Chapter Seven

L angton's kitchen looked as if an earthquake had hit it. There was broken crockery, dirty dishes stacked in the sink and on the draining board. The fridge door had been left open and now wouldn't close thanks to the ice blocking the door latch. Dirty pots and pans littered the floor and a garbage bag was spewing out its contents.

'My God, your kitchen is disgusting,' Anna said, from the doorway of his bedroom.

'I fell over in there yesterday. Just leave it all, the girl that cleans the flat upstairs is dropping by this afternoon to do the place over.'

That was easy enough to say, she thought as she walked back into the kitchen. She'd have to wash up some of the plates left in the sink, and there was no way she could prepare their breakfast until she had wiped down the surfaces and done a partial clean-up.

Carrying in the tray of the menu he'd requested, smoked salmon and bagels with fresh black coffee, she asked if he could at least clear a space on the bed for her to rest the tray. He did so by shoving all the newspapers and files onto the floor with one sweep of his arm.

'There you go!'

He was obviously hungry, as he devoured his bagel and smoked salmon so quickly he made himself burp.

'Excuse me. Delicious, just what I fancied.'

She nibbled hers as he drank his coffee, leaning back against the pillows.

'Okay, give me the lowdown.'

She told him about the garden design centre and that she still wanted to talk to Andrew Markham as there was a possibility Henry Oates could have worked for him, and that she would investigate the two boxers who'd been friends of Oates.

'I wouldn't bother with Markham, I interviewed him.'

'Really?'

'Yep. He used pals that worked at Kew Gardens to help with the work on the excavation.'

'Terrific. You know his name doesn't even feature in your files!'

He frowned and said that it must be some oversight because he had talked to him personally. He then changed the subject and asked about Oates. Anna told him that he was still in the prison hospital after the assault and as yet Kumar had not asked for a psychiatric assessment.

'Is he still acting up? Oates, not that prick Kumar.'

'He stopped eating for a while, said he was feeling very depressed, so to be on the safe side they put him on suicide watch.'

'He's pissing them about so he can stay in the hospital wing and have an easy time.'

'Gives us more time to find the evidence.'

'You've not done too well so far. Listen, if you or Mike don't find anything against Oates for the Flynn or Jordan girls you will still have to interview. If he killed them then a full confession to everything that happened is the only way forward, so I want you to talk to Mike. If I'm right, Oates is the kind of bastard that likes to gloat. Now he said . . .'

Langton leaned over the bed and rooted around before he retrieved the copies of the original interviews with Oates from when he was first arrested.

'He said he remembered Rebekka because of all the press statements about her being missing, right? You with me?'

'Yes.'

'Tell Mike to draw him out, test his memory, say he just needs to see how he could recall her name and the date she disappeared so clearly. Pictures of her posted up every-where, right? Ask him if he can – because of the media attention – remember what she was wearing. I told you the one thing we held back.'

'The hair band?'

'Correct. See if Mike can tease out what Oates can remember – you know, make sure that he was being honest when he said the reason he remembered Rebekka was because of the television reconstruction.'

'Okay, I'll make a note of it to tell Mike.'

'If Oates describes the pink hair band, you know he came into contact with her the day she disappeared.'

'But he could have seen her wearing it any time before she went missing?'

'No he couldn't. Emily Jordan had only bought it the previous day and Rebekka had never had, or worn, a pink Alice band before.'

'Sorry but I wasn't aware of that.'

'Well it's in the case file.'

'Right. Anything else?'

'If you're not going to finish your bagel I'll have it.'

Anna passed him her plate and took the tray back to the kitchen. She wanted to leave, so didn't bother washing up, just hovered in the doorway of his bedroom.

'I'm off now as I really want to get on with checking out those two boxers, all right? You've fresh coffee in the percolator and . . .'

She hesitated. He lay back and closed his eyes.

'Do you mind if I take that doll's house into the station?'

He opened his eyes. 'Why?'

'It gives a clear indication of how the house and garden looked before the extension.'

He sighed and said she could take it and not to bother bringing it back. Kitty didn't want it and he hated looking at it.

'Well you know where I am,' she said as she walked out.

'You know where I am!' he yelled back.

She went into the kitchen and dug in a cupboard for a large carrier bag. There were so many plastic bags tossed inside, the cupboard door wouldn't close. She returned to his bedroom.

'This cleaner . . . when she gets here tell her to clear out the kitchen cupboards. I'm taking a big John Lewis carrier bag, okay?'

He held out his hand and grinned. 'Come here, you.'

She moved closer and he leaned forwards to catch her hand.

'Thank you. And will you call me if you get anything from these two boxers?'

'Of course.'

'Leave your mobile on?'

'Yes I will.'

'Okay. You go off then and see you later maybe.'

She hesitated, turning back to look at him. She wanted

to say to him that she wouldn't be seeing him later, that she wasn't prepared to be at his beck and call to pick up groceries, cook for him and feed him, but he looked so vulnerable, so untidy and in need of a shave and a bath that she thought better of it.

'Hope you feel better soon. Bye.'

The doll's house wouldn't quite go in the bag, but in the end she managed to cover the roof and first floor. She had to rest it on the bonnet of her Mini as she unlocked it, as it was very heavy, and she couldn't get it into the passenger or back seats as it was too wide. In the end she folded the rear seats flat to make the boot bigger and managed to fit it in the car. She slotted the little bags of tiny furniture and figures in beside it.

Joan and Barbara had to hold open the incident room double doors for Anna to carry in the doll's house. She placed it on an empty desk and both of the older women stood around to admire it. Joan was especially taken with it.

'I used to have one, though not as well built as this. It's lovely and with a spot of paint it'll look even better. Is it home-made?'

'Yes.' Anna removed her coat and then had to go back to her car for her briefcase as she'd been unable to carry it before. When she returned the two women were still opening and closing the doors of the house, and Joan was inspecting the little bags of furniture.

'If it's not a rude question, why is it here?' Barbara asked, heading back to her desk.

'Could be used as evidence, but I'm not sure about it. Maybe get it down to the property lockup later.'

'Do you know something?' Joan began. 'I was telling Barbara the other day about some episodes of *CSI*, that TV series from America. They had this killer and he sent in small doll's-house-size rooms showing how he killed his victims.'

'Really?' Anna sat at her desk.

'My mother never misses it. They showed teeny little knives in one doll, one was shot and another poisoned, all hand-made by the murderer.'

Barbara rolled her eyes as Joan was still bent over the doll's house.

'You know the windows open and shut.'

'It's actually about the garden. Rebekka Jordan's parents had a big extension built, but as you can see there isn't one here.'

'It's been damaged.' Joan was now checking out the back garden area and squatting down on her heels.

'It must have taken someone hours and hours to make this.'

'Was it Rebekka's?' Barbara asked.

'Yes.' Anna said, eager to get on with her work. She didn't mention that she had brought it in from Langton's. Now she turned to the big bag of posters and programmes from York Hall. The musty smell made her sneeze as she spread them over her desk. None of the posters featured Henry Oates's name, so she put them aside and began to sift through the programmes. She found one with the name of Timmy Bradford from about fifteen years ago, but still had no joy with Henry Oates. There were numerous programmes mentioning Ira Zacks, both as a semi-pro fighter and an amateur. He appeared to go from middle- to heavyweight. The last programme she checked out had Henry Oates down as a light middleweight amateur boxer and his opponent was Timmy Bradford, also an amateur.

Anna added the information to the incident room board. She put in a call to Timmy Bradford but there was no answer, so she next rang Ira Zacks and hung on waiting for an answer for almost four minutes. Eventually a deep guttural voice growled, 'Yes?'

Anna explained who she was and that if it was convenient she would like to speak to him regarding his friendship with Henry Oates.

'Who?'

He sounded half asleep and she constantly had to repeat herself before he finally admitted that he used to know Oates, but hadn't seen him for years. She asked if he knew Timmy Bradford and he said that he did, but again had not been in contact with him for years.

It took a while before Ira agreed to see Anna. He said he'd had some business at a nightclub and hadn't got home until the early hours, so it would be best if she came that afternoon. He gave her an address in Hammersmith. She asked if Timmy Bradford still lived at the address in Bromley she had and he said he couldn't tell her. All he did remember about him was that he worked for a security firm.

Anna tried the phone number for Timmy Bradford again and this time it was answered by a woman who said she'd never heard of him and she'd lived at the flat for the last four years.

Joan was given the job of calling York Hall to see if they had a date of birth for Timmy Bradford so she could try and locate him through the benefits office at the Department for Work and Pensions or other agencies.

'You know we got a bit of a break with Fidelis Flynn?'

Barbara said to Anna. 'Barolli and Joan spent hours going through adverts for flat shares from the *Evening Standard* and *Time Out*, around the time Fidelis disappeared. They checked through hundreds.'

'And?'

'Came in late last night. Barolli got a hit. It was a bedsit in a converted Victorian house in Shepherd's Bush.'

'What? You are kidding me?'

Joan looked across at them.

'Girl fitting Fidelis's description went to see the flat, said she would think about it and call that evening. Never rang back.'

Joan got up to point out the exact location on the blown-up map now on the incident board.

'It's not far from the stables,' Joan said.

Anna was buzzing.

'She turned up at four-fifteen,' Barbara went on. 'The woman who owned the premises said four women had applied to see the room and they viewed it on the same day. She recalled Fidelis as being Irish, that she carried a small rucksack and said that if she took the room she would want to move in straight away.'

'Never called back?'

'Right. So we now have a sort of description of what she was wearing – we didn't have anything to go on before: blue anorak, jeans, dark-coloured jumper and knee-high boots.'

'Hmmm ... this girl who owns the lease has a very good memory. I mean, it was eighteen months ago.'

'She said she pays particular attention to anyone coming in to see the room as they would obviously be sharing the kitchen and bathroom.'

'She recognized her straight away,' said a new voice.

Anna turned as Barolli walked in.

'This is good work, Paul.'

'Thank you. I needed to get my mind off sneezing from the bloody hay at the stables. As you can see, the Shepherd's Bush flat is not far from Ladbroke Grove and within walking distance of the Tube station and the stables.'

'Don't thank me,' Joan said mournfully. 'I've been on the phone for so long my ear lobes are ringing.'

'Great work, all of you. Congratulations,' said Anna, with feeling.

Anna went in to see Mike and filled him in on that morning's conversation with Langton. She also suggested they send some flowers to Pete Jenkins' home address for his wife and new baby.

'Anything more from Kumar?' she asked.

'Nope. He went over the disclosure stuff and left without saying a word. I spoke to the prison for an update on Oates. The governor says he's stopped playing up and should be moved to solitary in the next couple of days for his own protection and be closely monitored.'

'Be good if we could crack either Fidelis's or Rebekka's disappearance. I'm not having much luck so far, nothing new, but it's a big development on the Fidelis Flynn case. I'm trying to contact two boxers that knew Oates way back, see if I can get more on his background. One of them lives in Hammersmith close to the Jordans' place.'

Mike nodded and then opened out a large map, covering his desk. They had investigated building sites across West London, on the possibility that Oates had worked in the Shepherd's Bush area. They were now sifting through any likely building sites and companies that might have hired unskilled or cheap labour over the last six years. Parts of the map were circled with a highlighter pen.

'It's not unusual to use Eastern European guys paid on a daily rate for less money than a skilled labourer. Day's rate for a builder, carpenter, anyone with training, is around a hundred and ninety quid, but these casual workers will accept a hundred.'

'Cash?'

'Yeah. The obvious site is the Westfield Shopping Centre, which was started in 2003 and took five years to complete, so it fits the time span for Rebekka, but not for Fidelis.'

'The security on Westfield must have been massive?'

'It was, so it doesn't look likely he could have put Rebekka's body there. Barolli's spoken to the contractors to see if Oates ever worked on site but they're being very cagey. But here's one Paul reckons we should look into.'

Mike pointed to a red-circled area just off Shepherd's Bush Green.

'What is it?'

'Multi-storey car park built as an overflow for Westfield and the timing is right for Fidelis's disappearance. Two years ago they had a big rebuild and put in footings and supporting pillars going down twenty feet. They built lifts, used tons of concrete and heavy mixers, but they didn't really need guys with qualifications.'

'What was the security like?'

'One night guard in a Portakabin.'

'Terrific. Good luck.'

'Thanks.' Mike smiled and cocked his head to one side. 'So how is he?'

'Langton?'

Mike nodded.

'Pain in the butt. He keeps on calling me to get in groceries for him, his place is a pigsty, and he looks worn-out, but he told me he's getting a cleaner in today.'

'Where's his wife and kids?'

'Apparently at his place in the country. You know how he keeps his private life close to his chest, so I have no idea where it is.'

'I'll call him and give an update about the Flynn girl.'

'Don't mention I said anything, will you?'

'As if I would. I might even drop in to see him. I owe him a visit.'

Anna walked to the door and then grinned. 'He likes his vodka!'

'Listen, if it'll keep him out of my hair I'll get him a crate!'

By the time Anna was back at her desk, Joan had succeeded in tracking down Timmy Bradford. He had changed address, having been made redundant six months ago. Unemployed, he was now living back with his mother on a council estate in Kingston.

'Terrific. Thank you, Joan.'

'My pleasure.'

The Kingsnympton estate was huge, with a warren of lanes, but very well maintained and it was apparent that a number of the flats were privately owned. Anna parked and walked to the block where Mrs Bradford lived. It was unlike many of the council estates she had been to previously. This block was clean and the stairs were freshly painted; all the front doors looked as if they had just been painted too.

The bell had a jingle like a nursery rhyme and the bright blue door was opened by a pleasant white-haired woman wearing a tracksuit and fluffy slippers.

'Mrs Bradford?'

'I was, dear. I remarried. I'm Mrs Douglas now and you are the detective lady, right?'

Anna showed her ID and introduced herself as Mrs Douglas led her across a floral-carpeted narrow hallway through frosted glass doors and into a sitting room. There was more floral carpet and a velvet suite with a large foot-stool and in the corner of the room was a huge plasma TV. Glass-fronted cabinets were filled with china and orna-ments, and there was an electric coal-effect fire glowing against one wall.

'Do sit down. Timmy's just popped out for some fresh milk. I used to get it delivered, but bottles would go miss-ing. Kids, you know . . .'

Anna almost disappeared into the deep cushions of the velvet chair. Mrs Douglas came closer to her, evidently anxious.

'There's nothing wrong, is there? He hasn't done any-thing wrong, has he?'

'I am just here to ask for his help in an enquiry. He knew the person we are investigating and nothing more.'

'That's a relief. Poor boy needs a job, but it's been years on and off. Every time he stays with me he says it's just for a few weeks, but this time it's been over six months. He lost his savings, you know, with that bank that closed down. He lost every penny he earned and he'd been saving to buy one of the flats here; there's a lot coming up for sale. It would mean we're not on top of each other – not that I mind, he's a good boy.'

'Is your husband at home?'

'Oh no, dear. He passed on two years ago. And that was another thing – they never got on. He called him a bit of a freeloader and maybe he was right, but he's my only son. I suppose I should be glad of the company, but to be honest, he's very untidy and I like things to be just so. He says I'm obsessive, but I'm the sort that's up and ready by seven, always do the crossword in the paper, and nothing gets me more irritated than the newspaper all split up before I've even read it.'

She hardly drew breath, but thankfully Anna heard the front door opening and Mrs Douglas hurried out.

'She's in here, dear. Did you get the biscuits too?'

'Yeah.'

Anna could see them through the frosted glass doors and waited. Eventually Timmy Bradford walked in. He was also wearing a tracksuit, with a black T-shirt and trainers, and he was obviously very fit. He was blond, his hair cut in the odd new fashion, cropped and razored at the sides and floppy on top. He had a gold earring and a thick gold necklace. Similar in looks to his mother, he had a very chiselled face and had at one time broken his nose. It was now crooked, which gave him an added toughness, even more so as he had a front tooth missing.

He moved over to Anna and shook her hand, asking if she would like a cup of tea.

'Had me nipping out to get biscuits. I don't eat them, but she insisted. She'll be in in a minute with a tray and lace cloth.'

He grinned and sat opposite Anna on the edge of the other big velvet chair. 'She's eighty-two, in her forties when she had me.'

'Good heavens. She doesn't look it.'

'She's busy doing nothing, but she's on a diet, lost over

a stone since I've been here. She's a devil for sweet stuff, though – chocolate orange biscuits, she can eat a whole pack of them.'

He smiled and then gave a sigh.

'I dunno ... grown man my age having to live off her pension. It's driving me nuts. I keep active, down the gym every day working out, and if I'm not there, I'm at the job centre. I hate being on the dole.'

Anna nodded then opened her briefcase and took out Henry Oates's picture.

'I need to talk to you about this man. Do you know him?'

Timmy jumped to his feet as his mother called to him from the doorway. He swung open the door and took the tray from her.

'Thank you, Ma. Now just leave us for a minute, will you?'

He fussed around with the tray, which did have a lace-`edged cloth, with a silver teapot and matching milk jug, and a plate of plain biscuits. The cups and saucers matched and were covered in roses.

He poured a cup for Anna and passed it to her and then offered the biscuits. He didn't pour a cup for himself or take a biscuit, but reached over for the picture of Henry Oates.

'Henry, yeah I know him, or I used to know him well. Long time ago now when I was boxing at the club in Bethnal Green. I've got a deviated septum, used to bleed like a stuck pig at the smallest tap. Gave it up, had to, but I used to train and spar with him, even fought him in the London Boys Club Championships. He was a tough little bastard – excuse me – but Henry was a good athlete, had a lot of potential.'

He handed the photographs back to Anna.

'When did you last see him?'

Timmy shook his head and then leaned back.

'Maybe seven years ago, bumped into him at York Hall watching the ABA championships. He still looked fucked-up – excuse me, sorry. I knew his last ever fight had been a real hard one, but he was the type that wouldn't go down. Even his corner man wanted to throw the towel in, but he boxed on, got smashed up badly.'

'Was he still boxing when you last saw him?'

'No, he'd given it up a good few years before, looked like he'd hit the bottom, drunk out of his skull. I was never close to him. To be honest I didn't think anyone was really. He'd got a chip on his shoulder the size of a boulder. Mind you, rumour had it that he'd got involved with a wrong 'un.'

'Who do you mean?'

'His wife.'

'Eileen?'

'I didn't know her name, and this is all what was repeated to me. He married her because she said she was pregnant – you know, he done the decent thing.'

'He was very abusive towards her, wasn't he?'

'I wouldn't know, but what I was told was that he thought the kid wasn't his. Had the look of a darkie.'

'So you didn't know that as a fact?'

'She put it about a bit for cash, you know, on the game, they said, and again I'm only repeating what I heard, but apparently he only found out about her other job after he'd married her. She denied it, said he was definitely the father, but he was never sure. I mean, it could have been anyone's.'

'Did he find out? Do a DNA test, anything like that?'

Timmy shrugged. He remembered that Henry had gone to Liverpool to find his mother so he could get a passport, but he had never caught up with the rest of the story.

'Do you recall the man who trained Henry, perhaps an ex-boxer?'

'Oh I know who you mean, old Mr Radcliff, yeah, yeah, he was a great character. He took Henry in to live with him. He'd been one of the best all-rounders forty years before, but got busted for doing illegal fights.'

'He died while the club was on tour?'

'Florida, yeah, I was there, big heart attack ringside. The rest of the tour went ahead though, in his memory, like, and they shipped him back with us. I remember the funeral, big turnout, Henry was there. I think it hit him very hard, especially not being with him when it happened. Radcliff was sort of like a surrogate dad to him, to all the kids, but after he was gone it meant Henry had no place to live and he'd doss down anywhere he could. To be honest . . .'

Timmy frowned and then cracked his knuckles.

'Remember that fight I told you about, when he took a lot of punishment? It was after, I think, after old Mr Radcliff had died. When I say he wouldn't go down I mean it. Talk about a "Raging Bull" episode. He was totally outclassed and was walking into the punches, leaning on the ropes and then holding on as the punches hammered into him; then he dropped his fists and bam! Hard right and he was down and out for the count.'

'Go on.'

Timmy made a broad gesture, and said that it had to have been a while after that he was told Henry had given up, but that more than that the boxing had done his head in by the time he was in his late twenties.

'Punch-drunk, they said, not that I believe in all that stuff. He was always a bit of a nutter. There was a fighter called Ira, heavyweight, lot of people in the business reckoned he'd go all the way.'

'Ira Zacks?'

'Yeah, that's right, Ira Zacks. We was all at the same club together in the East End. It was him that told me, said he'd seen Henry wandering around like a dosser.'

'So Ira Zacks knew Henry Oates well?'

'I dunno about that. I'm just telling you what he told me.'

Anna put her cup and saucer back onto the tray.

'Would you like a refill?'

'No, thank you, you have been really helpful.'

Anna stood up as Timmy jumped to his feet.

'You mind me asking, what's he done? Something bad?'

'Yes, he's been charged with murder.'

'His wife?'

'No, not his wife. Thank you very much for your time, Timmy.'

'No problem. I've got a lot of that right now, time.'

Anna headed towards the door, Timmy moving quickly to open it.

'Have you ever married?' she asked him.

'Once. Didn't work out so not tried it again.'

He opened the door as his mother appeared.

'Are you going?'

'Yes. Thank you for the tea and biscuits, Mrs Douglas.'

'My pleasure.'

The old lady went to collect the tea tray as Timmy opened the front door. Anna noticed she had changed into a smart dress with a pearl necklace and earrings.

Timmy jerked his head towards his mother.

'She's gone and got all dressed up for you. God forbid she'd go out at all, got me running errands all day for her. Anyways, you know where I am if you need me again.'

'Yes I do. I hope things work out for you, Timmy.'

'So do I. I hope you don't mind me saying this, but you are a very pretty woman.'

'Thank you.'

Anna returned to her car and sat for a while. Starting up the engine, she wondered just how much of a liar Eileen had been. Timmy's version of her life with Oates was very different from the one she had described. The composite picture of Henry Oates's background could almost make someone feel sorry for him. However, the brutal murder of Justine Marks left little room for compassion. But she still had no new evidence that implicated him in the disappearance of Rebekka Jordan. The team was moving ahead with the Fidelis Julia Flynn case, whilst she languished behind. She knew if she didn't come up with something soon to connect Oates to Rebekka's abduction and murder, the investigation would return to the cold case files.

Anna headed from Kingston towards Lambeth and the forensic lab, keeping to the south side of the river, and arrived just before twelve. As she headed down the corridor towards Pete Jenkins' office she couldn't fail to notice a big display of pink balloons floating up to the ceiling, with messages of congratulations attached by pink ribbons. It made her wish she'd stopped off and bought something for his baby, even though Mike had promised to organize flowers from them all.

*

Pete was surrounded by his team. They had a bottle of champagne open and there were even more balloons. He was still wearing his overcoat so Anna presumed he had arrived just ahead of her.

'Anna!' he called out, opening his arms and giving her a bear hug.

'How's Matilda?'

'Brilliant. She's gorgeous. Let me show you.'

Pete went over to a computer that already featured a picture of his baby. She had a shock of thick black curls, but was so tiny and with so many tubes attached it was hard to really see her little red face and her eyes were closed.

'Good heavens, she is so small.'

'This big.' Pete gestured with his hand, cupping his palm.

'And she's all right?'

'Yes. We had a scare last night when the alarms rang out, she's got a bit of a cold and they breathe through their noses when they are this young, don't know to open their mouths. It's hard when she coughs as it sets off the alarms because they are so sensitive. Anyway, she's rallied round and you see her fists, she's boxing smart already.'

Pete actually looked worn-out and as he shrugged out of his coat he admitted he'd not slept for three nights; he would be back at the maternity hospital to sit with Matilda again later.

'I just have to be there watching her. In fact I can't take my eyes off her, it's the most amazing feeling. I keep on saying to myself, she's my daughter, I've got a little girl. Christ, if anything went wrong now I don't know what I'd do. She's already got such a strong personality.'

Anna managed to keep smiling but Pete carried on

gushing, at one point growing so tearful that he had to wipe his eyes.

'Listen, Pete, I don't mean to interrupt the celebrations, but I've got an interview at four.'

'Right, let's crack on.'

They put on lab coats and latex gloves then went into a large ante-room where four rows of white laminated trestle tables were lined up covered in sterile brown paper. Each table bore different items brought from Henry Oates's basement flat. On one were the female garments: knickers, brassieres, slips, tights, a pair of boots and two filthy torn dresses.

'Okay, we have done a wearer DNA test to compare with your victim Justine Marks; no match on any of these items. There's no blood-staining, but there is semen and, on a couple, vomit, again no match found to your victim. The semen has tested as a match to Henry Oates though. We've been sent a description of the clothes possibly worn by Fidelis Julia Flynn and Rebekka Jordan and we have no match.'

'I guess you will need DNA samples from the Jordan and Flynn families for comparison?'

'Just the Flynns', thanks. We already have the Jordans' on file from the original enquiry.'

They moved on to a table littered with men's worn clothes: sweaters, trousers and coats. The smell from the garments was hideous, a mixture of beer, body odour and mothballs.

'I think these are your suspect's. We've found no blood-stains on anything. Part of the stench is urine, looks like he pissed in his pants.'

On another table were the knives, hammers and screwdrivers – all the tools taken from Oates's flat. Everything was tagged. Pete picked up a brutal-looking knife with a roped handle and a very sharpened blade about ten inches long.

'Unpleasant. No bloodstains. Further along we have the large pump spanner found in the back of the van Oates was driving. You probably already know from DCI Lewis that we found Justine's hair and blood on it along with a palm print matching Oates. There was also vaginal discharge, suggesting he used it—'

'It's okay, Mike told me,' Anna said, deliberately interrupting Pete.

She quickly moved on to the fourth table. This was filled with an array of children's clothes and shoes, all of them well worn and stained. There were a number of broken plastic toys that were grouped together with a moth-eaten teddy bear and a broken china doll's face.

'A lot of children's stuff here,' Pete observed.

'He has two girls so a lot of it may be theirs, or – and I dread to think it other victims'.'

'Well there's no blood or semen stains on anything you see here. I can test it for wearer DNA but it will take time, and they are so soiled it may not be possible to get a profile due to degradation. You may want to check your budget as to do all this stuff is going to cost big-time.'

'Hold off until I speak with Mike Lewis then.'

'Fine. Anyway, back to this lot. I don't think there is a toy intact and they were all thrown together in a cupboard along with broken cutlery and old saucepans and frying pans with no handles. We also have a couple of old-fashioned leather boxing gloves and a more modern right-hand glove, no left hand. There's also some boxing boots.'

Pete had moved to the next section of the table but Anna leaned forwards.

'Wait, just wait one second.'

Amongst the broken toys was a small wooden head, no bigger than a small marble.

'What's that?'

Pete looked and picked up the list of items on the table.

'Listed as miniature doll's head, hand-painted, and I think we had a leg . . . hang on a moment . . .'

Pete swiftly searched around in the group of children's toys.

'Yes, here it is, not sure if it belonged to the head, but it's painted. Let me see if it's a match.'

He carefully picked up the doll's head and then held the leg beside it.

'Yeah, I'd say it might have been part of the same doll. It's very small, whole thing must have been only two to three inches, if that.'

Anna could feel her body shaking. Was it possible that these two items came originally from Rebekka Jordan's doll's house?

'I need to take these two things with me, Pete.'

'Sure, but I need to swab them for DNA and take some paint scrapings first.'

He looked at her and then rested his hand on her shoulder.

'What is it?'

'I can't be certain, but I think Stephen Jordan may have carved the doll for Rebekka. If so, then it will be the first direct evidence that connects Henry Oates to her disappearance.'

Anna had to sit down. She was so wound up her heart was racing. She explained to Pete about the doll's house and how she had brought it in to the incident room that morning.

'Well you know what they say about coincidences.'

'That there aren't any, just evidence,' she said quietly.

Chapter Eight

Fired up by this latest discovery, Anna raced back to the station. She was eager to sort through the items in the little plastic bags that she had brought in that morning from Langton's. So far she'd only taken a fleeting look over them but now she wanted to check to see if any of the small figures matched the tiny head and leg from the lab.

The incident room was quiet, as half the team was in the canteen having their lunch. The doll's house was still on the desk. Quickly she took off her coat and opened her briefcase as Barolli walked in eating a hamburger.

'We're going to get the experts in to investigate that car park,' he announced. 'I've got a forensic archaeologist on standby. They have these groundpenetrating radar machines that can detect if there's anything buried in the concrete.'

Anna wafted her hand in acknowledgement that she had heard him.

'Could be a bit like looking for a needle in a haystack and take weeks, but Mike says it's got to be done.'

Barolli sat at his desk and swivelled in his chair as Anna tipped out the contents of one bag; small pieces of furniture tumbled out – a tiny fridge, even plates with food on them.

'If it's not a rude question, why are you playing with dollies over there?'

Anna turned, shook her head, and swiftly brought him up to speed on the findings at the lab. Paul got up to stand beside her as she sifted through all the items; there were no small figures to be seen. She moved on to the second bag.

'I'm right, I'm right, I know I'm right. I keep on thinking I saw one of the small figures.'

She and Barolli carefully checked all the little pieces of beds and wardrobes and there was even a tiny lampshade. But there was no figure. Anna sighed in frustration.

'You can always ask her parents.'

'I know, I know. I just want to be sure ... wait a minute ...'

Anna opened up the doll's house and she and Barolli leaned in, their heads close as she checked the contents room by room.

'Damn it. I was so certain. Wait, WAIT ... just give me a bit of space.'

Anna peered into the kitchen.

'Yes, yes!' She brought out a small carved wooden figure of a woman, perfect down to the hand-stitched dress and glued-on hair, though some of the paint on her face was peeling and she had lost one arm. Thin pins attached the arm and legs to the body, the head was secured with a small Phillips screw.

Anna, afraid it would shatter, carried the figure as carefully as if it was made of crystal and laid it down on a sheet of paper on her desk, and then opened her briefcase. Her hands were shaking as she removed an evidence bag containing two small Perspex boxes in which Pete had placed the doll's head and leg, to protect them from further damage. Side by side, the similarity between the figure from the doll's house and the pieces from the lab was obvious.

'It's a match. These aren't shop bought, are they?' Anna asked, looking for assurance.

Paul shook his head and said that he was no expert, but to him they looked as if the same person had carved them.

'You know what this means? Henry Oates could have got them from Rebekka Jordan's home, maybe she even had one with her when she went missing, but it is the first bit of tangible evidence we have that links him to her.'

This was a major step forwards for Anna. She told Barolli to photograph the woman figure then find an evidence box and get it over to Pete Jenkins so he could take some paint scrapings to compare with samples from Oates's squat. Anna realized she would need Stephen Jordan to confirm that he'd carved the tiny head and leg. It was certainly going to be hard for Oates to explain how he came by them. At last the jigsaw was starting to take shape, but there was still a long way to go before it could be proved Oates was involved in Rebekka Jordan's disappearance.

Buoyed by her discovery, Anna was feeling very confident, but didn't have time to share the development with Mike Lewis. She had to meet Ira Zacks, so Barolli was left to feed the details to the team. The hunt was on, the entire murder team was beginning to feel positive. They had made a lot of headway on the Fidelis Flynn case and now they had a breakthrough with Rebekka Jordan.

*

Ira Zacks lived in a surprisingly smart apartment building overlooking the river a short distance from Hammersmith Bridge. It was also not that far from the Jordans' house. A caretaker buzzed Anna into the spacious reception, and instructed her to go to the second floor. The lift was immaculate and thickly carpeted, with one wall consisting completely of mirror. She checked her reflection before the lift opened onto the same dark red carpet in a wide corridor hung with paintings and a gilt-framed mirror.

After a moment a door was swung wide open and Ira Zacks' massive frame virtually filled the entire doorway. He was mixed race and at least six feet four, with wide sloping shoulders and his hair in dreadlocks down to below his shoulders, tied back with a black band. He was wearing a T-shirt that showed off his muscular arms, track-suit bottoms, and had bare feet.

Anna introduced herself and showed her ID, but he hardly glanced at it, ushering her inside into his hallway, which was filled with posters from his boxing past. He towered above her as he gestured for her to continue to the drawing room. Yet again she was surprised by how luxurious the flat was, with stylish ultra-modern furniture and a view from a wraparound window overlooking the river. Outside, she could see a balcony with tables and chairs and a furled parasol tastefully accompanied by plants and trailing ivy.

'You have a beautiful home,' Anna said as he waited to take her coat. He gave a wide smile, showing two gold teeth, as he neatly folded her coat and placed it over the back of a lounge chair.

'Unexpected, huh?'

She smiled and nodded, at the same time wondering how he could afford such an elegant and clearly expensive place on a doorman's salary. She sat beside a glass-topped table and placed her briefcase on top of it while he crossed to an ornate bar and opened a fridge, taking out a small bottle of chilled water for her. He took a paper napkin and put it on the table beneath the bottle.

Ira then picked up a hard-backed chair, turning it around with one hand to sit astride it, and leaned his elbows on the gilt frame.

'Just in case you think I got all this from ill-gotten gains, I ain't no drug pusher, this is down to hard graft. I used to work the doors on nightclubs in the East End as security, then decided to start my own business. I now provide over two hundred registered door supervisors to pubs and clubs across London. Recruited a lot of the old boxers and pals and then got into working as an extra on movies and TV, so nowadays they do all the hard graft and I make a nice living, thank you.'

'Congratulations.'

Anna took out the photograph of Henry Oates and passed it to him. He did no more than have a glance before handing it back to her.

'Henry Oates.'

Anna explained her reason for wanting to talk to him and he listened, occasionally twisting his head to loosen his hair.

'Basically I need to know when you last saw him,' she concluded.

'Few years back, three, four, maybe longer.'

'Did he work for you?'

He shook his head and gave a wide-handed gesture.

'Nah, we tried him, but he couldn't be trusted to turn up and to be honest, though he could handle himself, he was on the short side and he could lose it just like that.

Working the doors you got to have a big presence; you also got to know who's who if it's one of the smart nightclubs, know what I mean? Movie stars can turn up looking like scruffs and dealers can look like dummies outta Burton's. I train my guys up. They're smart, savvy, and Oates was a bum. I got contracts for West End clubs, couple in Stockwell, one over in Kilburn and another about to open in Kensington.'

'So this last time you saw him, did he come here?'

'Nah, wouldn't let him through the door if he did. He was a mess, but I felt sorry for him. Years ago, when he was on the amateur circuit, he got himself mixed up with a right whore, everyone at the old club knew what she was, but he was always one sandwich short of a picnic, know what I mean?'

'So where was it you met up with him?'

He closed his eyes and then drummed his fingers on the back of the chair.

'I'd closed a deal at a local pub when he sees me and comes over looking for a handout. I took him for a burger at the McDonald's off Shepherd's Bush Green.'

'So you met him around here in Hammersmith and then took him to Shepherd's Bush?'

'Yeah. I was goin' to the BBC at White City. I said where I was off to and he asked if he could cadge a ride there. Said he had a chance of getting some work, an' he stunk out my car, but like I said I felt sorry for him. He ate three cheeseburgers, I remember that, said he was no longer with his wife and that she'd taken his kids to Scotland.'

'Did you know his wife?'

'Not really. I didn't say anything but I wasn't surprised they'd split. Everyone knew she put it about. They said the daughter looked nothing like him, more like me. Don't get me wrong, I never slept with his missus, she was a minger.'

'Did Oates say anything else to you?'

I asked where he was living and he said he'd found a squat somewhere. To be honest I couldn't wait to get rid of him. I gave him fifty quid and that was the last I saw of him.'

'He never tried to see you again?'

Ira shook his head, then showed his wide toothy smile.

'Well he said he'd pay me back as soon as he got a job so that'd be a reason to stay away.'

Anna made a note in her notebook.

'I remember watching one of his fights. Took a terrible pasting, his face was like a squashed tomato; ref had to stop the fight because he was bleedin' so badly. He only had a go at the ref, wouldn't go down, but that was his last bout.'

'Do you think he's punch-drunk?'

Ira laughed and pointed one of his thick fingers.

'Listen, that's old wives' crap. In the old days maybe, cos of the illegal fights, bare knuckle ones with no holds barred, you got hurt bad in those days, but we got strict rules and regulations, you get knocked out and they got you down the hospital for a brain scan. I know I was no Lennox Lewis, but I had a chance and had a couple of professional bouts, though the reality was I couldn't keep up the training, it costs, and without a lot of money backing you there's no way. In those days I was working the doors every night and you can get injured tossing out drunks. They can come at you with iron bars, not worth the aggravation. Besides, I started my own business.'

'Are you married?'

He nodded and held up two fingers.

'Was twice. Got a couple of kids that live with their mother.'

'Do you live alone?'

He gave her a cold look.

'Why you asking me about my private life?'

'Just out of interest.'

'Well for your interest, ma'am, I live with someone, a model, Swedish, been together three years. What about you, are you married?'

'No.'

'Live alone?'

'Mr Zacks, I am sorry if you think I am being too personal, but we are investigating the disappearance of two young girls and strongly suspect that Henry Oates was involved in their abduction. He has recently been charged with the murder of a woman and he said in interview that he had committed two others—'

'What?' he interrupted.

'One was Rebekka Jordan, the other Fidelis Julia Flynn.'

Anna passed over the girls' photographs, which Ira studied for some while. Finally he asked, 'Jesus Christ, how old is she, the little one?'

'Thirteen.'

'Is it recent?'

'No, Rebekka disappeared five years ago. She was last seen leaving the riding stables in Shepherd's Bush. Fidelis went missing a year and a half ago in Kilburn.'

'Don't make sense to me, why are you asking about them now?'

'Because we have never found either of them and Mr Oates is now a suspect. Can I take you back to when you said you last saw him? You said he told you he was looking for work in the Shepherd's Bush area?'

Ira rubbed his head.

'He implied that he was — I mean, I had just left the pub and was walking to where I'd parked my car. I was unlocking it when he come up to me, I think I sort of said something like I didn't have much time, you know, I wasn't that eager to rap with him.'

'So he didn't have a vehicle?'

'No, just looked like shit. I felt sorry for him.'

'Did he mention anything about stables, or what kind of work he was looking for?'

'No, I think we talked about the old days and if he'd ever gone back to the boxing club or York Hall to see any fights. Listen, I told you all I can about the last time I saw him, and I wish I could give you more, but I've not seen him since.'

Anna closed her notebook and took back the photographs to replace in her briefcase. She stood up and Ira fetched her coat.

'You know, I'll ask my guys about him; if I get anythin' can I contact you?'

She took out her card, and wrote down her direct line.

'I'd be most grateful, and thank you for your time, Mr Zacks.'

As she passed a cabinet she noticed some photographs in silver frames.

'That's my mum, my dad was Jamaican — he'd gone off by the time I was six, never heard of him since. These are my kids, and this is my woman.'

The 'woman' was a stunning blonde, and Anna noticed his gentle tone of voice as he indicated her picture.

'She's a good 'un, love her to pieces — maybe third time lucky!'

Ira ushered Anna into the corridor and pressed the

button for the lift, standing beside her like a perfect gentleman.

'It's been nice meeting you,' she said and meant it. She just wished he had been able to give her more. The only thing she had gleaned was that three or four years ago Oates had been in Hammersmith and then in Shepherds Bush, possibly looking for work.

Back at the incident room, Anna had plenty to tell Mike.

'When I heard about the doll thing I was surprised you didn't get your skates on straight away and visit the Jordans – it's a big breakthrough,' Mike commented.

'Well I'd arranged this meeting with Ira Zacks at his place in Hammersmith and he recalled bumping into Oates three or more years ago. Oates said he had a chance of work in the area, but Zacks has no idea what he was actually doing. It could all be a coincidence, but you are looking at a chance he worked on the building of the multi-storey car park.'

'Yeah, we've had meetings with the contractors, talk about shelling out work this way and that, but Paul's tracking down as many as possible of the men that worked on the rebuild to see if they remember Oates. The company have admitted to using a lot of cash labour, mostly Polish, so they're even harder to track down as they move around and share properties . . .'

'Paul said you had a forensic archaeologist ready to go with a radar of some sort.'

'Ground-penetrating radar, it's costly and time-consuming. I'd feel better if I had some evidence that he actually worked there, so the archaeologist is on standby at the moment.'

'Did you see Langton?' Anna asked with a sigh.

'No, he was being taken to hospital for a check-up, maybe catch up with him tonight.'

She smiled and he caught it, giving her a grin back.

'Yeah, lucky you.'

'See you in the morning,' she said as she headed for the door.

Mike paused. 'This Ira Zacks, you reckon he was telling you the truth?'

'Yes I do. Very expensive, tasteful flat, worth a packet.'

'By Hammersmith Bridge, right?'

'Yes, but he didn't know or recall anything about Rebekka Jordan. He did say he'd ask around his friends to see if they knew anything.'

'Is he dealing?'

She hesitated.

'Come on. He worked doors and now lives in a place you say was worth what, how many thousands?'

'He has his own security business. I didn't think he was lying. He also works as a film and TV extra.'

'All the same, run a check on him. I'd say he was dealing drugs . . . only way you get out of the world of doing heavy muscle on club doors is supplying gear to the kids.'

'Okay, I'll look into it. Goodnight.'

Barbara was just about to leave when Anna asked if there had been a CRO check on Ira Zacks for any previous criminal record. It felt as if Mike had been having a small dig at her, but he was right . . . she knew she should have run a check on Zacks and Bradford before visiting them. It had totally slipped her mind. She didn't think that Ira Zacks was a drug dealer, but then she had also believed Eileen Oates.

'Joan was dealing with the boxers,' Barbara had told her.

'She's in the Ladies, but I'm off. Mike said it was okay, I've got a dinner party.'

'Goodnight, have a nice evening.'

Barbara was already heading out of the door and Anna overheard her say to Joan, 'She's still here so I wouldn't bother putting your coat on yet!'

'You want me?' Joan said, coming over.

'Did you run a check on any criminal record for Ira Zacks?'

'No, did you want me to?'

'Yes, and run one for Timmy Bradford as well.'

'Anything else?' Joan sat at her desk, taking a squirt of moisturizer from a container she kept by her computer. She rubbed her hands together and patted them with a tissue from the box she always had on her desk.

'No, just get them as soon as possible,' Anna said, more abruptly than she'd intended, but she was already trying to compose herself for the difficult call to the Jordans.

Stephen Jordan answered and Anna quickly explained her reason for wanting to see him as soon as it was convenient, so they agreed she would drive over that evening. Anna decided she'd fortify herself with a quick bite to eat first. She knew she should have chosen something light like a salad, the canteen's steak and kidney with chips made her feel ill just looking at it. She took a few mouthfuls and then pushed her plate aside. She just about managed to finish her strawberry trifle, but knew deep down she was intensely agitated. She absolutely dreaded the thought of facing the Jordans and explaining how they had discovered the tiny broken figures, which would further reduce any hope they had of Rebekka still being alive.

*

Joan was sitting with her coat on ready to leave when Anna got back from the canteen. She gave one of her flushed looks.

'Both of those men have criminal records. Timmy Bradford, when he was a juvenile, for assault and burglary and a six-month sentence for handling stolen property. Ira Zacks has had a number of run-ins with the law. Ten years ago, again an assault charge. He apparently used too much force ejecting someone from a disco, but more recently he was flagged up by the Drug Squad. Suspected of being involved in a cocaine ring; they've been monitoring the gang for eighteen months.'

Anna sighed, resting her head in her hands.

'I'm sorry, ma'am. I should have checked them out earlier.'

'It's all right, Joan, don't worry about it. I'm as much to blame.'

'Here's all the details and if you want the contact for the Drug Squad officer there's his mobile and office number.'

'Thank you.'

Joan hovered and asked if she could get off home and Anna nodded, more interested in reading the reports.

'It's just I have to do a grocery shop for my mother.'

'Goodnight, Joan.'

Anna was furious at herself; it was a real oversight. But even knowing their backgrounds didn't really change the fact they both denied seeing Henry Oates for a number of years. Unless of course they had both lied, but she could see no reason why, as neither would benefit from it. What concerned her was her lack of intuition. It was even worse that Mike Lewis had been onto Ira Zacks' possible drug connection without even meeting him.

She opened a bottle of water and fished around in her

desk for a packet of aspirin and took three. Sitting sipping the lukewarm water that had been on her desk all day she picked up the phone and rang the Drug Squad. The officer Joan had mentioned was not at work so she left a message, hoping that she hadn't in any way compromised their operation by visiting Zacks at his home address. If she had, she knew Langton would go ballistic at her failure to carry out basic procedures.

The aspirins were beginning to do their job as she headed towards Hammersmith and the Jordans' property. Was it coincidence that Ira Zacks lived not far from them?

'Stop it. Just stop it,' she told herself. She had to be in total control for her meeting with Stephen Jordan as she knew it would be wretched.

Stephen Jordan opened their front door a moment after she had rung the bell. 'Emily's out with some friends at the theatre,' he said as he led the way into the kitchen.

Anna put her briefcase down on the granite-topped counter and then quietly told him how she had discovered the figures. She brought out the plastic evidence bag, laid out a piece of sterile paper and carefully removed the wooden pieces from their Perspex boxes, first the tiny head and then the leg.

'Do you recognize these, Mr Jordan?'

He didn't touch either, but stood staring down at them. After a long pause he had to cough before he could speak.

'Yes. I carved them. They are made from plywood and the head I remember painting. See the small hole at the top of the leg? I used very fine pins from my wife's sewing kit to attach them to the bodies.'

'Are you absolutely certain? These are the ones you made?'

'Yes, one moment.'

He quickly turned and she heard him running up the stairs. Although it was only a few moments it felt like an age before he returned. He held out in the palm of his hand two tiny dolls; one had on a little white dress and black painted shoes, her pigtails made of woven yellow cotton. The other doll was incomplete, just a head attached to a post, the face half painted.

'I was working on these for Rebekka's new doll's house.'

He laid them down beside the head and the leg and they were without doubt identical in shape and size.

'May I take these with me, Mr Jordan?'

'Yes of course. I have more if you need them.'

'No, this is enough.'

Anna carefully replaced the figures in the boxes, which then went into the evidence bag.

'It's almost over, isn't it?' His voice was hardly audible.

'I'm sorry?'

'This man, this suspect, it's him, isn't it?'

She closed her briefcase.

'This is very incriminating evidence, but we have nothing to indicate that Rebekka did in fact have the figures with her on the day she disappeared.'

'They'd fit in her pocket. She often used to take them with her to school.'

'Yes I know, but this is not yet confirmation. Our suspect could say he found them.'

'Oh God, it's unbelievable . . .'

'Thank you for seeing me, Mr Jordan, and I will be in touch as soon as I have anything further to tell you.'

He could hardly speak as he followed her down the hall back to the front door. Finally he choked it out:

'I see her every day. I wake up and she's standing out there on the path in the drive ... Bye-bye, Daddy ... that was the last time I saw her and I will live with that moment for the rest of my life ... Bye-bye, Daddy ...'

Anna gently touched his arm and could almost feel the grief that tortured him.

'Goodnight.'

'Goodnight, Detective Travis. Thank you.'

Chapter Nine

It felt as if her brain cells were being hammered. Pictures fractured and split into jagged fragments like shards of glass. Broken dolls, horses, the faces of her team and victims all flashed by as Rebekka Jordan called out, 'Bye-bye, Daddy.'

Anna was woken by the sound of her landline. It was five-thirty! Her answerphone clicked on but the caller didn't leave a message. It was no good going back to sleep so she went into the kitchen to have a coffee. Mug in hand, she checked the answer machine and then pressed for the caller's number to be displayed; it was withheld. She suspected it was Langton, but made no effort to call and see if she was correct.

She was dressed and had just made herself some tea and toast when her kitchen phone rang. She snatched it up.

'Yes?'

'You up?'

'Yes,' Anna replied sharply at his lack of apology for the 5.30 a.m. call.

'Mike came round last night and I spoke to Stephen Jordan after he left. He told me you'd been to see him.'

Anna, wanting to eat her breakfast, put the phone on speaker.

'Yes.'

'Very monosyllabic this morning, aren't you?'

'Yes,' she said whilst tearing her slice of toast in two.

'I would have liked to hear the update from you. Why didn't you call me?'

'I'd had a long day at work, unlike some people!'

'So what's on the agenda for this morning?'

She sighed, knowing that Langton had always been impervious to sarcasm.

'I need to discuss with Mike how we use the discovery of the dolls in an interview with Oates. If you spoke to Stephen Jordan, you know he matched the wooden pieces with ones he was making and said without doubt they belonged to Rebekka.'

'If you find that Oates did work at or nearby the Jordans' you can bet Kumar will throw in that Oates found the doll parts. Be good to have further evidence, like exactly when they were made. If it was just before Rebekka disappeared the evidence will be stronger.'

'I am aware of that.'

'I asked if he'd ever thrown any of her toys out and obviously as I was given the doll's house for Kitty this could muddy the waters. Stephen said that she'd often taken the wooden dolls to school with her.'

'Wait, hang on a minute. Are you suggesting that by you having the doll's house at your flat, there could be a legal problem with the evidence from forensics?'

'Yeah. You took it from my place into the incident room, so his sharp bastard solicitor could imply you planted the evidence. Were there any dolls or similar bits in the bags with the furniture?'

'Not in the bags, just the two pieces lying inside in the doll's house. Barolli was with me when I found them.'

'Did you record it in your notebook?'

'Of course, and I'm sure the Crime Scene Manager will have a record of the exact time when Oates's basement was cleared and all the items will have been listed and photographed in situ as well as at the lab.'

As she said it she knew that she hadn't looked in all the little bags as she was so excited when she found the doll parts. When she had spotted the small doll's head at the lab, the toys were in fact jumbled together. She very much doubted that each individual item would have been recorded in the exhibits book and photographed. Fearing Langton's anger she didn't tell him.

'Let's hope the CSM does have something written down that will prove they removed them from the basement.'

'I'll check the paperwork first thing when I get in and call the lab on the way,' Anna said, nervously writing a reminder in her notebook.

'Okay, talk later.'

She managed to reach the assistant who had been part of the team checking the items from Oates's property.

'It's very important, double-check your copy of the submissions list and photographs from the suspect's flat and see if there is a shot with the doll's head and leg in focus.'

The last thing Anna wanted was to be accused of tampering with evidence. As she hadn't actually mentioned that she had brought the doll's house in from Langton's, she wasn't too concerned that Kumar might suggest the possibility that she could have planted the items, but if more pieces were found in the little bags it could pose a problem. If the question did arise, they could argue that Langton could not have planted the incriminating evidence, as he was incapacitated and unable to leave his flat. But Anna also realized that

Kumar could say Langton gave her, or someone else, the doll pieces to plant as evidence or, worse, that she acted alone.

Anna was spreading everything from the little bags over her desk when Mike Lewis made her jump. She hadn't heard him come out of his office.

'We might have a problem with that.' She pointed to the doll's house.

'Langton said he'd been given it for his stepdaughter and you brought it in from his place,' Mike told her.

'Yes I did.' She blushed.

'Are there any more of the dolls here?'

'I don't know, that's what I'm looking for. It's mostly bits of furniture for the various rooms. Maybe Langton should check with his stepdaughter if there were any more dolls when she got it?'

'Yes, you'd better ask him to do that. It was a big break-through and the last thing we want is for it to slap us in the face.'

'Mike, I've got something.'

Anna held up a tiny arm, half the size of her thumb. 'It's part of one of the dolls, and it still has a pin attached. Mr Jordan said he used his wife's sewing pins.'

Mike sighed and held out his hand to take it.

'We have no reason to think that Rebekka Jordan had one with her when she went missing.'

'I know but she could have had it in a pocket and her parents wouldn't have known. Her father said she often took them to school.'

He handed back the tiny limb. 'Well if it turns out Oates was in their property working on the excavation he could say he found the bits. One step forward, another major one back!'

'That's what Langton said.'

171

'Look, for now just put that arm into the system and put me down as finding it with you. It's so tiny you missed it first time round; no big deal, it could happen to anyone. We may not need to use it as evidence anyway.'

'Thanks, Mike.'

Barolli made an entrance, beaming.

'Just come from a contractor. He put me in touch with some of his regular workers that were on the multi-storey car park job ...'

Everyone turned expectantly.

'Didn't have much luck at first but kept digging away as you do ...'

'Get on with it, Paul!' Mike shouted.

Barolli gestured towards the mug shots of Henry Oates on the incident board.

'Polish lad, Pavel, identified him as working on site near completion, very confident, said he remembered him because he was Oates's supervisor. Said he was a lazy worker and they didn't get along. Oates was helping to finish off the ground-floor pay station area by the lift. He'd only been there for a few days and then left. Pavel reckoned it was about a year and a half ago.'

Barolli gave a mock bow.

'I'm going to double-check with the contractor. According to my Polish informant he said a couple of times guys would hang around the site asking for any work. He thinks Henry Oates was employed that way.'

Mike clapped his hands and told them that now Paul had narrowed down the area where Oates was working he would get clearance for the forensic archaeologist's team to get started with their specialist equipment to see if there was a body buried in the concrete.

*

During Barolli's self-congratulatory speech, Anna's phone rang. It was Andrew Markham, saying, in a very pleasant upper-class voice, that he had just returned from his holiday and was available should she wish to speak to him. Even though Langton had questioned him previously, Anna felt that she would still like to eliminate him for her own satisfaction.

Mike and Barolli arrived at the multi-storey car park just after midday. It was closed while the search took place, which was causing a lot of aggravation from the owners, let alone the customers, especially the ones that had private parking bays.

They met up with the forensic archaeology team by the lift area. It was a much larger space than Mike had imagined, especially as the ticket machine had been moved out for the search. The floor was covered with plastic grid sheets and looked like a giant chessboard. One member of the team was slowly moving the ground-penetrating radar over the grid while the lead archaeologist viewed a laptop monitor that was linked up to the radar. They had been working since nine, moving inch by inch over the floor, but as yet had found nothing suspicious. Mike and Barolli stood side by side looking at the monitor screen. Barolli, inquisitive as ever, asked how it all worked. The lead archaeologist explained that the GPR emitted and received reflected radar signals up to a thousand times per second, in effect creating a map of what lay beneath the surface. The information was relayed to and stored in the laptop, allowing the team to interpret any images or unexplained spaces that they found.

Although Mike had been told it would only take a day or so to search the area with the radar, he had not been warned that if anything was found, it would then take much longer thanks to the need to be cautious so as not to damage any human remains during excavation. He decided that Barolli could inform the owners that the car park might be closed for longer than was originally anticipated and he would return to the office to catch up on his paperwork.

Meanwhile, Anna drove over to Markham's garden design centre, only to be told that he was at his home. Mari gave her directions and added that they were going to be busy later as Markham had had a very successful buying trip and they had to clear part of the barn for the deliveries coming in.

Markham's home was set back off a small lane, with very ornate gardens and a paved drive leading to a white stucco thirties-style three-storey house. A wood of fir trees was on one side and a small lake on the other. The elaborate pillared porch had vast urns with a profusion of plants and four white stone steps which led up to a pale blue studded front door.

A woman wearing a raincoat and headscarf, two spaniels on leads beside her, appeared from around the side of the house.

'If you're the detective that wants to see Andrew he's out by the greenhouse. I'm his mother.' She loosened her headscarf and shook out her dark hair, then removed a leather glove to shake Anna's hand. She was very well presented, with dark red lipstick, small drop pearl earrings, a pearl necklace and a whopping diamond on her ring finger. It was all rather at odds with her big green wellington boots.

'Make him take you inside, dear, it's quite chilly this morning.'

She strode off, leaving Anna to walk around the narrow pathway to the rear of the house. There was Andrew Markham, in old cord trousers, a polo-neck jumper and green wellington boots similar to those his mother was wearing. He had a brown cloth cap on and was digging out what appeared to be a small trench beside the green-house.

'Hello.'

He turned, surprised.

'I just met your mother, she said you were out here.'

'You must be Detective Travis?'

He took off a big old gardening glove and shook her hand.

Anna didn't have to suggest they go inside; he removed the other glove and propped them on the spade's handle.

'Follow me. It's a bit muddy, I'm afraid, but I've got to get a new drainage system as the old one has packed up, so I'm going to run some new pipes from the garage.'

He was a very good-looking man, tanned and fit, and very tall. When he got to the back door, he had to bend his head to enter. He held the door wide for Anna to go through.

The huge kitchen was warm and yet looked as if it needed some decorating. The old green paint was peeling in places and the walls were yellow with smoke. There was a double Aga in one corner with an array of copper pans on hooks beside it, and dog baskets and dog bowls took up a lot of space around it. Anna noticed an old bookcase spilling out an array of cooking and gardening books.

'Would you like some tea?'

'Yes I would, thank you.'

He removed his cloth cap and tossed it onto what looked like an old church bench. He had thick dark curly hair similar to his mother's, worn quite long. He also had a gold looped earring.

Andrew insisted they take their tea into the sitting room as his mother would be back and they'd have wet paws all over them as well as his mother's attention.

'We refer to her as the Queen Mother. Do sit down, please.'

The room was gorgeous, high-ceilinged, with lovely old green velvet drapes and matching well-worn sofas and chairs. A stone fireplace held the residue of a wood fire; beside it was a stack of chopped logs ready to light.

There were Persian rugs scattered around the wide polished oak floors. Oil paintings covered the walls, many of horses and hunting, with one very large painting clearly that of his mother as a young woman. The gilt frames were somewhat worn and chipped, but the feel of the room was one of jaded elegance.

Anna sat on the edge of the sofa as Markham handed her tea and some scones. They were freshly baked, he said, but she refused. He sat opposite her, munching on one.

'I was interviewed years ago about Rebekka, it's something I don't think you ever sort of forget. Not the interview, I mean about her disappearance.'

'Did you meet her?'

'Oh yes. She was often in the garden with her brothers watching us all work, but they were never a problem. I had to move a small pond – you know, drain it – and they helped catch the fish. We had them in a sort of big old bathtub until we had the new pond ready.'

He sipped his tea.

'She was very concerned about the frogs. I told her they'd hop over to the new one when it was built, but she wanted to catch them all. She said there were six she knew and had given names.'

He leaned back.

'Frogs, every time I see one, reminds me of her.'

Anna finished her tea and took out her notebook. She asked about the excavation of the Jordans' garden and he got up and crossed to an oak desk, searching around and then pulling open drawers. Eventually he returned to sit beside her with a drawing book.

'These were my original designs. They were the sort of basic to start off from.'

Anna turned over page after page of sketches and notes.

'Have you found her?' His voice was soft and quiet.

'No.'

'It was a long time ago, maybe five or six years now.'

'Yes.'

'May I ask why you wanted to see me?'

She closed the drawing block.

'Do you recall if you ever, whilst you were working there, saw any children's toys or got rid of anything the children might have been playing with?'

'No. I don't think so. The Jordans hadn't lived there for very long and I think they had done a bit of clearance before I started. It was a major job though. I mean, Stephen Jordan sort of cleared old garden furniture and stuff like that, but we had to take down the back fence of his garden to get the diggers in and the rubbish out.'

'When you say "we", how many of you were working on the project?'

'Well there was me and two friends I worked with at Kew Gardens who helped out. I hadn't really started out on my own then but was just doing some extra weekend work on the side, so I had to rely on anyone I could get to give me a hand. Pay was better than I got at Kew so I took a week off to do the initial work. To be honest it turned out to be a much bigger job than I had anticipated.'

'The builders recommended you for the job, didn't they?'

He nodded and smiled. 'Lovely guys, those brothers, and yes they did. Met them in the beer tent at the Chelsea Flower Show in May, a few weeks before starting at the Jordans'. Said I was thinking of starting my own business and gave them my number. In fact I've worked on and off for them ever since.'

He leaned back and folded his arms behind his head.

'We have a possible suspect,' Anna said. 'These two people who worked alongside you, do you have their names?'

'Yes, somewhere. I think one went back to Australia, but the other still works in the hothouse at Kew.'

Anna opened her briefcase and took out the envelope with Henry Oates's photograph.

'And you only ever used these two friends to work with you, no one else?'

'No, the three of us did the job. When the initial excavation of the tree and other shrubs was completed the brothers began digging out the foundations and I was working on my own. I had to demolish a brick wall and dig out the area for the new pond. Couldn't do a lot more until the building work was completed. It was a big job for them as well, good-sized extension took up almost a quarter of the garden.'

'So you went back after the extension was built?'

'Yeah, for a couple of weeks to put up a new wall, rebuild the pond and also finish the overall landscaping. My own company was up and running by then but I worked on my own – not enough money coming in to employ staff back then.'

She passed him the photograph of Henry Oates.

'Have you ever seen this man before?'

He stared at it, frowned and then ran his fingers through his hair.

'Jesus Christ. I'm sorry, I'm sorry.'

Her heart missed a beat. He shook his head, but still stared at the mug shot.

'I completely forgot. I'd forgotten, Jesus Christ, I had forgotten this guy, this man.'

'Do you recognize him?'

'Yes, yes I do. Shit, I don't believe it.'

The door burst open and the two sodden spaniels hurtled into the room while Mrs Markham screeched for Andrew to get them out and not let them onto the sofas. The dogs chased manically around the room, skidding on the carpets, jumping on and off the chairs as Mrs Markham appeared.

'Get them out, for goodness' sake, they've been rolling in manure. GET OUT! GET OUT! Why did you leave the kitchen door open?'

Andrew grabbed one by its collar as his mother chased the other out of the room. Anna could hear him shouting at the dogs before he walked back in and slammed the door shut.

She was impatient to hear what he had to say, but he fetched a decanter of Scotch and poured a good measure.

'Would you like one?'

'No, thank you. Please, this is very important, Mr Markham. If you recognize this man—'

'Just a second . . . I need a drop of water with this.'

Anna wanted to scream, but he came back quickly.

'Okay. I have to piece this together because it was a long time ago, but . . .'

He picked up Henry Oates's photograph.

'Remember I said that I had to dismantle a wall at the Jordans' . . . well, I was wheeling the bricks out to my van, as they were nice old ones and I knew I could re-use them and . . . he came up to me and asked if there were any odd jobs I could give him.'

'You never mentioned this before?'

'No, the reason being he wasn't employed to work at the Jordans' and without this photograph . . . I just didn't think. I gave him twenty quid to help stack up the bricks in the back of my van.'

'Do you remember his name?'

'Yes, Henry . . . Christ, I am so sorry, but you know, when I was first questioned I'd finished off the garden work at the Jordans' almost six months previously and I was expanding my own company. I mean, if they'd shown me this photograph of course I'd have said something, but it was really more to do with where I was on the day Rebekka disappeared. I gave them the names of the guys who had helped me on the job and they were questioned, I think, but this . . .'

'So on this day when he helped you wheel out the bricks, did he go into the Jordans' back garden?'

'Yeah, he would have had to, shit!'

'Is that the only time you saw him?'

'No. It must have been about one, maybe two weeks later that he turned up here looking for work. He looked down on his luck, I felt sorry for him and paid him fifty quid to clear out our septic tank as it was blocked up.'

'How did he know where you lived?'

'From the time before with the bricks. He came back

here in the van to help me unload them. I was going to give him more odd jobs to do but Mum had a set-to with him.'

Mrs Markham walked back in with a towel.

'Have they marked the sofa? How many times must I tell you to always keep the kitchen door closed as they dive in here at the slightest opportunity. You'll have to hose them down, they're filthy.'

'Mother, do you remember this man?'

Anna couldn't believe it. Mrs Markham picked up the photograph and pulled a face.

'Yes I do, ghastly creature, I wanted him off my property. You remember I found him skulking around in the kitchen. He smelled dreadful and I said to him, what do you want, and he said a glass of water, I said I had taken a jug out not ten minutes before. It was the time the septic tank was blocked.'

Anna stood up and took a deep breath.

'Could you both please sit down, this is very important. The man you have both recognized is a suspect in a murder enquiry. It is imperative I get the dates and times you remember seeing him as we believe he could have been involved in Rebekka Jordan's and another girl's disappearance.'

'Oh God, this is terrible. He was in my kitchen!'

She grabbed Andrew's Scotch from his hand and downed it in one.

Over at the multi-storey car park, Barolli now knew the dates when Henry Oates had worked on the construction site. The last one was the day after Fidelis Julia Flynn was known to be alive. They'd established that Oates was working the ticket machine area alone, with

Pavel occasionally checking on him. His job, which he had completed, had been to finish digging out the area then pump in two foot of ready-mix concrete. He was supposed to turn up the next day when the cement was dry to help tile the floor, but he never showed up at the site again.

The archaeologists were almost finished with their GPR analysis and had found nothing that might suggest that a body was buried under the concrete. They told Barolli, who had remained at the scene throughout, that there was nothing more they could do and once they had finished the last section they were going to call it a day. Barolli then rang Mike Lewis to give him the bad news. Mike was naturally very disappointed but thought it strange that if Oates had abducted and murdered Fidelis he should turn up for work the next day, especially if he'd actually buried her there. The day's events suggested that Oates might have hidden her body elsewhere. Before hanging up, Mike asked Paul to keep the two archaeologists on site as he not only wanted to come and thank them personally for their time and effort but also to seek their advice on further searches of the area.

By the time he got there the archaeologists had set up arc lights and one of them was in the lift shaft.

'Wasn't the lift built before Oates ever worked here?' asked Mike.

'Yeah, and we weren't going to bother looking, but I remembered a manslaughter case I was involved with a few years back,' Barolli began.

'Paul, this is a murder enquiry ...'

'I know, but the job was a health and safety case. Engineer was working on a lift that had broken down between two floors. He left the door open, no safety tape, no nothing, some poor bloke walked straight in and fell three floors down to the bottom of the shaft.'

'And your point is . . .'

'There's a recessed area, like a car inspection pit, below the ground floor, big enough to put a body in. So we thought it was worth a look. The archaeologist's taken a hand-held radar down with him.'

Mike was impressed and patted Paul on the back.

They watched the monitor screen, grey and fuzzy as the GPR inched slowly across the lift-shaft floor.

'I've been staring at this all bloody day,' Barolli moaned.

The lead archaeologist pointed to the screen.

'We've got something.'

Barolli and Mike leaned closer, not really sure what they were looking at. The archaeologist hit a button on the laptop and a three-dimensional image started to appear. Like an ominous shadow a dark shape began to form. They were unable to detect exactly what it was, just that it was some kind of figure just below the surface of the concrete.

'Is it what I think it is?' asked Mike.

'That's what I'd expect to see with a buried body,' said the archaeologist. 'As to who it is ... well, that's up to forensics and pathology.'

Barolli gave Mike an admiring glance. He had certainly grown in confidence – maybe not having Langton breathing down his neck all the time was paying off.

Although time was of the essence, it was almost dark and the archaeologists had been working all day, so Mike was hesitant about continuing the work through the night.

The two archaeologists were both now on a high and keen to keep going. It was agreed that they would get some colleagues in to continue the excavation while they took a couple of hours' break.

'This is gonna cost,' Barolli said.

'I know,' said Mike slowly, 'but I think we may have just found Fidelis Julia Flynn.'

Chapter Ten

It was 7 p.m. when Anna joined the entire team in the incident room as Mike was giving a briefing update. He brought out photographs of the lift shaft and a copy of the picture from the monitor screen showing the shrouded shape encased in concrete. The identity could not be confirmed until they had completed the excavation and removed the body to the mortuary for full forensics and a post mortem examination. Digging out the body was not going to be an easy task and would take some time. Not only were they working in a confined space using specialist cutting equipment, but the archaeologists would have to slowly and painstakingly cut round and under the body to try and remove it as a block.

He explained all that he and Barolli had learnt about Oates's employment on the site. On the day Fidelis disappeared he had completed digging out the ticket machine area and left work at six in the evening. The next day he filled it with ready-mix concrete pumped in by hose from a truck and was due to return the following day but he never turned up for work again. Mike went on to say that as the car park was near completion the site barriers had been removed and overnight security consisted of a guard in a Portakabin who was supposed to patrol the grounds every hour.

Barbara raised her hand and said that if Oates had gone to the site at night, thrown the body down the lift shaft and covered it with concrete the next day then surely someone would have noticed the new level the following morning!

'Good point, Barbara, but the lift was already completed and in working order, so nobody ever had a need to look inside the shaft. Oates would have to have used some kind of transport to get the body to the site so he probably borrowed, or more likely nicked, a motor. Joan, I need a list of all lost or stolen vehicles in London on the day Fidelis went missing.'

Listening to Mike and watching the expressions on the faces of the team, Anna realized what she had missed while on Specialist Casework. She could once again feel the buzz of excitement and adrenalin rush through the room when an investigation suddenly made a major breakthrough. She hoped that what she was about to tell the team would add to the euphoria. Mike looked over to her as she came forward.

'I have a big development. I went to Cobham to interview Andrew Markham who runs a garden design company. He excavated the garden for Rebekka Jordan's parents.'

Anna pinned up the 'before' and 'after' pictures given to her by Markham.

'There was this brick wall and tree that had to be removed before the builders could dig out the earth and lay the foundations for the extension. Mr Markham dismantled the wall brick by brick, they were Victorian and he decided rather than get rid of them in the skips he would retain them for himself to use in his work.'

She could sense a lack of enthusiasm around the room, and Mike pointedly looked at his wristwatch. She decided to get straight to the point.

'This work was done late June or early July 2006, some four months prior to completion of the Jordans' extension. Mr Markham identified Henry Oates as the man he paid to wheel out and load the bricks onto his van.'

There was a murmur from everyone and then silence. Anna, who now had their full attention, opened a bottle of water and sipped a few mouthfuls.

'There's more. Although Mr Markham was questioned about the disappearance of Rebekka, he had an alibi for the day she went missing, as did his two assistants, one of whom had already left for Australia. Bearing in mind that Oates was not a suspect at the time and Mr Markham had only ever met him briefly, it is, I suppose, acceptable that it was something he could forget. However, as soon as I showed him a photograph he was certain that Oates was the man he had hired, and was able to recall his Christian name.'

Barolli let rip applauding, and she held up her hand.

'Markham said that Oates was in and out of the Jordans' garden removing bricks and it was possible that Rebekka came into the garden while Oates was there as she often checked on her frogs when she returned from school.'

Anna told them about the two ponds, and that Markham had taken Oates back to his house in Cobham where he had helped unload the bricks. Markham then took him to the local train station and gave him extra money for his fare back to London.

'Bloody hell!' Mike shook his head angrily; he couldn't believe that Markham had not come forward with the information years ago.

'Okay, time frame. Markham first worked at the Jordans' at the end of June 2006 and Oates helped with the bricks, he thinks, on a Thursday. It would be reasonable to assume that Oates may well have seen Rebekka in the garden.'

Anna was interrupted by Mike, who was now standing by the incident board. He pointed to Rebekka's details.

'Rebekka didn't go missing until March 2007, so I don't see how this fits.'

'Can I just finish?' she said irritably.

Anna continued, explaining that about two weeks after helping with the bricks Oates turned up at the Markham house looking for work at eight in the morning on a Saturday. He was asked to unblock the septic tank but during the morning Mrs Markham, Andrew's mother, caught him in her kitchen. She thought he might have been looking for something to steal so she asked her son to get rid of him. Andrew Markham paid him and asked him if he wanted a lift to the train station, which he turned down, saying he would walk as it was a nice day.

'Do the Markhams know if Oates had any contact with Rebekka around the time she actually went missing?' Mike asked impatiently.

'No. However—'

'Then I really think we need to move on.'

Anna ignored Mike and continued.

'Acting on the possibility that Oates may have stolen a car in order to return to London, I went to the local cop shop and spoke to the duty sergeant. She was not only interested in what I had to say but as it turned out was very helpful.'

It was clear to everyone in the room that Anna was not only having a dig at Mike for yet again interrupting her but her tenacity had obviously uncovered further evidence. She looked at Mike, who raised his hands apologetically and nodded his head for her to go on.

'I asked the duty sergeant to check back through the records for any motor vehicles that were stolen within a two-mile radius of the Markham house from July to September 2006. The area is not a hotbed of crime and only one car was reported stolen on a Saturday, about two miles from the Markham house. It was a 2004 silver Jeep Grand Cherokee, which has never been recovered. The owners were away at the time when someone broke into their house, stole some property and the Jeep keys. The report also gave details of a man matching Oates's description knocking door to door in the area looking for odd jobs to do.'

The room was very quiet apart from the clerical staff monitoring the phones. No one interrupted Anna as she pinned up a picture of a silver Jeep and wrote the registration number next to it.

'Although no fingerprints were found at the Jeep owner's house I think Oates may have committed the burglary and stolen the vehicle. As it was never recovered he could have sold it on, scrapped it or maybe dumped it somewhere. I know it's a long shot but he might have decided to keep it for a while, which would mean putting false plates on it. We need to find out what happened to it.'

Anna instructed Joan to run a computer check on all crimes reported in the London area for one year from August 2006 where the words 'Cherokee' or 'Jeep' came up, and to firstly concentrate on any reports where such a vehicle had made off without paying for petrol from a filling station.

Anna knew this would not be an easy task but was encouraged when Barbara volunteered to help. Joan had just started to run computer checks on the suspect vehicle when her phone rang and she answered the call. She waved at Mike to get his attention.

'They've uncovered the remains of a decomposed left hand,' she whispered, handing him the phone.

Mike and Barolli headed for the multi-storey car park in a patrol car with the siren blaring. Anna, left in the incident room, felt exhausted. She sat at her desk, her head in her hands. Both cases were now being galvanized into action, and the evidence against Henry Oates as the killer of Rebekka and Fidelis was mounting up. The similarities in the two cases were coming together, and the incident board, with its coloured arrows linking Oates to each victim, was beginning to look like a Tube map.

'Coffee?' Joan placed a mug down on her desk.

'Thank you. I need it.'

'I was going to go home, but I want to wait to see if Mike calls in with an update. They said it was a human hand, but I don't think they can tell if it was male or female.'

Anna didn't feel like talking, so she sipped her coffee.

'You know, when I was about seven, my mother lost me in Woolworths,' Joan said. 'I'd just wandered off and then I got panic-stricken because I couldn't see her anywhere. I went outside and I will never forget what happened when she eventually found me, she was hysterical and gave me such a slap, she'd never done anything like it before and I was crying, and then she started crying as well, saying that she thought someone had run off with me, and—'

Anna interrupted her. 'Is there a point to this, Joan? I've got a terrible headache.'

'Just that I'd only been gone ten minutes. What her parents must be going through, have gone through, over five years waiting and hoping, it's heartbreaking.'

'Yes.'

'Same with the Flynn girl – her parents keep on calling, you know, asking Mike if there's any news.'

Anna ignored her desk phone as it began to ring. Joan asked if she was going to answer it, it could be from Mike.

'No, I'm going home. You can tell whoever it is I'm not available.' She had an intuition that it was Langton calling.

Joan reached over to answer the phone as Anna picked up her coat and briefcase.

'Incident room, DCI Travis's desk.'

Anna paused.

'Good evening, sir.' Joan put her hand over the mouthpiece and mouthed that it was Langton. Anna gave a waft of her hand to indicate she didn't want to talk to him.

'I'm sorry, sir, she's not available. Can I take a message for her?'

Joan came round to sit behind Anna's desk.

'Well it's a big update; they found skeleton remains at the multi-storey car park.'

Langton was clearly listening, making only the odd interruption to clarify dates, and Joan was enjoying being the focus of the Chief Superintendent's attention. She'd never in all the years she had worked for him had such a lengthy conversation.

The arc lights lit up the dank lift-shaft pit, the drills carefully working their way in to the concrete around the skeleton. They now knew from the original car park plans that two foot of extra concrete had been added to hide the body. The archaeologists had drilled down a further six inches into the older layer, allowing them to use small controlled explosive charges to split the two levels apart. Lifting pins with eyes like giant needles had been drilled into the concrete around the body and chains attached to allow the removal of the concrete coffin to the ticket machine area on the ground floor, which was now covered in heavy-duty white plastic sheeting.

Dressed in protective clothing they used small chisels, hammers and special saws to chip and cut away the concrete without damaging the badly decomposed remains. The smell was intense now that the body was open to the air. The archaeologist explained that because it had been entombed in concrete no air could get in or out and although the lime mix in the concrete aided the decomposition there was nowhere for the body fluids to fully soak away. There were shreds of clothing left intact, and one boot was hardly damaged.

'She was last seen wearing a dark sweater – that looks like wool to me, and isn't that a part of a leather sleeve?' wondered Mike.

Barolli peered closer; he could see strands of wool that might be described as yellow-ish. The head and strands of hair were clearer, but the cement had got into the open mouth and eye sockets. The encased remains were eventually light enough to be wrapped in a body bag and taken to the mortuary. It would be some considerable time before they would have confirmation of the identity, but the body appeared to be female.

Anna went straight to bed as soon as she arrived home, knowing the following morning was going to be busy. It was clear that Oates would steal a motor vehicle if he needed to, so uppermost in her mind was the hope they could trace the Jeep, doubtful though it was. Oates's remark to Eileen, that he had been shovelling shit, began to make sense, as he could have been referring to his work emptying Markham's septic tank.

Anna realized that they still had no clue where Oates had been living or any employment he might have had after that job. They knew he had worked on the multi-storey car park site eighteen months ago when Fidelis Julia Flynn had disappeared, but she had yet to discover exactly where he was around the time Rebekka Jordan went missing. She wondered if Oates could have been living rough around Shepherd's Bush.

There was no information about the Jeep the next morning. It was quite possible that the number plates had been changed, or even that it had been broken up, but it was a very long and tedious task to check all Cherokee Jeeps of that year and colour used in crime, sold or crushed in breaker's yards.

Anna rang the Drug Squad again about Ira Zacks, and this time was put through to the officer who was dealing with the investigation into his drug dealing. They had a lengthy discussion, during which she described the luxury flat. To her relief the Drug Squad was not carrying out surveillance on the address as they were not aware of it. The lease, it turned out, was not in Zacks' name but his girlfriend's, and they had been waiting for him to turn up at a known associate's address to arrest him when the deal went down. Whether or not Anna's unconnected visit had made Zacks wary, the Drug Squad officer said he had gone 'walkabout'. The name Henry Oates had not surfaced anywhere in their investigation. The officer thanked Anna for her information, saying he would get a search warrant for the girlfriend's address, then, if and when they tracked Zacks down, they would be in touch.

It felt very much as if everything was on hold, and the team was now waiting for the pathologist to examine the skeletal remains. The priority was to get an identity as soon as possible. The dental records of Fidelis Julia Flynn had already been forwarded from a dental practice in Dublin some months ago and were on her 'Misper' file. The concrete around the mouth area was being chipped away very slowly to avoid any damage, so that the forensic odontologist had the best chance of making a match. Mike decided that he would hold off interviewing Henry Oates again until they had confirmation, either by dental records or DNA, that the remains were indeed those of Fidelis Julia Flynn.

Mike had a very terse conversation with Adan Kumar, who was clearly fishing to see if there was any more evidence.

'I keep getting calls from my client. As you are no doubt aware, Mr Oates is on suicide watch and is clearly not fit to be interviewed. I think he needs to be further assessed by the prison psychologist.'

Mike couldn't keep the sarcasm out of his reply.

'Well he must be unstable if he keeps calling you . . . and yes, having spoken with the prison I am aware he is on suicide watch, which is about to be lifted.'

'Have you found any evidence that implicates my client?'

'Our investigation is ongoing, Mr Kumar, and all will be disclosed to you when we are ready to re-interview Oates.'

Mike cut off the call. Thanks to his daily contact with the prison governor he knew that, contrary to Kumar's assessment, Henry Oates had settled down, and although he was still segregated he had had no violent mood swings. He was eating three meals a day and sleeping. Even though he remained on suicide watch and unable to be interviewed, Mike was not overly concerned by this as it gave him more time to put the evidence together. Oates had no visitors apart from Kumar.

Mike left his office to study the incident board. 'Zacks has done a runner,' Anna informed him, putting down her marker pen. 'Drug Squad think that my visit might have worried him. I really need to narrow down the date he last saw Henry Oates. He was vague about it when I spoke with him, said it was three or more years ago. Oates didn't have a vehicle then, so if this meeting occurred shortly before or after Rebekka Jordan went missing he may have got rid of the Jeep.'

'There's a lot of difference between three and five years,' Mike retorted.

'I know but I don't think he was really concentrating on what I was saying, especially if his drug dealing was on his mind.'

'Kumar called,' Mike said gloomily. 'He wants Oates reassessed by the prison psychologist. I think he's trying to get the suicide watch extended so we can't interview him. I don't want to be caught out; we need to look at all the evidence together then get Oates back in police custody for interview.'

Anna shrugged. She felt like the investigation was beginning to stall but she knew that it could move rapidly forward if they could only get Oates to open up and reveal more about his crimes.

'Have you thought any more about the Behavioural Investigative Adviser?'

'I'm not sure. Langton was dead against it . . .'

'What have we got to lose?'

'Well for one it could all backfire on us if the BIA thinks Oates is nuts. I don't want all our time and effort wasted.'

'How about we ask him to stick to advice on an interview strategy only?' Anna suggested.

'Who's the best?'

'Guy called Edward Samuels, doctor of psychiatry, works at the Bethlem Hospital. I've not met him personally but I have heard him lecture and also recommended him on a few cases; he's a cool customer with a lot of experience. Feedback's always good . . .'

'Then go ahead, unless Langton disagrees – I'd run it by him.'

'Yeah, right, I'll do that,' Anna said with sarcasm and laughed.

'Sorry, stupid suggestion. We'll keep it to ourselves for the time being then. I'll make DVD copies of the interviews with Oates and all the relevant statements and get them couriered over to Samuels.'

'Thanks, Mike, I appreciate your help. I'll ring him and brief him on the case and what we need,' Anna said.

Glad that Mike had agreed with her, she couldn't help wondering if he would back her if and when Langton found out.

'By the way . . . sorry for interrupting you during the meeting yesterday. What you had to say was a leap forward for the investigation, but you do go the long way round to get to the good bits.'

'You know me, Mike, I like everyone to know all the facts.'

*

While Mike headed off to the canteen for breakfast, Anna took the chance to use his office phone to speak to Samuels. After a lengthy conversation she went back to her own desk in the main office to try and concentrate on discovering how long Oates had lived in the basement squat. She knew from his ex-wife that he had at one point lived in Brixton, and basically survived off benefits and working odd jobs for cash in hand. She and Joan contacted social security, employment and National Insurance records, finding that Oates had been working the system and making various claims for years.

During the initial search of Oates's squat the scene of crime officers had removed a stack of claim forms and old rental receipts dating back years. Joan and Anna set to work to try and make sense of them all. Anna couldn't believe how long Oates had worked the system; the number of different addresses, let alone assumed names, made it difficult to compile a straightforward list. He appeared to be able to move from one area of London to the next, constantly claiming unemployment and benefits in a variety of names. It seemed from the dates on the seized documents that he had stopped making false claims three years ago. Did he think he was about to be caught or had he become bored, she wondered. What amazed Anna was that Oates, over a five-year period, was always one step ahead of the authorities, and had never been arrested for any benefit fraud offences. She wondered if they had all underestimated Oates's level of intelligence – clearly he was clever and able to plan his crimes.

To discover how long he had lived in the basement took yet another round of calls by Joan. The house was under a protection order and had been empty for six years; numerous squatters had lived in the property, so to try and trace anyone who could confirm just how long Oates had been there seemed impossible. There were old computer records of the police being called out, as neighbours across the street had made complaints about squatters on a number of occasions. These were from six years ago, shortly after the owners had moved out and the squatters moved in.

'You know, I'm going round in circles, because Oates's squat was due for demolition and the houses either side are also under the same order, so he could have been ejected and then moved back into the basement after things calmed down,' Joan said to Anna.

Anna sighed, and suggested they get some of the team over there to ask the local residents if they could recall seeing Oates.

The dental records for Fidelis Julia Flynn had now arrived at the mortuary, where the forensic odontologist was taking dental X-rays from the body for comparison. It had taken hours of painstaking work to excavate the body from its concrete tomb. The remains, now laid out on the mortuary table, had been cleaned, with the last residues of cement carefully washed away. The remnants of clothing had been removed and parcelled up ready to be sent to the forensic lab: scraps of wool, one boot, part of a sleeve from a blue anorak and fragments of material from what might have been a skirt or jeans.

They had measured the body and determined that their victim was five feet six, and the shoulder-length hair, which had now been washed through, was clearly auburn and still reasonably undamaged. They had recovered a small gold crucifix on a chain still snagged to one of the woollen remnants. It had been swabbed for DNA, photographed and then put in an evidence bag so Barolli could take it away with him to show Fidelis's two known boyfriends.

The forensic pathologist could not determine time or cause of death because of the level of decomposition. Although there didn't appear to be any broken bones or stab wounds he couldn't rule out the use of a knife and also suggested she might have been strangled or suffocated to death.

Mike had put off contacting Fidelis's parents until the odontologist had checked out the dental records. Finally, at five that afternoon, he had a confirmed match, and not only from the dental records: the DNA comparison to her parents showed that the remains were those of Fidelis Julia Flynn.

They now had evidence that Oates had worked at the construction site on both the day before and after their victim went missing. What they did not have was any witness that saw him with Fidelis.

By six that evening the team of three detectives had returned from interviewing the residents in Oates's street. Shown a photograph, one neighbour was able to confirm that he did live in the basement, and she could give an exact date she knew him to be living there because he had helped her husband put up new gates. Oates had been living in the basement for even longer than they had anticipated, for at least five and a half years, because the gates had been bought in March 2007. She also said that he came and went and was sometimes absent for days or even weeks on end, but as he was no trouble and often helped wash cars for cash, no one bothered making a complaint about him. She had never seen Oates with any children, and as far as she could recall she'd never seen anyone else entering or leaving with Oates. She also implied it was disgusting that the house had been left unoccupied for so long because the owners were waiting for planning permission to demolish all three buildings and build a block of flats. She had never seen Oates with a car, or a Jeep, but claimed he was always helpful and pleasant and had shovelled up the snow from her pathway the previous year.

Although the evidence linking Oates to Rebekka Jordan and Fidelis Julia Flynn was mounting, they still had no eyewitness who had seen Oates in the company of either girl. The hope of finding any forensic evidence from Fidelis's remains or clothing that might implicate him was slim.

'Could he have killed Rebekka in the squat?' Anna wondered.

Barbara pointed at the photographs of the house, boarded up on three floors.

'I know this neighbour said she never saw anyone coming or going apart from Oates, but don't tell me she was at her window twenty-four seven. He could have snatched her, hidden her body in the house.'

Anna came over to stand beside her.

'It's possible, but how did he get her there? We still haven't established that he was driving the Jeep – the neighbour never saw it parked up and we have no witness that saw him in it. We suspect he stole it, but only by supposition because someone saw a man fitting his description outside the owner's house. We have no proof that it was Oates that took it.'

'Still no trace of it either,' Joan said, joining them.

She had been contacting every garage, auction house and dealership, plus the wreckage yards, and there was no trace of it.

'Any luck with the crime reports?' Anna asked.

'I've given all the details to the station crime analyst and I'm waiting for her to get back to me.'

Anna went into Mike's office.

'Did the search team who went over Oates's place look under the floorboards?'

'Yeah, they used an optical cable attached to a monitor. Nothing untoward, though.'

'So they didn't lift the floorboards?'

'No, they thought using the lens would be quicker.'

'Rebekka could be buried under the floorboards! I want Oates's basement stripped, in fact the entire house – pull the bloody place apart.'

'Wheels are already in motion.'

'What?'

Mike gave a wide-handed gesture.

'Langton, he implied the house should have been searched properly as soon as the doll parts were discovered. We didn't realize they had cut corners so the search team's going back in tomorrow morning. Crime Scene Manager's going to keep an eye on them.'

'Good, but he should have been there to supervise the first search.'

'Langton had a lengthy conversation with our Joan and she brought him up to date. I'll give him a visit tonight; let him know we have identified the recovered body as Fidelis.'

'Don't let him use you as his housemaid.'

'Listen, can you do me a big favour, the Flynn parents are flying in and I'd appreciate it if you could see them over at the mortuary.'

Anna was so wrong-footed she wasn't sure how to react.

'But she's been identified by dental records.'

'I know, but they insisted. It's a grotesque sight, and the remains are not recognizable as their daughter.'

'Okay, what time are they due?'

'I've got a car picking them up from Heathrow and taking them straight to the mortuary, should be there around eight tonight. Barolli left this on my desk. You might want to take it with you,' Mike said, handing her an evidence bag containing the crucifix and chain.

'Was this on the body?'

'Caught in some clothing. Probably Fidelis's but we need to be sure.'

Anna went back to her desk. It was not yet seven, so she decided to grab a bite to eat, then go straight to the mortuary. Joan and Barbara had already left. Written up on the board were the details of the search teams for Oates's flat, and she could see ten officers were assigned to the job. She suspected Mike's budget was going through the roof. She partly wished she had taken the call from Langton. It really irritated her that even holed up unable to walk he was overseeing the cases. Her case specifically.

At eight-fifteen, Anna was waiting in a small ante-room off the mortuary set aside for relatives. By eight-thirty there was still no sign of Mr and Mrs Flynn, and Anna was becoming impatient. What was left of Fidelis's body was now shrouded in a white sheet and laid out on a trolley in the chapel of rest. All that could be seen of her was a skeletal face and her auburn hair. The mortuary assistant played with the light dimmer in a futile effort to dull the shock that awaited the Flynns before pulling the shroud up over where her face had been.

Anna was about to call flight arrivals at Heathrow when Mr and Mrs Flynn were ushered into the room. Their flight had been delayed owing to fog, and they were very apologetic, but their nervousness made it even more difficult for Anna to prepare them for what they would see. Mr Flynn was a robust man with a barrel chest, and bright very blue eyes; in contrast his wife was ashen-faced, with deep circles beneath her eyes, and she clutched a tissue, close to tears.

In as gentle a way as possible Anna told them how their daughter's body had been found and that her dental records had identified her. They didn't interrupt but sat tightly holding each other's hands. Anna then explained to them that Fidelis's body was badly decomposed and what they were about to see would not look like the daughter they so lovingly remembered. Mr Flynn put his arm around his wife and said that perhaps it would be best for her to stay in the waiting room.

Mrs Flynn refused, so Anna escorted them into the chapel of rest. It was wretchedly sad as they stood side by side holding each other, both trembling with the anxiety of what was to come. Anna nodded for the assistant to ease away the sheeting from the skull, which he did very carefully, and there was a terrible pause. They did not move closer but remained standing a little away from the body.

'When they are finished will they let us take her home?' Mr Flynn asked, and Anna assured him that it would be arranged. He then gave a small nod of his head, and the sheet was drawn back over what was left of Fidelis Julia Flynn's head.

They walked slowly back to the waiting room, holding onto each other for comfort. Anna asked if they would like a cup of tea, and they accepted. It was a relief because it meant she could leave them alone for a while. She heard Mrs Flynn begin crying as she closed the door.

Tracking down the tea-making facilities took a while, but at least it gave the Flynns time to compose themselves before the next part of their ordeal.

As they sipped their beakers of tea, Anna took a small plastic evidence bag out of her briefcase.

'Is this your daughter's crucifix?' she asked gently.

They asked if they could take it out to have a closer look. Mr Flynn cupped it in the palm of his hand; the chain was broken in two places. He stared at it, and then held it out to his wife.

'I've never seen this before, have you?'

'No. I have never seen her wearing this. Is it gold?' Mrs Flynn touched it lightly with her forefinger. She gave a nervous look at Anna. 'Do you mind if I pick it up?'

'Do, please.'

Mrs Flynn held the cross in her hand, turning it over to look at the back; she rubbed it with her thumb, and then chewed at her lips.

'I don't think this could belong to her, it's rolled gold, and she was allergic to anything that wasn't real gold. You remember the St Christopher?' she asked her husband.

'No.' Mr Flynn watched her as she continued rubbing at the cross.

'My sister gave it to her for her sixteenth birthday, but it left a terrible rash on her neck just like the swimming medals she won. Doctor said it was the nickel in them that gave her eczema. I tell you it was the same with her pierced ears, they got itchy and started weeping because the posts weren't real gold . . . It's the ones where the posts go through the ear I'm talking about.' Mrs Flynn handed the cross and chain back to Anna.

'So you never saw her wear this and doubt that she would have worn it?'

'That's right.'

Anna replaced it into the small plastic evidence bag. She knew that she had to say something, knew that they would be thinking this meant that perhaps the remains they had just seen were not their daughter's.

'I'm afraid the dental records sent from your daughter's dentist in Dublin were a confirmed match. Also we've compared the DNA samples you sent over. I'm very sorry, and if there is anything I can do whilst you are here ...'

Somehow, through all of this, the couple were able to maintain control over their emotions, impressing Anna with their quiet dignity.

As soon as she got home, Anna called Barolli, who had been to see Fidelis's boyfriend Barry Moxen, the nurse at Charing Cross Hospital, about the crucifix; she repeated the concerns of Mr and Mrs Flynn.

Barolli said that he had shown Moxen some photographs of the crucifix and although not one hundred per cent certain he 'thought' that it did belong to the victim.

'Thought isn't good enough, Paul, you have to go back with the actual crucifix itself and get him to look at it, also go to the ex-boyfriend who worked at the garage and her flatmates and see if they recall her wearing it.'

'Right, will do, have you still got it with you?'

'Yes, I'll bring it in first thing in the morning; you do realize the importance of this, don't you?'

'Course I do – if she wasn't wearing it, then it could belong to the killer.'

'Exactly.'

She replaced the phone, and closed her eyes, sighing. Nothing she knew about Henry Oates led her to believe that he would wear a crucifix, let alone a cheap rolled-gold one. The chain was broken, as if it had been snapped, the tiny links flattened. She knew if it had not been worn by Fidelis, or Oates, then they would have yet another massive round of enquiries to trace its origin, unless they struck lucky and got a hit for Oates with the DNA swabs taken from it. But if the DNA on it was unknown, or absent altogether, Anna knew it would open up the door for Kumar to allege that Oates was not their killer.

Chapter Eleven

It was mid morning and Anna was in the incident room with Mike Lewis, going over the details of her meeting with Mr and Mrs Flynn and the conversation about the crucifix. Paul Barolli entered the room looking annoyed and slammed the crucifix in its plastic evidence bag on Anna's desk.

'Bloody Moxen. Now he's seen the real thing he's not so certain. I pressed him on it and he came out with a load of crap about another girl he knew who had a similar one that was silver.'

'Thanks for going back to him,' Anna said.

'It doesn't get any better. While I was out I also visited the other ex-boyfriend who worked in the garage and her former flatmates. Not one of them recognized the crucifix as ever being worn by or belonging to Fidelis.'

'Well, the plus side is that it's now more likely that it belonged to Oates himself,' Anna reminded Paul.

'Yeah, but the lying bastard is never going to admit that, and there was no DNA on it.'

'So we keep digging until we find the connection,' Mike said in an effort to lift Paul's mood.

Mike asked Joan if she had spoken with the Polish worker Pavel who had supervised Oates at the work site.

'Yes, guv, and he's been very helpful and given us a list of contracted and casual labourers who worked on the car park. Barbara and I are trying to track them down.'

'Good. So we can ask them if they knew Oates and if he ever wore or had a crucifix like the one that was recovered,' Mike said with enthusiasm before Barbara interjected.

'Well, tracking them down is not proving as easy as it sounds, bearing in mind they are all now on different jobs, moved house or gone back to God knows where in Eastern Europe!'

'Keep up the enthusiasm, Barbara,' Mike said as he walked off towards his office.

Barbara looked at the others, who were now all laughing.

Anna anxiously checked the time, as she knew that Samuels would have received the DVDs and documents Mike had sent to him by now and she was eagerly awaiting his reply.

Barbara handed to Barolli the details to be passed on to the officers checking out the crucifix.

'It's unbelievable, they're all working in different parts of London or have gone home to Poland,' Barbara went on. 'Personally I think it's a waste of time. I mean, it could have been dropped there by anyone.'

'Not at all,' Anna snapped. 'On the contrary, it could prove to be invaluable evidence. In case you are not aware of it, Barbara, the crucifix was found snagged to clothing on the body. So it coincides with her body being carried and dropped into the lift shaft, and the cement being poured on top of her at the same time, all right?'

She got up and put her coat on. Sometimes it really ratted her, not having her own office so she could have time alone.

'Where you off to?' Barolli asked.

'Going over to see how the search is getting along.'

She had a good idea that they'd be talking about her as soon as her back was turned, but the reality was, the Rebekka Jordan case was now very much lagging behind the discovery and identification of Fidelis Julia Flynn. Although she had uncovered new evidence, there was still no tangible proof that Oates had abducted Rebekka. No witnesses. No sign of the Jeep. Even then they had no sighting of him driving it, they could only assume he'd stolen it.

The police vans were lined up outside the house. The team had already started the second search, this time lifting floorboards and taking down false ceilings. A few neighbours stood watching the comings and goings, and two of the officers were standing outside in white suits drinking coffee.

When Anna showed them her ID, one smiled, suggesting she use a face mask as there was a really pungent stink inside, especially in the basement. She hesitated.

'Pungent?'

He put up his hand, and said it was not the smell of a decaying body, that smell was different. This, he said, was sewage.

Anna carefully stepped inside the hallway; floorboards had been lifted up and stacked, leaving a narrow passage. The search teams were literally ripping the house apart, dismantling all they could find in every room. It was hazardous walking around and Anna knew she should have worn a hard hat, but it was too late now. She turned back to the hallway and then through a narrow door heading down into the basement.

*

The stench was disgusting – urine and sewage; it was a filthy hovel. As the officers were busy, she tried to not get in their way. The main room where it appeared Oates had slept and lived had already been searched, as the floor-boards lay stacked against one wall by a filthy floral bedhead. The iron bed was turned on its side, the springs showing the rusted frame, since the mattress had been taken to the lab. Cardboard boxes contained broken mugs, teapots, and plates. She could see a dresser with its draw-ers hanging open, and a broken mirror, which was part of the wardrobe door.

Anna had seen, and smelt, enough, so she spoke with the Crime Scene Manager to make sure the search was done properly this time then left the officers to get on with it. The fresh air outside came as a huge relief. Opposite was a terraced house, the garden of which had been paved over to use as car parking. A Ford Escort was parked on it, and the gates closed. She crossed the street, glanced back towards the derelict house, then looked up to the cur-tained windows. No other house on the terraced side had gates; this had to be the one with the 'helpful neighbour'.

Anna unhooked a gate, closed it, and walked up the neat paved drive to the immaculate front steps and dark green front door. She rang the bell, observing a notice for no circulars above the letterbox. Two clean empty milk bottles stood by the thick doormat.

'Yes?' The door was opened by a stern grey-haired woman.

'I'm Detective Anna Travis from the Met; could I have a few words with you?' She showed her ID.

'They're making a mess over there, dust'll be every-where, and they've been at it since eight this morning.'

'I'm sorry for any inconvenience.'

'Is it the developers? They've been supposed to do something for ages, that's three houses left empty for almost six years.'

'Could I come in? I'm sorry, you are?'

'Adele Murphy. Wipe your feet.'

Anna did so, and stepped into the hallway. The smell of lavender polish was very strong, combined with some kind of floral air freshener.

'We can sit in here, or in the kitchen.' The woman indicated a closed door.

'Whatever is convenient?'

'Well the kitchen's best as I've just hoovered and cleaned in the front room.' Anna followed Mrs Murphy into a kitchen with green linoleum floor, pine tables and chairs, pine cabinets and a big white range cooker. The sink and draining boards looked new; everything was polished to within an inch of its life.

'Thank you for seeing me, I know you were previously asked about the resident of the derelict house opposite.'

'I wouldn't call him a resident, he was a squatter, but not like the others we've had, hooligans drinking and playing loud music. We've all called the police out numerous times, they board up the place but they come back, well they did. We had an officer with a dog that used to patrol the neighbourhood; he sort of made sure the place was cleared.'

'But you have stated that Henry Oates lived in the basement opposite your house?'

'Yes, told them all about him, and he was no trouble, and he kept himself to himself.'

'You apparently used him for odd jobs?'

'Yes, my husband did, he helped put the gates up and sometimes washed the car.'

Anna went over all the previous questions, and Mrs Murphy answered them without adding anything new. She also said that she had never seen Oates with a car or any other kind of vehicle. She calculated that he had been squatting in the basement for over five years, possibly nearly six as the house had been empty for that long.

'They moved out families, you know, and then do nothing. One by one they've been bought up, all three of them. At first it was just the house opposite. They're still arguing over the protection order in the courts.'

'Did you ever see Mr Oates with anyone, male or female?'

'No.'

'So he came and went, never entertained anyone, no friends?'

'That's right.' Mrs Murphy then frowned, and ran her finger along the pine table top.

'I was thinking about him since the other detective spoke to me, and my husband and I talked about it, and then he reminded me about one time. I'd forgotten about it.'

She pursed her lips.

'It was a long time ago, not long after he moved in, and I know it was just before he helped with the gates, as they were delivered at the end of March 2007.'

Anna waited as Mrs Murphy still tapped the table with her finger.

'I've always had trouble sleeping, I often get up to make a cup of tea, and I was standing with the cup in my hand just looking out into the street. It's such a shame those houses standing empty, I mean it's not right, and it had to be two-ish or even later in the night, and I saw him.'

'With someone?'

'No, no, I've said I never saw him with anyone, but it was just strange. Maybe it was the streetlights, but it was like seeing a ghost.'

'How do you mean?'

'He had like white, powdery white stuff over him. He was just walking down the road, then he went inside the house. It probably was just the way the lights made him look, I don't know, but, like I said, it made him look sort of ghostly. It was even in his hair, on his face.'

'Did you speak to him about it, ask what the white stuff was?'

'No. I never had anything to do with him until – I've told you, about him giving my husband a hand putting up the gates in late March 2007. They weighed a ton, we didn't think they'd be that heavy, and he was strong. It was hard lifting them up onto the hinges, and then he'd also helped mix up the cement for the posts, they had to dig down quite a way so the posts could hold the gates up.'

'So the work went on for some time?'

'Yes, they had to let the cement dry, it all took a few days.'

'So during this time you must have got to know him quite well.'

'I wouldn't say that, he didn't ever come inside the house and we never crossed the road to go into his basement. I did give him some sandwiches and cups of tea, bottles of water. He was stripped to his waist, digging, and he was paid in cash!'

Anna turned as a small white-haired man appeared at the kitchen door.

'I thought I heard voices. I was having a nap upstairs.'

'This is my husband. Ronald, this is Detective . . .'

Anna introduced herself, and he shook her hand.

'She's asking about Henry from over the road.'

'Can either of you recall when he helped you with the gates or any time you saw him if he was wearing any neck jewellery?'

'Don't think so, do you, dear?' Ronald said as he looked to his wife, who shook her head.

'My eyesight's much better than his, and my memory, for that matter.'

'Would you both look at this photograph, please, and tell me if you ever saw Mr Oates wearing this.'

They both looked at the photograph of the crucifix, and neither could remember ever seeing Oates with anything like it.

'There's a lot of action going on over the road,' Ronald remarked as he drew up a chair and sat between them.

'I've been asking your wife about the time Mr Oates worked with you putting up the gates.'

'Strong as an ox. I couldn't have done it on my own, we paid for the paving stones to be laid by a company. I just reckoned I'd be able to put the gates up by myself. I'd sized it all up, made the order and they delivered them. Left them propped up by the wall, said it wasn't their job to hang them.'

'What did you make of Mr Oates?'

Mr Murphy shrugged, and said that apart from needing a bath, he was very helpful. He nodded at his wife.

'She wouldn't let him inside here, he was very scruffy, but then I'd also seen him all scrubbed up. He used to go swimming in the local baths. I often saw him with a rolled-up towel under his arm.'

'Did you ever see him with a vehicle?'

'No. You know, the other copper that came here asked a lot of questions about him, said it was connected to a murder enquiry, but we've not had any details, not seen it in the papers.'

'Mr Oates has been charged with the murder of a woman called Justine Marks, and we are also making enquiries into two other cases that we believe he could be involved in.'

'Bloody hell! Are they looking for bodies in the house opposite, like in the Fred West case?' he exclaimed, looking at his wife in shock.

'They are looking for evidence, yes; did you ever see him with anyone entering his basement or anyone visiting him?'

'No, he was a real loner, though he'd always be friendly, wave over to me if I saw him. This is very worrying. I said having those houses empty was bound to create trouble.'

'But they weren't all empty when you used him to help you with the gates?'

'No, the two either side got boarded up quite a while after, they had a bunch of squatters in the middle house that were causing problems and they were moved on, then the sitting tenants were moved out from the houses either side.'

Mrs Murphy was clearly becoming quite agitated and Anna asked if she could just confirm that Henry Oates was living in the basement in March 2007, and that it was before the other properties were boarded up. Both agreed. Next she asked again if they had ever seen Oates driving a car, or possibly a Jeep. They both were certain they had never seen him with any kind of vehicle.

Next Anna had them confirm that Oates had helped mix cement for the gate posts and Mr Murphy said that he was glad that he had helped him as he was very professional, knew exactly how much sand was required. Oates had explained to Mr Murphy the importance of getting the right consistency.

'So do you think he was working on a building site then?' Anna asked.

'Might have been, and I'll tell you why. I mentioned to him, when he was helping me with the gates, that he'd given my wife a bit of turn, that she'd seen him coming home looking like a ghost. He said to me that that was chalk dust, he said something about a bag dropping on him!'

'Chalk dust?'

'That's right, then he went on complaining about trying to get work, said the Poles were taking all the available jobs and accepting lower wages. I never said nothing to him; I mean, he was obviously capable of getting a job but I reckon he couldn't be bothered if the giro cheques kept coming.'

'Did he get post delivered to the house?'

'No, he'd collect from our local post office, often saw him in there,' Mr Murphy said.

Lastly Anna showed them the photographs of the victims. They went very quiet, but could not recall ever seeing them. Mrs Murphy was shocked when she looked at the photograph of Rebekka Jordan.

'She's just a young girl.'

Anna was now eager to leave, and knew that if she stayed any longer they would start asking more questions about the murder enquiry. Mr Murphy walked her to the gate, opening it for her and pointing out the cement-filled area around the posts.

'You won't have to dig all this up, will you?'

Anna smiled as she told him there was no need for him to worry about his gates or driveway.

She was still standing there when she noticed Barolli parked up opposite in an unmarked police car, and the Crime Scene Manager handing him something through the driver's window. Anna crossed the road and opened the passenger door.

'You heard?' Barolli asked her, as he took from the CSM a large square plastic box in an evidence bag. 'This was found stashed up the fireplace; I'm taking it straight over to forensics to check for fingerprints and DNA.'

'What's inside it?'

'Load of jewellery trinkets, could belong to a victim or just junk stuff, but as the place had a load of squatters at one time or another we need to see if Oates's dabs are on the box.'

Barolli nodded over to Mr Murphy, who was watching them intently.

'Get anything else from them, did you?'

'Not really. I'll be interested to see what's inside that box, though.'

'Likewise, but I'm not touching it until it's been dusted.'

Anna was about to do a web search for 'chalk + building' when Mike arrived back at the incident room.

'You hear about the box found in Oates's basement?' he asked. 'Hidden in the fireplace. Paul said it was full of jewellery. He's having it individually photographed then the lab can get to work on it.'

'Yeah, hoping to get prints off the box.'

Mike ruffled his hair.

'You know what it could mean?'

She nodded as her desk phone rang, and coincidentally it was Pete Jenkins. They had been able to get some good prints from the plastic surface of the box, and as they had already taken prints from Oates when he had been arrested it wouldn't take long to do a comparison.

'You know what my gut feeling is about this stuff?' Pete said. 'I've examined tokens like this in other murder cases. You want to come in and see for yourself?'

'Be right there. I had the same feeling. Give me half an hour or so.'

Anna set off at once, but as she drove to Lambeth, she couldn't shift the dread that the prints would not match with Oates's.

But they did. It was a perfect match: three left fingers, a right palm and left thumbprint all belonged to Oates, and no other prints had been found.

Pete was standing in the section of the laboratory that had been given over to the Oates murder enquiry. Many items had been discarded, but that still left a vast amount of clothing and bed linen. There was even a filthy rolled-up towel and swimming trunks. Everything was being carefully checked over, tagged and bagged.

Anna asked if any items of clothing had chalk dust over them and explained her conversation with the Murphys. Pete said that as far as he knew there was nothing and, given that Mrs Murphy had said that it had been in March 2007, a minimal trace would be worthless as evidence and not even worth looking for.

Laid out neatly on brown paper was the square empty plastic box and beside it, an array of jewellery: cheap brooches, bracelets, necklaces, pendants, single earrings, a couple of rings and a string of fake pearls. Many pieces were broken, stones were missing out of clasps; nothing appeared to be of any great value.

Anna examined the hoard using plastic lab tweezers to look more closely at each item.

'I've had individual photographs taken back and front where necessary,' Pete told her. 'I'd say the thing of any value is the bracelet, which is hallmarked gold. This is the one item you can concentrate on first because . . .'

Pete, wearing gloves, picked up the gold bracelet. The clasp was broken and missing some stones, and a safety chain held the two bands together. He took a magnifying glass and Anna moved closer.

'It's engraved,' he said. 'Angela 1999 from Mum and Dad.'

Anna sighed; she knew what she was looking at – days, weeks of backtracking through unsolved case files, missing persons, burglary and robbery and lost property reports in an effort to identify all the items. She and Pete couldn't help coming to the same conclusion: these items could be the sick tokens of a serial killer. That left Anna little choice but to return to the station to speak to Mike.

Mike closed his eyes at the news.

'Jesus Christ, if there are more murdered women out there our cases could spiral out of control.'

'Well, we can't be sure until we identify the jewellery, and that won't be until the photographs and details are sent over in the morning. So I don't know about you, but I need to go home, get ready for the shit to start hitting the fan tomorrow.'

Anna had just started up her Mini when Mike tapped on the window to say that Dr Samuels had just rung the office to let them know that he had nearly finished going over the Oates file and would come to the station in a day or so to advise them on the best way forward with the interviews. Just at that moment Anna's mobile rang: 'Does he know about Samuels yet?' demanded Mike. Anna shook her head as she answered the phone.

'You avoiding me?'

'No, it's been quite an eventful day.'

'I'll be waiting to hear the details, so get over to me as soon as you can.'

'I'm really tired.'

'So am I, tired of not being kept up to speed, all right?'

'Okay, I'll come straight over.'

'Good. Have you eaten?'

'No.'

'I'll fix us something. Bye.'

At least he hadn't asked her to schlep over groceries, and she was certain he'd order a pizza delivery. In some ways it was better for her to share that afternoon's depressing discovery with Langton, rather than go home alone, and more than likely order a takeaway Chinese.

Chapter Twelve

Langton had set the table in the living room, even if the cutlery did look as if he had half-heartedly thrown it onto the cloth. Napkins, wine glasses and an open bottle of Merlot had been dumped alongside HP and tomato sauce.

The main front door had been buzzed open, and the flat door had stood ajar for her to walk in.

'Get a glass of wine, won't be a minute.'

She was surprised that his voice came from the kitchen.

'Anything I can do?'

'Nope, I'll tell you when I need you.'

Anna poured two glasses and arranged the cutlery and napkins into place settings, turning as Langton appeared. He looked remarkably well, shaved and wearing a grey loose tracksuit; he smiled, and lifted his walking cane.

'Plaster's off, but the worst part, and I've never felt such agony, was bending the leg. Bloody hell, Travis, it was excruciating, but hardly a twinge now.'

'That's marvellous.'

'Stuff's on a tray if you could just carry it in.'

He walked a trifle unsteadily, but considering how he had been when she last saw him it was obvious he was well on the road to recovery.

'Stairs are still hazardous but I'm doing exercise gradually.'

He eased into one of the hard-backed chairs at the table. Anna found the kitchen is some semblance of order, and a tray with a Pyrex dish of shepherd's pie and a bowl of vegetables.

'Don't tell me you cooked this?'

'I'd be lying if I did. I've got a freezer full of easy meals, but I have to watch it as I've put on weight.'

She put the tray on the table, and returned to the kitchen to collect plates and serving spoons. By the time she had filled first his plate and then her own he was already wading through his portion, eating with his usual haste.

'Right, let me have it, cheers to you, Travis.' He lifted his glass and she raised hers.

'To recovery,' she said.

He almost drained his entire glass, topping it up as she ate, with his trademark tangible impatience. Slowly she gave him the update, between mouthfuls of food and sips of her wine. He helped himself to another serving of the tasty shepherd's pie, squirting ketchup over it, and listened attentively without his usual interruptions. As Anna described the task of tracing the owner of the gold bracelet he let out a sigh, shaking his head.

'Dear God, you know it could open a can of worms. If this is a collection of sick tokens it'll be weeks of work. What's happening with Oates?'

'Suicide watch is about to be lifted but Kumar wants him reassessed. Mike's going to get him back in police custody any day now.'

'The two of you need to sit down and go over all the evidence you have so far.'

'We've already agreed to do that and prepare the interviews together.'

'Good. You see, you don't need some prick profiler or behaviour adviser thingy as you call them.'

'No, I guess not,' Anna said, avoiding eye contact by looking down at her plate of food.

'I used a profiler on a stranger's murder a few years back. He was a useless self-opinionated pain in the arse. Made the evidence fit his bullshit theory and sent us miles off course, then to top it all the bastard had the cheek to hit us with a three-grand bill.'

'I can guess what you told him to do with his bill.'

'Too right. Samuels, I said, go fuck yourself! Enjoyed saying it but still had to pay him in the end.'

Anna nearly choked on her food and gulped her wine to clear her throat.

'You all right?'

'Sorry,' she gasped between breaths. 'Food went down the wrong way.'

Langton poured himself another glass of wine, offering to top hers up but she refused as she was driving.

'So nothing new with the Rebekka Jordan enquiry?'

'Well, I have confirmation that Oates was living in the basement at the time Rebekka went missing. The search team are still working on the three houses but they haven't found anything other than the jewellery.'

'But nothing has come up evidence-wise that could actually move your enquiry forward?'

Anna hesitated, and then described how Oates had looked on the night Mrs Murphy had seen him returning home. This possibly around the date Rebekka Jordan went missing.

Anna got up and showed Langton her notebook of

dates. The Murphys knew when Oates had helped with the gates because they were delivered in the last week of March 2007, and this was when they got to know him because he had helped to put them up. Mr Murphy was certain that it was two weeks before when Oates was seen by his wife.

Langton looked at the scribbled pages and shook his head.

'Well this is all very crossword puzzle, you seem to have a lot of cryptic clues but nothing that fits right in your time frame.'

'I know, but—'

'The forensic lab has found no blood or DNA of Rebekka's on any clothes or shoes from Oates's basement.'

'Well he probably threw away the clothes he wore when he abducted her.'

'He worked odd jobs on building sites, which could account for any chalk on his clothing.'

'That's my point. If the Murphys are right about the gate delivery date, then the time she saw Oates covered in chalk was the same week Rebekka went missing. If he was working on another site at the time he could have buried her there during the night.'

Langton closed his eyes and yawned.

'Sorry if I'm boring you!' she said, closing her note-book.

She stacked their dinner plates onto the tray along with her wine glass. Anna felt she needed some breathing space before her temper exploded.

'I'll take these into the kitchen. Do you want a coffee?'

'No.'

Anna calmed down as she washed the dishes and left them on the draining board. The remains of the shepherd's pie she covered with tin foil before going back to find he'd now moved to sit on a sofa and was irritatingly thumbing through her notebook.

'The bastard gets multiple giro cheques, benefits and Christ knows what other handouts. If the Work and Pensions fraud squad had got their act together they could have had him locked away years ago.'

Anna sat herself opposite him.

'He was pretty adept at working the system. We found numerous claim forms under different names, and heaps of addresses he'd dossed down in, but they did throw him out of a council flat – he was subletting the rooms!'

Langton tapped his hand with her notebook.

'Doesn't sound like a man who's not the full ticket, does he?'

'We've underestimated him. He doesn't just abduct a woman off the street and kill her on the spur of the moment. He's a planner who knows exactly what he's going to do.'

'Rebekka, though, doesn't seem to fit his MO – she was only thirteen, the other two girls were a lot older.'

'His wife Eileen caught him touching up their daughter when she was ten!'

'What about the other case – Fidelis?' he asked.

'Still no eyewitness, crucifix didn't belong to the victim. Yeah, he was working at the multi-storey car park but no paperwork with his name on it to confirm the exact dates. Mike says it's still all circumstantial and the CPS may say there isn't enough evidence to charge.'

'Are you any further forward on the Jeep?'

'No.'

'I think with the amount of money already laid out on this and the first Jordan investigation, unless you come up with something soon or Oates makes a full confession then you may have to call it a day.'

She swiftly reached over to retrieve her notebook and put it into her briefcase, then picked up her coat.

'I won't give up. I disagree with you, and I think we are accumulating enough evidence. So it's taking time, so it's costing, but look how much we have uncovered so far. We are nearly there.'

'Nearly isn't good enough.'

'No, but if this box of trinkets really does contain sick tokens and Oates has killed, not only our three known victims but others, we have a duty to continue this enquiry.'

'You going?'

'Yes.'

'Come here.' He patted the seat on the sofa beside him.

She sat down, keeping her coat and briefcase on her knees.

'Sometimes, Anna, as hard as it may seem, you have to reach a conclusion that you've done as much as possible to gain a positive result.'

She turned towards him.

'If Rebekka Jordan was your daughter, how would you feel if you were told that?'

'Don't go there,' he said sharply.

She stood up angrily and hurled her briefcase down beside him.

'Yes I will, because I am not giving up. You brought me onto her case and I am confident I will get a result, contrary to what you believe. She was thirteen years old, her parents deserve to have closure and I'll get it for them.'

He watched her pulling on her coat and pointed at her briefcase.

'You've got nothing in there, Anna, that'll stand up in court. All you have is dates and times and possible connections, but admit it, you have no hard evidence. Do you think that I didn't feel the same way as you when I had to leave the case open? Yes, they have a right to closure, every victim's family has that right, but sometimes you just have to accept you are not going to get it.'

'Oh really, so we find a gold bracelet that belonged to a girl called Angela and we just drop it – a bracelet found in a stinking basement where we know a killer lived?'

'Go home. You're giving me a headache.'

'If everything boils down to how much it costs I may as well quit. How can you put a price tag on a thirteen-year-old girl's murder ... or anyone's, for that matter! You want to close the case, do it, and live with it, because I couldn't. And don't even begin to think I will be the one who tells the Jordans.'

She yanked open the front door and banged it hard behind her. He could hear her thudding down the stairs, and would have liked to run after her, but he couldn't. He clasped the sofa arm to ease himself up and then reached for his walking stick, poured the remainder of the wine into his glass and drained it. It had become consistently harder to control budgets and he had already had a lengthy discussion with Mike Lewis, warning him that it was becoming tough for him to constantly get more financing. The archaeologists, the specialist police search teams and the mounting forensic work were all costly, and he had to approve more and more officers to be attached to the investigation. He turned as if to pace the room the way he always did and almost fell over. He swore, gritted his teeth and, with determination, began walking slowly up and down the room. He paused by a photograph of his stepdaughter. Anna had implied that if it had been Kitty who had disappeared he would not have left the case on file. It wasn't true. He had worked twenty-four seven trying to get a result on this one. He had becomes friends with her distraught parents, he had wanted to give them some kind of peace, but the weeks had turned into months, and the longer Rebekka was missing the smaller, he knew, were her chances of being found.

He had felt guilt. He had lived with the fact that he had been unable to find any suspect; it had been the most frustrating investigation he had ever headed up. If he was honest, the case had never truly been over for him and now it had reared up again. He began to go over in his mind the entire conversation with Anna, eventually conceding that she had touched an extremely raw nerve.

Anna was at the station by seven-thirty the next morning. Mike arrived shortly after, so she asked to speak to him in his office. She was very tense, her hands clenched.

'I had dinner with Langton last night.'

'Oh, how is he?'

'Let me ask you. He is not overseeing my investigation, he's on sick leave, isn't he?'

'Yes, but he's had his finger in the pie all along. I already told you that as far as DCS Hedges is concerned both cases are Langton's.'

'He is getting ready to close down my enquiry and by the sounds of it yours as well. He maintains we only have circumstantial evidence.'

'Maybe we do, but we haven't even re-interviewed Oates yet. When we present him with what we do have, he might cough up.'

'If he doesn't?'

'Where are you going with this, Anna?'

'I am just warning you he's going to withdraw officers. He says the budget's out of control, and that it's all about finances.'

Mike ruffled his hair distractedly.

'I'm refusing to back off, Mike, and I want you to also refuse, because I truly believe we are close to proving Oates is the killer of both Fidelis and Rebekka.'

'Listen, I know you've been doing a lot of work, and with results, but I also have to consider the facts.'

'He's already called you, hasn't he?'

Mike flushed.

'Oh my God, I don't believe it, don't tell me you agree with him?'

'Whatever my feelings are, Anna, Langton makes the rules. At the moment, though, he's just considering it, so in the meantime we don't slow down.'

'He shouldn't even be considering it.'

'The investigation right now is costing a fortune. We had a full-scale search of not one but three properties that—'

'Resulted in the finding of a box of jewellery that could belong to other victims, a box with only Oates's fingerprints on it, a bracelet with a girl's name engraved on it. We got a result, Mike.'

Mike slapped the desk.

'If Oates is guilty of more murders, the fact is we have him charged with that of Justine Marks and he will stand trial for her murder. If we do not have proof beyond circumstantial evidence for the other cases you know the CPS will not proceed.'

Anna stood up. Mike had obviously been got at by Langton so she didn't think there was anything more to say.

*

Anna couldn't sit still after such a start to the morning, so she decided to visit the swimming pool in Hackney known to be used by Oates. She was completely wired, extremely angry, and also very disappointed by Mike's reaction. Half of her doubted she would gain anything useful from going to the pool but she recalled Fidelis's parents saying she had won swimming medals. On the pretext that the young woman might have met Oates there she got out of the incident room as fast as possible, only pausing to ask Joan to run a web search for chalk production – how and where it was mined, and its use on building sites – and leave the printed results on her desk. Anna was surprised at how large the sports complex in Hackney was. It consisted of not just a swimming pool, but facilities for karate training, trampolining, and dance classes from aerobics to modern ballet. The gym was well equipped and private training lessons were available. There were pre- and postnatal classes and a crèche where mothers could leave their children to do painting and pottery. Altogether it was a very well-run centre funded by the council. There was even a café serving hot meals, with windows that overlooked the swimming pool, where plenty of attendants supervised schoolchildren taking swimming lessons in roped-off lanes.

Anna waited at the reception desk and watched two pleasant girls working at computers and answering the telephone, before she was led to the manager's office. Jim Banks was a fit-looking man wearing a tracksuit top with a badge of the centre's logo, dark trousers and training shoes. He shook her hand and indicated for her to sit in a chair opposite his smart desk, on which computers and telephones and papers were neatly arrayed. Behind him was a wall of cups and trophies.

Anna explained about the investigation into the murder of Fidelis Julia Flynn. She showed him Fidelis's and Henry Oates's photographs, asking if Banks recalled either of them.

'Yes. He was a regular up until about a year ago. Never seen her before, though.'

Banks turned to his computer.

'I was a swimming instructor when he first joined. In fact, it was shortly after we opened six years ago.'

'He was a member?'

'Yes. I'll just see if we still have his particulars.'

Banks tapped a few keys and scrolled through the past and present membership lists.

'Nothing on here for Fidelis Flynn, but yes, there you go, details of his joining date, membership number and photograph.'

He printed out the information and passed it to Anna. At the top of the page was a star and the words *NOT APPROVED FOR FURTHER MEMBERSHIP*. Banks next went to a filing cabinet and withdrew a folder.

'I keep a file on people who we have complaints about or who've been barred for one reason or another. The girls at the desk also have a copy because of the photograph.'

Anna was hardly able to contain herself as she asked why Mr Oates was no longer approved for membership.

'We have a policy: anyone using the swimming pool has to go through the shower and foot bath before entering the water, it's all about health and safety.'

She waited.

'Mr Oates was to say the least rather unkempt, and I recall him very well because when I worked the pool area he had obviously not showered. I think he was working on a building site and I caught him coming into the swimming pool area from a staff door. He had not used the shower and so I sort of earmarked him as someone to watch. I did on a couple of other occasions turn him back to go through the disinfectant foot bath; his feet were filthy. We also had a couple of complaints from other swimmers and he was warned that if he didn't shower he would not be allowed to use the pool.'

Banks went on to say that Oates was a very strong swimmer, and would do up to a hundred lengths every time he used the pool. He also used the gym, where again complaints had been made about his appearance. In fact, the list of complaints also included using someone's shampoo and sitting around too long in the café.

'He was warned a couple of times that he would not be allowed to use the centre and his membership would be revoked. There was some altercation on a running machine once. He was quite athletic and would be on the treadmill for hours.'

'Did you ever see him approaching young girls?'

'I think a swimming instructor did give a memo about him taking too much interest in a group of schoolgirls.'

Anna remarked to Banks that the list of complaints against Oates was extensive, yet he had still been allowed to use the premises.

'We are a council-run club, not private, and we have a three-warnings rule, but in actual fact we didn't ask him to leave due to his hygiene or behaviour – we had a spate of thefts. Tracksuits and shoes went missing, and we did a Miss Marple, cross-checking the members that were signed in when the thefts occurred. Overall, Oates was top of the list.'

'Did it get reported to the police?'

'No. It was nothing of value really and often the stolen item wasn't missed immediately. We did install some interior CCTV cameras and, if my memory is correct, it was just before we had them installed that Mr Oates was asked to leave. We always had them in the car park, but not inside the club.'

'So he was never caught on camera stealing?'

'No. One of our instructors was in the gym for a one-to-one workout with a member, said she had taken her crucifix off and put it on the windowsill. When her class was finished . . .' He paused and shook his head.

'No, sorry, it was the young lady's, she had taken it off because it got in the way when she was doing press-ups and Judy the instructor filled out the lost property report for her. Again it was not of great value, more sentimental value really.'

He frowned and stood up.

'Just in case I get the facts wrong she still works here if you would like to talk to her.'

'Thank you, I would, and I need to take the file you kept on Oates.'

Anna was so excited she burst into the incident room. Barolli physically jumped, as he was closest to the door.

'I got a result, one you won't believe.'

Anna dumped her briefcase down as people around paid attention.

'Henry Oates was confronted by a fitness trainer at the sports centre where he went swimming but he also worked out in the gym there. They'd had a spate of thefts – running shoes, tracksuits – and one of the members left her gold crucifix on a window ledge. Oates was running on a treadmill; he was the only other person in the gymnasium.'

Anna had taken off her coat and was opening her brief-case.

'When Oates was confronted and accused of taking it, he became very abusive and threatening. The manager was called and said Oates refused to allow them to search his bag – in fact swung it at him and ran out. He was subsequently barred from the centre.'

Anna crossed to the incident board and picked up a marker pen.

'The lady who owned the crucifix is a Sabrina Holt and I went to see her on my way back here. It was stolen eighteen months ago. Sabrina said it was rolled gold, not real gold, and that it had a chip mark at the bottom of it.'

Anna pointed to the picture of the crucifix on the board and circled a small chip mark, which was in the same place described by Sabrina Holt.

'She said it could not have been taken by anyone else as Oates was working out when she started her class and left before it had finished and no one else entered the gym.'

'Did she report it to the police?' Barbara asked.

'No, she said it was not that valuable.'

'Nobody actually saw him with it though, did they?' Barolli said.

Anna snapped that the necklace was stolen two days before Fidelis went missing and had now been recovered snagged to her clothing. It was obvious Oates had taken it.

Joan had been on the phone during all of this, but now called out: 'I got a hit!'

Anna turned towards her.

'I did as you asked about the chalk and building sites. Basically raw chalk itself isn't really used on site but it is used to make cement, lime, mortar and so on. Oates told his neighbour it was chalk dust on him so as a bit of initiative on my part I started ringing round working chalk pits near London. Been onto a chalk quarry near Marlow – that's sort of past Heathrow Airport, M40-M4 – it's only semi-running at the moment, but the manager was really helpful. Worked there for over twenty years.'

Anna was so impatient she wanted to shake Joan.

'Did Henry Oates work there?'

'No, but I also ran by the manager, amongst other names, Timmy Bradford – remember him, ex-boxer associate of Oates?'

'Yes, and?'

'In 2006 Bradford worked there briefly as a driver, and he brought a friend along who was looking for a similar position, but the friend was unable to provide a driving licence.'

'This guy has a bloody good memory,' Barolli said.

'I thought that, but he recalls "the friend", who matches Oates's description, as being trouble. When he was refused a job he became belligerent, screaming and shouting about wasting his time and the next minute the two of them were fighting.'

'Which two, the manager and Oates?'

'No, Timmy Bradford and Oates. They had to be separated, which is why he remembers the incident. Oates cleared off and Bradford only lasted a few more weeks before he left.'

Anna still had the marker pen in her hand.

'Joan, hit me with the dates this happened.'

'Well, the manager thinks it was late June, early July 2006.'

Anna tapped her teeth with the pen. The date didn't match when Mrs Murphy had seen Oates covered in chalk dust but was around the time he worked at the Jordans. She hesitated before writing down the information.

'What's this place like, Joan?'

'I don't know, it's called Taplow Quarry. I'll get some pictures of it up on the web. Some parts of it are disused, or so the manager said.'

Anna leaned on the back of Joan's chair as she brought up the pictures on the website. It was like an alien world – colossal, with towering white cliffs of chalk and a quarry hundreds of feet in depth and width. The dumper trucks looked like small toys in comparison. They could see huge open-sided barns with loading bays and conveyer belts, which Joan said were to move the blasted chalk into a crusher before it went on to the cement and lime factories. The disused area was also massive, with a large pond, trees, bushes and abundant moss.

Anna went back to her desk but couldn't concentrate. The quarry had given her an eerie feeling – the hairs on her arms were raised. She doodled on her notepad. Why had Henry Oates been seen covered in chalk dust nearly nine months after he had applied for work there?

'Paul, will you do me a favour?'

Barolli looked over.

'I'd like you to bring in Timmy Bradford for further questioning.'

'Sure, and good work on tracking the crucifix down. Do I have a reason for wheeling Bradford in?'

'Yeah, he lied.'

Timmy Bradford sat nervously in front of Anna, who had Barolli beside her. This time he was outside the comfort zone of his mother's flat, and there was no tea and biscuits on offer.

'You fed me a load of lies, Timmy, didn't you?' Anna began, in no mood to mess about.

'No.'

'Listen, Timmy, I've looked at your record. You're not sitting here because of another petty juvenile crime. You're very close to being arrested on suspicion of murder, so you need to start telling me the truth.'

'I ain't done nothing.'

Anna opened her notebook and began to flick through the pages.

'You said you last saw Henry Oates seven years ago at York Hall.'

Bradford leaned forwards.

'I was telling you the truth. I ain't seen him for years, that's God's truth.'

'What about the time you took him to Taplow Quarry?'

'What?'

'You were working there.'

Bradford leaned back in his chair and shook his head.

'Are you shaking your head because you didn't work there?'

'No, it was bloody years ago, and I only lasted a few months cos the work was shit, and the money was no good. You got covered in the crap, in your hair, up your nose ...'

'Tell me about the time you took Henry Oates there.'

Bradford sighed, looking down at the table top, unable to meet Anna's eyes.

'He was looking for a job. I met him at a boxing match. I told him I was working there and he asked if I could take him with me.'

Bradford's gaze wandered around the small room.

'Like I said, it was years ago the last time I saw him and I just forgot he went with me to Taplow.'

'You had a fight with him, didn't you?'

Bradford shrugged.

'Yeah, we had a punch-up. They wouldn't let him drive one of the trucks like I was doing cos he had no driving licence. Like I said, I had a job and he wasn't gonna get one. He was all uptight, blamed me for wasting his time; he told me I had to take him back to London, but I told him to fuck off or wait for me to finish workin'.'

'Don't swear, Mr Bradford,' Anna said firmly.

'Sorry, but you know you got me hauled in here, my mum's frantic, she won't believe it was for nothin'.'

Anna glanced at Barolli and closed her notebook. Bradford had confirmed what they had been told by the chalk pit manager.

'I dunno how he got back to London, maybe thumbed a ride, but that was the last time I saw him.'

'But how do you think he got back to London?'

'I dunno. I swear before God I never saw him again. He bloody swung a punch at me and hit me in the face. Knowing him, he could have even walked back. As it turned out, I left the job a few weeks later like I told you, but I never wanted to see him again. He's got this temper and he could just let fly. I mean, I could hold me own with him, but he caught me off guard.'

'Are there any other contacts with Henry Oates that you may have "forgotten" about?'

Bradford hesitated and then gave a slow nod of his head.

'Yeah, forgot this an' all, sorry, but it was before the fight at the quarry. I'd had this run of bad luck. I'd been saving up and looking for a place to live, but I was stupid. I took a punt on a dog, got told it was a certainty, lost five hundred quid.'

'What about the savings your mother mentioned, that you'd lost the money you'd saved for a flat?'

He pulled a clownish face.

'Yeah well, that was a bit of a lie, she'd have never let me stay with her if she'd known I'd blown what I'd got on a fucking dog. Excuse me, sorry, she's very careful with her savings. I know she's got quite a packet from her last husband, and . . . I completely forgot this. I've had to move in with her off and on for years, it's the gambling doing me in always, and then when I get a bit of dough I move out. Me and her husband didn't get along either, but since he passed on I've been staying with her more and more.'

Anna waited patiently.

'Go back to the time you say something had slipped your mind.'

'Right, yeah. It was when I was taking him to the quarry, he came to Mum's flat for me to drive him there. I don't even have the car any more, had to sell it.'

'Go on.'

'Well, he was early so I let him in and told him to wait in the hall. Of course Mum was hovering around, it was only six-ish but she's always up with the birds.'

'Did she meet him?'

'Christ no, he was stinking out the hallway and she'd have gone apeshit about me being with his type. I just grabbed my overcoat and we left. I was tellin' you the truth, cos I honest to God haven't seen him since that time at the quarry.'

'Thank you for coming in, Mr Bradford.'

He had the audacity to smile. 'Had an option, did I?'

'What's so important about this chalk pit?' Barolli asked after Bradford had been allowed to go.

Anna explained that Oates couldn't have been working at the chalk pit when Mrs Murphy said she saw him covered in dust. She thought it unlikely that the elderly couple would be nine months out, particularly as Mrs Murphy recalled the exact date the gates arrived.

'It's the chalk pit, something about that place. But if they are right about the dates Oates helped them put their gates up, it was March 2007 that Oates explained to Mr Murphy about the chalk dust. Mrs Murphy did say her husband's memory was not so good. Maybe he did get the timing wrong.'

Joan was in tears, her shoulders shaking as she slumped at her desk.

'What's up with you, Joan?' Anna asked.

'Just got a dressing-down from the Chief Super.'

'Langton?'

'No, the one who's standing in for him.'

Anna leaned close to Joan, who was wiping her eyes with a tissue.

'What happened?'

Joan tearfully explained that she had, although not specifically instructed to do so, run a check through missing persons, searching for the Christian name Angela.

Anna tensed up, leaning closer still as Joan passed her a report. She sniffed.

'Angela Thornton, "Misper" from Epping over five years ago, and as you can see from the description of the clothes she was wearing they also include a gold bracelet, a present from her parents for her twenty-first. It was engraved with the inscription, "Angela 1999 from Mum and Dad".'

Anna couldn't believe it. She perched on the edge of Joan's desk.

'Good work, Joan, but tell me what Hedges said that's got you so upset.'

Joan said that she had left early the previous evening so had come in that morning very early and had decided rightly or wrongly to check out the bracelet.

'I mean, it's the most obvious because of the inscription.'

'Absolutely, yes I agree.'

'I'd just got a result when I picked up the phone and it was him, Chief Superintendent Hedges. He asked me for an update. I mean, he usually speaks with Mike, but I was the only one available and so I told him.'

'About the bracelet?'

'Yes, and he went ballistic. He said that he had not given the go-ahead to open up any further missing persons cases and as such I had overstepped my position.'

Anna patted her shoulder.

'Leave this with me, go and get yourself a cup of coffee in the canteen. As far as I'm concerned you've done nothing wrong. If Hedges had been more of a presence and kept up to date with our investigations he'd have realized the recovered jewellery had to be followed up.'

As Joan left the room Anna became more irate as she recalled how Mike Lewis had told her that Hedges had said that as far as he was concerned both investigations were now Langton's. She decided that if Hedges should complain to her or Mike about Joan's behaviour she would remind him of his remark to Mike and his total lack of interest concerning the investigation of a possible serial killer.

Anna, still annoyed about Hedges' attitude, sat at her desk reading the Essex Police report about the missing girl. The case had been left open on file, with no suspects and no clues as to her whereabouts. Angela Thornton had last been seen in June 2007 on CCTV footage with two friends leaving a nightclub in the Mile End Road. The friends had said that they had all been drinking heavily and as they lived locally together they walked home, leaving Angela to get the Central Line Tube home to Epping. By the time she left the club the last Tube would have already gone. Anna looked at a map of the area and noticed how close Mile End was to Hackney and Oates's squat.

Turning around, she could see that Mike was on the phone in his office, and so she picked up the report and knocked on his door.

'Can I see you for a second?'

He gestured for her to come in and returned to his phone call.

'I understand, sir, yes, yes.' He rolled his eyes to the ceiling.

'I understand, sir, and I will take it up with her, but now the ball has started rolling I won't know until I have had the time to—'

Mike pulled at his tie.

'Yes, sir, well as I just said, leave it with me, and let me get back to you.'

Mike eventually replaced the receiver, and pointed to the report in Anna's hand.

'If that is what I think it is, I've just been told off because we are apparently attempting to open up yet another murder enquiry when we are snowed under with the ones we've already got.'

'Mike, you can't walk away from this. Angela Thornton's bracelet was in the hoard of stuff we removed from Oates's basement.'

'It's not a question of me walking away, Anna, she's an Essex "Misper" so it's not in my hands to say whether or not—'

His desk phone rang.

'Yes? What? Bring him in straight away when he gets here . . . yes, to my office.'

Mike stood up.

'She was last seen in Mile End, which is close to where Oates . . .' Anna began.

'Let me deal with the Angela thing later. Right now we've got Edward Samuels coming in, he's ten minutes away. Get Joan to arrange some tea. He's also asked for sandwiches.'

Mike's phone rang again and he snatched it up.

'DCI Mike Lewis, incident room . . . Good morning.'

Mike covered the mouthpiece and said it was Langton, the last person he wanted to have to talk to, so Anna made her escape fast.

Half an hour later Barolli ushered the diminutive Mr Samuels into the incident room as Anna was asking Joan if she could also rustle up some sandwiches. She was very eager to hear what Samuels thought of their prime suspect, and hurried to join him in Mike's office.

Samuels turned to shake her hand, his own almost the same size as hers. He was wearing a grey pin-striped suit with a white polo-neck sweater and had very highly polished black shoes. He drew his chair closer to the desk and opened his laptop.

'I'll obviously have my report typed up, but for now we can discuss, from my notes and observations, what I believe is the best way forward when you next interview Mr Oates. I have been quite thorough going over the paperwork and viewing the DVDs you sent me, but firstly let me explain how behavioural assessments work . . .'

Before he could continue, Joan entered with the teas and a plate of sandwiches. Samuels thanked her, saying he was hungry as he'd not had time for breakfast. Anna was quite intrigued by the way he ate – very quickly, in big bites, each of which he chewed rapidly before hesitating a moment then swallowing. It was rather like watching a hamster as his cheeks bulged and he held the sandwich in front of him poised for his next mouthful. Anna gave a glance towards Mike, who also appeared fascinated watching Samuels consume three sandwiches then reach for his tea, taking quick rapid sips before he let out a sigh of relief.

'Ahhhh, good, feel a lot better now. I usually have a big breakfast, but this morning I skipped it, always a mistake. My mother, God bless her, always said breakfast was the most important meal of the day, sets you up.'

Anna smiled, and Mike murmured his agreement, but he was obviously a little bemused by Samuels.

'Right, let's get the show on the road. Now obviously I have made an assessment of Mr Oates's personality, behavioural and lifestyle characteristics.'

'Dr Samuels, Anna and I really appreciate your help but we wondered if you could stick to the interview strategy as we—'

'DCI Lewis, I have not had a doctor-to-patient psychiatric session with your suspect so I am not giving any opinion regarding his fitness to plead. It is not my place to dictate how you, or DCI Travis, should conduct the interview, but I can suggest how to approach it and hopefully connect with Oates. To achieve this you must have some understanding of the person you are dealing with, particularly if you want positive rather than negative outcomes.'

Mike and Anna looked at each other, both realizing that Dr Samuels was very much on their side but his opinions and advice had to appear unbiased. He went on to explain that although the information about Oates's family background was limited and to a large extent influenced by his ex-wife Eileen's statement, he felt that she might be lying about some elements of her life with and without Oates.

'In respect of the suspect's childhood and the abuse that he endured at the hands of his mother, her lovers and in care, his wife, in my opinion, would have no reason to make these incidents up. He could have lied to her but, and this is off the record, I made some enquiries through my contacts and Henry Oates was in and out of care homes because of physical abuse. He suffered a wretched childhood and although he seriously assaulted other children he was replicating what his mother did to him. It brought him the attention he craved although he never sought pity or spoke about his abuse to his carers, so he may respond to sympathy.'

Samuels told Mike and Anna that abuse in a child incited feelings of hurt and, almost inevitably, that hurt led to a feeling of hate and a longing for revenge. He believed Oates's running away from the care home at sixteen was an attempt to escape those feelings and make a new life for himself. Certainly at the outset he seemed to have succeeded. He found a way of suppressing his anger through boxing, held down a job, made new friends and, in Eileen, found someone who he loved and no doubt believed loved him.

'The death of Radcliff, the boxing coach and father figure, must have been a setback for him, but he had others around him at the club who also grieved the loss. Boxing was in his mind the only thing he was good at, it gave him self-purpose. The gym was his home and his family so he continued to box and then he met Eileen.'

Whilst Samuels continued with his assessment, Anna glanced towards the window that divided Mike's office from the incident room. She drew a quick intake of breath and looked at Mike, trying to get his attention, but he was focused on Samuels. Eventually, she coughed and at last she caught his eye. She jerked her head towards the incident room, and made a small gesture with her hand. Mike now glanced towards the window and back to her, not understanding what she was trying to tell him.

Too late, the office door was opened and Anna got quickly to her feet, as Langton, wearing one of his immaculate grey suits, pristine shirt and a dark navy tie, walked in. She was surprised to see that he didn't have a walking stick; in fact he looked fit and healthy, and his manner seemed very breezy.

'Edward Samuels, how nice to see you again. Thankfully it's been a long time.'

Samuels turned and peered at Langton, who now took Anna's chair so she had to stand. Samuels appeared unflustered and only acknowledged Langton with a disparaging nod of his head.

'You don't mind if I sit in on this, do you?'

Mike shook his head. Samuels had already returned to his laptop screen.

'Shall I continue?' He asked.

'It's all been very beneficial so far, sir,' Anna said as Mike nodded in agreement.

'Well let's hope it's all worth the cost this time,' Langton said with a false smile as he gestured for Samuels to continue.

'Right. I'd been explaining that in order to prepare an effective interview strategy you first need to consider the behavioural characteristics of Mr Oates.'

Samuels gave Langton a swift résumé of what he had already told Anna and Mike and then continued where he had left off.

'Eileen Oates's description of her life with Henry may or may not be true in parts, however I believe she lied about him forcing her into prostitution as her criminal record shows a soliciting conviction prior to the time they met. He married her because he believed the child she was carrying was his, he set up home with her and saw less of his friends, and his boxing career was not progressing. Discovering his wife was a prostitute ignited not only the belief that the child was not his but all the feelings of anger he had suffered as a child.'

'Excuse me interrupting,' said Langton, 'but I think we are all aware of this background detail. Basically I am asking you to cut the bullshit and get to the point of your assessment.'

'I don't regard anything I have so far stated as bullshit, Detective Langton,' replied Samuels with some dignity. 'Yes you may be well aware of his background but what you do not understand is how or why he has become what he is today. If you do not understand someone or something then how can you possibly ask the right questions in the context of your investigation?'

'That may be, but time is of the essence and as I said you are not telling us anything we haven't already considered ourselves.'

Samuels gritted his teeth with annoyance.

'You are missing the point. During his childhood, teens and to an extent in his marriage, Oates has pushed his anger to the back of his mind, hiding it from public view, but it continued to grow in the shadows like mould on a wall. Eventually it all boils over and the backlash starts . . .'

'We all get angry at one time or another, but it doesn't give us the right to abduct, rape and then murder women and children when we feel like it!' Langton said whilst fidgeting in his chair.

'I am not condoning his actions,' Samuels pointed out. 'What I'm saying is that his mother and wife created in him a seething desire to harm women. He sees them as objects, mere tools to vent his anger. Tell me . . . wouldn't you like to see Oates repeatedly beaten to within an inch of his life or maybe you'd like to personally inflict his pain to relieve your own anger?'

'Too fucking right I would!' Langton shouted, and then let out a deep sigh of frustration, realizing that Samuels had used his own short fuse to make his point. He got up out of his seat.

'I need to stretch my legs!'

'I believe that Oates has killed more times than you are aware of and if you want him to talk to you in interview, then you need to approach him in a structured manner,' Samuels suggested. 'Aggressive, accusatory tactics will not work with him. There is also the danger that if you push him too far he may have a total breakdown.'

'Carry on without me,' Langton said as he left the room.

'Off the record, do you think he's a psychopath?' Mike asked.

'I take it that you are referring to Oates.'

Both Mike and Anna could not help but laugh and were glad that Langton had left the room.

'Without a full psychiatric assessment it's impossible for me to make an accurate diagnosis, but there are clear signs of antisocial, borderline and other personality disorders. The symptoms can lie dormant for years, then suddenly manifest themselves in early adulthood and are often related to traumatic events during childhood.'

Samuels was of the opinion that Oates's mood swings drifted between mania and depression. He explained that either state of mind could last for minutes, hours, days or even weeks, rising and subsiding suddenly. It sounded to him as if Oates's behaviour on the night of his arrest and during the interviews ranged from elated to volatile, and was arrogant, attention-seeking and at times depressed. Furthermore, Samuels believed that Oates's skill at multiple benefit fraud showed his intelligence and ability to plan a crime.

'He must have made plenty of money out of it but he lives a life of squalor. Why do something you don't seem to benefit from?' Anna asked.

'It's not the money,' Samuels explained. 'It's the ego trip of being able to do something wrong and get away with it. He probably only stopped because he became bored with it.'

Langton returned to the room, bringing a chair in with him. He sat facing Samuels.

'Why do you think he made a partial confession then retracted it?' Langton asked.

Samuels stared at him as if it was a trick question, but replied anyway.

'This is not a criticism of DCI Lewis but the interview

strategy was all wrong. Oates knew the game was over as soon as Justine Marks' body was found in the back of the van. You went in blind so he lied about her manner of death but when you said you were going to search the squat he became visibly agitated. He then said that he had killed two other women, Julia and Rebekka. You pushed him for answers and you were aggressive, whereas he wanted to be in control, for you to show him respect and listen to what he was about to tell you.'

Mike looked dejected and said nothing. Langton could see this and said that for what it was worth he would have interviewed Oates in the same way.

'He started to admit the other murders because he thought we would find the pieces of the doll and the jewellery hidden in the fireplace,' Anna said.

'Yes, but when you didn't he decided to really start playing games. You missed the clues, he felt in control and decided if you think I did it, prove it.'

'So what's the best way forward?' Langton asked.

Samuels handed him a folder. 'You should try and connect with him first through general chitchat then gradually approach the sensitive subjects, but wherever possible encourage him to tell his story. Do not be aggressive with him, and look for any physical signs that he is becoming agitated or is lying. Oates does not know all the evidence against him, you do, so keep him guessing . . . drip-feed it into the interview,' Samuels said and looked at Langton, inviting a reply.

Langton handed the folder to Anna.

'Best you two get on with the prep work then we can get Oates in.'

'I would be careful about using DCI Travis in the interview . . .' began Samuels.

'I am perfectly capable of planning and conducting a suspect interview,' Anna snapped.

'Sorry, I didn't mean to offend you, it's just that Oates harbours a distrust and hatred of women and may react by ignoring you or becoming immediately aggressive.'

'Well surely that would show exactly what type of man he is.'

'Yes, but it could also backfire on you with him saying nothing, but it's up to you.'

Langton much to everyone's amazement apologized to Samuels for his earlier outburst then shook his hand and thanked him for coming in. Anna took the behavioural adviser back down to reception. As they headed down the corridor, she asked him about his bill, but he said he owed Langton one so there was no charge.

There was an uneasy atmosphere when she got back to the incident room and Mike's office was the object of much furtive attention. The team could hear raised voices and Anna was surprised to hear Mike arguing with Langton. She had never known him to stand his ground with him before.

Barolli nodded over at the closed blinds.

'Been having a real go at each other in there. It's about time. Langton's always stepping in and looking over Mike's shoulder, but reality is he's on sick leave and isn't chief on this investigation, Hedges is, and so he shouldn't even be here.'

'Correction, Paul,' she said, 'Rebekka Jordan was Langton's case, so like it or not, he does have a right to be here. Myself, I'm amazed that he is even on his feet considering he's just had surgery.'

The level of interest escalated as Detective Chief

Superintendent Hedges now made an appearance. He grunted a brusque 'Good morning' to everyone before he joined Mike and Langton in the office.

The team were even more intrigued when Area Commander Leigh also arrived in the incident room, acknowledging Anna as she did so. Mike called for a tray of coffee to be taken into his office and Joan said she would arrange it.

'Getting crowded in there,' she said with a rueful smile.

Meanwhile Barbara came over and handed Anna some computer printouts.

'What are these about?'

'Your checks into Cherokee Jeeps paid off. Three hits in London for making off without paying for petrol, same model and colour as the stolen vehicle but using false plates.'

Anna looked through the printouts. All three incidents occurred after the Jeep was stolen in Cobham, and the last one was in Shepherd's Bush the day before Rebekka disappeared.

'Any CCTV of the drivers?'

'No. Usual thing with that type of crime – garage attendant reports it, no one bothers to investigate it. There's a verbal description taken when the report was made and each one is the right age group for Oates but other details differ.'

'This is fantastic work, Barbara. Well done,' Anna said excitedly.

'Thanks, Anna.'

One hour later, Commander Leigh left with DCS Hedges. They didn't speak to anyone, but walked straight out of the incident room. Langton eventually emerged from the office with Mike, who looked very tense as he asked for everyone's attention and to gather round for a briefing. Anna watched Langton ease himself into a hard-backed chair. If he was in any pain he was going to great lengths not to show it.

The outcome of the briefing was that not only would the team continue their investigations into the murders of Fidelis Julia Flynn and Rebekka Jordan, but they would also be joined by ten more officers to assist in the investigation of any other cases arising from the findings in Henry Oates's basement.

'The ongoing searches will continue,' Mike told them, 'and we will use the two outer rooms to accommodate everyone, so we will be setting up desks and computers this afternoon.'

There were a lot of looks flying round the room, but not from Langton, who sat with his head bowed, staring at the floor.

'It will be an opportunity for everyone involved to cross-reference all the evidence gathered to date, and let's face it, we've got a lot going on,' Mike concluded. 'Any questions, save them for this afternoon's briefing, which we will kick off at three. Lastly, but not least, Henry Oates will be brought in for interview tomorrow, so let's get this show on the road.'

Much disruption followed this announcement as desks and chairs were found and brought in, and computers set up. Langton remained sitting by the incident board despite the mayhem that surrounded him, making copious notes. Meanwhile, Anna put in a call to the Murphys. Mrs Murphy was not at home, but her husband answered. Anna asked if he could recall again in his mind the time his wife had seen Henry Oates returning home covered in chalk dust. Mr Murphy without hesitation repeated that he was certain it was two weeks before his gates arrived. Although he had noticed Oates around for some considerable time previously, he had had no interaction with him. He maintained he remembered the date because it had scared his wife and he spoke with Oates about it when he helped with the gates. He also confirmed it was very late at night because his wife couldn't sleep. Anna thanked him and then crossed to the incident board, where she underlined the words 'chalk dust' and 'Taplow Quarry'.

'What's that?' Langton asked, watching her.

'Henry Oates was seen by a neighbour that lived across the street from his basement. The same week Rebekka Jordan disappeared, he was spotted walking home at two o'clock in the morning, covered in what he later claimed was chalk dust, said that a bag of it had fallen on him.'

Langton stared and then shrugged his shoulders.

'It's a massive quarry, and he tried to get work there, so he knows the area,' Anna persisted.

'How far from London is it?' Langton asked.

'It's in Buckinghamshire, up the M40 and M4, not far from Heathrow.'

Langton sucked in his breath. 'Point being?'

'I think Oates was still using the stolen Jeep. He changed the plates,' Anna said, pointing to her notes on the board about petrol thefts.

'Try me again, what is the point?'

Anna chewed her lips. 'It's just supposition.'

'I gather that,' Langton retorted.

'Well it's just such a vast open space, and a good hiding place for a body, even the vehicle you transported it in.'

He nodded.

'You been there?'

'No. I can bring it up on my computer for you to see.'

He eased himself to stand upright. 'Let's go and take a look.'

'To the quarry?' Anna asked, surprised by Langton's suggestion.

'Yes, to the quarry, not a lot we can do until everyone is gathered.'

Surprised but pleased, Anna agreed.

'Where's he going?' Mike asked and Joan shrugged.

Barbara indicated with a pencil.

'They were talking about Taplow Quarry.'

'What?'

Mike gritted his teeth and glanced over at Anna's scrawled writing with her arrows in different colours linking locations and dates.

'Well so long as he is kept out of my hair that's fine by me.'

'Henry Oates applied for a job there six years ago,' Joan said.

Mike, still obviously very rattled, snapped back, 'Six years! Jesus Christ, what bloody good is that to us?'

Joan flushed. 'Angela Thornton, the girl that maybe owned the gold bracelet found in Oates's basement, she disappeared shortly after Rebekka Jordan.'

'Get Barolli to show it to her parents.'

Mike slammed into his office and took out a bottle of aspirin. His head was thudding, the kind of headache that cuts right across the eyes. He had accused Langton of interfering and overstepping his position, and had thought for a moment Langton was going to punch him, but instead the DCS had told Mike bitterly how he was overstepping the mark bringing in Edward Samuels without telling him. He had been, in case Mike was unaware of it, the chief investigating officer on the Rebekka Jordan case, and as such he had every right to be privy to information now the file had been reopened. Mike sighed. Now it appeared the old bastard was digging into the Angela Thornton disappearance as well.

Mike swallowed three aspirins, and drained the bottle of water. He was not looking forward to this afternoon and he knew he would have to get his act together. Langton wasn't just looking over his shoulder, he was sitting on it.

Chapter Thirteen

Langton collected his walking stick from the duty sergeant at the station's reception desk. Anna smiled –
typical, always the macho man refusing to let anyone see
that he was still recovering.

'How you feeling?' she asked as she bleeped open the
Mini passenger door and then moved the front seat as far
back as possible for him. 'You know we'll be cutting it a
bit fine to be back for three.'

He ignored her flicking through his notebook.

'You and Mike seemed to have been having a bit of a
confrontation,' she tried.

'He didn't drop you in it about Samuels, took the blame
himself. Anything else you might have missed?' he said
sarcastically.

'Nope, just that he's been run ragged with the case and
the mounting finances; his budget must be in trouble.'

'It isn't now, that's why I came in today.'

'That's good.'

'Yes, means I am still given enough kudos by the powers
that be. To be honest, if this was to hit the press it
wouldn't look good for any of us, but it'd be worse for
Mike as he's heading up the investigation. Just looking out
for his best interests and at first he didn't like'– he gave a

257

short humourless laugh – 'quote, my continual interference, but I slapped him back down about Samuels.'

'Very informative though.'

'Well I am glad you feel that way, Travis, and contrary to Samuels' advice you will be doing the main interview with me.'

He rested his arm along the back of her seat. 'I'm looking forward to confronting the little creep.'

Anna betrayed nothing, but she was amazed that he had already appointed himself to lead the interviews.

'Did Mike agree to it?'

'Course he didn't. This is a very big case for him, but you know experience will out. Anyway, at first I'll just be monitoring how it goes from the viewing room. If there's a problem I'll step in. I would say it's going to be a very long hazardous interview, minefield time. If Oates starts losing it, you'll have to be ready to deal with it and calm the waters.'

He fell silent, leaning back against the headrest and closing his eyes, so that she thought he was asleep. Eventually she took the turn off the M40 towards the chalk pit, her satellite navigation directing her.

'Christ, doesn't that voice send you crazy?'

He tapped the small screen.

'Bloody dangerous things, you know. If you look to see if you are on the right road following that little red arrow you could have a crash.'

'That's why you follow her instructions.'

The chalk quarry was much as depicted in the photographs on the computer, but far far larger, in fact dauntingly huge. They drew up beside a security gate and it took a while before a guard came up to the red-and-white pole.

Langton lowered his window and showed his ID, explaining briefly that he would need to talk to whoever was in charge as he was from the Metropolitan Police murder enquiry team.

Anna got even more of an eerie feeling as she drove down a long dirt track towards a cinder block that housed the offices. Numerous trucks were being driven to and fro, loaded up with crushed chalk. A huge conveyor belt was shifting blocks above the pit into a hanger.

'My God, the size of the place,' Langton said quietly. Whether or not he felt the same skin-prickling sensation as Anna, she couldn't tell, but the sheer vastness of the quarry was in itself intimidating. It transpired that the manager was not available, but one of the workers showed Anna and Langton various maps, on which he indicated a vast disused part of the quarry. It would take considerable time to be shown around everywhere and they would also need overalls and boots. Gradually Langton raised the possibility of someone entering the quarries without supervision. They were told that at night the place did have a semblance of security, but to secure the entire area would be impossible. The entrance they had used was supervised, but even that was difficult. The CCTV cameras were in position to cover working areas, which were sealed off to the public by wire fencing. They were very wary of anyone dumping waste, but they had had no recent problems.

'Tell me about the disused quarry – can anyone have access to it?'

'Yes, but it's a sort of nature reserve now, what with the pond and all the trees. Sometimes we get kids in messing about on mountain bikes.'

Langton hesitated, but time was pressing so he decided

to elaborate on the reason for their visit: the possibility of someone burying a body. Because of the size of the place it looked as if it could be easily done. Now, armed with this added information, the young man called up his superior and asked for permission to drive Langton and Anna to the disused quarry.

As they returned to Anna's car, Langton was silent, rubbing at his hands; the feeling of chalk grit made them dry and itchy. What they had seen was a vast empty quarry, a steep cliff of reddish clay and a cavernous pit the size of Leicester Square. Explosives had blasted away the old track into the basin of the pit, leaving it impossible to get down there without safety equipment.

Woods bordered a high ridge, and to detect visually if anything had been buried there would be almost impossible. Potholes three and four feet deep were half filled with water and chalk-covered rubble, like waves of foam in the ocean.

'Take the back route, see what that wooded area looks like from the road,' Langton instructed. Anna was loath to do so as it meant leaving a tarmac surface and going onto a dirt track with deep ruts full of mud.

'I'm never going to get the car clean,' she groaned.

They moved slowly, bumping and dipping, and Anna swerved as much as possible to avoid the potholes.

'It's further than I thought,' Langton said irritably.

'Do you want me to turn back?'

'No. Keep going, it looks less bumpy further along.'

There was a field on the driver's side with a wire fence and barbed wire threaded in loops along the top, rusted and with many gaps revealing rotting wooden posts that had fallen down.

'This must have been one of the lanes they used to get to the old quarry,' Langton said.

Anna made no reply, becoming more uptight the further they went. They rounded a bend, from where they could see that the track continued up ahead for miles and now the edge of the wood was coming into view on the passenger side.

'Here's the wood,' Langton pointed out, and Anna sighed with relief as the dirt track opened onto what had once been a tarmac lane, but which was now in almost as bad shape as the track. There were wide cracks and plenty of dips, but at least they were no longer churning through old deep muddy lorry tracks. The wood became denser, and here a wire fence had been erected around it, then the road widened. Old signs read 'No Admittance, Private Property', yet still they drove on before coming to a crossroads. Left would be virtually heading into the wood itself and turning right looked as if it might lead back to the main road.

'I think we should go straight on here,' Anna said, moving the car forwards along the lane.

Langton nodded. His knee was clearly bothering him as he kept on rubbing it.

'Well that was very informative,' she said sarcastically.

'I tell you what is – what a place to dump a body. It'd never be found and you could come this way . . .' He indicated the track ahead.

'You'd have to know the area quite well.'

'Yeah, but nevertheless, drive up to the wood, climb over that fence and you'd get to the disused quarry.'

They continued to drive and now Anna was able to pick up speed as the road, although rough, was smoother, even though grass sprouted up between the cracks in the tarmac. They drove past derelict huts and old troughs, and rather unnecessarily she murmured that at one time this must have been farmland.

Anna braked suddenly, so unexpectedly that Langton lurched forwards, swearing. The road had opened out onto a field where a number of small camper vans and trailers were grouped, with broken-down vehicles littered behind the trailers. Two grey thickset tethered ponies grazed beside a moss-covered horsebox. Near the horses was a precarious pile of scaffolding poles and orange cones. As she slowly passed the entrance to the field she could see washing lines filled with clothes. She reversed to bring the Mini directly up to the entry to the site.

'What, what?' Langton demanded as he lowered his window.

'Do you see it?'

'What, for Chrissake, what? It's just a gypsy camp.'

Anna got out and went over to the old barred gate. She pointed to a pile of vehicles, many minus wheels or doors, some on their side, others stripped down, most rusty. Car seats were stacked up next to the wrecks.

Langton eased himself out, glad to be able to straighten up.

'I'm sure I'm right,' she said.

'About what? We've obviously got them irritated, they're coming out of their trailers.'

Three men were standing staring towards them, their expressions and folded arms making it clear that they didn't like the intrusion. Then a woman came out and gestured towards Anna and Langton, and then she too folded her arms.

Anna leaned towards Langton.

'Between the wrecked green van and the red car on its side, isn't that a Cherokee Jeep?'

'I dunno. I can only see a door hanging off. Anna!'

'Stay here – the ground is too uneven and muddy for you. Let me talk to them.'

She waved to the group and one man headed towards her as she took out her ID and held it up. Contrary to what Langton had expected, the man appeared to be very civil as Anna spoke to him. He saw her point to the wrecks and together they headed past the other men, whose sullen expressions never wavered, but at least they did not make a move as Anna struggled to keep her balance in the muddy field.

Langton leaned against the car, watching as bits and pieces of vehicles were tossed aside to open up an area around the rusty silver Jeep. It lay on its side, with no wheels, no seats or number plates, and it was heavily dented, with broken windscreen and headlamps, and one wing missing. He saw Anna bending down to where a number plate should have been, plainly keeping up a conversation throughout as the big man cleared as much away as possible for her to take a good look.

Eventually Anna returned and asked Langton if he had a couple of twenty-pound notes; her face was flushed as he opened his wallet and handed her two ten-pound notes and one twenty. She made her way back to the group, who were now talking animatedly to each other. There was a lot of nodding and pointing and then she was shaking hands and handing over the cash as the woman began to take in her washing.

Returning to the car, Anna tried to scrape the mud off her shoes, but gave up as Langton eased himself back into the passenger seat. When she finally got in beside him she was still flushed.

'What did you need the forty quid for?' he demanded.

'Had to pay for information . . . and the vehicle. I'll put money on it, that's the Cherokee Jeep that was stolen six years ago in Cobham. I phoned the locals and they're sending someone down to sit on it until the transport guys arrive. There are no licence plates, but we can get the forensic lab to check out the engine and chassis numbers while they give it a going-over.'

She started up the Mini, waved at the group of men, and then slapped the steering wheel with the flat of her hand before driving off.

'I know I'm right, I know it. By the way, this is a legitimate site. They've been there for fifteen years, farmer leases them the land. I'd say it did have licence plates on it when they found it, but I wasn't going to get into that with them. The main man, the one I was talking to, is called Reg Green; his son found the Jeep – wait for it – about five years ago.'

'Bloody hell.'

'It was crashed into a tree. He said that whoever smashed it up also tried to set light to it, the back seats were melted, but the petrol tank didn't blow. Two front tyres were buckled, the two rear ones he said had been slashed – whether that is true or not . . . probably sold them.'

'Did he report it?'

'What do you think? Of course he didn't, he said he towed it back to the site. I've taken some pictures of it on my mobile.'

She was smiling and he couldn't help but find it contagious. He rubbed the back of her neck with his hand, resting his arm along the seat.

'Well spotted, Travis, but if you'll just let me have a quiet word, not to dampen your enthusiasm in any way, but I would say finding a print, finding any evidence connecting that rusted wreck to Henry Oates will be a miracle. It is, I presume, the reason for your excitement that he possibly stole it, but without a witness it's supposition.'

'You are the one that always says there are no coincidences. Jeep stolen six years ago, same type of vehicle on false plates in Shepherd's Bush the day before Rebekka Jordan disappears. Oates seen returning home covered in chalk dust. I think he drove it from Cobham to London and—'

'All right, all right, just take things easy.'

'But that is why no one has ever traced the Jeep and if Oates had met Rebekka when he worked on their garden—'

'Shusshh, shusshh, just relax.'

'I am relaxed,' she snapped, but her hands were gripping the steering wheel. She also hated the way his hand was touching the nape of her neck and she shrugged it away.

'You know to even attempt a search of the quarry is near impossible; it'd take hundreds of officers, let alone digging machinery, and it's dangerous. We don't have a shred of evidence, not one witness that saw Oates. Did you ask them if they'd seen anyone?'

'Yes of course, but they only saw the smashed-up Jeep.'

'They remember exactly when they saw it?'

She sighed for the second time, 'At least five and a half years ago.'

She lapsed into silence as she followed the directions Reg Green had given her and eventually they saw signs for the M40. It was with some relief that she got onto the motorway at last.

'Just an added thought. It's a hell of a long way back to London from there,' Langton murmured.

She made no reply because she knew it. All the same, Oates could have thumbed a lift or nicked another car.

It was almost four-thirty when they drove into the station car park. Mike had grown even more agitated having had to wait for them to arrive, but Langton didn't bother going into detail about the discovery. Instead he ordered everyone to draw up chairs. By now the team had been joined by the ten extra detectives so the incident room was jammed.

The tension was running high, as it was very obvious that Langton and Mike were not on good terms. Langton, having already ordered his usual bacon and chicken roll with no tomatoes, sat himself between Mike and Anna in the centre of the horseshoe row of chairs that faced the newly enlarged incident board, which stretched for virtually the entire length of the room.

At four-forty-five Mike started the briefing. He began with the details of the investigation into the murder of Justine Marks and the discovery of Henry Oates in the children's party van. The new members listened attentively. Next, Mike introduced Barolli, who stood up to take them through Fidelis Julia Flynn's disappearance. As he talked he used an old chopstick to point to pictures of the recovered body encased in cement. Langton glanced over at Anna, but she was reading a text message. He couldn't tell if it was important, but then he could see her replying. It irritated him that it could be personal rather than connected to the investigation. But he found it hard to fault her diligent detective work, since Barolli constantly referred to how DCI Travis had brought in result after result, such as the theft of the crucifix from the sports club Oates used. Barolli looked at Mike, who now stepped forwards and said that there was a lot of work to be done trying to trace the owners of the jewellery found in Oates's squat but that he would discuss that later in the meeting. He now asked Anna to tell them about her investigation into the disappearance of Rebekka Jordan.

Yet again Langton was made more than aware of Anna's competence as she took the floor with a very confident attitude. She was much more detailed than Barolli, listing her evidence in chronological order, starting with the discovery of the small doll's head and leg, and the similar figures from the doll's house. The contact with Andrew Markham led to the revelation that Oates had worked at the Jordans' property and therefore could have met Rebekka. She reminded them of the confusing statement from Oates's ex-wife, that he had told her he was 'shovelling shit', and she explained that Markham had used Oates to shovel out and clean a blocked septic tank. This then led to her discovering that a Jeep Grand Cherokee was reported stolen from Cobham in July 2006 on the same day Oates cleaned out the septic tank. Although the theft of the Jeep took place eight months before Rebekka disappeared, she had wondered if Oates could have changed the number plates, hidden it somewhere and used it when he liked.

'This was important to me because to snatch a young girl off the streets without anyone seeing it and then transport her any distance would have required the use of a vehicle. Barbara ran some petrol theft checks for me over a one-year period after the vehicle was stolen. There were three in London matching the model and colour of the stolen Jeep and using the same false plates. Importantly, one of the thefts was in Shepherd's Bush the day before Rebekka went missing.'

Langton, knowing all this already, was able to watch from a different perspective to that of the team. He had known Anna from her first murder enquiry. Rightly or wrongly, he had had a relationship with her, and they had continued to work alongside each other on many other murder enquiries. He had wrapped her in his arms when he'd had to tell her about her fiancé's death and advised her to take time off work, which she had refused to do. He had loved her passionately, then in an almost fatherly way, and he still cared for her even more than he admitted to himself, but watching her now gave him an inordinate feeling of pride. In front of him was a woman whose confidence and astute working methods out-stripped everyone else's. He remembered her tottering behind him in her high-heeled shoes covered in mud, he remembered her fainting at her first autopsy, her distress when the appalling injuries to the victim in the Red Dahlia case had moved her to tears. He noticed that her shoes were muddy now from the chalk quarry and the gypsy site, but she appeared to not even be aware of it. Her hair, scraped back in a knot, had strands loose. He had always found it touching the way she fiddled with her hair, making sure she looked presentable. Now it was obvious that, like her muddy shoes, her hair was of no importance. What he was watching was a woman fired up, her determination explicit, and her cohesive delivery of the facts made everyone pay close attention to her every word.

'I believe that Henry Oates has killed at least four, maybe even more. We are dealing with a devious killer, a man who preys on young women and prides himself on his ability to remain undetected. So far we have only recovered two bodies. Justine Marks from the back of the van and Fidelis Julia Flynn encased in concrete in the lift shaft. Earlier today DCS Langton and I uncovered evidence that may lead us to where the other bodies are.'

She hesitated and gave a small satisfied smile.

Langton leaned forwards, now attentive to what she was saying.

Anna stood beside the map of the quarry she had pinned on the board. As Mike and the team were not yet privy to what had happened that afternoon, the room went very quiet.

'You can see on the map a gypsy camp six miles from the disused quarry, on the wooded side. The camp is legal, as they have permission from the farmer and have been camped there for fifteen years. Five and a half years ago, and this is of utmost importance, because it was five and a half years ago that Rebekka Jordan disappeared, they found a Cherokee Jeep. An attempt had been made to burn it after it had smashed into a tree by a ditch near the wood. They towed the Jeep back to their campsite and the virtual shell of it has remained there. The seats, wheels and any part that could possibly be sold on, including the number plates, have gone. However . . .'

Everyone waited as she put up a picture of the burnt-out Jeep on the board and then turned to her captive audience with an almost theatrical flourish.

'Forensics have confirmed from the chassis and engine numbers that this was the same Jeep stolen from Cobham. Finding any further forensics is a long shot, but the steering wheel, windows and doors are still intact. They will not know until later if we have any identifiable prints that match Oates. It is also doubtful that they will be able to recover any DNA, but they are working on it.'

*

In fact Anna had only just received this information in a text message from Pete Jenkins. She had managed to reply before taking the floor, asking him to make sure they covered every inch of what was left of the Jeep for prints and bloodstains. Now, she ended her lengthy speech by indicating the dates on which Oates was seen covered in chalk dust.

'His basement was a filthy hovel, but nothing that could link him directly to the chalk quarry was found. His slip-up was Mrs Murphy seeing him looking "ghostly" at two in the morning. Oates told Mr Murphy that it was chalk dust his wife had seen on him. She cannot be sure of the exact day but I have narrowed it down to the week Rebekka went missing . . . Added to this is the confirmation from one of his associates that he had attempted to get work driving the trucks in the quarry, and this means Oates knew the area.'

A murmur broke out as she returned to her seat and Mike Lewis stood up once more. Like everyone else, he was taken aback by the revelation of such vital pieces of evidence. But to calm things down, he stressed that they were still without a single witness for two of the murders Oates had claimed. Without doubt, they had him for the murder of Justine Marks, but even with the considerable amount of circumstantial evidence, they would still have difficulty in proving Oates murdered Fidelis Julia Flynn and Rebekka Jordan. It was at this point that Mike looked at Langton. There was an embarrassing delay as Langton found it difficult to get to his feet. Barolli had to give him a hand, which he clearly hated, but he covered it by making a joke about stiffening up due to waiting so long to say his piece. He adjusted his tie and firstly apologized for keeping everyone waiting for the briefing to start. He then gestured to the incident board and as always gave a theatrical pause for effect.

'The cost of this triple enquiry has escalated and it has been difficult for me, being out of action, to oversee everything that's been going on, especially the Rebekka Jordan case. However I congratulate DCI Travis as she has uncovered vital evidence that five years ago I was unable to bring to light. Acting on admissions from Henry Oates regarding the two unsolved murders, you have all shown incredible dedication, but even considering your achievements it has still been a major problem for me to get the green light to continue.'

A murmur broke out and Anna clenched her hands. Surely he was not going to pull them off their cases at this juncture? But then he gave one of his flashing smiles.

'But we have the go-ahead, and now with extra staff and total commitment I know you will find the evidence to put Oates away for every murder he has committed.'

He indicated the photographs of the items removed from Oates's basement.

Anna was relieved and sat back in her chair as Langton continued, informing the team that in the morning they would be getting Oates back in police custody for interview. He reminded them they were dealing with a man who had killed and who enjoyed the power it had given him to outwit the law. He went into detail about the cost of searching the quarries, and warned that it might be impossible to mount such a big operation due to the time and manpower it would require.

Anna was nonplussed. One moment he was opening up their enquiry and the next it felt as if he was closing it down. Langton started to loosen his tie before taking a chair and turning it around so he could remain standing but lean on the back of it.

'If we can find further evidence, in particular from that bastard's trophy box, I believe it will be the key to breaking him down in the interviews. It will be imperative we move slowly, if we want him to admit his sick prowess, but with encouragement and tenacious psychological questioning, I believe Oates will crack ...' He crooked his finger and smiled.

'Get the fox out of his lair, get him so fired up with his cleverness he will want to reveal his brilliance, and it will be Oates himself who will take us to the poor souls' graves. I have lived for five years with the face of little Rebekka Jordan, I felt I failed her and her family, but I truly believe we are close to uncovering what happened to her, uncovering this man's sick perverted pleasures. So, good work everyone, keep at it, and we will get the result we all want.'

The briefing broke up. Langton had, as he always did, given everyone a boost of confidence, an energy boost. Anna could see that he was tired out, and was about to offer him a lift when he disappeared into Mike's office, asking Joan to order a car in fifteen minutes.

Barolli sidled up to her desk and nodded towards Mike's closed door.

'You think Mike is up for this?'

'Up for what?'

'Getting the fox, as the guv said, out of his lair.'

'You got that wrong, Paul, he's got to think we don't know what we are doing, not him, it's going to be up to Mike to draw him out.'

'Langton should be the one to do it.'

'No he shouldn't. This is Mike's investigation, he has to take the lead, but Langton will be in the viewing room.'

'You in for the interview with him?'

'Samuels said it might be a bad idea, so you might have to do it.'

'Who, me? You know more about all the cases than I do.'

'What's wrong, Paul – not up for it?'

As Paul hurried off, Anna laughed. Langton had already said she would be in the interview with Oates. The truth was, she was unsure about Mike's ability to conduct the type of interview Samuels had recommended, but it was not her place to say so, and she knew that if she was sitting beside him rather than Langton he would have the opportunity to prove himself.

Langton left without saying goodnight, and Anna and Mike found themselves still working at nine o'clock, preparing for the following morning.

'Christ, there's so much here to get through, it's going to take all night,' Anna said.

Mike, visibly drawn and tired, hesitated and then ruffled his hair.

'You think Langton should steer the interview?' he asked Anna.

'No, this is your investigation and you've led the team from day one. He'll probably be looking over your shoulder from the viewing room and he'll proffer advice along the way, but believe me, Mike, you are ready for this.'

He smiled and had no idea she was lying.

'Thanks for that. Can we just go through some more strategy before you leave? I've got a shedload of notes from Langton and I'd like to run them by you.'

'Sure, and we need to work out a signal between us when one or other of us takes over questioning Oates.'

'What did you and Langton have?'

She smiled and said Langton would close his notebook to indicate that she was to open hers. Other times he would tap her on the knee beneath the table. It wasn't a question of good cop, bad cop, it was simply exhausting work trying to draw out truthful answers from the depths of a twisted mind. Since everything was filmed and recorded, they had to go by the book.

'Another one of Langton's tricks is to use a fountain pen,' Anna remembered. 'He'll take it out of his pocket when the interview starts, remove the cap and use it to write something. He then replaces the cap to look as if he's finished. It unnerves the suspect as they think the questioning is over and they feel relieved, only for it to start again as he takes the cap off. I've seen him put that pen in and out of his pocket numerous times – again it unnerves the suspect – but the signal to take over is when he lays the pen down flat by his notebook, and if he taps the table twice with the pen he wants to take over the questions.'

Mike leaned back in his chair. She could tell he was very unsure of himself, and again she encouraged him, reiterating that no matter how nervous he was, she would be right beside him and together they would make a strong team. He opened a desk drawer and took out a fountain pen, held it up and smiled.

'I'll put some practice in, top off, top on.'

Anna suggested that they re-read the report from Samuels and pay very close attention to his interview advice. Mike agreed and together they went through the file he had left with them.

'I reckon you should start off by asking Oates about the Justine Marks case first,' Anna said.

Mike was puzzled as he had already done this and he didn't think it would take them any further.

'Remember Samuels said Oates knew the game was over as soon as Justine Marks' body was found in the back of the van but you went in blind and were too aggressive,' she prompted.

'Thanks for reminding me. My confidence needed boosting.'

'My point is that this time you're not blind. Her case is the one with the strongest evidence out of all of them. It's the freshest in your mind, isn't it?'

'Yes.'

'Well it's the same for him, but the difference is he's revelling in it, still getting his rocks off dreaming about it every night. To Oates Justine is still a fresh kill.'

'So you're saying if I can draw him out about Justine's murder using his behavioural patterns he may let it all out . . .'

'Then the rest will follow and he will be dying to tell you about all the other murders.'

'That's brilliant, Anna, thanks for that.'

'Just in case it doesn't work, don't disclose the doll pieces, trinkets box or crucifix to Kumar. Oates doesn't know about them either and still thinks we haven't found anything. To him they're murder trophies, so it'll be like dropping a bombshell when we reveal what we know.'

It was after eleven by the time Anna collected her briefcase and coat ready to leave, and even then some of the team were still working. Tomorrow was a big day, and she could see the trolley of files stacked up for Mike to select and check through. The mug shots of Henry Oates had been enlarged and pinned up. Having never met him, Anna stared at his face: the blue eyes set wide apart, the flattened boxer nose, the thick-lipped mouth. The face could not be described as foxy, there was no cunning in the vacant eyes, but she knew that inside Henry Oates was a vicious animal and that if they drew him out too fast, he would bite them and retreat back into his lair. To lure and keep him out of his lair they would have to stroke, cajole and encourage him and it would take time and patience.

Tomorrow she would meet him face to face. Her emotions were very mixed, but shockingly she was actually looking forward to drawing out the fox.

Chapter Fourteen

A dan Kumar arrived at Hackney Police Station promptly at eight-thirty. He was as usual overconfident and ingratiating, smiling and shaking hands with both Mike Lewis and Anna as they at first discussed the murder of Justine Marks. As he was already well aware that his client was charged with her murder, he listened without interruption. He had not, as they feared he would, requested a psychiatric assessment of his client. Kumar did however express concerns about his client's physical and mental state, but Mike informed him that on his arrival earlier this morning Oates had been seen by a doctor who had declared him fit to be interviewed.

It was a shaken Adan Kumar who was led through the disclosure of his client's connection to the disappearance of Rebekka Jordan and the murder of Fidelis Julia Flynn. He made copious notes and often asked for Mike to repeat himself, which he obligingly did. Kumar appeared hardly able to digest the bulk of evidence mounting against his client. He did attempt to argue that he should have been given prior access to the documents, but Mike pointed out that the enquiries were still ongoing and it was hoped that his client would be able to assist them.

Kumar, now visibly nervous, was given access to Oates

to discuss the disclosure evidence and, to the surprise of the team, he returned after spending only half an hour with his client, to inform them he was now ready to be interviewed.

Langton was already set up in the viewing room with Barolli. The interview would be filmed and recorded to DVD. Whilst they waited for Oates to be brought up from the cells, Mike and Anna checked through the trolley filled with files and made sure that the photographs and statements for the Justine Marks case were laid out. Mike glanced at Anna. She had her notebook out and a row of sharpened pencils beside it.

'You all set?'

'Yes.'

They had only a few more minutes to wait before they heard footsteps outside in the corridor. Kumar entered and sat opposite Mike Lewis. He took out his notes and took one of the bottles of water provided on the trolley. The solicitor said nothing, but he gave a couple of anxious coughs and looked at his watch. Heavier footsteps sounded from the corridor as two uniformed officers approached with Henry Oates between them. One opened the door, the other stepped back to allow the suspect to walk into the room. He was wearing prison-issue denim jeans and shirt and black slip-on trainers. He was smaller than Anna had anticipated, no more than five feet nine, but he was well built, with broad sloping shoulders and a slim waist, and the jeans without a belt looked loose.

'I sit here, do I?' he asked, nodding to the only vacant chair.

'Yes, please,' Mike said, without looking up.

'Opposite her,' Oates said, smiling.

Anna forced herself to return his smile and stared into

his face. His wide-set very blue eyes were unnerving, babyish, the nose even more flattened than in the photographs, as if the entire bridge had been crushed. His flared nostrils tilted upwards, giving his cheeks a strangely flat appearance. His thick lips were pinkish, and from his smile she could see that his teeth were gapped and stained. He wore his hair in a dirty blond curly crew cut which revealed that one of his ears was much thicker than the other.

Mike quietly read through the police caution, gesturing first to the tape recorder and then to the cameras. It was ten-thirty-five. He started off by asking Oates if he could call him Henry, to which the prisoner nodded in agreement. Mike said he was sorry to hear about the assault on him in prison and that he hoped Oates was now feeling better. Oates said nothing but just sat looking around the room. Anna knew that Mike was trying to soften him up as Samuels had suggested, but so far this was not bringing any noticeable response from Oates.

'We have here, Henry, your original statement when you were arrested,' Mike went on, 'and I would like to draw your attention to certain paragraphs in which you told me how the body of Justine Marks came to be discovered in the rear of the van you were driving.'

Oates listened attentively, slouching in the chair.

'I need to go over what happened with Justine again.'

'Why? I already told you it was an accident.'

'Yes, and we appreciate your honesty, but last time I didn't really give you an opportunity to tell your side of the story and there are a few things I didn't understand.'

'All right, fire away then,' Oates replied with a yawn.

'You said that you stopped to offer Justine a lift home but she was rude. How was she rude?'

'Bitch told me to fuck off when I was just trying to do the right thing.'

'She must have liked you, though, as she obviously changed her mind.'

'Yeah, but I had to tell her I was okay, like nothing for her to get worried about.'

'You must have really turned on the charm to persuade her to have sex with you,' Mike suggested.

'Well, not a lot. I think she was just up for it and fancied me anyway.'

'Wish I was so lucky.'

'Well you got it or you ain't,' Oates replied with a wink of his eye.

Both Anna and Mike noticed that Oates had started to sit more upright as the conversation went on. He was now leaning forwards making eye contact with Mike as if he was having a lads' chat in the pub.

Langton sighed. This was going to be a very long day. He found it extremely irritating to have to sit and listen to Mike being all namby-pamby with a man like Oates, but he knew there was a purpose to it and that it had to be done if Oates was to fall into the trap. He was actually impressed with Mike's tactics and the way he was drawing Oates onside. He did wonder how much of the strategy was down to Travis's advice, but either way the fact that they had planned the interview and were now executing it together was good to see.

'You said that after willingly having sex with you Justine suddenly became hysterical and attacked you . . .' Mike was saying.

'Kicked me in the balls.'

'That must have pissed you off, let alone hurt like hell.'

'It did piss me off. I thought, you ungrateful slag. I give her a good shagging and she then throws a hissy fit.'

'If I were you I think I'd have slapped her as well.'

Kumar suddenly interrupted.

'DCI Lewis, I really think this line of questioning is leading—'

Before he could finish his sentence Oates with a look of rage in his eyes turned quickly and poked his solicitor firmly in the chest.

'You don't ever interrupt me again!' Oates shook his head in annoyance then turned back to Mike, who resumed at once.

'I was saying I could understand you losing your temper like that and hitting her with the spanner.'

'It was just there beside me. I was really wound up, I picked it up, she turned like this, didn't she, to avoid the thingy. I just let her have it . . . but only once.'

He had the audacity to swivel round in his chair, indicating the back of his head. Mike was finding it hard to restrain his own anger with Oates but knew he had to continue in the same vein, especially as Kumar was unlikely to interrupt again.

'Sounds like the slapper deserved it, Henry.'

'Fucking right she did.'

'So after you hit her, did it shut her up?'

'Well, she wasn't screaming no more, just sort of moaning and gurgling.' Oates smiled as if he was enjoying recalling the moment.

Mike said nothing; he simply acted as if he too was enjoying what Oates was saying and nodded to encourage him to go on.

'I realized I'd hit her a bit hard, shook me up a bit, it did, but I thought I'd better take her to a hospital.'

Mike leaned forwards as Oates shook his head, acting bewildered.

'At what point did you discover she was dead?'

'When the moaning stopped.'

'So the drive to a hospital would have been pointless?'

'I guess so.'

Oates was still obviously lying but he had gone from a visible high in describing the sex and assault on Justine Marks to a sudden low. He clearly thought that Mike was genuinely sympathetic and believed his lies. Anna thought Mike looked drained and wondered if it was the right time for her to step in and take over the interview. She reached over to the trolley and picked up the pictures of Justine Marks that had been taken in the van and during the post mortem. She tapped Mike's knee beneath the table, and he slowly closed his notebook without looking at her.

'I would like to ask you some questions, Mr Oates,' Anna began.

Oates raised his head and looked at her with contempt.

'Oh here we go, now we get the woman's point of view. How could you do a thing like that, the poor defenceless girl. Doesn't matter the bitch kicked me in the nuts, does it!'

Anna held the pictures as if she were a croupier about to deal a pack of cards. She turned the first one over and laid it on the table. It showed the rear of the van with the doors open and Justine's body wrapped in the bin liners.

'Justine's blood was found smeared on the outside of the rear doors, on the bumper and the floor of the van,' she said.

'I told you, I hit her on the head in the van.'

Anna now turned over the next picture, which was a close-up of the scuffmarks on Justine's boots.

'From these marks on her boots and the direction of the blood patterns on the outside of the van, the scientist says that she was hit on the back of the head before she was dragged into the van.'

Oates said nothing. He started chewing his bottom lip and tapping his right foot on the floor as he had done in the interview after his arrest when asked if he had abducted and killed Rebekka Jordan.

'You attacked Justine in the street with the spanner,' Anna persisted. 'She was already dead when you dragged her into the back of the van, wasn't she?'

Again Oates said nothing. There was a long pause before Kumar broke the silence.

'Are you suggesting that Mr Oates is a necrophiliac, DCI Travis?'

'I'm saying what the evidence suggests, Mr Kumar. Only your client knows the answer to that.'

'I am bloody not.'

She turned and looked at him.

'Do you know what Mr Kumar means, Henry?'

'Yeah I know what the word means, and no way, screwing a dead body, do me a favour.'

'Why don't you tell us the truth about what happened that night? It may dismiss any ideas we have that you did have sexual intercourse with Justine after she was dead.'

'She was alive when I fucked her.'

Adan Kumar could see that his client was becoming agitated and he turned to have a whispered conversation with him, holding his hand up to cover what he was saying. Oates leaned closer to him and then nodded. Anna promptly leaned towards Mike and whispered to him in a similar way, hiding her mouth by holding up her notebook.

'Wait a minute,' Oates said and pointed to Mike. 'You know I'm telling the truth, she wanted to have sex with me.'

Kumar gestured for him to sit back, but Oates wafted his hand away.

'I am not one of them sick perverts, she was alive. I never done it to her when she was dead.'

Langton pulled a chair in front of him to rest his leg on as Barolli passed him a coffee, asking, 'What's all this necrophilia stuff, what's the angle?'

'She's needling him, she never said he's a necrophiliac – Kumar did. Doesn't like it though, does he?' Langton sipped his coffee, watching the monitor closely as he knew exactly where she was leading Oates. Oates's ego was such that he wouldn't like the implication he was a necrophiliac. He liked women to know exactly what was happening as he first raped them and then killed them. The forensic evidence had shown he had abused Justine Marks only after he had raped her, possibly in anger that she was unconscious and didn't respond to his violence. Anna and Mike's intention was to draw Oates out into the open by firstly siding with him through empathy and then by Anna attacking his lies.

Langton couldn't believe how well things were going. He watched with satisfaction the way Oates answered questions, unwittingly revealing his deep contempt for women.

'He's talking and reacting like Samuels said he would ... didn't think it would happen so fast. That bit with Kumar was something else.'

Langton sipped his coffee in satisfaction.

*

Like Langton, Anna was surprised how quickly Oates had opened up. He was very self-assured, almost cocky, yet agitated. She knew that Oates felt in control when Mike questioned him, but now that an object of his hate, a woman, had taken over, she was worried he might say nothing more, but Oates continued.

'This is exactly how it went down. I liked the look of her, right? And seeing her walking all by herself was like an open invitation.'

'One you took advantage of, didn't you?' Anna said encouragingly and Oates nodded, going on to explain how he had stalked Justine for only a matter of yards before he hit her on the back of the head with the spanner then dragged her into the van.

'She was all dazed and her head was bleeding. I got her inside the van within seconds. In fact, if it had taken any longer someone could have walked past, a pub's a busy place. I drove off sharpish, but she came round, started to scream and yell, and so I pulled over and parked and went to shut her up.'

He recalled very specifically how he had gripped her by the hair and hit her with his fist, rising out of his chair to demonstrate how he had shaken her and then thrown her hard onto the floor of the van. He banged his fist into his hand to imitate the sound as his face twisted into a grimace.

'I didn't want it to go down like that, I liked the look of her, but these things happen. I got stuck in and she started to come round again just as I was full on and I pulled her bra up round her throat.'

He raised his hands in a twisting motion towards Anna. She didn't flinch, but kept up a steady gaze, nodding to encourage him to keep talking. He explained how he had realized she was dead and that it made him angry because he liked it when she struggled and had planned to have much more time with her.

Anna knew the next question could be a provocative one coming from her and at this point she didn't want Oates to fly off into a rage, so she tapped Mike's leg.

'Angry enough to insert this inside her?' Mike asked, placing the photograph of the spanner onto the table, and Oates nodded, puffing out his cheeks.

'Yeah, that was a bit over the top, but she really pissed me off, dying like that. Anyway, I got back into the front, sat there for ages. I was in a quandary, understand me? I had to do something with her, I had to get rid of her, cos me mate wanted the van back.'

'When did you wrap her body in the plastic bin liners?'

Oates sucked in his breath.

'Oh right, I done that straight after, they was in the back with all the balloons and stuff. Sometimes they want about twenty of them blown up and these giant-size bags can hold up to ten.' He gave a laugh.

'I was doing some deliveries for me mate one time when I got out of the van with a bunch of them and off they go up in the air and I was running around trying to catch the strings. You gotta tie them in a special way so the knots come out easy, parents get pissed off if they can't hand out a frigging balloon to each kid.'

'Yeah I know, I've got youngsters – party bags, balloons. So, there you are with a van that needs to be returned – what were you planning to do with the body?'

'Well, that was it, wasn't it? Sitting like a prick when the coppers come and knock on me window.'

'You must have had some plan for disposing of her, though?'

Oates raised his hand, pointing his index finger to the ceiling.

'Felt the Lord looking down at me and I just wanted it to be over.'

In the viewing room Langton swore under his breath. He didn't want the 'good Lord' coming into the interview – that, or any hearing bloody voices.

'To be honest, I was relieved, you don't go through something like that and live with yourself easily,' Oates explained.

This was not going the way Anna had hoped, but Mike carried on with his questions.

'That surprises me, Henry, you're an intelligent man, you must have had some kind of plan in mind?'

'Nope.' He fell silent, licking his lips.

Anna kept her fingers crossed that Mike wouldn't start to ask about the other victims; they had to know what he had planned to do with Justine first.

'I'm glad, to be honest, glad it's over.' Oates appeared ready to carry on. 'I've not been sleeping because of it, you know; it was something that took me over and I know by my admitting to doing what I did I will be in prison for a long time.' He bowed his head and made the sign of the cross. 'God forgive me.'

'Well, Henry, I have to say I admire you for telling us the truth about what really happened to Justine,' Mike said, managing to keep his voice sincere, 'but just out of curiosity, though, let's say the police hadn't stopped you that night and you had the chance to dispose of Justine's body, what would you have done with her?'

'I just told you. I acted on impulse, it's not as if I ever done anything like it before. It was something that happened and, like I said, the coppers caught me red-handed.'

Mike was now tired of being Mr Nice Guy, knowing as he did that Oates was playing games with them and enjoying every minute of it, and so he put down the pen, cap on, beside his notebook to indicate to Anna to take over.

Anna remembered what Edward Samuels had said about Oates not knowing all the evidence against him and to keep him guessing.

'I overestimated you,' she told him. 'I imagined that a man with your experience and intelligence would have made a very clever decision as to where or how you would dispose of a body. Not somewhere where you worked or had visited – that would be plain stupid.'

'Lemme tell you, if I had, you'd never have picked me up, right?'

'Maybe not, as you had no police record, no prints or DNA on file ...'

'I worked all over London, I know places that I could have used, but like I keep saying, I was caught before I had got me thoughts sorted out.'

'Well if that's true, give me some indication of these possible dumping places, because for the future I'd like to know, be a good career move for me to have the knowledge.'

Oates chuckled and leaned towards her.

'I could have been a contender! You see that film with Marlon Brando? He said that. Well, I could have been a professional, it was down to me being depressed about the death of a man who was me mentor. I lost the fight, lost me confidence, and then with a wife who was a lying bitch things got on top of me, but I've kept up the training all these years, work out at a gym, swimming, I'm bloody fit for my age.' He tapped his forehead. 'This is always ticking. I might not have the education, but there's not much that I can't get to grips with.'

'It must have been really annoying when you were accused of stealing a necklace from the sports centre you frequented.'

'Too fucking right it was. I was there every week and it wasn't a necklace, it was a cheap piece of crap, a crucifix, not even proper gold, left on a windowsill. I never knew it even belonged to anyone and the stiff that called himself the manager there had a right go at me, said not to come back. I'd like to have thrown a right hook at him, but he had these two other pricks with him.'

Anna had tapped Mike's knee under the table and he brought out the photograph of the crucifix.

'Is this the item you took?' she asked.

Oates glanced at it, then nodded.

'Piece of crap like I just said, and it meant I lost me membership.'

'What did you do with it?'

'Lost it somewhere, threw it away, can't remember.'

'What work were you doing at this time?'

'Part-time labour finishing off the multi-storey car park in Shepherd's Bush. They were hiring fit blokes to dig out areas for cementing.'

He suddenly pressed himself hard against the back of his chair, making it creak. He shook his head.

'Fucking walked into this one, haven't I? Eh? I think you are the clever one.' He wagged his finger at Anna. 'I tell you what I'll do, I'll make a deal with you: you tell me what you got and I'll tell you what I know. Depending on how good you are, I might help you out.'

'I am not making any deals with you, Mr Oates, but I believe that you killed this girl.'

Mike put the photograph of Fidelis Julia Flynn down on the table, but there was no immediate reaction from Oates.

'Never met her in my life,' he said eventually.

Mike quietly told him that when he had been arrested he had made a statement admitting to killing two other women, one of whom he could only remember as being called Julia. Before he could continue, Oates clapped his hands.

'Right. Back on that, are we? Well, I have already told you I'd seen the missing posters for them two girls and I was having a laugh with you lot.'

Anna slid the photograph away from him but Oates gave a chuckle and put his hand out to draw the photograph back to be in front of him.

'Pretty, very pretty.'

In the viewing room Langton sighed, sensing that Anna and Mike were now going backwards rather than making progress. He stood up and stretched, wishing that he was in the interview room; he was more than sure that he would have had Oates confessing by now.

'I guess if you didn't know her then someone else working on the same building site, at the same time as you, must have murdered her and then put her body in the lift shaft,' Anna suggested.

Oates slowly looked up from the picture of Fidelis with a grin on his face. Anna leaned forwards and whispered as if she were telling him a secret.

'The crucifix, Henry, you messed up. You dropped it beside her body before you covered it in cement.'

'You are a good little detective, aren't you? Yeah, I take all that, but you don't know how or where I killed her, do you?'

Adan Kumar tapped Oates's arm and warned him to give no further details, as the discovery of the crucifix and body had not been disclosed to him.

'I'm fucking helping her, all right?'

In sickening detail Oates described meeting Fidelis Julia Flynn on a lunch break from work. He had gone to his regular place, the McDonald's by Shepherd's Bush Green, and sat at the same table as her. She had told him she was looking for somewhere to rent and he had said that he lived in an old house that had spare rooms and if she came back after he had finished work he could take her to see it.

He was sweating, clearly enjoying himself as he recalled waiting for her and then taking her back to his basement flat. It had been dark and there was no one about. His anger had been triggered when she said the place was a pigsty and she called him a fucking animal. He calmly spoke of how he beat her unconscious then raped and strangled her. He had put her body in an old suitcase, carried it up to the main road late at night, got a taxi and took her to the building site, because he had noticed the security was bad there.

'I knew I had to fill the ticket machine area with cement the next day so I put her in the bottom of the lift shaft. Once it was done I thought no one would ever find her. I didn't go back there, Polish supervisor didn't like me anyways, said I was lazy.'

He showed absolutely no signs of remorse. On the contrary, he seemed to be having the time of his life, directing much of his explanation at Anna. Exhausted by the effort of keeping him talking, she observed he got through two bottles of water, and was sweating and wiping his face with the cuff of his shirt throughout. He had the audacity to toss the empty water bottles into a bin and then smile.

'Anything else you got for me to help you with?'

This was what Langton was waiting for, the chance for the interview to move on to the case of Rebekka Jordan. But Oates asked for a bathroom break before they could begin. It was now one-thirty, so Kumar requested that the break also take in lunch as his client was hungry and had been at the station since early in the morning. Oates asked Kumar if he could get him a Big Mac but his solicitor said it was not allowed.

Oates was led out, not tired in the slightest – quite the reverse, as he jumped to his feet to be accompanied by two uniformed officers down to the cells and toilet facilities.

'See you later,' he called out to Anna.

Mike had organized sandwiches to be brought into the viewing room, and so Anna joined him and Langton as they were pouring fresh coffee.

'Good going so far,' Langton said, choosing a sandwich.

Anna wasn't hungry but sipped her coffee. Having been sitting hunched at the interview table for so long it was good to stretch her legs.

'I think he's going to tell us about Rebekka. I just hope the break doesn't stop the bastard talking,' Langton continued.

'I doubt it,' Mike said, taking his second sandwich.

Anna was not as confident as she felt Oates would be more reluctant to confess to the murder of a thirteen-year-old girl. After she had finished her coffee, she announced she was going to take a walk outside the station and get some fresh air.

'You all right?' Langton asked.

'Yes, I'm fine, thanks, it just sickened me having to keep up the encouragement and be pleasant to that creature. He makes my skin crawl.'

'But it's worked, you're keeping him buoyant, his ego is such that he can't keep his mouth shut.'

'Well I'll try not to deflate it,' she said sarcastically as she walked out, passing Barolli as he came in.

He brought the news that they were getting results back from their enquiries into some of the 'trinkets' found in Oates's basement. Two cold cases were being re-opened, along with the Angela Thornton investigation. He explained that he had tried to speak with Angela's parents but they were away on holiday and wouldn't be back for a few days. Langton poured his second cup of coffee.

'Christ, how many do you think the scumbag has killed?'

Barbara tapped on the door with a message from the forensic lab. Pete Jenkins had found no prints on the windows and doors of the wrecked Jeep but had decided to try the driver's seat adjuster as it would have been reasonably protected from the fire and from the wind and rain over the last five years. He had recovered prints of a middle and right index finger matching Henry Oates's, and they were now going to search the Jeep for traces of blood. Langton swore, passing the report to Mike. He had hoped for some evidence that Rebekka had been in the vehicle. All this meant was that Oates had stolen a car and dumped it at the chalk quarry.

Anna walked around the car park, smoking a cigarette from the pack in the glove compartment of her Mini. She didn't smoke on a regular basis, but sometimes she just felt she needed one and this was one of those times. After stubbing it out she went back into the station and to the Ladies'. Barbara was there and passed on the information from Pete Jenkins.

'You were right then about him using it with false plates,' Barbara said.

'I guess I was.'

'They're also bringing up some cold cases that may be connected to the box of stuff taken from Oates's basement.'

'Dear God, how many?'

'Two, and then the bracelet belonging to Angela makes it three, but nothing has been confirmed. We have to get verification from all the case files of missing items.'

'I'd better get back,' Anna said, drying her hands.

'You had lunch?' Barbara asked as she herself was leaving.

'Not hungry, thanks.'

Alone, Anna rested her hands on the sink, staring at herself in the mirror; she looked tired. Taking out a comb she undid the elastic band holding her hair in a ponytail. She replaced the band, drawing her hair tightly away from her face, then she opened her make-up bag, ran a powder puff over her nose and cheeks, and added some lip gloss. She still looked ashen-faced so she rubbed her finger over the top of the lip gloss and added a little to her cheeks for colour.

Mike was standing in the corridor in the throes of a heated discussion with Adan Kumar. As Anna approached the solicitor stormed off into the interview room, slamming the door behind him.

'What's up with him?'

'Annoyed about the lack of full disclosure, said we only

gave him some new stuff on the Marks case. I reminded him we decide when and what we want to disclose, not him. Anyway, forget Kumar, you all set?'

'Yes, and I've heard the good news about the finger-prints.'

'After you,' he said to Anna and opened the interview-room door.

Anna returned to her seat, Mike beside her. Kumar, sitting opposite, opened his notebook. They all turned to the door as the heavy footsteps sounded on the stone flags, then Oates entered the room.

'Sit back in the same chair, do I?'

'Yes please, Mr Oates.'

Mike reminded him that he was still under caution, and the cameras and recorder were started up as he gave the time the interview was resuming and who was present.

'I had steak and kidney pie, mashed potatoes, carrots and gravy and a custard tart,' Oates announced.

'I'm glad you enjoyed it,' Anna said

'I never said I did – it was horrible, prison food's better. Did it come from your canteen?'

'I believe so.'

'What did you have?'

'Sandwiches and coffee.'

'What was in them?'

'Mr Oates, can we continue the interview, please,' she said quietly, as Mike placed onto the table the Rebekka Jordan file.

'Just making conversation,' Oates said, disgruntled.

Rather than go down the usual route of displaying pho-tographs and asking if the suspect knew the victim, Mike and Anna had discussed presenting the bulk of evidence they had accumulated.

They kicked off with the discovery of the doll's head and leg found in his basement, explaining that these had been identified as belonging to the young girl who went missing five years previously.

'Rebekka Jordan,' Oates said.

'Correct.'

'I remember that case, which was why I brought it up when I was arrested.'

'Because you did, Mr Oates, we began an extensive enquiry.'

'Read about it in the papers.'

'I am sure you did – it was a very big media story, the missing girl was only thirteen years old.'

'Why I remembered it, but it had nothin' to do with me.'

'How did the pieces of doll get into your basement flat?'

'I don't know – in fact, how do I know you didn't put them there? I told you last time you'd try and fit me up.'

Anna continued to talk, quietly giving details of the Andrew Markham connection, showing that they knew that Oates had been in the Jordans' garden, and that they had confirmation that Oates had been to the Markhams' house on two occasions: once to help unload bricks and the other two weeks later when he cleaned out the septic tank.

Oates nodded and then leaned towards Anna.

'You've put fresh make-up on.'

'Yes, that is correct. I knew I'd be coming back to talk to you and I also combed my hair, very observant of you.'

'You look better than you did earlier.'

'Thank you.'

Mike brought up the subject of the stolen Jeep, but

Oates gave no reaction and concentrated on staring at Anna.

'We have your prints from the stolen vehicle,' Mike told him.

Kumar tapped the table, saying he had not been given this information, and Mike replied that they had only just heard it themselves.

'What is the connection between my client and this Jeep?'

'We believe that your client abducted Miss Jordan using this stolen vehicle.'

Oates shook his head, smiling.

'So I nicked the Jeep, I admit it, but they're lousy things to drive, and it wasn't automatic, I like automatic cars. I just dumped it along the A3 somewhere and I left the keys in the ignition so who knows who nicked it after I done.'

'We discovered your hidden box of jewellery and are checking it out right now. I bet we find that the items belonged to women who have been reported missing.'

'Rubbish, I get that stuff off car boot sales. Is there any murder you might have missed that you think I done?'

Anna smiled. 'A lot, a lot more, Mr Oates.'

Mike felt her nudge him under the table and he let her take the lead.

'How do you get along with your neighbours across the way?'

'Oh, swift change of subject, right? Getting nowhere with the Jeep, right? Well I get along just fine.'

'You clean their car, don't you?'

'Yes, ma'am, I do. I also, as you probably know, helped the old geezer put his gate posts up, mixed the cement.'

'Do you know you scared Mrs Murphy?'

'What, me? Never, I hardly had two words with her,

gimme a cup of tea and biscuits, but God forbid they asked me inside their house. She's got polishing mania, that woman, the brass strip of her doorstep is like glass.'

'She said she thought she had seen a ghost, all white and walking down the road at two o'clock in the morning; frightened the life out of her and she told her husband. He said she was dreaming, must have been the way the lights were shining.'

Oates laughed, nodding his head.

'Yeah, right. He asked me about it – funny, he said she was scared I was a fucking ghost, right, but it was just—'

He pulled back and wagged his finger.

'Fuck me, you nearly made me say something then, didn't you?'

'Like what?'

'That I was covered in chalk dust.' He wafted his hand and then laughed again.

'There you got me, didn't you?'

'Was it chalk dust?'

'Yeah.'

'Where did you get it from?'

'You tell me.'

'No, Mr Oates, I need you to tell me.'

Langton was tense, his fists clenched.

'Where the hell is she going with this?'

Barolli murmured that she was trying to get Oates to say he was at the quarry.

'Why doesn't she just come out with it?'

'I dunno.'

Langton leaned back as the game continued in the interview room.

*

Anna then brought up Timmy Bradford, who had when interviewed said that Oates had tried to get work with him at the quarry. Oates refused to rise to the bait.

'He said they wouldn't give you work because you didn't have a driving licence, which I have to say surprised me as you are a very competent man and I'm amazed you were unable to pass a simple driving test.'

'I never needed one, I never went with him.'

'But you obviously did, to try and get work. It must have really made you angry to go all that way and then get turned down, and Timmy didn't even offer to drive you back to London, did he?'

'Listen, that guy's a prick, and not a good fighter, he's got a glass chin, always getting knocked out.'

'He told me about a fight, one when you were punched so badly the ref tried to stop the fight.'

'Right, but I never gave up, I kept getting back on my feet, nobody knocked me out.'

'So when they said you couldn't work driving the trucks, but he could because he was clever enough to have a licence, maybe that big fight did something to you – you know, made you punch-drunk.'

'I was never that – he is, Timmy is, his brain's scrambled, fucking taking me all that fucking way and then dumping me.'

'Got you again, haven't I?'

'What?'

'Well, now you have just admitted that you did go to try and find work at the chalk pits.'

Before he could get angry with her she switched to admiring him.

'But you managed to get a ride back, never bothered with him again, right? It must have taken you hours, though.'

'Yeah, bloody miles from anywhere.'

'Did you walk a long way?'

'Yeah.'

'Well, with you being so fit, I'd say you could have run all the way.'

'Yeah, got fucking lost, though.'

'Was that the only time you'd been there?'

'Yeah.'

'So how did you get covered in chalk dust all that time after, months after? In fact it was March the 15th, as Mrs Murphy recalled the exact date she saw you walking home.'

Anna knew she was chancing her luck when she dropped in the lie about Mrs Murphy knowing the exact date but thought it was worth the risk.

'It was cement, something or other, and her seeing me as a ghost, it was a joke.'

He shrugged.

Anna glanced at Mike, feeling it was his turn again.

'Did you keep the Jeep and change the number plates on it?' he asked.

'I told you, I dumped it on the A3 – someone else must have found it and done that.'

'Why dump it so far from where you lived?'

'Because I didn't like it not being automatic, for Chrissake, and I'm telling you, some of the drivers on that A3 are like lunatics, seventy, eighty miles an hour, flashing their lights at you.'

'The same type of Jeep was used with false plates to drive off without paying for petrol. The description of the driver in each case matches you.'

'Then someone who looks like me was using it.'

As they couldn't get Oates to admit he had kept the

Jeep they had to move on. If he had abducted Rebekka in it he would have had to have driven it into and possibly out of London.

Anna watched as Mike brought out the photographs of Rebekka Jordan, placing them in front of Oates. Then she felt her mobile phone vibrate in her pocket. She hesitated, and at that moment there was a knock on the door. Langton gestured for Anna to leave the interview room.

'This is Rebekka Jordan, Mr Oates,' Anna said.

'Well, if you say so. I mean, I recall her name, but nothin' else and—'

He swivelled round in his chair as Anna stood up and spoke into the tape recorder to say she was leaving the incident room. She stepped out into the corridor, where Langton was very agitated.

'Pete Jenkins found something in the rear of the Jeep. It was in the boot well where the spare wheel's kept, reckons that's why it survived the fire.'

'What? What is it?'

Langton had to pause to get his breath, he was so hyped up.

'He reckons it's part of one of the dolls.'

Anna closed her eyes.

'You are kidding me.'

'It'll be here in fifteen; you've got the other two items, haven't you?'

'Yes, the head and leg, but I got no reaction from him when I brought them up earlier, other than that he thinks we're trying to frame him. As for the jewellery, he said—'

'I know, got it from car boot sales. I'm watching from the viewing room. The bastard must have killed Rebekka, then put her body in the boot well of the Jeep before dumping her.'

Anna gasped, then nodded – it made sense. 'You will come and get me as soon as the evidence arrives, won't you?' Langton agreed. Before she went back in she checked her mobile and there was a text from Pete telling her about the toy. Closing her eyes, she had to take a few moments to compose herself before re-entering the interview room.

When the police courier arrived at the station Barolli was waiting to sign for the sealed security bag. He ran with it to the incident room where Langton was waiting. Langton cut the seal and opened the bag and there inside was the tiny piece of doll, in a Perspex box. He held it up: it was a tiny left arm with the remains of a pin attached where it would have been joined to the shoulder of the doll. The little hand had been crushed; minuscule jagged pieces of wood were all that remained of it. Langton stared at enlarged images of the head and the leg on the incident board, and he could make out an identical pin at the top of the leg.

Anna was hardly able to contain herself while she waited. Mike had attempted to draw Oates out by showing him more pictures of Rebekka and asking why he thought it would 'be a laugh' to say he had murdered a thirteen-year-old, but Oates continued to sit back, glancing at Mike without any show of emotion.

'Listen, I'm sorry about this girl, but, you know, I've admitted to you about the others, and I wouldn't hurt a little girl, no way would I do that, I got daughters.'

Anna nudged Mike's leg, the signal for her to take over.

'I know about your daughters, Mr Oates, you were very close to one of them, so close you were accused of sexually abusing her so—'

'That's a fucking lie, that's my wife – she's a lying bitch. Corinna wasn't even mine but I raised her like she was. I wouldn't ever have harmed either of them. If she says different, get her to say it to my face cos she wouldn't dare.'

'Wouldn't she? Because if she did you'd knock her out, isn't that why she left you and took the girls as far away from you as possible?'

Oates clenched his fists, but before he could answer there was a rap on the door. Anna's hand was shaking as she looked into the sealed bag. Langton said he was certain the arm was identical to the bits of doll found in Oates's basement, but Pete Jenkins had taken a paint sample from it for testing to be sure. She nodded. But there was no time to waste as Langton had already turned to go back to the viewing room, leaving her to resume the interview with Oates.

'Mr Oates, you claimed earlier, when these items were shown to you, that you had never seen them before.' Anna took the boxes containing the small head and leg from the trolley and placed them on the table.

'Yeah, yeah, we're going round in circles here. I said I never saw them. If they was in my place they was planted, just like the box of stuff you say was in me fireplace. I go on weekends to car boot sales and—'

Anna pushed the boxes towards him.

'You have also claimed that on the day you stole the Jeep, you didn't drive it into London but left it on the A3 with the keys in the ignition, speculating that anyone could have picked it up and used it.'

'Yes.'

'Would you look at this item which has been recovered from the Jeep, please?'

Anna opened the sealed bag Langton had given her and placed the box with the little arm next to the other pieces of doll.

Oates leaned forwards and grimaced.

'I dunno what it is.'

Anna placed some white tissue paper on the table then removed the tiny head and leg from their containers and laid them down on the tissue. Next she put the latest find beside them.

'As you can see they are from dolls, very small dolls, as made for Rebekka Jordan by her father. The pin in the leg is identical to the pin in the tiny arm – they are actually sewing pins cut to measure by Mr Jordan and used to join the bits together. This bit, a left arm, was found in the Jeep you stole.'

'Listen, you don't expect me to believe this shit – you must have fucking planted that, it's wood, isn't it, so it would have burnt up in the fire.'

'Burnt up? What are you referring to?'

Oates twisted his head as if his neck was constricted.

'I know what you are talking about, because I know you have lied,' Anna went on. 'You didn't leave the Jeep on the A3, did you? You drove it back to London and put false plates on it so you could use it when you needed to go looking for your next kill, which was Rebekka Jordan.'

Oates was so fast. He pushed his chair back so hard it hit the ground and his legs came up as he somersaulted back-wards, then sprang up, raising his fists like a boxer.

'Come on, come on then, hit me, hit me.'

Mike hit the panic button and stood up quickly as Oates pranced in front of the table and began shadow-boxing.

Kumar ducked down and crouched against the wall, plainly afraid he was going to be punched. The door opened and Langton came in with two uniformed officers as Oates became crazed, hunching his shoulders and punching wildly. As they grabbed both his arms, he struggled and started kicking. They twisted his arms behind his back and he howled in pain. Only after they had managed to push him forwards so that he was bent almost double did he suddenly deflate and sink to his knees.

They could still hear him as he was led down the corridor to the cells. It was a screeching howl, so high it sounded like a wounded animal. Langton suggested they put everything on hold until Oates calmed down. Kumar was shaken and said that he doubted if they would be able to continue. Langton snapped at him that it was all a big act, no doubt encouraged by Kumar, and he would get the police doctor out to examine him. He would decide if Oates was fit to be interviewed again.

Half an hour later and Oates had stopped screaming but was sitting on the cell bed rocking backwards and forwards, moaning at the top of his voice without making any sense. The police doctor had still not arrived to examine him as he was busy at another station some miles away. Barolli went to the cells to check up on the prisoner as Mike and Anna went over the interview. Anna didn't say it, but what had occurred was the very thing Samuels had warned them about: Oates had flipped. Barolli returned to say that the screeching had stopped, but the prayers were now in full flow. Oates was on his knees, claiming God was talking to him, the voices were calling to him, and he wanted a Bible.

*

Anna had joined Mike in his office when Langton came in to inform them that the police doctor had still not arrived and there was nothing further they could do until he had assessed Oates. He checked his watch.

'Maybe gives me enough time, but if I'm in the cells and the doctor arrives, stall him. Take your time explaining why we called him.'

Mike looked at Anna in surprise and then turned to Langton.

'There are cameras all over the custody suite.'

'Not in the cells.'

'Where is Kumar?'

'Oates's antics scared him so he's gone for a walk to calm his nerves.'

Langton hurried out and Anna sighed.

'What do you think he's going to do?'

'Well he's not going to say a few prayers with him, is he?'

'He could jeopardize the whole investigation. All our hard work gone because he has a personal agenda with Oates.'

'I think between you and me we just keep our noses out of it,' Mike replied as he flicked up his blinds. Langton appeared to be deep in conversation with Joan.

Chapter Fifteen

'I printed off some pictures and as much coverage as I could get up, but he was in such a hurry,' protested Joan as Mike looked over her shoulder at her computer screen.

'Thanks, Joan.'

Mike crossed to Anna's desk and perched on the edge.

'Langton's gone down to the cells. He told Joan he was taking Oates a Bible.'

'To hit him with, most likely. Oates has lost it, Mike – it was pretty obvious, which is why I trod so carefully with him, and now Kumar will ask the courts for a pre-trial psychiatric assessment. You know they nearly always fall on the side of the defendant.'

'That's if we ever get him to trial, shadow-boxing with the judge! Wouldn't go down well. On the other hand, he was being a smart alec throughout until you showed him the doll's arm found in the Jeep. That threw him – you saw the way he reacted: he knew when he said about the toy being burnt that he'd trapped himself. So he could be faking it.'

'Well if he is, he's going to have to keep it up. In the meantime, let's get onto these other cases.'

'Already checking them, but it's getting late and I don't know about you, but I am drained.'

'Yeah, well let's see what happens.'

Langton was having a quiet conversation with the young officer outside Oates's cell. He told him he had a Bible for Oates and he'd keep an eye on him while the officer had a well-earned coffee break as a reward for putting up with the shouting and moaning for so long. Langton looked at his watch.

'Fifteen minutes, okay?'

The officer nodded and moved off as Langton unlocked the cell. The young man turned back, unsure, watching for a moment, but then did as he was told. It was against regulations, but Langton had never been one to stick by those.

Oates was kneeling by his bunk, eyes closed, when Langton walked in, threw the Bible on the bed and then inched the door closed with his foot.

'You can stop the act now, it doesn't work with me.'

Oates opened his eyes and started crying.

'May the good Lord forgive me for doing the work of the devil. I can't help it. When he speaks to me he controls me and I am helpless.'

'I just wanted to have a quiet word as after that performance I very much doubt you'll be declared fit for trial. I know I won't contest it, no way, and we've got a doctor on standby who will sign you out of our hands.'

'The Lord giveth his blessings and taketh away, and I am deservedly waiting for him to give me peace,' Oates informed him.

'I bet you are, but before you get the Lord to comfort

you, I just want to give you a bit of a lowdown on where he will be having to comfort you.'

Oates bowed his head and clasped his hands in prayer.

'You'll be on your way to Broadmoor,' Langton continued, 'and I guarantee you won't be getting out. You'll want to, believe you me you will want to, as they don't have wings there, you know, no one's segregated, part of their rules.'

Langton passed him a picture.

'Take a look. You know who that is? No? That's Sutcliffe. Good-looking fella, isn't he? Neat black beard, nice hair, looks quite the man, doesn't he?'

Oates glanced at the picture and then looked away.

Langton held up a second picture, shoving it in front of Oates's face.

'Take a look at him now: skin like a patchwork quilt. He's been bottled so many times, he's bloated like a stuck pig; he's lost his teeth, he's deaf from a blow to the head and he's been kicked in the testicles so often by the inmates he walks as if he's got a trolley between his knees.'

Langton shoved the most recent pictures of Sutcliffe directly under Oates's nose, but he turned away, waving his hand. Then he leaned closer, whispering.

'I do the devil's work, I need to pray.'

'I will make sure you get there, Henry, and this is what you have got to look forward to for the rest of your dirty disgusting life. You'll be able to trade prayers with him, he might even come on to you, they can't keep their hands off fresh meat, even with all the surveillance and officers trying to protect the poor demented souls. You will get knifed, razored, bottled and raped, they'll give you medication to dull your whimpering crying and you will never get released – that's what they do to inmates that can't take the mental strain: crush it, crush you.'

Langton turned to the cell door, folding the pictures and stuffing them into his jacket pocket.

'You say your prayers, Henry, you are going to need them. They'll be taking you away tonight, unless . . .'

Oates's wide frightened eyes blinked rapidly.

'You can assist us. Tell the police doctor you're fine and it was all an act. Then if you help close our cases you could end up in a nice secure prison with your own private cell, TV, computer games, we can sort that, make sure of it if you help us; we notify the authorities, tell them this guy is not all bad, he's intelligent, he's not a crazy, no way is he mentally unfit, he's too sharp, too clever, and he deserves some respect because without his help we'd never have nailed him.'

Oates sucked in his breath. Langton glanced at his watch.

'You've got five minutes before I call the wagon to get you carted back to prison, then it's on to Broadmoor when that solicitor of yours insists you are incapable of standing trial. You are going down for the murder of Justine Marks, for the murder of Fidelis Julia Flynn, you know that, no way out of that, but get the others off your chest, Henry, come clean with us and stop fucking around.'

Langton had his hand on the cell door, ready to leave, when Henry Oates whispered, 'I want to make a statement.'

Mike was furious as there had been a press leak. This meant he'd had to get hold of the press office, who wanted a statement they could release regarding the arrest of Henry Oates. Mike kept it very brief: they had a suspect in custody following the disappearance of Fidelis Julia Flynn, but as yet no charges had been brought. The press officer asked if this was also connected to Rebekka Jordan, as there had been enquiries from Fleet Street. Mike admitted that their suspect was also being questioned about her disappearance, but gave no more details.

Anna had listened and could see how riled-up Mike was, but leaks happened, it could even have come from inside the prison. She felt he had handled it well, but hoped the press wouldn't speculate further. It could create a lot of media attention, and they really didn't want that at this stage.

Langton walked back into Mike's office, leaned against the door and smiled. Anna turned, half expecting him to call it quits for the night at least.

'Henry Oates wants to make a statement. He's quiet now and the police doctor's with him. Give him another fifteen minutes, cup of coffee, get him brought back up from his cell. If he acts up again or refuses to answer any further questions, charge him with Fidelis Julia Flynn's murder then call it a day and take him to the magistrates' court in the morning.'

Mike looked at his watch – it was already five-fifteen, and the thought of conducting another round of questions with Oates made him feel sick.

'How about we do this in the morning?'

'No bloody way, get some black coffee down you and get the energy up,' Langton retorted.

Anna said nothing, but like Mike did she found the thought of going back into another session with Oates daunting. She stood up and said she would arrange the refreshments. She would also talk to Kumar to let him know they were about to continue the interview of his client.

*

Kumar was astonished, and pointed out that it was almost six o'clock. He was also peeved that he had been left in the reception area waiting to know what was happening.

'Your client wants to make a statement,' she said, almost enjoying his reaction.

It all took slightly longer than Langton had anticipated and it was six-thirty before they reconvened in the interview room to wait for Oates to be brought up from his cell. Kumar had complained sulkily that he should have been told sooner that his client wanted to make a statement. Mike replied curtly that he was almost as surprised as Kumar was, especially after the performance they had all witnessed.

'Performance? My God, it was perfectly obvious that my client was breaking down and incapable of even talking coherently.'

Before Mike could answer the heavy footsteps sounded in the corridor outside and the interview-room door opened. Oates did not appear to be suffering any adverse effects from his 'breakdown' as he sauntered in and sat in the same seat without saying a word.

Kumar asked him if he would like to have a private consultation before the interview began. Oates shook his head and then looked at Mike and Anna.

'You don't have to show me nothing. I don't need to see anything you got, I'm gonna tell you the truth and get it over with.'

He didn't look as if he was unstable, or even close to it, but there was a strange look about him that made Anna and Mike apprehensive of what was to come. He folded his hands in front of him on the table.

'Shall I start now?'

Anna kept her voice low and controlled as she very

quietly said that when he was ready he could begin, but if he wanted she could repeat what they had been discussing before he had halted the last interview session.

'Strange it didn't burn when I set light to the Jeep. That doll's arm was wood and you'd have thought it would burn. I never even saw it, didn't know it was there, it must have fallen out of her pocket.'

Oates closed his eyes.

'The other things I found in her jacket; the head and the leg, I think it was. I got rid of everything else, but I kept those items – stupid really, but they reminded me of what I'd done. Sounds odd, I suppose, that I ever needed to be reminded, because I never forgot anything, forgot nothing, but I always kept a little something. Sometimes I would play with them, not like a kid, no, I'd just lay the stuff out and look at it. Gave me a sense of power, do you understand? It made all the shit in my life go away.'

Anna glanced at Mike. He seemed unsure as to whether or not he should interrupt, but Anna knew they had to get some direction in the rambling monologue.

'Mr Oates, when you say you had a feeling of power, was this over your victims? Explain to us about the feelings you had about Rebekka Jordan.'

Oates nodded and took a deep breath. In the same monotone he described working for the Jordans in their garden, how he had seen Rebekka when they were taking down the wall and he said she looked forward to the new pond for her frogs. He said she was such a pretty little girl and she had spoken to him in such a nice voice. After he had had the argument with Mrs Markham he was angry and didn't want to walk all the way back to London so he broke into a house nearby, found the keys and stole the Jeep. He said that he had intended to dump it but he liked it so he parked it some distance away from his squat and got false plates for it the next day. He didn't use it often, just if he was going out looking for work, and he never parked it near his flat. He admitted that it was him who had driven off without paying for the petrol in Shepherd's Bush, and that he had been going there on and off for a few days looking for work at Westfield, or on nearby building sites, as sometimes they needed extra workers and would give you cash in hand.

'I'd finished what I had to do and they let me leave early. I went and got the Jeep from a back street where I parked it. The traffic was really busy, all single file and going really slow; that's when I saw her, standing at the lights.'

His voice had taken on a softer tone and when Anna looked at him his eyes were glazed over, staring not at her, but straight through her. The alteration in his voice bothered her, and again she went back to Samuels' assessment that Oates potentially had several different personality disorders. He was certainly behaving very differently to any previous interaction. He seemed very depressed, and hardly moved his hands, but kept his fingertips pressed against the edge of the table. She forced herself to pay closer attention as Oates described seeing Rebekka.

'She was looking so sweet, in her riding boots, carrying her hard hat, and she had this pretty Alice band, pink it was, made her face glow. She was so unsure about when to cross.'

He gave a sigh and lightly ran his fingers along the table's edge, almost as if playing a piano.

Anna knew that the Alice band was the one piece of evidence that Langton had kept out of the press. She made a note and then looked back at Oates as he had paused for a few moments.

'"Hello, Rebekka," I said, and I leaned over and opened

the door. She remembered me and she said she was going home so I said to her that I was going that way and I could take her there. She got in beside me. I had a car behind tooting at me to get moving cos the lights had changed so I drove off.'

Oates continued, describing how Rebekka had chattered on to him about her new pond and how he had driven all the way around the roundabout as if he was going to head to Hammersmith but took the wrong turning.

When Oates spoke as Rebekka, his voice was childlike. He described how suddenly she had become afraid, saying that he was not going the right way and she knew how to get home as her father always took the same route when he collected her from the stables. His hands went still and he dropped them into his lap. He told them how she started to get more and more frightened and nothing he said would calm her down, so he had been forced to do something drastic. She had been trying to get out of the Jeep and he had no option but to do it.

Oates clenched his left fist, and demonstrated a vicious punch, just as he had before. He had struck Rebekka a few times until she went quiet.

'I think, I am not certain, but I think I broke her neck.'

The silence was hideous. Neither Mike nor Anna could speak, and Kumar had his head bent forwards as if unable to take in the horror he was forced to listen to. It didn't end, it took Oates a few more moments of silence before he described his own terror, knowing what he had done, and knowing he had to do something to make sure he wouldn't be caught with the child in the car.

'You know, I was in a stolen Jeep, I wasn't even sure where the hell I was, but then it all became clear – I knew where I could take her, where she would never be found.

I saw an alleyway round the back of some houses so I went down there and threw out the spare wheel and put her body in the boot well. I went along Western Avenue, then on the M4 past Heathrow. I'd been thumbing lifts that one time trying to get back home from the quarry and I reckoned that would be the best place to take her. It was getting dark and I was sweating in case I'd be picked up for going too slow.'

He smiled, shaking his head, and continued to describe how he had eventually reached the quarry where he had tried to get work, but then changed his mind and found a back road and made for the disused quarry, passing a heavily wooded area.

'I was getting into a right state. I didn't know where the road came out, but then I reckoned as there was no one around I'd get rid of her there.'

Oates chewed at his wet lips and this time drummed his fingers on the table.

'Now, how about this? Left in the back of the Jeep was a spade, a big shovel – talk about lucky. Was I lucky? And she was feather-light and easy to carry.'

In the viewing room Barolli and Langton remained silent, listening as Oates professed his luck as he carried his little victim over his shoulder and made his way through the woods. What surprised him was that after only a short while the wood thinned out and he was looking down into the disused quarry. He told them he had intended to toss the body in at first, but lost his footing and slithered down the embankment; it was by now pitch-dark. He had the girl by her hair and the spade in the other hand and as soon as he had found firmer footing he dug a grave.

*

There was another lengthy pause as Oates opened a bottle of water and drank in gulps. He gave a ghastly smile.

'Thirsty work.'

His eyes were bright, no longer glazed, and so Anna asked if he had removed Rebekka's clothes. He snapped at her that she should mind her own business, and she could see the Oates she had first questioned returning with a vengeance.

But it wasn't over. It took a lot of carefully structured questions, stroking his sick ego, to see if he could recall the exact location. He swore that he could easily find it again as he'd climbed all the way back up and then nearly killed himself.

'I didn't see the fucking ditch. I was in the wrong fucking gear and instead of going backwards I shot forwards smack bang into the fucking ditch and there was this soddin' big fir tree; the bonnet buckled up and it started smoking and the more I tried to rev it up and back out the more it got stuck.'

Oates described how he'd set the Jeep on fire, worried he might have left evidence inside, and then he ran and kept on running until he made it back onto a road and thumbed a lift. He was gloating again, saying that no witness had ever seen him and all the press about the missing girl never mentioned her getting into a Jeep.

'I was so in the clear it wasn't true, but when I went back there I saw the fucking thing had gone. I thought the police had found the Jeep but then I saw it at the gypsy camp with no plates or wheels on it.'

He hesitated and drank more water. Replacing the cap he shook the bottle.

'Why not get it all off me chest, right?'

*

It was almost ten when Langton and the team gathered in the incident room. They now knew that Oates had returned numerous times to the same location – he even knew the gypsy camp and had seen the stolen Jeep broken up amongst the other wrecks. He said he was certain there had been three more car thefts, three more victims, and he had become adept at stealing vehicles, dumping the bodies and leaving the cars in a side street or anywhere he chose. He had kept the shovel hidden in the woods and he came to know the area like the back of his hand.

Oates was returned to his cell for the night as the exhausted team went over in some detail what the next move would be. There was no feeling of accomplishment or exhilaration; their depression hung heavy. Langton said that they would need to arrange for a search team and Oates to be taken to the quarry as he had claimed he knew exactly where he had buried his victims. Rebekka Jordan's was the only name he could recall, managing just a sketchy description of the other women. He had made it very clear that he had not molested or sexually abused 'the little one', only the women.

It would take time for a search of the quarry to be organized and any bodies found to be exhumed. First they needed another session with Oates to see if he could remember any more details of the other victims and who the 'trinkets' he had kept might belong to. They would then transport Oates with armed officers to the disused quarry and from his directions uncover the graves. Mike queried why they would need armed officers with Oates in handcuffs, and Langton said that as much as he disliked doing it he had to be aware of Oates's safety in case a disgruntled member of the public took a pop at him.

Everyone was tired. Langton suggested to Anna that she accompany him early the next morning to give the Jordans the news about their daughter, as it was too late to call on them that evening. It was a duty that he had dreaded having to perform, but at least the Jordans might now be able to have closure. If their daughter's remains were uncovered they could arrange a funeral, but first the body would have to be carefully exhumed by a forensic archaeologist, followed by a full post mortem.

'Let's hope to God we find her,' he said quietly.

Anna nodded as they walked out of the station together. She gave him a sidelong glance.

'So what made Oates make the statement?'

Langton shrugged and said that he'd elaborated on what life would be like in Broadmoor.

'But it's closing down, isn't it?'

'Yeah, but he doesn't know that. I showed him these.' He passed her the folded pictures that Joan had printed for him from her computer. She bleeped open her Mini, threw her briefcase onto the passenger seat, and opened the pages, staring at the photographs of Peter Sutcliffe, the notorious Yorkshire Ripper. The second picture had been taken after he was seriously assaulted with a razor blade by another inmate in Broadmoor. The hideous distortion of his features and his bloated face made him almost unrecognizable. Anna refolded the pages and put them on the seat beside her. Sutcliffe now looked the embodiment of evil and whatever punishment had been forced on him, he deserved. Henry Oates would deserve as much, if not more.

Chapter Sixteen

Anna had never known Langton to be so emotional. Not that he said anything; it was the way he constantly touched the knot of his tie and kept on giving a light cough as if clearing his throat. The morning papers had been full of the news that a man was being held on suspicion of multiple murders and they had mentioned Rebekka Jordan's name. Langton was furious and extremely concerned that Mr and Mrs Jordan might have read about it before he and Anna had had time to warn them.

The Jordans' front door opened before they even had time to ring the bell, and it was clear at once from the way they both stood there expectantly that the couple had seen the papers. It was Stephen who asked them to come in and Anna noticed the way he reached out for his wife's hand as he drew her into the kitchen.

Langton didn't waste any time. He couldn't, there was something heartbreaking about their tense frightened eyes.

'We have a development. It's not good news: we have made an arrest and I'm afraid the suspect has admitted to the murder of your daughter.'

'Where is she?' Stephen Jordan asked, all the while

tightly gripping his wife's hand. She was shaking so much, he had to put his arm around her shoulders.

'We have a location, a disused part of a chalk quarry, and we will be searching for her and as soon as we know for certain we will contact you.'

'I don't understand.' Stephen looked so confused, it was pitiful, as Langton attempted to explain in as comforting a way as possible that their detainee had admitted burying their daughter. He added that they also suspected that the same person had been involved in other murders and he had agreed to help the police recover the bodies. Langton was so hesitant and unsure of himself that Anna couldn't help but move closer to the distraught couple. She took over.

'The reason we are here is that the press have been informed of the arrest and we wanted to make sure you were aware of the possibility we will find Rebekka. If it is any comfort to you, the suspect has adamantly denied that she was in any way sexually abused and we will endeavour to bring you details as soon as we have confirmation we have found her. Right now we just have the suspect's statement admitting to her abduction and murder.'

Stephen helped his wife to sit down. She was gasping, taking short breaths, her face was stricken, but it was as if she had already shed so many tears she was now unable to cry. The dreaded news they had been waiting for was now confirmed. Five years of waiting and hoping were over. It was wretchedly sad and neither Anna nor Langton could ease the pain. They left as soon as it was apparent the Jordans wanted to be alone.

Langton remained silent as they drove towards the station. Eventually, without looking at her, but staring out of the passenger window, he said quietly, 'You shouldn't have said that.'

'Said what?'

'We don't know if he was lying – you said there had been no sexual abuse; we don't know that, we don't even have her body. He might have cut off her bloody head.'

'For God's sake, I was trying to give them some comfort.'

'I know that,' he snapped, pinching the brow of his nose and sighing. 'Sorry, but comfort or not, you should never give out details that you are not certain about, and until we find her and the post mortem has been completed we won't know if it was a broken neck that killed her, or . . .' He paused, shaking his head. 'You know what really got to me? His describing that fucking pink Alice band. As soon as he described it I wanted to put my hands round his neck and squeeze the life out of him.'

She agreed and continued driving as he got out his mobile phone, barking out instructions to Mike to begin coordinating the search of the quarry and organizing POLSA and underwater search teams along with firearms officers for Oates. He then rang his surgeon for an appointment to see how his knee was recovering so he could get a clean bill of health. No sooner had he cut off that call than his mobile rang again. As he answered Anna noticed his voice changed.

'Good morning, ma'am.'

Langton listened to his caller and then gave her a brief update of the latest developments. He must have been asked about his health as he assured her that he would be fit and well that afternoon. He repeated his thanks, and then said that he would be available and looked forward to the meeting. When he shut off the mobile he was smiling.

'Good news?'

'You could say that. Area Commander asking to see me – she's given clearance for whatever we require for the search but wants a full update, so drop me off at the Yard. It'll be a big security job and I want a slew of men, plus a helicopter with all the new-fangled camera equipment. If that bastard buried his victims in the quarry we're going to find them.'

He was back to his brusque delivery. In the previous call he'd used a very soft cultured tone – not exactly arse-licking, but close. It reminded Anna of something she had thought of when interviewing Oates during their last session.

'You know Samuels suspected that Oates could have many different personality disorders with highs and lows, well did you notice how different he was when he was describing his abduction of Rebekka? His voice was lighter and he changed the way he tapped along the edge of the table with his fingers.'

'Don't go there.'

'Pardon?'

'I said don't go there. Right now I couldn't give a toss if he was talking like Gloria Swanson – he's talking, that's all I care about, and we keep him in whatever character he wants to play until we get what we want out of the little turd.'

The press were already picking up on the scent now that they had a serial killer under arrest. A few reporters and photographers had gathered outside Hackney Police Station and Mike was under pressure to give a press conference to control the media furore. Wherever the leaks were coming from, it was obviously someone close to their investigation. The last thing they needed was any press attention when they searched the quarry, so Mike intended to keep that under wraps when he agreed to hold a mid-morning press conference at Scotland Yard.

Barolli had been instructed to check on Oates and make sure that he had been given breakfast and then interview him about cases of women going missing over that last six years. In readiness Barbara prepared photographs of the women in question and Barolli set up the interview room with the items from the jewellery box. He laid them out on white paper, including the gold bracelet they now knew belonged to Angela Thornton. Her parents had returned from holiday and confirmed it had belonged to their daughter, as they had given it to her as a twenty-first birthday present.

Oates had been given bacon and eggs and fried bread and two mugs of coffee. He was affable and very talkative and all those coming into contact with him were warned to keep him sweet. It was ten-thirty when he was brought into the interview room, where Kumar was already waiting.

Barolli explained that they had some missing persons photographs for him to look at and see if he recognized any of the women as his victims.

Oates sat as the photographs were spread out in front of him. Again he appeared to be enjoying the attention. It was sickening the way he dismissed one after the other, muttering derogatory remarks about the women, shoving the pictures aside as he went through them.

*

Anna slipped into the viewing room with a bacon roll and coffee. There were a couple of other members of the team there already, taking the opportunity to observe Oates, and it was almost as if they were watching a film in a private cinema. With Mike at the press conference she had spent the morning coordinating the upcoming search of the quarry. Costs were no longer an issue now they had clearance from the Deputy Commissioner to use whatever manpower was necessary. The forensic archaeologist, specialist POLSA and underwater search teams and the foot officers and their sniffer dogs all had to be ready to go when they received the call, along with sufficient transport. Even caterers had to be organized. If they were to work in bad light or into the night they would require arc lamps and high-powered torches. Protective suits and footwear would be needed, as the chalk quarry was likely to be bogged down after heavy rain. They would also have to bring abseiling equipment and ropes to access some areas of the massive quarry as Oates claimed he had buried his victims deep down. By now Anna had been supplied with detailed Ordnance Survey maps covering the area, and all they were waiting for was the green light for the convoys to go.

'What have we got so far?' Anna asked.

The way they were working the interview was that as soon as Oates identified a victim this was fed directly back to the incident room, then they could get the missing woman's file brought over from the station that did the original investigation.

'We've got two so far,' a young fresh-faced officer said, as he stood up to allow Anna to take his seat.

Oates had selected two photographs of missing girls: Kelly Mathews, aged twenty-two, who had disappeared four years ago, and a curly-haired redhead, twenty-one-year-old Mary Suffolk, missing for three years. Anna watched as Oates continued dismissing one photograph after another before he started to laugh. His hand was covering a photograph of a dark-haired girl with buck teeth.

'This one reminded me of my bitch of a wife – yeah I did this one.'

'Has he identified the girl that owned the gold bracelet? Angela Thornton?' Anna whispered.

Just as she mentioned the name, they saw Oates hold up the last photograph – it was Angela. He seemed irritated, saying he thought there had only been three, but this meant he'd miscalculated. There must have been four victims.

Barolli stopped the interview shortly after this when Oates had said he was hungry and asked for lunch. He came back up to the incident room, totally worn-out. That afternoon they would proceed with the viewing of the jewellery and ask Oates to place each item he recognized next to the victim to whom it belonged.

'My face feels stiff from giving the bastard encouragement. He's enjoying himself, loves the attention; he's stuffing his face down in the cells. I can't face eating, he sickens me.'

Barolli slumped into his chair at his desk. Meanwhile, Barbara and Joan had the task of arranging the photographs of the dead girls Oates had claimed he'd killed in a row across the interview-room table. They all now had names: Kelly Mathews, Mary Suffolk, Alicia Jones and Angela Thornton. From the missing persons reports it appeared they didn't live in the same area of London, and had no connection to each other bar the fact that Oates, by his own admission, had abducted them. At this point there was no information on the vehicles Oates claimed to have stolen. He could not remember the makes of the cars, just that he had taken them from various car parks and streets in and around London. He had always dumped them after returning from the quarry.

The afternoon was taken up with Oates going through all the items discovered in his basement. He seemed to like the way he was asked to put on the light latex gloves. He joked that they were too small, that he had fighter's hands, but eventually he seemed satisfied with a pair that fitted and then prodded and inspected one item after another.

'Bit like a car boot sale, this, isn't it?'

Barolli smiled, nodding.

'So what you want me to do? Eh, you remember that old game show they used to have on the TV? They have this conveyor belt, right, and they'd pass along all these things, like a teddy bear, a toaster, a cream jug, pair of gloves, and then the contestant had to remember what they were, and if he or she was able to remember, they got them all at the end of the show.'

Barolli forced himself to look interested.

'Yeah, it was terrific, but my memory is rotten – I'd never get anything, but I bet you can though. Play the game, Henry, let's see if you can match these items to the girls you took them off.'

'Are you gonna time me?'

'I haven't got a stopwatch – just see if you can do it.'

Anna was back in the viewing room observing Oates acting like a teenager, laughing and joking. He also kept up a light shuffle with his feet. Langton walked in and stood behind her chair, watching.

'We've got four, not three,' she said quietly.

'I know. I'd stop this fucking farce in there, but he likes it, and we don't want him refusing to take us to the bodies in the quarry.'

'Kumar's been sitting in on it, started taking notes, but he looks as if he's filled his notebook.' They both glanced at Kumar to the side of the screen, sitting head bowed, his notebook on his knee.

'You think the press tip-off came from him?'

Anna looked at Langton, then back to Kumar.

'I wouldn't put it past him, this case is going to be front-page news for days.'

He withdrew from his coat pocket a copy of the *Evening Standard* and passed it to her.

'Trying to get photographs of the Jordans, the bastards, and they've dug up all the old pictures we used of Rebekka.'

Anna sighed as she read the front page and was about to turn over when Langton tapped her shoulder.

'Look what he's doing.'

Oates was performing his silly prancing shadow-boxing dance, choosing one piece of jewellery and placing it on the photograph of the victim's face. He was very fast and his tongue pointed out of his mouth like a child's as he concentrated.

He didn't speak, but surveyed his handiwork and then with one hand swept the rest of the bits and pieces aside.

'They belonged to me wife, me kids, left them when they ran away from me; only these things belong to each of my girls.'

Anna stood up, believing he was telling the truth as laid on top of Angela Thornton's photograph was her gold bracelet.

In small piles by each of the dead women were hair slides, rings, cheap broken necklaces, earrings and bracelets.

'How do you check if I'm right?' he asked Barolli.

Barolli told Oates that forensics had already taken what samples they could and now they would see what the reports on the missing girls gave them.

'I get a prize, do I?'

Barolli could hardly break into a smile, but he gave a small nod and clapped his hands as if applauding Oates's effort.

'Okay, we are going to take you back now and I reckon it'll be fresh doughnuts and a nice cuppa.'

Oates thanked Barolli, and then he glanced at Kumar.

'You enjoy yourself, did you?'

Kumar stood up as Oates waited for the interview-room door to open.

'Mr Oates, you also agreed to further assist the police by directing them to where you buried the victims.'

Oates frowned, then pursed his lips.

'I never agreed to do that. Isn't it enough what I've been doing here all bloody day?' He was back to his snarling unpleasant self.

Barolli could have slapped Kumar. This was not the time to discuss the search and he knew that Oates, like himself, had been working all day. He glanced at the two uniformed officers waiting by the open door, then pulled himself together to save the situation.

'Well I don't know if that would be on the cards.'

Barolli wasn't sure if he was saying the right thing. He had been instructed to keep Oates sweet, but now the prisoner looked surly and angry.

'What do you mean not on the fucking cards?' Oates snapped.

'Well we've got everything agreed – helicopters and search team, cameras . . . it'll be a massive expense and has to be done.' Barolli was sweating, knowing full well he was on his own as the tape and monitor screens had been turned off.

'Helicopters?' Oates asked suspiciously.

'Right, this is a big operation, Mr Oates, you are big news, and the coverage, let alone the security, will be massive. But if you are against it then they can maybe do it without you.'

Oates interrupted him, raising his hands, and Barolli stepped back, fearing the former boxer was about to lash out at him.

'I never said I wouldn't do it, I'm well and truly up for it, and besides, no one else knows but me where the bodies are buried. You tell them they can't go without me.' He gestured to Kumar. 'I want to be on that search. I got a right to be on it, so you make sure it goes ahead, you hearing me?' He smiled at Barolli. 'I was only joking just now. Honest, I'm looking forward to the day out.'

'Good. Well you'll be informed as soon as we get the green light.'

As Oates was led out of the room Barolli gave a sigh of relief. Kumar clicked opened his briefcase.

'I will want to be present, officer, so I sincerely hope that I will be privy to when this search is set to happen.'

'I am sure you will be contacted, Mr Kumar.'

Kumar picked up his cashmere coat and folded it over his arm.

'You must be creaming yourself.' Barolli couldn't stop himself.

'I beg your pardon!'

'Well, let's face it, this is a whopper of a case for you, media's already all over it like a rash.'

Kumar gave a tight-lipped nod, and asked to be taken to reception. Barolli said he would escort him personally.

'The monitor and tapes were off and I got to tell you, I was sweating, but I played up how much it was gonna cost, helicopters and all the security we'd need.' Barolli was lapping up the team's praise as he repeated the altercation between Oates, Kumar and himself.

'All right, all right,' Mike said brusquely, and then with everyone present apart from Langton, he gave them the details. The fact that Anna had coordinated everything was not mentioned. Mike turned to a large new board marked out with maps and aerial photographs of the quarry and all the equipment the search would need.

'This is a huge operation and we can't afford any mistakes or screw-ups. We set up the search areas, Oates will be transported in a blacked-out armoured police wagon with armed guards following behind, and to ensure we get as much daylight as possible we leave here at five in the morning. Oates will leave in the wagon at six with motorcycle outriders to stop the traffic so he should be at the quarry by seven.

'We've got to keep this under wraps. We absolutely do not want any media interference so we're calling this "Operation Pits"- okay, I know that's not terribly inventive. Now most of you have been working flat out for almost twenty-four hours, so off you go and we'll see you first thing in the morning.'

As everyone prepared to pack up and leave for the night, Barolli grabbed Mike for a whispered conversation in which he hinted that the leak could have come from Kumar and suggested they leave it until the last moment to inform him when the search was happening.

Anna was one of the last to leave the incident room. Pinned up on the board were the photographs of the victims: Rebekka Jordan, Kelly Mathews, Mary Suffolk, Alicia Jones and Angela Thornton, and as always the faces of the dead seemed to radiate a chilling energy. Beside them the photographs of Justine Marks and Fidelis Julia Flynn were somehow no longer as haunting, maybe because the discovery of their bodies had in some ways brought them a tragic peace.

'Goodnight,' Anna said as the night duty officers set to work and the main lights were lowered. In the centre of the board were the enlarged mug shots of Henry Oates, with his wide pale eyes, his flattened nose and thick lips, his face dominated by an evil energy of its own. Only a few more days and if everything went according to plan they would be able to take his photograph down and rip it to shreds.

Chapter Seventeen

In the darkness of the early morning, the preparations were well under way. The forecast was gloomy and heavy rain was expected, so teams of officers were being kitted out in protective overalls and boots. The catering wagon 'Teapot One' had already opened up. It was very cold and the caterers would be kept busy all day with so many people to serve. On one side of the quarry there was a vast area of flattened ground, which became the operation's main base as the vehicles could park up with ease.

Fifty metres from their base was the cavernous quarry pit with many ridges and smaller pits, and a crumbling cliff edge. Officers began to cordon off the area with crime scene tape. Anyone entering the location would have to show identification. The two sniffer dogs and their handlers remained in their van, and the barking of the animals echoed across the vast quarry.

Mike had commandeered a large tent, inside which there were tables and chairs, and a board propped up on two easels with photographs and maps of the area divided into squares. Four of the search teams were already exploring the easiest route down to the deep pit. Abseiling equipment, rope ladders and steel extendable ones were being unloaded. A coach with more officers drew up and twenty men and women alighted to await instructions. The marine support unit van was also on site with two large inflatable dinghies and dredging equipment to search the large water-filled areas at the lower end of the quarry. The divers were busy putting on their wetsuits and testing the breathing apparatus. Mike gave them the go-ahead to start searching the pond area as soon as they were ready.

Anna arrived in her Mini and parked beside the coach. Remembering the state of her shoes after her last visit, she was wearing wellington boots and a thick fleece jacket with a hood. She joined Mike and Barolli for a coffee at the catering wagon just as Mike received a call on his mobile to say that Oates had left the station and was on his way with a large escort. They made their way over to the big tent and Mike pointed to the map of the wood.

'We get him here and then, as he says he came up to the quarry from the wooded side, we start from there, let him guide us to where he says he tipped the bodies over. He claims he also went down into the main pit. How the hell he got down there and back up he'll have to show us, but it's bloody steep.'

Anna looked around.

'I suppose if he'd parked near here someone might have seen him, so coming in via the woods would have been better cover for what he was up to.'

Mike made sure his earphones were working as his phone began to ring constantly. He used a microphone attached to his earpiece to relay messages to the teams, which were still arriving. The police helicopter, *India 99*, was on standby at its base in Lippitts Hill, Essex, all ready to take off when required, although the thermal image sensor on board would not be of much use unless Oates had recently buried a body. But even after five years they would be able to identify from the air possible ground disturbances in the open parts of the quarry and the Nitesun high-powered searchlight would also help the officers on the ground.

'Is Langton going to show?' asked Barolli, who'd just arrived.

Anna smiled and said she doubted that he would miss such a big event.

'Well he should watch out for himself, this place is lethal – there's potholes everywhere and the clay makes it like an ice rink.'

'Yeah, but at least the rain is holding off.'

A large tent with rolled-up sides and a tarpaulin floor had also been erected for the forensic team and they were unpacking boxes of equipment inside. At the same time officers from the POLSA support van began taking out the huge arc lamps.

'Well it looks like everyone's here except the star of the show,' said Barolli. He looked around, impressed: this was a major operation. 'Eh, look who's driving up – his nice shiny BMW's gonna be caked.'

Adan Kumar was showing his identification to the uniformed officers standing by the cordoned entry to the parking area and was directed to park alongside Anna's Mini. They watched as he got out and looked at the ground. He was wearing his cashmere coat and toggled leather shoes.

'Silly bugger's not got wellington boots, and it's a pity we don't have any extra protective gear to help him out.' Barolli grinned.

Mike glanced at his watch. 'He made good time, I only gave him the location an hour ago, woke him up. Mind you, I never mentioned it was gonna be a mud bath.'

They laughed as the elegant Kumar threaded his way

across the potholed muddy ground, side-stepping and hesitant. The hem of his beautiful coat was already covered with white splashes of chalk and he drew it up to avoid a really slithery area as he reached the duckboards set down around the catering van.

'Do you have any extra boots?' he demanded.

Mike shook his head and apologized. 'I regret to say they're all allocated to the officers. I suggest you sit in your car, Mr Kumar – nothing will be happening for a while, as we're waiting for your client.'

Kumar asked for a black coffee and brown toast. He then did a tripping dance back to his car with his breakfast balanced on a paper plate. By now the back of his coat was covered in stains as well.

'Well, that's him out of the way,' Barolli said and then he looked up.

'That's not ours, is it?'

Mike and Anna followed his gaze skywards. A helicopter was making a slow circuit around the perimeter of the pit.

'It's not fucking press, is it?' Mike said angrily.

'Can't see, but it's moving off.'

'Can we check with air traffic control if there's clearance? If it's press it'll be a bloody pain in the arse.'

'I don't think you need permission to fly at certain heights, but it's moved well off now.'

Their attention was then drawn to the black-out armoured wagon surrounded by police motorcyclists. It was held at the cordon and they saw an officer gesturing for it to drive on towards the coaches. Behind this was an armed response vehicle, with two armed officers on board. Oates would be handcuffed at all times and the armed guards would be close at hand.

Oates looked clean and well in a police-issue grey track-suit. He had asked to have a shower and for clean clothing before leaving the station on what he referred to as his big day out. He was asked to remain in the wagon and given hot chocolate with, as he requested, four teaspoons of sugar. The marine unit had warned that the climb down into the pit would be very hazardous. They had attached abseiling ropes to deeply buried anchor poles, but it was a steep drop down to the bottom of the quarry. As more ropes, harnessing and descending equipment were laid out it began to look like a mountaineering expedition. The last vehicle to enter the cordon was an open-backed Land Rover with a high-powered rear winch. The winch was to be fitted with a stretcher and body bag, ready to be lowered when required. It was also decided that the winch could be used alongside the abseiling ropes to lower officers down into the quarry and speed up the descent time. The forensic archaeologist had told them that bodies buried in chalk for a year or more would be badly decomposed due to the limestone content, but the bones themselves should remain in good condition. They felt they had covered every possible problem that could occur and Mike didn't want any further delays.

It was almost seven when the operation began. Anna and Mike joined the armed officers in their van and were driven along the dirt road leading to the wooded area. They drove for almost two miles, half the perimeter of the quarry. The officers with Oates radioed back to warn them they were close and to slow down as the prisoner thought he recognized the area where he had usually pulled over. The wood had become much more dense and they could see that the wired fence had a break in it.

'This is it,' Mike told them. He turned to look back as the prison van stopped. Their own vehicle backed up a few yards to halt directly in front of the police wagon, which was now parked between the armed officers and the backup team of six more men.

Anna and Mike got out, and the armed officers followed as they took their positions by the rear doors of the prison van. Oates had now been given an all-in-one protection suit and wellington boots.

'Can you step down, please, Mr Oates.'

Oates, with an officer either side of him, his hands cuffed in front, was helped down the steel steps of the wagon.

'I was gettin' claustrophobia in there,' he said irritably.

Mike apologized and with himself and Anna either side of Oates they all turned towards the ditch and the wood.

'You see that big tree there, one with the black marks up it?'

They did.

'That was from me setting light to the Jeep, so I know I'm in the right place, it's been my marker, but mind the ditch, it's wider than you think.'

It was. Anna jumped over, and Mike helped Oates steady himself before he too jumped to the other side. Oates stood peering at the trees, then he pointed.

'Just a bit further up, there's a gap between two firs.'

They made slow progress as the ground was very uneven, but after a short distance they found themselves on a narrow path covered in thick rotting leaves and branches. There were thick brambles with sharp thorns on either side, making it necessary to walk in single file. The wood was becoming increasingly dense and Anna was growing suspicious, it seemed impossible that Oates could have come this way carrying a body.

'You sure you're on the right track?' Mike asked Oates, who was now leading them.

'Trust me, I can be certain in a few minutes. All right, everyone halt.'

Oates held up his handcuffed arms and everyone behind him stopped. It would have been comical if the reason for their being there hadn't been so dreadful. Oates turned around, squinting upwards, but the branches were so dense they could only see glimpses of the sky.

'No, not yet, forward.'

Mike threw Anna a look and she shrugged.

They continued walking slowly and whether or not Oates knew where he was going they could do nothing but follow in silence. He was like a little sergeant major and obviously enjoying himself as he kept on stopping and looking up, before ordering them to get going once more.

'How much further?' Mike asked.

'Not sure, but I'm on the right track. I'll know for certain in a minute. See, the trees are wider apart now.'

It was true, they were. Yet again he stopped and turned around, looking upwards, but then shook his head. On they went for another fifty yards or so before he did the same thing, stopping and looking upwards. This time he gestured for them to look up.

'See, I'm right, there in that tree, can you see it?'

'What are we looking for?' Mike came close to Oates.

'Can't you see it?'

'I don't know what I'm looking for.' Mike was getting tetchy, but Oates lifted both hands to point.

'It's up in the big branch that curves over your head.'

'Is it a ball?' Anna asked, gazing upwards.

'No, it's a riding hat. See, the strap is caught, the chin guard is hooked over a branch and it's probably full of water by now, but that's my marker.'

'How did you get it up there?' Anna asked.

'Threw it, of course, chucked it up. I mean, you'd never notice it was there if you didn't know about it, right?'

They left two officers to get the hat down, while the rest of them walked on.

Oates still led them and gradually the wood began to get less dense and the ground beneath their feet grew soggy. It looked as if at one time a number of trees had toppled into the quarry, as there were many dangerous roots just waiting to trip someone up and a couple of trunks lay on their sides rotting in the wet clay. There was a shout from behind them and yet again everyone halted. It turned out to be the officers who had retrieved the riding hat, which they now handed to Anna. The velvet was covered in moss, and inside it was full of cones and broken twigs. She gently rubbed the moss away from the protective padding and although it was badly faded she could make out the name Rebekka Jordan written in marker pen. She asked one of the officers to take the helmet back to the forensic tent. Oates was getting impatient. 'Come on, what are we waiting for?'

The path was now wide enough for Anna and Mike to walk either side of Oates and then it opened up onto flat ground.

'Watch your step, this is all crumbling, so take it easy cos you slide and you're going down into the pit,' Oates warned.

Rather ominously they were now at the edge of the wood overlooking the giant quarry. From their position they could see all their vehicles and men waiting across on the other side of the quarry. To their right, about two hundred metres away at the lowest part of the old quarry, they could make out the pond area and the marine unit busily working away searching through the cloudy water.

'Step back, please, Mr Oates.' Mike was concerned he would jump and kill himself, but he laughed.

'You'll have to get a bit closer, pal. Look down and you'll see a ledge, it's about twelve feet down, then there's another one below that, and then it's free fall to the bottom.'

Oates was not at all out of breath and made a gleeful point of telling everyone that he was more athletic and fitter than any of them. He indicated where he had slithered over the sloping side of the quarry.

'I was shit-scared, I admit it, cos it was pitch-black and I didn't know if I was done for, but I was on me back as I slid and I almost dropped her. I had her by the hair and we just came to a stop. Got to remember I had the shovel in me hands as well.'

Mike sighed; this was going to be a more formidable task than anyone had anticipated as the gradient of the slope was not only extremely steep but everything was dangerously wet and slippery. To bring in the winch vehicle or heavy excavating equipment through the woods would be impossible. The uniformed sergeant, who was the search adviser from the POLSA team, suggested to Mike that they drop further abseiling ropes from where they were standing down to the ledge. This would allow one of his men to descend to the ledge and then drop rope ladders and harnessing equipment to the bottom of the quarry. His team, who were still at base, could then go down into the quarry pit using the winch and abseiling lines already set up by the operation's base on the opposite side. They would then be able to cross the floor of the pit and climb up to the ledge indicated by Oates.

Oates told them he had buried Rebekka somewhere along the first ledge, and then he had dug another grave further along and the others were on the second, wider ledge.

'How did you get back up from down there?' Anna asked.

'Clawed up, used the shovel as a chisel – ground was quite hard then, so I could get a good grip. It took me a long time, but there are lots of tree roots to hang onto so that made it easier. I also got another route to show you, one I found later; it's easier, but it's further along and that's where I took the other girls.'

They followed Oates along the crumbling edge of the wood to another section, which was less steep, and with a vast amount of roots. Now there was another ledge visible.

An hour later they were driving back to the base. Everyone was covered in clay and chalk dust, their boots thick and crusted with it. Oates was taken back to the police wagon, where he would be given a hot drink and some food. It was nine-thirty.

Mike was surrounded by his team as he pinpointed on the map the areas where Oates claimed to have buried the bodies. As the search adviser had anticipated, it was felt that it would be less dangerous to go down into the main quarry, cross and climb upwards rather than attempt to go over the ridge, as it would be difficult to get all the equipment over there and through the woods. They already had the ropes in place ready for the men to abseil down. Mike now gave the order for the helicopter to circle the quarry and use its high-definition cameras to look for any noticeable ground disturbances in the areas indicated by Oates.

Barolli was still concerned that the other helicopter, which they'd noticed earlier circling the quarry, wasn't one of theirs. They had been unable to see it whilst walking in the woods, but now Mike watched as it came into view again. It circled the entire perimeter of the quarry and swooped audaciously low over the gaping pit, at which point they could read on its side: *News Flight Aviation*.

'It's the fucking press!' Mike shouted above the noise. He wondered helplessly how they could get the damned thing ordered out of the area.

'When our lads fly in, they'll put the wind up them,' Anna said, glancing over to the parked BMW. Kumar was sitting in the passenger seat staring at them. 'Somebody bloody tipped them off and I wouldn't put it past that slimeball.'

Barolli agreed. Kumar had ventured out from his car twice, to get refreshments, but otherwise nobody was speaking to him. He had been seen on his mobile phone a great deal. Mike asked if Anna would go and talk to him, to inform him that his client had been of assistance. It almost choked him to use the word assistance, as it had been obvious to them all that Oates was thoroughly relishing all the attention.

Kumar lowered his window and then turned in surprise as Anna opened the passenger door and got in beside him. She liked the fact that her mud-covered wellington boots left thick stains on the car's pale blue fitted carpet.

'Mr Oates has been very informative and has given us the locations where he claims he buried his victims. We have also retrieved Rebekka Jordan's riding hat; he used it as a marker to find the way to get rid of his other victims.'

'I would like to talk to him.'

'I'm afraid for security reasons you will have to have armed officers present, so any consultation will not be private. He is being very helpful and we may need to take him down into the quarry, but if you wish to climb down as well I am sure I can arrange for you to do so.'

'I don't think that will be necessary.'

'Can I also ask that you do not use your phone as we have our helicopter coming in to check the area, so mobiles have to be turned off.'

'Really?'

'Yes, really, Mr Kumar. As you may have seen, we have another helicopter circling which belongs to the press. Extraordinary, isn't it? But some idiot must have tipped them off that we were here. Let's just hope there isn't some God-awful accident, but we'll get the local air traffic control onto them as soon as possible.'

'I've heard it circling.'

'Have you now – sad, isn't it? We are here trying to uncover the victims your client claims he murdered and buried. And yet it's possible that before we are able to identify the bodies and inform relatives there could be photographs splashed over every paper.'

Kumar turned away from her.

'You know the names of these women,' Anna went on. 'If it is leaked in any way that we are looking for their remains, then it must be obvious the information came from someone very close to the investigation. I know it's none of my team, so that leaves . . .'

'I don't like what you are implying, Detective Travis.'

'Really? Well I dislike intensely anyone who feels that media attention will be beneficial to their career. You'll get your moments of hype at the trial of your client. Meanwhile, keep off your mobile or I'll have you arrested for obstructing a police investigation, not to mention the more serious offence of perverting the course of justice!'

'Would you please get out of my car?'

'Can't wait.'

She slammed the door so hard the car rocked, then she headed back to where Mike and the search teams were gathered ready to begin the climb down into the quarry pit.

Marked up on maps were crosses indicating where Oates said he had buried the victims. Mike decided that the first body they should attempt to exhume would be Rebekka Jordan's. Although on a high ledge it looked more secure than the other areas pointed out by Oates. The police helicopter observer radioed down to Mike that they couldn't see any unusual disturbances in the area, but there was a lot of moss covering the ledge, which had obviously re-grown over the five years since she was buried. Mike was keen to avoid taking Oates down into the quarry and across onto the ledge, as he knew if anything happened to him there would be serious repercussions. He decided that a team of four plus the archaeologist should go and examine the ledge for any signs of evidence that might pinpoint the exact spot. The archaeologist chose this moment to tell an increasingly agitated Mike that he suffered from vertigo and there was no way he could go near the edge or down into the quarry. He hadn't admitted this before as he hadn't thought the pit would be so deep.

Anna stood by watching as the four search officers began abseiling down into the quarry. The winch vehicle was brought in to lower the equipment the men needed and then they made their way across to the opposite side and attached themselves to the abseiling ropes that had now been put in position. The police helicopter came in low, hovering above the team base, the blades creating a storm of chalk dust. The air grew thick and many officers began reaching for their face masks so Mike radioed to the helicopter to go higher.

It was almost two o'clock by the time two of the team had abseiled down into the quarry to join their colleague who had already descended to the ledge from the wooded side. He had fixed two rope ladders and pulleys to haul up not only all the digging tools but also additional safety equipment to harness themselves to the ledge. It was all frustratingly slow. The quarry walls were breaking up and the ledge, already extremely slippery in some areas from the moss, was crumbling away. The rain started spitting at first, which in some ways helped as it kept the chalk dust down, but it also added to the dangers as the ledge became even more slippery.

Mike banged on the wagon door. The team on the ledge had found nothing unusual to indicate the location of Rebekka's body so he decided he had no option but to ask Oates if he would be willing to assist the search team further. Oates agreed to be winched down into the quarry and then climb up the other side onto the ledge and point out the burial site. Kumar had been present and Oates had been very positive, but the search officers were wary about him joining them on the ledge. Kumar, egged on by Oates, complained about his client's safety if he had to continue to wear handcuffs. Mike and Anna conferred, but they really had no option but to agree as it was very obviously a steep climb up and down from the ledge.

Mike told Oates that the handcuffs would be removed but the armed officers would accompany him. If he pulled any stunts then he would be returned to the police wagon and they would continue without him.

Oates was behaving himself, smiling and showing off. He had to wait for the armed guards to reach the bottom before he was allowed to make his way down via a harness attached to the winch.

Anna and Mike looked down as Oates was winched to the bottom of the quarry and then crossed with the officers to the ledge opposite where a safety harness was attached to him before he climbed up the rope ladder. He was very fit and agile, using his physical strength to pull himself quickly up onto the ledge to join the search team. Mike passed his binoculars to Anna and she was able to see Oates waving his hands around and then guiding the search team further along the ledge. She saw him pointing downwards and nodding.

'Christ, he's even helping them dig – take a look.'

'I can see,' Mike snapped, clearly frustrated at not being a part of the physical activity. He turned up the collar of his protective suit. The rain was still coming down, thankfully not heavily, but it was nevertheless making visibility more difficult, especially for the two cameramen recording the entire operation. Mike was in constant radio contact with the helicopter, explaining that if a grave was uncovered they could have another flight to check over the lower ledge.

Anna lowered the binoculars. Even without them she could see four men digging and one who was hacking at the side of the ledge as Oates kept digging alongside them. Then he was shaking his head and turning this way and that.

'I don't think they've got the right spot ... they're moving further along. This is ridiculous, Mike – he couldn't have spent all that much time digging up there by himself. The chalk and clay is pretty hard, so it had to have been somewhere more shallow.'

Mike turned away, pressing his earpiece.

'They got something.'

The excitement was awful; it was so inappropriate to what was happening. But the team on the ledge gave the thumbs-up, and then they put down their spades and started to use their hands to clear the surface clay and chalk as the forensic officers made their way down into the quarry.

'Bring him back,' Mike ordered.

The first thing the team found were Rebekka's riding boots. As the clay was delicately scraped back they could see they had a very decomposed body, virtually a skeleton. Oates climbed back down and made his way across the quarry to be winched up. As he reached the top he was handcuffed again.

'I found her,' he said, smiling.

He didn't like being taken back to the wagon, and complained once more that he was claustrophobic, but after they cajoled him and arranged for food to be provided, he acquiesced and went inside.

It took a long time for the body to be excavated by the three forensic officers who were now working on the ledge. Eventually the remains were placed into an airtight body bag and lowered down into the pit and then taken across to a metal caged stretcher, which had been attached to the winch. They could not use the helicopter to lift the body as the downdraught would be too dangerous for anyone on the ledge, but by four-thirty the body was finally lifted out of the quarry. They carried the body bag into the forensic tent, where Anna and Mike stood outside watching.

The helicopter went back into action, scanning the lower ledge as the forensic team began to descend for a break. The rain was still coming down and rain capes had been handed out. At least it stopped the dust.

As the black body bag was unzipped Anna moved closer. It was without doubt Rebekka Jordan, even though her long hair, caked in clay, was no longer attached to her skull. The jodhpurs, riding boots and sweater were still in reasonable condition. The jacket was in shreds. Nobody touched her; the bag was zipped up and she was taken to the mortuary van.

'One down, four to go,' Mike said quietly.

The helicopter circled for the fifth time. Suddenly they radioed that they had found an area of possible disturbance near a small very narrow pathway that was invisible from the forensic tent.

'Big enough for us to get through?' demanded Mike.

Back came the distorted voice, warning that it was doubtful, but that it was conceivable a dog could make its way round to the ledge.

Not long after this news, Langton's old brown Rover came splashing through the puddles and parked behind Kumar's BMW. Barolli plodded over with a rain cape and boots. Langton pulled on the boots, but ignored the rain cape. He waved across to Anna before he headed over.

'Mike sent me a text saying that you'd found Rebekka. I've been trying to track down who instigated that bloody press helicopter. I'd place a bet that it's Kumar hoping for front-page news so he can allege Oates won't get a fair trial. Anyway, air traffic control is onto it now.'

'Yeah, I'd put my money on it being him too,' she said, pulling her hood up as they made their way over to the mortuary van. Langton took a long time looking at the remains of the child it had taken five years to find. He asked that they take her straight to the mortuary, as he wanted a post mortem done as soon as possible.

'Maybe wait – when we find the other bodies they'll need to be taken to the mortuary as well,' Anna suggested.

'There's a second van on standby and judging by how long it's taken you to find her I doubt we'll be uncovering the others until . . .' He looked at his wristwatch. 'Christ, it'll be getting dark soon. I've not got this whole circus for another day, you know. Why is it taking so long?'

Annoyed with him, she walked off without answering. If he'd seen what they had been up against all day he'd have bloody known.

Langton, still refusing to put on his rain cape, joined Mike, who was at the catering wagon ordering sandwiches and coffee. They had pulled out a canopy for shelter, but the rainwater was flowing off the sides as if it was coming from a tap, creating an ever-deepening muddy puddle. Anna, who was with Barolli, could see that they were having a heated argument. Barolli pulled at his cape as the rain was dripping down his neck.

Mike came over to report that Langton wanted the burial sites found today, so he could cut the number of officers at the quarry by half and the digging-out could be done the next day. Anna remarked how Langton had already complained to her about the time they were taking. Mike was not happy.

'I'd like to see him bloody climbing up and down those frigging rope ladders; it's already very slippery and the rain's getting worse.'

'I doubt he'll attempt a climb with his knee, but at least he's now driving himself.'

'It's not him I'm worried about, it's the guys doing the hard work on the ledge.'

Anna turned the binoculars onto the search team, who looked like black ants climbing up and onto the lower ledge. Some had already begun digging.

'They got the sniffer dogs up there now,' Mike told her, 'but the handlers didn't like it, they had to go round past the woods and miles on foot to the far side; it's just a small narrow path and crumbling fast.'

There was a lot of action, but no radio feedback that they had found anything. All they could do was stand and wait as the ground all around became like a bog. Anna sat in her car for a while to warm up; her feet were freezing cold. She could see Mike pacing up and down, and Langton and Barolli sharing binoculars as they monitored the action on the ledge. Mike constantly had to fiddle with his earpiece to get reception.

'Mike,' Langton called over, from where he was sheltering under the canopy. Mike sloshed through the puddles towards him.

'What's going on over there?' Langton demanded.

'They're having no luck; it's a big area. One of the dogs got excited but it was a dead animal. I think it's becoming too dangerous up there with the weather, so I'm thinking of calling them back.'

'Get him out there. We'll lose the light soon and it's not going to be easy, arc lamps on or not. Get the pilot to do

one more circle and to stand by with the searchlight; it'll
help the team on the ledge to see what they're doing.'

Although Mike felt Langton was wrong to continue the
operation he said nothing. As the senior officer present it
was now Langton's decision alone whether or not to use
Oates again. Langton finally put on his rain cape and
looked up to the cloud-darkened sky. In the distance they
could see a flash of lightning, which was eventually followed by a low rumble as the sound waves travelled across
the grey sky.

'Looks like that storm is heading our way,' Mike said in
an attempt to dissuade Langton from continuing the
search. But Langton walked off, leaving Mike to signal to
the armed officers, who were sitting in their vehicle waiting for instructions.

'Get him out!' he shouted across to them.

Langton, back under the caterers' canopy, watched as
Oates was led to the edge of the quarry. He saw them
remove his handcuffs and watched him clamber down,
accompanied by the armed guards, to the floor of the
quarry.

Anna, who was by the winch vehicle, turned as
Langton came to stand beside her and Barolli.

'If my knee wasn't shit I'd be down there. Look at the
little prick.'

Oates was shadow-boxing again, dancing around the
two armed guards, fooling around.

'He's bloody loving it, isn't he?'

Anna nodded as they watched Oates climbing up to
join the search teams on the ledge.

'Athletic little sod, though, isn't he?' Langton said.

*

Mike had ordered the huge arc lamps to be moved into position, and their iron tripod stands sank deeply into the clay. They had four lamps altogether, spaced around the quarry, each connected to the portable generator, ready to be switched on.

'Is that ours?' Langton looked up at the helicopter coming into view.

'No it's that News Flight one,' Anna said. 'It's been in and out, hovering around us like a gnat.'

Langton snatched her binoculars, and swore loudly.

'They got a fucking camera; they're filming us. This was supposed to have been bloody sorted.' He moved away, shouting into his mobile phone, heading for the cover of the caterers' canopy to protect his phone from the rain.

Oates could be seen moving amongst the search team. He bent down a couple of times and gestured for them to move further along the ledge. He repeatedly leaned forwards, staring closely at the ground, and then straightened up, looking to his left and right along the ledge.

Anna passed the binoculars to Barolli.

'You know, I think he's stringing us along. He's moving this way and that and it looks as if he doesn't know what he's doing. Maybe he never intended us to find the other victims.'

Mike returned, by now very worried about the encroaching lightning and the safety of everyone on the ledge.

'Might be lucky – Oates could fall off,' Barolli said.

'Christ, don't say that, Paul.'

Anna pointed across the quarry.

'You know what I don't like – that narrow path the dogs were let loose on. I'm just concerned that all this could be Oates setting us up; he's got no handcuffs on, what if he did a runner? He said he knows this area like the back of his hand, maybe that was the way he got to that ledge because it's a long way down from the first ledge and we're supposed to believe he carried the bodies.'

Mike sighed and said that even if Oates attempted to escape, with two armed guards he wouldn't get far.

'I'd like to blow his head off,' Barolli said, stamping his feet.

There was another ominous low roll as the thunder got closer. *India 99* was again hovering above them, shining its Nitesun searchlight in the direction of the ledge, illuminating the area like a floodlit football pitch. The noise was deafening as it echoed around the massive pit and the blades created a downdraught that even with the rain created a thick mist of chalk. The press helicopter was hovering at a slightly higher altitude over the middle of the pit when suddenly it turned and moved off at high speed away from the quarry. At first they thought that air traffic control had been onto them at last, but then the police helicopter radioed to say that they, like the press, had to clear the area and return to base due to the incoming weather.

Langton shouted to Mike as the lightning and thunder got even closer.

'Get the arc lights lit and give it another half-hour.'

'The helicopter's been grounded because the weather is getting worse. It's dangerous out there in the open with the lightning so I think we should call it a day,' Mike protested.

'I make the decisions, Mike, it's not on top of us yet. If they find anything we can dig it out fully tomorrow.'

The electricians started the portable generator, powering up the four huge arc lamps. One was focused towards the ledge and ladders, another shone down onto the base of the quarry and the two others lit up the winch and rope ladders used at the operation base. They could see very clearly Oates and his armed guards preparing to make their way down from the ledge, while the officers still on the ledge continued to dig.

It looked as if it was going to be a disappointing end to a long day when Mike received a radio message that set everyone alight. The dog handlers had been returning through the woods, following the markers, and when they reached the point where Rebekka's riding hat had been recovered one of the dogs had begun to react, barking and pawing at the ground. Mike went over to Langton.

'I think the bastard lied to us – the dog handlers have found a spade and a garden pitchfork hidden in the woods. The dogs have also sniffed out a possible grave.'

There was another, louder rumble of thunder as Langton told Mike and Barolli to go over and secure the area for the search team. Mike would have been happy to seal the site and continue in the morning but he could see no point in arguing with a very determined Langton.

'This is madness,' Anna said to Mike.

'Well why don't you try and make Langton see sense?' Mike said and walked off.

Kumar, eager to find out what was happening, blew his car horn, flashing his lights as he wanted to pull out, but Langton's car was parked across the rear of the BMW.

Oates made his way across the pit between the two armed guards, reaching the winch just as the search team were beginning their descent from the ledge. One of the armed officers was winched out first, followed by Oates, and by the time he had reached the top the storm was directly overhead. The second armed officer had attached his harness and was slowly being pulled up.

Just then the arc lamp that had its beam of light directed at the basin of the quarry began to wobble, as one foot of the heavy iron tripod holding it up had sunk, over-balancing the massive heavy light. Almost in slow motion it toppled forwards, pulling taut the thick cables that linked all the lamps to the generator. The electricians were shouting and yelling for help to steady the arc lamp, when it suddenly lurched downwards and slid over the edge, dragging the other lamps with it. The front lamp stopped briefly, swinging in the air like a moving spotlight, but before anyone could react the cable to the generator gave way and the lamp began to tumble through the air, causing the search team below to scatter. The other lamps began to follow, the sound of the lights popping and blowing hardly noticeable above the thunderstorm. The second armed officer was dangling from the winch as one of the tripod legs smashed into his head, knocking him unconscious.

In the mayhem it took only seconds: Oates, still uncuffed, punched the first armed officer with such force that it instantly broke his jaw and knocked him senseless to the ground. It gave Oates enough time to take the officer's gun, a 9mm Glock with a 17-round magazine. Screaming for everyone to back away from him, he started to pull the trigger repeatedly, and bullets sprayed the air as he began to run while everyone ducked or hit the ground. Barolli, still at base, was in an unmarked patrol car waiting for the search adviser to join him when suddenly he saw Oates was heading straight for him. He threw open the door and clipped Oates, who tumbled forwards then turned and kept on firing as Barolli got out of the car and moved towards him. There was no control – he didn't even aim the gun but just kept on firing round after round, the recoil sending the bullets flying everywhere.

Oates threw himself into Barolli's car, and to everyone's horror he drove forwards, churning up the ground as he pressed his foot flat down on the accelerator and the car hurtled through the barrier and into the lane. No one could give instant pursuit as everyone was boxed in by a row of cars that belonged to the search team who were still down at the bottom of the quarry.

In the shocked few moments that it took to register what had happened, it was Anna who realized that Paul Barolli still lay flat on the ground, his face in the mud. She immediately ran to him and, panic-stricken, turned him over. Blood streamed from his mouth as he gasped for breath and she felt thick sticky blood on her hands, but couldn't tell if he had a head or a chest wound. Langton moved her aside as he cleared the area and another officer hurried across with a medical kit. Someone shouted for a stretcher and eventually Barolli was carried into the armoured police wagon. It seemed horribly incongruous that he was taken to hospital in the same vehicle that had been used to transport Oates safely to the scene.

By the time anyone managed to call the incident in or set off in pursuit from the quarry, Oates had a good head start, and with no police helicopter in the air, due to the weather, he had an even greater chance of a successful escape.

Anna was shaking as she asked how bad it was. Langton reported that Paul had taken bullets to his chest and abdomen, so it wasn't looking good. Then to her anger he turned and began barking out orders for the men to start taking action.

'Start searching the fucking woods.'

Everyone looked at each other in confusion and a young officer spoke out.

'We've only got torches, sir, all the arc lamps are at the bottom of the quarry and—'

'Shut up and get moving.'

Mike was ashen-faced as Langton swore that they'd have Oates back within the hour, as there was no way he'd be able to get far. The important thing was they needed to finish up and concentrate on the reason why they were all there.

'Travis!' he shouted, gesturing for her to get into the coach with the other officers. As they headed out towards the woods she saw through the window Langton having a real go at the electricians, looking as if he was going to punch them. He was obviously angry. But she missed his final show of fury when Kumar, now in a state of shock, shouted at Langton for parking across his BMW so that he was unable to get out. Langton picked him up by the lapels of his cashmere coat and threw him at his car. Yet the solicitor still thought to warn Langton that he had better control himself. It was a mistake; Langton took hold of his lapels a second time and gave him a head butt so hard Kumar's nose cracked.

'Sorry, I slipped in the mud.'

He turned away and Kumar could feel his nose dripping blood. Terrified that he might get another whack, he announced he would report Langton for assault as he hurriedly got into his car, shrinking back as Langton held the door so he couldn't close it.

'Try it, because one, you have no witnesses, and two, if

I find out that you have been tipping off the press I will screw your career and have you up for perverting the course of justice. Now fuck off out of my sight.'

Langton got in beside Mike, who was waiting to drive him over to the woods.

'They picked him up?' he asked, calming himself down.

'Not yet.'

They headed out and Mike felt comforted as Langton rested his arm along the back of his seat.

'Not your fault, son, not your fault. These things happen.'

Chapter Eighteen

The lightning storm passed, and the search team used hand-held battery-powered work lamps and torches to continue combing through the woods late into the night. The archaeologist was brought in to help identify sites where any bodies might be buried. Observing any areas of change in the plant growth and disturbances by foxes or badgers, the dog handlers carefully made probe holes in the ground using large metal rods, allowing the cadaver dogs to get a better scent of what lay beneath the surface. Wherever the dogs gave a strong positive reaction the area was cut and cleared away by the search team, allowing the surface soil to be removed and any remains exposed.

Four victims' bodies were uncovered buried in a semi-circle around some thick-trunked pine trees, close to where Oates had thrown Rebekka Jordan's riding hat to act as a marker. It was too difficult a task to remove the tragic discoveries using torches. The remains were carefully covered with plastic sheets so that the archaeologist and forensic teams could complete the exhumations in daylight. The forensic pathologist, odontologist and scientists would then have the job of identifying not only who each body was but a cause of death. There were five in all, just as Oates had claimed, but only Rebekka Jordan's body had been buried in the quarry itself. Now her remains were already at the mortuary and had been formally identified by her dental records.

The bad news was that there had been no sighting of Oates. The fact that he was using an unmarked police car with a radio on board, allowing him to listen to the police response, did not help matters. The police helicopter was eventually back in the air and roadblocks had been set up in an attempt to stop the vehicle, but there were so many back lanes and other routes Oates could have used that it was impossible to cover them all. It appeared, according to witness accounts, that he had even had the audacity to use the blue roof light to clear the traffic ahead of him. Most worrying of all was that he was still in possession of a loaded firearm. The Area Commander was not happy about the whole incident and decided to give an urgent press and television appeal asking for public assistance in tracing the stolen vehicle and Oates. She warned that Oates was armed and should not under any circumstances be approached.

Eventually, in the early hours of the morning, the stolen police car was found abandoned close to the Hammersmith flyover, but Oates was nowhere to be seen. Evidently he must have dumped it recently as the engine was still very warm. It was some consolation that found left on the passenger seat was the firearm, with five rounds still in the magazine. Although tragic that Barolli had been shot, and was now having emergency surgery, it was a miracle that more officers had not been hit or killed.

*

Oates's basement had been one of the first places the team had checked, but there was no sign of him. Despite all they had accomplished, the escape of Oates was front-page news in all the morning tabloids, with his photograph and blazing headlines that he was 'on the run with a gun'. The Commander had ordered Langton to give a further press conference on breakfast news, impressing on the public that the firearm had been recovered and that if they saw Oates to contact police on either 999 or direct lines they had now set up in the incident room. Langton again warned that Henry Oates was a very dangerous, volatile individual who should not be approached.

Anna had only managed a couple of hours' sleep before she was back at the station. It was already midday and everyone was eager to find out about Barolli's well-being. All they did know was that he was in a life-threatening condition. He had a shoulder wound that was not serious, but the wound to his abdomen was of great concern and he was still undergoing surgery to remove the bullet that had lodged in his spine, having perforated his stomach wall. Until he was out of surgery no one would know if he would survive and even then there was the risk of paralysis from the spinal injury. He had also lost a lot of blood.

Exhausted from having no sleep for over forty hours, Mike Lewis called it quits for the day. Under terrible pressure from the media outrage, Mike was not only very tired, but the fact of Oates's escape and the shooting of Barolli weighed heavily on him. He strongly believed that the whole incident could have been avoided if Langton had stopped the search when he first suggested it.

*

It was not until early evening that the exhumation of the four remaining bodies was finally completed. The post mortems and identification processes were to start the next morning. From Oates's confessions, and his recognizing photos as well as the jewellery, they were sure the bodies were those of Angela Thornton, Kelly Mathews, Mary Suffolk and Alicia Jones. However, this would have to be confirmed by dental records and DNA.

Langton had been a very visible presence all day, overseeing much of the search for Oates, and attempting to give the team stability. In a briefing he chose not to mention how Oates had escaped, but congratulated the team on their successful recovery of the remains of five victims. He concluded by saying that wherever Oates was hiding out, it would only be a short time before he was arrested again. He was unable to give any further news on Barolli, but he would be going to the hospital personally on the way home. Anna asked if she could accompany him and he agreed.

It turned out that Barolli was out of surgery and was being monitored in intensive care. They had a long discussion with the surgeon, who said that the luck of the gods must have been on Barolli's side. The bullet to his shoulder had narrowly missed any arteries; if it had been a fraction closer to his neck it could have been fatal. The injuries to his abdomen had not affected any vital organ, but the bullet, which had perforated his stomach wall, had lodged in tissue within a fraction of his spinal cord, amazingly without causing any lasting damage. He would need to remain in hospital for at least two to three weeks, but he would most likely make a full recovery.

*

Barolli was still very groggy from the anaesthetic and had an oxygen mask to help his breathing. His face had a yellowish pallor unlike his usual ruddy hue. He didn't appear to be aware of any visitors; his eyes remained closed.

'Have his family been contacted?' Anna asked.

'Yes, they were down in Wales and local CID brought them up overnight,' Langton said. 'I told the detective to book them in at a nearby hotel and we'd foot the bill. Nurse said they sat with him for hours and left just before we got here.'

Langton leaned over the bed and gently touched Barolli's hand.

'Have you back with us in no time, son.'

Barolli gave no reaction. Langton straightened up, knowing of old just how long it could take; the trauma of being seriously wounded was not only physically but mentally very hard to get over.

Langton announced he was eager to get home and sleep and would visit Barolli's parents at the hotel in the morning.

'How's your knee holding up?' Anna asked as she bleeped open her Mini in the hospital car park.

'I'm fine, be a lot better when we pick that bastard up.'

She watched him in her rear-view mirror as he got into his Rover, noticing how he winced as he bent to get into the driving seat. Both cars were covered in chalk dust and clay clung to their wheels and bumpers; mud had sprayed over the doors and even the windows. Anna drove out after Langton, and decided that she'd go straight to a twenty-four-hour car wash and valet service in Waterloo.

*

Sitting in the garage's small waiting area, Anna read newspapers left on a small table for the customers. She yawned and tossed aside one paper after another. It took three quarters of an hour for her Mini to be returned polished and buffed, its interior hoovered and wiped down. By this time it was after nine and she picked up a takeaway Chinese, stopped at an off-licence and bought a bottle of wine.

The Chinese noodles were soggy, so she ate little, but drank two large glasses of wine. After taking a shower and blow-drying her hair, she watched the TV news as it covered the escape and the ongoing search for Henry Oates. Aerial shots of the quarry appeared, showing the massive search the Met had organized, and although the media were not yet privy to how many bodies had been uncovered or their identities, it was stated that Henry Oates was a serial killer on the run. They repeated clips of the news conference, stressing that an officer remained on the critical list after being shot by Henry Oates. Anna, feeling depressed, couldn't be bothered to watch any more so she turned off the TV by remote, switched off her bedside light and snuggled down under her duvet.

In the darkness she let her mind wander over the events of the case, recalling that Eileen Oates had said that her husband had attempted to join the Army, but had been kicked out. She wondered if he'd had enough time to learn how to use a gun. He had certainly fired off enough rounds, but she doubted he had intended to shoot Barolli. But then again, maybe he had.

Anna didn't give a moment's notice to how lacking in emotion she was. Of course she felt bad for Barolli; everyone did. There was also the depression they all felt at the escape, which would, she knew, have repercussions within the team. It was normal procedure for the Met's Department of Professional Standards to investigate the type of incident that had occurred, and she had no doubt the Independent Police Complaints Commission would be all over it as well. Every single moment of the entire operation would eventually come under scrutiny and be investigated. She was satisfied that nothing she had done could be held against her as unprofessional. On the contrary, if her part in the enquiry was to be reviewed she was satisfied she had handled herself with integrity at all times. She thought that Mike would probably be the scapegoat – someone had to take the blame, and not only within the Met. The public would want to know how a serial killer like Oates could have managed to not only get away but also with a police officer's gun. One by one she went through the incidents that had culminated in Oates's escape.

The relentless storm followed by the crashing down of the arc lamps, the mayhem and confusion that had ensued, Kumar blowing his car horn, the howling of the sniffer dogs and the sudden discovery that there were bodies in the woods. All of it combined together, followed by a brief few seconds of such chaos that Oates had used the opportunity to make a run for it. Barolli, although attempting to stop Oates, had left the patrol car with the keys in the ignition, and it was parked literally within yards of the top of the quarry, ready to head for the woods.

Anna yawned again and curled up on her side, confident that no blame could be cast in her direction. The selfish clinical appraisal made her realize how different she had become. The protective shield was in place: her only concern was for her own career position. The Anna who had been unable to hide her distress at a victim's injuries earlier in her career was buried deep. Her feelings were now totally under control, her vulnerability would be difficult to detect. She had been consumed by the loss of her beloved fiancé Ken Hudson, she had suffered such lacerating pain that she was determined to never allow the possibility of it ever happening again.

The press were surrounding the station waiting for news, so Anna muttered 'No comment' as she hurried inside, to where Mike was waiting for everyone to gather. He looked terrible; his eyes were red-rimmed as if he hadn't slept. Anna, coffee in hand, looked refreshed by contrast and was wearing one of her smarter black suits with a ruffled white shirt beneath it. As she had washed her hair the previous night she wore it loose and had even put on some make-up.

Mike told everyone that Barolli was on the road to recovery and was very fortunate that the two bullets had missed vital organs.

'Not hit his head then?' someone joked.

Mike smiled and suggested they have a whip-round to send him some flowers and then it was on to business.

They were waiting for the post mortem report on Rebekka Jordan and the four other bodies that had been recovered. The pathologist was finishing off the examination of Rebekka's body and would start on the other victims later that morning but to complete all the post mortems would take at least two days and he would need another week to write up his report.

*

Top priority was the hunt for Oates. Officers had been put on surveillance outside Oates's squat in case he turned up. Mike went through the possible areas Oates might run to, commenting that it was possible he'd try and contact his wife in Scotland.

'What we know is he has no money so he's got to steal, burgle some place, and with his face plastered over every newspaper we'll maybe get lucky and someone will recognize him. To date we have had twenty sightings, believe it or not, but none have proved valid, so it is basically a case of following every lead we get.'

Joan signalled to Mike that there was a call for him.

'Who is it?'

'Area Commander.'

'I'll take it in my office. Anna, you want to take over for a minute?'

Mike hurried into his office as Anna stood up.

'He's very used to living off the streets, but I think the locations we should check are those of the two known associates, Ira Zacks and his other boxing pal, Timmy Bradford. They appear to be the only two friends he has had any contact with in the last five to six years. I doubt he would get much help from his ex-wife – he would also have to travel some distance to get to her with no money for train or coach. He could thumb a lift, but again, as Mike says, his photograph is plastered everywhere and there's been a lot of TV coverage. He's also desperate, so as we have surveillance on his basement, double-check with the neighbours as he could be holding them hostage.'

Anna moved to the board to indicate the address of Ira's flat close to Hammersmith Bridge. 'We know the bird has already flown from there along with his girlfriend, so that would mean it's empty. He maybe could have broken in. They found the police car Oates stole abandoned in Hammersmith by the flyover. Sad as it may seem, we need to check on the Jordans and Markhams; again this is all down to where we know he knows. The other location is Kingston, the housing estate were Timmy Bradford lives with his mother. There are also numerous empty flats there that are being done up to be sold. Double-check the health club he used, any place we know Oates frequented.'

Anna hesitated and crossed to the large section of the board with the quarry pictures.

'He knows this area, quote, like the back of my hand – who knows, he might return there. There's also the gypsy camp – I don't know whether or not they'd allow him to hide out, but he's doing just that, he is hiding out. Oates can't risk going out amongst the public so he will probably move about at night. We need reports of any house break-ins in London. Prioritize the night ones, particularly where food, cash or clothing is stolen. He worked for Andrew Markham, so check the Cobham area as well. There are barns and outhouses, stables, lot of places to lie low. Mrs Markham had a greenhouse. We get as much manpower as we can to cover the known possibilities.'

Mike had been given clearance for a huge team of officers to coordinate and carry out the searches. Anna went into his office to ask if he wanted to join up with any of the crews, but he shook his head. Orchestrating the search would be very much down to her. He himself had been kept busy with Scotland Yard and the press office, not to mention that the incident room was being virtually deluged with potential sightings. Hundreds of phone calls were coming in, most from idiots, but every one of them had to be investigated and cleared. Four more clerical workers had been brought in to handle the calls and record the details of the alleged sightings on the HOLMES computers. Everyone was working flat out, but they were beginning to flag as one possible sighting after another proved unproductive.

Anna went through the list of all the locations that had been checked without any success. They had even had teams of officers from the Home Counties police forces searching woodland, farm buildings and outhouses outside London but no visible trace of Oates had been found.

Mike shook his head with frustration. He was under huge pressure, having to fend off not only the press but also the Area Commander. 'She's asked me to give her a detailed review of the operation, so obviously it's a total failure,' he told Anna.

'It wasn't a failure. For God's sake, we uncovered five victims and under horrendous circumstances. Don't let them wear you down, Mike, you have to speak up for yourself.'

He sighed and then put his head in his hands.

'Where the bloody hell is he?'

'He'll surface, he has to, and there is no way he can get far. Pump out more press on him, they've been screwing it up for us at the quarry. Turn it around on them.'

Mike looked up, frowning.

'That bloody press helicopter was screwing it up, make them know it,' Anna insisted. 'Put a portion of the blame on them, we want as much coverage as is possible. Oates's ego will blow up in his face.'

Mike sat back.

'Yeah. I guess I'm just tired out.'

'Then go home and get some sleep. I'll stay on here until late and you'll feel a whole lot better in the morning.'

'How come you look so good?' he asked, smiling.

'I had a full night's sleep.'

The calls were like persistent gnats all night, buzzing and often anonymous, but they kept on coming. It was intensely frustrating to have so many leads and all of them false. Every call had to be recorded and logged and Anna, along with Joan, Barbara and the extra clerical workers, were kept busy until at ten o'clock Anna said the night staff could take over. Joan had a large bunch of flowers she was going to deliver to Barolli with a card signed by all the team close to the enquiry.

'You'd better get them over there, Joan, they're wilting.'

Anna was packing up ready to leave when Langton arrived.

'I was just going home.'

'Come and have a drink with me.'

She didn't really feel like going to a pub, but he gestured to Mike's office and tapped his coat pocket.

Langton opened the drawers until he found a glass and poured a heavy measure of Scotch into it.

'Here you go. I'll use the bottle.'

'I can get a glass from the canteen.'

'It's closed.'

She looked at the Scotch and sipped; it hit the back of her throat like fire.

'My God. I need some water in this.'

She opened a bottle of water left on Mike's desk.

'I've been to the mortuary – the Rebekka Jordan report will be in tomorrow morning. You got a cigarette?'

371

'Yes I do actually; hang on, I'll get them.'

Anna returned to the incident room and picked up her briefcase. The phones were still ringing nonstop.

Langton was drinking from the bottle of Scotch as she took out the packet of Silk Cut and tossed it onto the desk. He lit up and then opened the office window. She also took one, and he leaned forwards to light it.

'I looked in on the other victims. They're mostly skeletons and a couple may have had animals at them. All lined up and laid out, just makes your heart sink to think that that piece of shit is still out there.'

She took another sip of her watered-down Scotch. They were using a dirty half-filled coffee beaker as an ashtray.

'What did the pathologist say about Rebekka?'

'Jawbone broken and fractures to the skull, all occurred before death and consistent with being punched repeatedly, so looks like Oates was telling the truth when he said he hit her. Only problem is, because her body was so badly decomposed he can't give a definitive cause of death or say if he sexually assaulted her.'

'So he will probably offer a plea of manslaughter, saying he didn't mean to kill her, just shut her up?'

'He won't get away with that, not with the similar evidence on the girls he's admitted raping and murdering so far.'

'Well that's something it's better they don't know.'

'The parents?'

'Of course.'

'Like the Flynns they want to see their daughter,' Langton groaned. 'I've asked if they can do something with the remains. If I was them I wouldn't, it's no longer their daughter, she's long gone apart from that hair; lovely hair. It's been cleaned.'

He took a long gulp of Scotch out of the bottle, and then put it down on the desk.

'Listen, Mike is going to be torn to shreds. I've spoken with the Commander, tried to make it less of a fuck-up, but it's hard, and no matter what excuses I make about the fucking arc lights blowing and toppling, somebody still has to be the fall guy. Then we've got fucking Barolli leaving the keys in the ignition of the unmarked car, and the biggest screw-up is that Oates had his handcuffs removed and took an armed officer's gun.'

'But you gave the order for that.'

His head snapped up.

'What?'

'You gave the clearance for the cuffs to be removed the second time. Oates was back in the wagon, Mike told you he wanted to call it a day but you overruled him. You told him to get Oates out again.'

Langton stubbed out his cigarette. She could see his tight-lipped anger.

'Didn't you tell the Commander there was no way he could have climbed into the pit and up the other side with the cuffs on? We succeeded in recovering Rebekka Jordan's remains because of him being up on the ledge. If we hadn't used Oates we might never have found her.'

Langton flipped the packet of cigarettes up and down, saying nothing. It was clear he had tried to offload the blame onto Mike and, incensed by what he'd done, she decided to stand up to him.

'You were there, the events that occurred to enable Oates to escape were not down to Mike's incompetence, but . . .'

'As you so tartly said, Travis, I was there, I am aware of exactly what happened.'

'Paul Barolli tried to stop Oates by using the car door, and then got out to try and rugby-tackle an armed man and ended up getting shot for his troubles. It may have slipped your mind but the cadaver dogs had found something and YOU told Paul, NOT Mike, to go over to the woods and that was why he was in the car!'

'I know that, I bloody know that.'

'Then you have to know that the blame cannot be pinned on anyone in particular.'

'The top brass don't see it as an act of God, so someone's got to take the blame.'

'Why? You were there, I was there . . .'

'I have no intention of taking the flak for this, Travis, you hear me? I haven't come this far to get rubbed out just when I am about to be recommended for . . .'

'Another promotion board, is it! You've missed out on Commander how many times now?'

'Yes it fucking is, and this case was in Mike Lewis's hands.'

'Not entirely. We did have Hedges, but you pissed him off so much he wasn't interested. Since Rebekka Jordan's name came into it you've been on Mike's back so—'

He interrupted. 'You want to step forwards? You're the DCI on the Rebekka Jordan enquiry, you want to put yourself forwards? Do you? NO, bet your sweet arse you don't want to. The reason I'm here tonight is so we can discuss—'

She went back at him angrily. 'You aren't discussing it. You're telling me that Mike is going to be the scapegoat because somebody has to be held responsible for Oates's escape. Too damned right I am not holding up my hand, but I will support Mike in this.'

'Let me finish, for Chrissake! What I wanted to discuss

with you was keeping a bloody united front, everybody singing off the same hymn sheet so that there's no one person who'll be singled out.'

She leaned back in her chair, knowing she had pushed the right button. Langton was basically making sure that he, as the most senior officer at the quarry, was not going to take the flak for the shit that had already hit the fan, and he wanted to find some way of sweeping the whole mess under the table.

Langton spread his hands out and, calming down, said they should now go over all the details that led up to Oates being released from his handcuffs not once but twice.

'It seems to me the main issue is whether the decision was right to get Oates out the second time, especially with the bad weather conditions and related safety issues,' Anna suggested to Langton.

'The weather changed for the worse after the decision was made . . .'

'Yes but you made it, not Mike,' Anna reminded Langton.

'I know, but none of you disagreed, and how could we have guessed what would happen next?'

'Well, there's a lot of the day's events on video so it might be worth going over it . . .'

'Well I hope the cameras were off when I head-butted Kumar.'

'You did what?' She was astonished.

'I slipped in the mud,' he said, smiling.

'You know, your car was parked right across his and he couldn't back out; he added to the chaos around Oates because he kept hooting his car horn. I wish I'd seen it.'

'Yeah, well, that's another point to make, but another is

the intrusion of the press helicopter. I want whoever authorized that to give us the person tipping them off about the entire operation. We can lean on them as part of the screw-up.'

'I already checked out the helicopter's logo. News Flight Aviation – they're contracted by independents or do film for themselves and sell the footage on. Whoever it was must be getting a big backhander from the aerial pictures sold to the press, never mind the TV. We all suspect that Kumar is leaking the information – proving it is a different matter.'

Langton nodded and then said they should get on with their so-called hymn sheet. He wanted all those involved to be aware that there could be a major enquiry, so they should be primed up and ready.

They sat together, smoking and drinking, making notes, and only when he was satisfied did he call it quits, saying that she could go home.

'Don't you have one to go to?' she joked.

He nodded to the bottle.

'Last thing I need is to be picked up over the limit.'

She left him in Mike's office, wondering if, like the old days, he was going to do an all-nighter. She was, as ever, impressed with his stamina – he was smartly dressed as always, albeit with a six o'clock shadow, but she wouldn't put it past him to have his shaving equipment in his brief-case.

Anna got into her car and could see that Langton's Rover was still filthy, unlike her own Mini. She tried to calculate when Langton had taken a break. He had been at the site when the bodies were uncovered, then at Scotland Yard over Oates's escape, and had then gone back to the quarry, leaving only at dawn. He had been at the hospital with her to see Barolli, and she knew he had spent time at the mortuary with the pathologist. She couldn't imagine when and if he had slept at all. She was used to him being a night owl when she had worked alongside him; they had all joked about his laundry and dry-cleaning bags stacked in his office.

She tried not to think about him. She hoped that the promotion he had hinted at was on the cards this time round, that it might be the reason he was putting so much time in, desperate to get that next rank, plus there was a big difference between a chief super's and a commander's pension. Deep down, Anna also believed that the Langtons of the force were now few and far between. He wasn't quite old school like her father, he was the next generation, but as he was coming up for retirement age she suspected that he did not want a blemish on his hard-fought-for career. She knew of a few incidents that were certainly more than blemishes, but that was yet again part of Langton's character. He did bend the rules; he did unleash his fury and was unafraid to have a go at the Kumars of this world. There was no other officer she had worked alongside that had gained the respect of everyone who had worked with him.

Even though she didn't want to be, Anna was still thinking about Langton when she let herself into her flat. His reaction when she had challenged him over making Mike Lewis the scapegoat interested her. He had denied it, but she still wondered if he would have been prepared to let Mike take the blame for the present debacle. He had been very fast to ask her if she wanted to step forwards and hold her hand up, and she had been equally fast to refuse. The truth was that Langton was the senior officer, and Mike, she knew, had been relieved he had shown up. By the time she was ready for bed, Langton was still occupying her thoughts. As well as everyone thought they knew him, and she believed that she maybe knew him better than anyone else, there was a part of Langton that was as unreachable as it was unpredictable.

Langton had rolled his coat into a pillow and was lying on Mike Lewis's office floor. He was always able to take cat-naps, often for no more than twenty minutes or so, and it always refreshed him, but tonight he felt dog-tired. He was fascinated by Travis, and he also realized just how much she had grown, and not necessarily apart from him, as he was certain their past would always be a strong link between them. But again he had seen that stronger force within her. She was a fighter, that he had always known, but now there was something else beneath it, ruthlessness and a quiet yet determined backlash against him. In a way he was almost seeing a mirror image of himself when he was around the same age.

He sighed, trying to make himself more comfortable, punching at the rolled-up coat beneath his head. He knew what had taken its toll on his emotions, and he had attempted to make Anna aware of what it meant not to grieve for a loved one. She hadn't, to his knowledge, ever let go, and it concerned him because he was certain that fury lurked beneath her controlled exterior. He himself had lost it completely when he had almost died after being attacked, and he had made sure the culprit who had tried to kill him paid the ultimate price. Anna, he suspected, knew what he had done, but it remained a subject they never spoke of. Besides, there was no way she could take revenge and justify the circumstances as he had done. The man she had hoped to marry had been brutally murdered and his killer would spend the rest of his life in prison with no hope of release. Langton suspected that there had been no release for Anna Travis, but that she had buried her fury, and he truthfully didn't know if or how it would manifest itself. Finally he wore himself out thinking about it and fell into a deep sleep.

Chapter Nineteen

Mike Lewis was one of the first to arrive in the incident room, to find that a cleaner was just clearing his office, the window wide open. In her cart were the empty glass and bottle of Scotch and the disgusting beaker filled with cigarette stubs. Mike could still smell cigarette smoke; he guessed instinctively that Langton had been using his office. Fifteen minutes later he knew for certain because he found him in the canteen eating breakfast.

'Good morning,' Mike said pleasantly.

'Glad you think it's good,' Langton grumbled. 'Bring me another coffee, would you?'

He looked as if he needed a shave and his tie was loose around his unbuttoned collar.

As Langton's breakfast tray was cleared Mike sat opposite him and got the singing-off-the-same-hymn-sheet discussion. Mike listened and agreed, but he was nevertheless nervous. He asked if there was going to be an inquisition and Langton laughed.

'Too bloody right – don't know about inquisition, but we're going to have the top brass breathing all over us, so better to be prepared and show a united front.'

Mike said he would get onto it straight away, and took

the remainder of his coffee with him, leaving a surly-look-ing Langton still in the canteen.

Anna was at her desk when Mike told her that Langton was up in the canteen. She was surprised; it wasn't even eight-thirty yet.

'I think he was in my office, stinks of cigarettes, and by the look of him he was there all night.'

'Old habits die hard,' she said, smiling.

'Yeah, maybe they do, but it's my office.'

'You see how many calls came in last night?' she asked.

Mike nodded, but none had given them any infor-mation they could use, most of them were time-wasters, but any remotely likely ones had to be checked out. Henry Oates had been 'seen' in Waitrose, at a petrol station, and at a variety of Tube stations, and every location had to be visited, enquiries made and any CCTV viewed.

Mike said he would give a briefing to the team as soon as everyone was gathered.

'Make sure we're all singing off the same hymn sheet?' Anna laughed, but Mike wasn't amused – it just confirmed that Langton had already discussed it with her previously.

Langton was having a shave in the Gents. He splashed cold water over his face and dabbed it dry with a rather seedy grey towel. His opened briefcase revealed some cologne and a laundered tie; he always kept a spare one in case he spilt food down himself. By the time he walked into the incident room, Mike was winding down his briefing.

'Good morning, everyone,' Langton bellowed as he banged open the double doors, tossed his briefcase onto Barbara's desk and clapped his hands, making his way to join Mike at the front.

'Right, let's make this a day to remember. He's out there somewhere and I want him tracked down.'

Langton pointed to the slew of calls and possible sightings and turned back to the expectant faces.

'I don't believe Oates is out and about living off the land. I think he is hiding and it's either in a fucking squat in some derelict house or he's homed in on some poor bastard. Now, what have we got? Who did he know? Who would be mad enough to let him lie low? We know he's got no money, he escaped wearing a police-issue grey tracksuit, and although he left his rain protective suit in the stolen police car, he would have still been wearing the boots we so helpfully provided. He'll want a change of clothes, new footwear – does he steal them? What reports have we got in from clothes shops that he may have been seen in, or thefts from clothes lines, and remember we've got petrol stations selling everything from underwear to Reeboks. What have we got?'

He took a look at the likeliest possible sightings, dismissed them bullishly and then gestured to Travis.

'These two known associates, what about them?'

Anna went to the board to read the reports from officers who had visited both addresses. Ira Zacks' elegant flat had been investigated. The information they now had on Zacks was that he had been picked up for drug dealing and was being held at Brixton Police Station. The flat was empty and there was no sign of a break-in or that anyone had been living there recently. Mr and Mrs Murphy, who lived opposite the squat in Hackney, had also been visited but they had not seen Oates. The three houses earmarked for demolition remained under surveillance in case Oates attempted to return to his basement flat. There had been no sightings of him at his old sports centre. Lastly, they had a report from the address where Timmy Bradford was living with his mother. The officers had not spoken to Bradford's mother, but Timmy had said he hadn't seen Oates and promised that should he make contact he would alert the police. Also up on the board was the number for DCI McBride in Glasgow, who had reported back that Oates had not attempted to seek help from his ex-wife. This was easily confirmed as Eileen was now under police protection, having given evidence against her so-called boyfriend.

Langton sighed as the room went quiet.

'Well we appear to be up fucking shit creek, don't we?'

Anna was still at the board. She turned.

'Can I just ask if the officers who went to Timmy Bradford's place searched it?'

A young DC stepped forwards to say that Bradford had been very civil, and had said that his mother was in the bath, that it was inconvenient, but if they wanted to come back they were welcome to take a look around.

'Did you?'

'Yes, ma'am, we went back about half an hour later and he let us in, we looked over the flat and left.'

'Did you look in the bedroom cupboards, under the beds?'

'We had a good look round, yes.'

'What about his mother, Mrs Douglas – did you speak to her?'

'No, ma'am, he said she had just gone to the corner shop.'

'How did Mr Bradford seem to you?'

'Like I said, ma'am, he was very civil and suggested if we wanted to wait we could.'

'So he didn't seem nervous or agitated in any way?'

'No, ma'am.'

Anna returned to her desk, tapping a pencil up and down as phones carried on ringing. Langton came over.

'Do you have a charger I can use? Battery's low.'

Anna opened her desk, where she kept various chargers, and he rooted through them, bending close to her.

'This is a total fuck-up,' he muttered.

She leaned closer to him.

'What's that cologne you've got on?'

'Don't ask me, Christmas present from Kitty. I just chuck 'em into my briefcase – you like it?'

The ground felt as if it was opening up beneath her. She knew exactly what it was: 'Happy' by Clinique – it was the same one that Ken Hudson had used.

'What is it?' Langton could see she had turned pale and had started shaking. 'Christ, it's not that bad, is it?'

'Excuse me.'

Anna had to get out of the room. She was finding it hard to catch her breath and her head felt as if it would explode. Langton watched her go and Mike had noticed her as well.

'What's up?'

Langton shrugged as he fixed the charger to his mobile, plugged it in and sat at her desk. On a notepad he could see she had scribbled 'mother' then underlined it twice.

Anna clung onto the washbasin rim, taking short sharp gasps of breath, not wanting to faint. It had hit her so hard and so unexpectedly. Langton wearing the same cologne was unbelievable, and would be funny if it didn't rip her heart in two.

'Calm down, calm down,' she said to herself like a

mantra, but she was too dizzy to release her hold of the washbasin. Her stomach lurched, and she almost bounced off the walls as she stumbled into the lavatory, where she was violently sick. Now her body felt cold, but at least she had stopped shaking and was eventually able to stand upright.

It was another ten minutes before she was capable of washing her face and hands and another few moments before she managed to walk out and back into the corridor.

Langton was leaning against the wall, waiting.

'You okay?'

'Yes, must have been the Chinese I ate last night.'

'You sure?'

'Yes.'

'You mean you went off and got a takeaway after we finished up here?'

'YES!'

He gestured for her to calm down and they walked along the corridor together.

'You've written the word "mother" on your notepad.'

'Yes.'

'You going to tell me why or do you want me to guess?'

She stopped and folded her arms.

'I met Mrs Douglas, Timmy Bradford's mother. She's neat and tidy and very house-proud. They have the first visit to her flat recorded at eleven-thirty in the morning, and it doesn't ring true to me that she would be having a bath at that time. I would think she's got her twinset and pearls on by seven, fully dressed and dusting.'

Langton pursed his lips.

'Does Oates know the flat? Has he been there before?'

'Yes, though Bradford said he'd never actually let him

in, but he's already shown himself to be a liar when it comes to Oates, so he could be helping him.'

Langton took only a brief moment before he decided that another visit would be on the cards. He also added that they would take it very carefully, first question neighbours, no uniforms and no patrol cars on show.

'They know you, right? The mother and son?'

'Yes.'

'Good, so you'll be able to identify Bradford. Now tell me about the time you were there.'

Anna repeated in detail her visit to Timmy Bradford's and his recollections of his boxing days with Oates, how he had lied to her about seeing Oates just the once and only admitted going to the chalk quarry with him when he was brought into the station for questioning. She added that his mother appeared to be a nice woman.

Back in the incident room they pinned up maps of the Kingsnympton estate, along with enlarged photographs on which the empty boarded-up flats could be clearly seen. It was a very well-maintained estate, but a very large one, with hundreds of flats. They also scrutinized a small row of shops frequented by the residents of the estate. There was an off-licence, a hair salon, a closed-down minimarket, a launderette and a newsagent's.

Langton suggested they start with a few discreet enquiries before upping the ante and bringing in the SO19 firearms arrest team. He stressed they were just working on a theory, and had no proof yet that Oates was hiding out at Bradford's, so it was imperative they play a very covert hand.

'Why take it softly-softly?' Mike asked.

'Because if I call in SO19 now the top brass will be all over this after what happened at the quarry. If Oates isn't there and the firearms go in throwing thunder flashes and waving guns about we'll look like a right bunch of pricks for not doing our homework, so I want some surveillance on the premises first.'

'But they searched the flat,' Mike pointed out.

'Never saw the mother, though. Oates could have been in the bathroom with her, keeping her quiet or tied up.'

'Timmy wouldn't risk his mother's life to grass on Oates under those circumstances,' Anna said, looking at them both.

By twelve o'clock Anna, with two members of the surveillance team, was in position in a high-tech police observation vehicle, which had been disguised to look like a painter and decorator's van. They were able to park unnoticed inside the estate and had a clear view of the balcony and door of Bradford's mother's flat. Langton had decided that as Anna knew Timmy Bradford, and vice versa, it was best she was out of sight in case he was assisting Oates and recognized her. If Timmy or Oates came out of the flat she was to notify Langton over the radio. After about twenty minutes' observation she reported that there appeared to be some movement inside, but owing to the net curtains she could not make out who it was.

Langton, Mike and Barbara were parked up nearby and out of sight in an unmarked police car.

'Quite eerie, isn't it?' Barbara said.

'What's eerie about an undercover observation in broad daylight?' Mike asked.

387

'Nothing. It's just eerie that the last person to drive this car was Oates after he shot Barolli,' Barbara replied as Anna's voice came over the radio.

'Shut up, Barbara, I can't hear what Anna is saying,' Langton said.

Travis informed Langton that there was movement in the flat and asked for further instructions.

'If Bradford comes out, one of the surveillance officers will follow him on foot and keep in radio contact. If Oates comes out I've got plain clothes armed officers ready to make the arrest,' Langton told her, making it clear he was leaving nothing to chance this time.

Leaving Barbara in the car, Mike headed for the off-licence and Langton for the newsagent's. Langton waited until the proprietor had served a customer before showing his ID and asking him to close the shop whilst he spoke to him. Nervously, the proprietor started to protest that he never sold cigarettes to underage kids, but Langton put his mind at ease fast.

'This is not connected to your sales unless you want it to be. I need to ask you a few questions about someone who may use your shop, so I'd like your assistance.'

Langton was first to return to the waiting Barbara. He got into the back seat and immediately radioed through to Anna.

'Okay, the newsagent said they get the *Daily Mail* delivered every day. Yesterday Timmy Bradford came in and got an *Evening Standard*, this morning he came back and bought the *Daily Mirror* and the *Sun*, plus two pints of milk, which he'd never done before. He also bought a sliced loaf, four packets of biscuits and six cans of Red Bull.'

'The mother likes biscuits; she offered some to me,' Anna replied, wondering what was so unusual.

Langton suggested that the extra newspapers could be of interest because Timmy might be following the story of his old friend's escape, while the extra milk and biscuits could mean they had a visitor.

Mike appeared by the open passenger window. 'Okay, Timmy Bradford is not a regular, but last night he came in and bought a six pack of beer, plus two bottles of cider.'

Langton rubbed his chin.

'Well, not exactly throwing a party, are they, but that combined with Red Bull means somebody's thirsty or needs to stay awake. Okay, round two, we need to speak with the neighbours, find out if they've noticed anything unusual.'

'We can't go anywhere near them – Oates knows us both. If he's in there and sees us from the window God knows what he might do,' Mike warned him.

'I have considered that, so Barbara here is going to canvas for the Green Party. Newsagent said they visit the estate regularly so they'll be used to knocks on the door,' Langton said as he opened a plastic bag and handed Barbara some Green Party leaflets and stickers that he had got from the newsagent's counter.

'I thought I was just here to be the driver?' Barbara replied nervously.

'I think this is all a bit Miss Marple, for Chrissake,' Mike said.

'He's killed seven women, Mike, he's a madman. Like you just said, God knows what he could do if he saw someone he recognized as police.'

'Well you said it, he's a madman, and I just think this approach is wasting time. What if he's not in there?'

'What if he is?'

'Right, and what if he is there and snatches Barbara round the fucking throat and drags her inside?'

Barbara looked at Langton. Mike had a point and she knew it.

Langton radioed Anna to let her know what the plan was, but it was a while before Anna saw Barbara come into view and walk up the communal stairs and then along the balcony. She went to the next-door neighbours' flat and rang the bell a few times but got no reply, then moved on to the target flat and rang the bell, stepping back as she waited. No response. She rang again, still no response. She was starting to move away when the door opened a fraction. She was very good; Anna could see her smiling and talking and showing the leaflets, but the door was only open about six inches and she couldn't make out who Barbara was talking to. Still smiling, Barbara gestured to the neighbouring flat, at which point the door closed. During all of this Langton was constantly on the radio to Anna, asking what was happening.

Langton then received a call from the station telling him that a wiretap on Bradford's home telephone had been approved and was up and running. It was going to take a little longer to set up a tap on his mobile.

'Check on who's calling who and any texts since Oates escaped then get back to me.'

Whilst he was on the phone to the station Anna had spoken with Mike on the radio to report that Barbara had gone into the other neighbour's and the occupier seemed fine and calm when he opened the door to her.

Langton had become so impatient he could no longer sit still and was pacing up and down the pavement. After about twenty minutes Barbara returned and got in the car, so Langton calmed down enough to join her and Mike.

'It was Bradford. He said it wasn't a convenient time and he'd never voted for anyone, especially not some rich bastard's son! And then as much as I tried he shut the door. I had no chance of even seeing past him. I could hear a TV on – a football match or something.'

'Do you think he suspected anything?'

'No, I asked if there was anyone else resident who voted; he said his mother but she was a Labour supporter.'

'How did he seem to you?'

'His eyes were red-rimmed as if he's not been sleeping. He also smelt very heavily of BO, and had terrible halitosis. Didn't seem to want me to see inside, never opened the door fully.'

'What about the neighbours?'

'Okay, no reply one side and on the other a Mr and Mrs Pearson: I told them I was a police officer but they haven't seen or heard anything unusual. They know Timmy's mother quite well but don't have much to do with him. There's a community hall on the estate used for bingo evenings and residents' meetings – they discuss any local problems. There was a meeting last night and Mrs Douglas usually does the tea and biscuits for everyone but she didn't turn up.'

'Residents' meetings?'

'Yeah, there's a lot of council properties, but also lots of flats being done up for sale: their beef is who is going to be paying for what as there's grass that needs cutting and garden maintenance and so on.'

'Did they knock to see why Mrs Douglas didn't go?'

'No, the neighbour saw Timmy coming back from the newsagent's this morning, he said his mum was under the weather and in bed.'

'Good work, Barbara.'

'Thank you, sir, and you might want this,' she said, handing him a Yale key. 'Mrs Pearson said Bradford's other neighbours are away and she goes in to water the balcony plants for them. I thought the key might come in handy.'

Langton smiled and praised her quick thinking, before contacting Anna to tell her that he wanted her to discreetly change places with Barbara in the observation van as Timmy now knew what the DC looked like.

Langton turned to Mike in the back seat.

'Give me ten minutes. I just need to stretch my legs and make some calls.'

A few minutes later and Anna was back in the car with Mike. She could see he was mad about something.

'Where's Langton?'

'I don't know what the fuck he's playing at. Do you?' Mike snapped.

Anna took a deep breath. 'What do you mean by that?'

'You two seem to like having cosy discussions without me.'

Anna sighed; sometimes Mike really exasperated her.

'Mike, don't you get it? He's protecting you, all of us, because don't you realize that the Deputy Commissioner wants a head to roll?'

Mike shook his head. 'In other words he's protecting himself.'

'No, you idiot, he's protecting you. If Oates is in that flat he wants you to get the kudos of a tight clean arrest.'

'Yeah, sure he does.'

Anna gave up, closing her eyes.

'He gave the okay to take the handcuffs off Oates, you know full well that I was hesitant about it.'

'Mike, you headed up the operation, and—'

Langton opened the passenger door and got inside.

'Bradford's made a call from the landline. NatWest Bank, New Malden, mother has an account there. She made an earlier arrangement for him to withdraw ten thousand in cash from her savings account. Bank said as he's her son all he needs is the signed cheque, a letter of authority and proof of identity. They have arranged that he can collect the money at four-thirty this afternoon. Now we go to work . . .'

'Arranged it over the phone? Surely that can't be right,' Mike said, surprised.

'Well I've got two officers going to see the bank manager to make sure it happens,' Langton informed them.

'Timmy told me his mother is always up and about early, and she seemed to me perfectly capable of going to the bank herself. From my conversation with her I doubt that she'd give him that much money. Something's not right,' Anna said.

'Oates is in there, it's the ten grand,' Langton said, his voice devoid of emotion as he turned and looked at Anna.

Langton drove off, and parked on Kingston Hill by the old gates that had once led into the estate in the days when it had been a big house surrounded by parkland. He got out and looked around. He could see for miles, but the spot was very exposed, not quite what he needed. Then he remembered just the place. Collecting Anna and

Mike, they set off for the Kingston Lodge Hotel, which was less than half a mile away from the Kingsnympton estate. It would make an ideal base for their operation. En route he told them that it had parking at the rear and a conference room that could be used for briefing the SO19 officers and other units they would need.

On arrival the three of them went and spoke to the manager. Langton was right; it was the ideal place, and they could come and go using the rear entrance without causing too much disturbance. The manager was more than happy to help and took them to the conference room and also arranged for coffee and sandwiches to be brought in. He seemed to be enjoying himself and said that whatever they needed just to let him know.

Anna and Mike watched and listened as Langton got on his mobile and phoned the Commander to let her know that DCI Lewis would be setting up and running the Gold Command base at the hotel. She obviously gave the go-ahead as he next phoned Central Command at Scotland Yard to request firearms and tactical support group officers in unmarked vehicles. He also asked for the technical support unit to bring their silent drilling and listening equipment. Lastly he phoned the Hostage Negotiation Unit and briefed them on the strong possibility that Oates was in the Bradford flat. He had covered every single base with all the correct procedures in an amazingly short period of time, and his ability to take control of a situation and think on his feet was quite breathtaking. When he had finished on the phone he put his hand out to Mike.

'Are we in this together?'

'Yeah, we're singing off the same hymn sheet.' Mike shook hands with Langton, and Anna was grateful their feud was over.

Whilst awaiting the arrival of all the teams at the hotel, Langton briefed Mike and Anna on what he felt would be the best course of action. Mr and Mrs Pearson, the neighbours, had been asked to leave their premises and come to the hotel. Within the hour everyone was assembled in the conference room. Radio contact had been maintained with Barbara, who was still in the observation van at the Kingsnympton estate. She confirmed that no one had left or entered the premises. The technical support boffins made use of the conference room projector to show everyone aerial shots of the estate on a large screen, along with pictures of Oates taken since his arrest. The firearms supervisor used a large map on the wall to mark the best vantage points for his officers, should they need to storm the flat or deal with a hostage situation. Travis was able to give them all a layout of the Bradford flat from her visit.

Langton stepped forward and introduced himself, then reminded them of what a dangerous and violent man Henry Oates was. He gave a brief account of the day's events so far and informed them that armed officers were already in place to make a street arrest should Oates leave the premises. This would be the best and safest scenario, however he felt Oates was unlikely to come out until Bradford had collected the money from the bank. Vehicle and foot surveillance on Bradford was the main priority at present as there was always the possibility, as slim as it was, that Oates could be holed up somewhere else and

Bradford was planning to take the money to him. Langton then introduced Mike as the DCI leading the investigation.

Mike, using a laser pointer, indicated on the screen the current position of the surveillance and firearms officers and added that Barbara Maddox would be able to inform them when Bradford left the flat from her observation point in the van. They expected Bradford would take the 97 bus route to New Malden. He would be followed on foot, with the surveillance officers continually changing places so that he remained unaware of what was happening. Surveillance vehicles, including a motorcycle, would also follow the bus. Mike impressed Langton when he raised the possibility that they might lose Bradford, and said that he had instructed a technical support officer and a detective to go to the bank to speak to the manager and have a tracking device put in the moneybag. Mike finished by stressing that no arrest was to be made unless authorized by him or DCS Langton. Langton again stepped forward and asked if there were any questions. No one spoke and in the silence the tension was obvious.

The monitored calls caused a flurry of activity when it was revealed that Timmy had called a local taxi company, Crown Cars, and asked them to send a taxi in fifteen minutes to pick him up by the row of shops. He wanted to be driven to the NatWest in New Malden and for the driver to wait and return him to the estate. The taxi company was based near the hotel, so Mike Lewis, who had not been seen by Timmy, would replace their driver.

Anna watched as the tech support officer fixed Mike up with a wire and gave him a small tracking device to put in the car. She moved closer.

'Still worried about the lack of action?'

He didn't answer as Langton took him aside.

'Radio back to us as soon as you're in position. When we hear you check with him where he wants to go we'll be ready for the off. You'll have a surveillance car on your tail.'

From the street map of New Malden, they could see that the NatWest Bank was on a corner. Langton told Mike to draw up outside the bank, drop Bradford off and wait in the street for him to return. There would also be an officer in the back of the bank monitoring everything on the CCTV.

'What if a traffic warden turns up?'

'Don't worry about that, there'll be a couple of surveillance officers in the street so if they see any they'll soon get rid of them.'

Anna noticed that whenever Langton was in conversation with Mike he turned to the SO19 and tactical support teams immediately afterwards.

'Okay, DCI Lewis has given the go-ahead.'

By doing this it seemed that all the decisions were coming from Mike Lewis, not himself.

Mike had instructed all surveillance units to use the code name 'Silver' for Bradford. Oates was to be referred to as 'Gold', should he be seen to leave the Kingsnympton premises.

Fifteen minutes flew past. Then came the message in from the surveillance officers in the van with Barbara watching Mrs Douglas's flat.

'This is OP one. Silver out of blue door, heading from premises . . . Fast pace . . . Towards lane by Block C.'

'Here he comes,' Langton said unnecessarily as it was pretty obvious.

'Silver in black BB cap, dark donkey jacket, blue jeans, white sneakers, carrying black holdall ... on foot towards shopping area.'

Mike had parked the Crown taxicab directly outside the small hair salon, where he sat reading a paper. He glanced up to see Bradford heading towards him. Bradford rapped on the passenger window, opened the door, got in and slammed it shut.

'NatWest, New Malden, was it, mate?' Mike asked.

Bradford nodded and as the taxi moved off, they could hear him telling Mike the direction he wanted to go, asking him to take a left and then go into Warren Road, and not to worry about it being a private road as the guy on the gates at the end would let a taxi through without stopping him. The surveillance car seamlessly moved into position behind the taxi.

Bradford told Mike to turn left out of Warren Road and then go right towards New Malden High Street. There was a slight moment of confusion as Bradford said Mike should pass the bank, keep on driving and turn left by Boots the Chemist, as he had to get something.

Mike knew that their conversation was being relayed back to base, but he nevertheless became concerned.

'I got you down for the NatWest Bank and then back to the estate?'

'Yeah, yeah, I know, but you just wait, I'll only be a minute. Go left at the lights, mate, and park it there.'

The surveillance car continued to follow, but held back as the taxi turned left and parked. A plain clothes officer got out to tail Bradford as he left the cab.

Mike was now parked on a double yellow line a few yards from the traffic lights. There was a pause, then the surveillance officer following Bradford made contact, reporting that Bradford had gone to the hair-styling section and selected a box of red L'Oréal hair dye and was now at the checkout counter.

Langton, listening in, glanced at Anna, wondering if it was for his mother. She smiled.

'I doubt it, dyeing it my shade? Quite clever: Oates's blond hair will take the colour easily,' she said.

Bradford paid for his hair dye and then came out from Boots to cross to a shoe shop on the opposite corner. Again he was tailed and back came the information that he was buying a pair of boots, which he hadn't even tried on! They also got the nod that he was very agitated, had dropped his wallet and was very impatient with the assistant, swearing at her to hurry up.

Bradford came out and tossed the purchases into the taxi. Mike turned towards him.

'Where to now?'

Bradford had his hand on the open door.

'Go to the bank now.'

'It's a no right turn,' Mike said.

'Then do a fucking u-ey, pal ... Wait, leave it ... I'll walk up to the bank, meet me outside on the corner.'

Mike let him slam the door shut and a different surveillance officer now took over as Bradford hurried along New Malden High Street towards the bank.

Mike did an illegal right turn, followed by the surveillance car, to the great annoyance of one irate driver who yelled out abuse as they came alongside the hurrying figure of Bradford.

'Silver now into bank.'

Waiting in the bank was the surveillance officer monitoring the CCTV. It was a small local branch, with just four cashiers behind the plate glass and a cordoned area for the customers to queue. There were two Japanese women, and an elderly man with a wheelie cart. Bradford took out papers from his jacket and was visibly sweating as he waited.

A cashier became available and he stepped forwards in front of the old man, who pushed his cart in front of Bradford.

'Get the fuck out of my way,' Bradford snarled.

A second cashier spoke into her microphone to say position number three was now available and Bradford elbowed past the old man.

The bank manager had already been primed to let the transaction take place without too many questions, as they didn't want Bradford to become at all suspicious.

'I'm here on behalf of my mother. She called you and I've got all the signed forms and my passport here,' Bradford explained.

In fact it would usually have taken considerably more time, with all the security questions and identification checks that were legally required, but Langton had pre-empted this. However, as with all carefully plotted and planned arrangements, there could always be a blip and this time it came from the cashier.

'I will have to speak to the manager to clear this, one moment.'

If Bradford was nervous so was everyone else. He was breathing very heavily, constantly looking over his shoulder and back to the empty teller's chair.

*

Langton threw up his hands in despair, asking what the hell was going on. But the wait wasn't over even when the cashier returned, as she asked Bradford to go into the small office as they didn't want to pass over such a large payment in the view of other customers.

It seemed an interminable length of time, but it was actually only five minutes before Bradford emerged from the office and hurriedly left the bank with ten thousand pounds cash. He almost ran around the corner to where the taxi was parked, and had a good look round before getting in.

'Get me back to the estate.'

'Yes, sir.'

As they drove off Mike noticed Bradford continually glancing in the passenger wing mirror and becoming increasingly agitated, so he decided to drive back via the Kingston Road and then up the London Road and back to the estate via Kingston Hill. Bradford didn't seem to notice the different route as he was so busy looking in the wing mirror.

The surveillance car behind radioed back to base the route they were taking. Langton wondered what on earth Mike was up to and worried he could blow the whole operation until he heard Bradford's voice over Mike's concealed radio.

'That car behind – do you know him?'

'What ya mean, do I know him?'

'It was behind us when we went to the bank and now it's back again.'

'Fuck off, you're paranoid, mate … unless you just robbed the bank,' Mike said, trying to ease the situation.

'The passenger in it, he was in Boots.'

'Look, they don't pay me enough to drive nutters, so I tell you what, I'll drop you off at the Kingston Lodge up there.'

Mike put his foot down hard on the pedal and swung into the hotel car park.

'What you bloody doing? Stop the car, STOP!'

Mike hit the brakes and, opening the driver's door, ran out of the vehicle and dived to the ground, knowing from experience exactly what would happen next and the last place he wanted to be was in the possible line of fire.

The surveillance car behind drew up almost bumper to bumper as two plain clothes armed officers rushed out and moved to the front and passenger side of the taxi, their guns drawn and aimed at Bradford.

It was over in seconds. Bradford was hauled from the taxi, dropping his shoebox and Boots carrier bag and forced to the ground at gunpoint. He was quickly hand-cuffed and roughly manhandled towards the rear entrance of the hotel screeching, 'What you think you're fucking doing? LET GO! LET GO OF ME!'

Bradford, with his arms held behind him, was forced to bend from the waist as he was pushed into a small side room where Langton and Anna were waiting.

He had a look of terror on his sweating face, and he was almost sobbing as he kept on repeating, 'What? What? What?'

Bradford was pushed into a chair as Langton confronted him.

'Who've you been shopping for, Mr Bradford?'

'Oh Christ, you don't know what you're doing, you've got to let me go.'

*

Mike swiftly went to the washroom and brushed himself down, before joining the others in the side room. Bradford was sitting by a table crying, the cuffs had been removed and Langton was holding out his mobile.

'Come on, son, just calm down, call him, say there's been a bit of a hold-up at the bank with the money.'

Anna updated Mike.

'Oates is in the flat. He's put Timmy's mother in the bathroom with a noose around her neck that's attached to a pulley ring above the bath.'

Bradford heard Anna and became even more agitated.

'Henry told me that he's left her standing on the kitchen stepping stool. He said he'd be watching out for me and if I come back with anyone or was late he'd go and pull the stool away and hang her.' Bradford wailed and put his head on his hands.

'Come on, straighten out, we'll make sure she's okay.'

'She's eighty-two years old. She can't stand up for long,' Bradford groaned, and blurted out that Oates had said he had to be back in an hour or he'd kill his mother.

'What were you doing in the chemist's?'

'He wanted red hair dye, said he's gonna dye his hair.'

'Were the boots for him as well?'

'Yes. You don't understand what you're doin' holding me here, he'll kill her.'

Langton drew up a chair so close their knees were almost touching.

'Now you listen to me, Tim, you've got to calm yourself right down because we need time to make sure we get your mother out of there alive.'

'BUT WE'RE WASTIN' TIME!'

'Shush now, look at me. Tim, look at me. You were a fighter, am I right, yes? Good one, from what I've been told. Now I want you to look at this like you were about to go into the ring, deep breaths, that's it, get yourself ready, keep looking at me, Tim, good lad, now this is what you do, because we need some time.'

Bradford nodded and Langton caught a full whiff of his disgusting halitosis.

'You make a call and you tell him there's been a hitch with the money withdrawal, person who deals with it is still in with someone else. Say it's going to take another fifteen minutes before they can hand it over to you, then you still get another ten to drive back to the estate, okay? You ready to do this, Tim?'

'Yeah, yeah, but I'm scared for my mum. He's got her on that stool.'

'Well, you are going to save her by doing this; here's your mobile, now let's call the bastard, shall we? If you get into a problem say the manager or the cashier will talk to him to confirm you're telling the truth, okay? Understand?'

Bradford nodded, his hand shaking as he pressed dial on the mobile. Timmy's landline had already been tapped so they knew the call could be recorded and Anna was on her phone, which had been linked in to listen to the conversation.

It rang and Oates picked up.

'It's me, Timmy.'

'You got the money yet?'

'I'm still here at the bank, there's a hitch. Cos it's so much money a cashier can't deal with it, the manager has to and I'm still waiting to see him.'

'You better not be fucking me about?'

'I'm tellin' you the truth.'

'How long do I have to wait, for Chrissake?'

'Said no more than fifteen then I'll come straight home. I got the taxi waitin'.'

'You better get a move on cos I'm starting to get edgy, man, and you know what happens when I get edgy—'

Bradford's voice trembled as he interrupted Oates.

'Yeah, you kill someone.'

'That's right, and the clock's ticking.'

As Oates replaced the phone, Bradford, sweating and shaking, cried out for him not to kill his mother. Langton gripped Bradford's shoulder.

'That was brilliant, and it gives us the time we need.'

The team were now galvanized into action, planning the best way to arrest Oates and get Mrs Douglas out alive. The neighbours, Mr and Mrs Pearson, were now at the hotel and had given permission for the police to use their premises for the operation. With the key Barbara had got from the Pearsons, tech support and firearms officers had gone into the flat on the other side while Oates was on the phone speaking to Timmy. Another group had gone into the Pearsons' at the same time. Being on the first floor, there was no rear entrance – the only way in was through the front door. They considered using a double for Bradford with his baseball cap pulled down, who would knock at the door; as soon as Oates opened it the armed officers would crash in and overpower him.

This plan became a no-goer when Bradford told them that he had the key to the front door and Oates knew it, so to ring the bell or knock on the door would be a clear signal that something was wrong. Langton, against his better judgement, decided that an all-out assault on the flat was too dangerous and Timmy Bradford should return to the premises and give Oates the money. There was still the danger that Oates might harm Bradford or his mother, but it was unlikely that he would leave the premises until late at night and this would give them breathing space to reassess the situation. Timmy was told to try and keep Oates in conversation about what he was going to do.

The tech support officers were now ready to drill from the Pearsons' bathroom into Mrs Douglas's. It would be a very difficult process going through at floor level to come out in the corner wall beside the toilet and would take at least half an hour, maybe longer. By using a fish-eye camera lens on the end of a thin optical cable they would be able to check on her condition and most importantly see if she was still alive. It was considered too risky to drill into the living room to see what Oates was doing. Bradford had described how his deceased stepfather had suffered from arthritis and so a pulley on a ring with a hand bar had been installed for him to grip onto to heave himself in and out of the bath. The ring was secured to the ceiling and Oates had tied a dressing-gown cord to the pulley, looping it round his mother's neck. She was balanced on a kitchen stool.

Keeping him calm, Anna and Mike sat with Timmy as he was given some very sweet coffee. He explained how Oates had found his mother's bank statements and forced him to make the arrangement to withdraw the money and then collect it or he'd kill her. He cried, and then wept even harder when he said that he'd never forgive himself for not being there the night Oates had got into the flat. He'd been out betting on the dogs at Wimbledon race track until late, not returning home until after midnight. He'd lost all his cash and had had to walk from the track, which was the reason he'd been so late. Oates had rung the bell and his mother, presuming her son must have forgotten his key, had opened the front door without a second thought.

'She's in her nightie,' he said pitifully.

'She's going to be okay, we'll get her out. Has he got any weapons?'

'He's got a kitchen knife he carries around all the time. Ten grand — that's all her savings, and you know if anything happened to her it's not how I wanted to get my inheritance.'

Anna nodded. The over-anxious son was worried about his mother but also about losing her money.

Langton gestured for Anna to come over.

'Hard to believe that in the middle of all this I get the hotel manager come up and give me the bill for the champagne and sandwiches the Pearsons ordered — bloody people...'

Langton held up the holdall containing the money.

'Too dangerous to wire up Bradford so we've got a pin-sized microphone fixed to one of the studs on the base of the holdall. The tracker's been taken out—'

'There's been some complications, sir,' the technical support officer said as he rushed into the room. 'The concrete is thicker and harder to drill through than we originally imagined so the team at the Pearsons' flat will need another thirty to forty minutes before they can get a camera lens into the bathroom.'

'We don't have that long,' Langton snapped.

The clock was ticking, and to keep Bradford in a calm state was far from easy. They simply didn't have the option of waiting, and Bradford was told to be ready to return to the flat.

Mike whispered to Anna that he wasn't sure Bradford was going to be able to keep himself together. She watched Langton yet again sit close to him and this time he really pumped him up.

'This is a fight, Tim, you up for it? Can you go in there and come out on top? We need you and we're doing it this way to protect your mum. You can save her, right? Look at me, Tim, you set to do this?'

Bradford nodded and he did seem to be up for it, licking his lips and nodding.

'Okay, here's the holdall with the money, the shoebox and the bag with the hair dye, you just act normal. Make sure you put the holdall down in the living room so we can hear everything. The sooner you hand this gear over to him, the sooner he's gonna walk out and we'll have him, okay?'

Bradford was driven up to the edge of the Kingsnympton estate, from where he then walked up to the flat with the moneybag, the boots and the hair dye. They watched him head towards the block, still with his baseball cap pulled down low, and he came into view once more as he headed along the corridor towards the blue front door.

'Silver at the door, letting himself in now.'

On camera they could see Bradford putting the key into the lock and stepping inside.

Meanwhile the drilling continued. They were almost through the wall, the specialist silent drills working carefully and, inch by inch, following the pipeline, getting closer so they could finally see inside the bathroom.

Langton signalled that they had a pick-up from the microphone hidden in the holdall.

'These my size?'

'Yeah, you said ten and a half, right? Try them on.'

'Very nice, they look like Doc Martens, don't they?'

'I need to see my mum.'

'You'll fucking see her when I'm ready. Now gimme the bag. I want to count the cash.'

'It's all there, ten grand. I done what you asked me to.'

There was then a long period where all they could hear was Oates counting the money. Langton had told Bradford to keep Oates talking but assumed that he was just sitting there paralysed with fear. There was no sound of a scuffle and it was nearly ten minutes before they heard Timmy's voice again.

'You got my leather jacket on.'

'Yeah, and your trousers. Here, there's a few quid for you.'

Oates laughed. In the hotel conference room everyone grew very tense as it appeared that Oates was preparing to move out.

'I'm sorry to tie you up, Timmy, it's just to give me time, right?'

'You said I could see my mum, she's fucking eighty-two years old.'

'Once you get out of these ropes you can. I guess you're hoping she's still alive?'

They could hear Bradford start to cry. Oates told him to shut up and then asked where the hair dye was. Bradford told him it was in the kitchen in the Boots bag.

Langton got the signal that the drills were through the wall and the camera was being threaded through into the bathroom. On the small screen they could see Mrs Douglas hanging motionless from the pulley ring. The kitchen stool lay on its side and her feet were dangling inches above the bath. Oates, it seemed, had already murdered Timmy Bradford's mother.

*

With Mrs Douglas obviously dead and Bradford's own life clearly under threat Langton turned to Mike.

'DCI Lewis, do we go in? Just give the signal.'

Mike nodded, and Anna knew yet again Langton was placing Mike in the driving seat.

'Let's do it.'

After such a tense long waiting game, the actual arrest was over very quickly. An SO19 officer used a hand-held metal battering ram on the front door and then threw in two thunder flashes, which went off with a massive boom, disorientating not only Oates but Bradford as well. Three more armed officers, one carrying a Taser stun gun, crashed into the flat, screaming out a warning that they were armed.

Oates was in the kitchen, red hair dye dripping down his face, the carving knife close to hand. As he turned towards them the officer with the Taser fired the dart-like electrodes into his chest, sending an electric current racing through his body. Oates's muscles went into spasm and he collapsed onto the kitchen floor and was quickly hand-cuffed. Oates was taken to Hackney Police Station under armed guard in a police van using its blue lights and sirens along the route from the Kingsnympton estate.

Anna followed hard on the heels of the armed officers and went straight to Timmy Bradford. She tried to be as diplomatic and as caring as possible as she untied his hands.

'I'm afraid your mother . . .'

'What? Is she okay? Is she all right?'

'No, I'm sorry, we'll have a medical team in straight away—' She didn't get the opportunity to tell him as Bradford started to push past her, heading towards the bathroom.

The door was now wide open and the pitiful body could be seen hanging from the pulley ring. Bradford stood there, mouth opening and closing like a fish, his eyes wide in disbelief.

'He's killed her. Why, why, why?'

'I'm so sorry.'

It was very obvious Mrs Douglas was dead. She was dressed only in her nightgown; her eyes protruded from their sockets and her face was a purplish red colour. Her mouth was covered with masking tape and her hands were tied behind her back with the same tape. It was a tragic, hideous sight and Bradford crumpled onto the floor, sobbing.

The flat was cordoned off for the forensic team to cut her down and then her body was taken to the mortuary as the distraught exhausted Timmy Bradford was helped from the flat. At one point he did become concerned about the moneybag, but was told it was safe and had to be kept for evidence. He agreed that he would go with them to give a statement at Hackney Police Station, where he was well taken care of. The police doctor came to see him and pre-scribed some sedatives, he was given food and a change of clothes and a family liaison officer sat with him until the team were ready to take down a full statement.

Oates was being held at the station in the cells and had hardly spoken to anyone. The entire operation had to be written up and reports submitted before they could move on and interview him again. Although they had made a successful arrest and prevented any harm coming to Timmy Bradford, the fact remained that Henry Oates had murdered Mrs Douglas after he had escaped from police custody. This was something that the media had picked up on at once, with headlines and stories of police incompetence leading to the murder of an eighty-two-year-old woman. The Deputy Commissioner, along with Langton, held a big press conference, which in truth was nothing more than a damage limitation exercise. They both praised the skill and efforts of DCI Lewis in apprehending Oates and saving Timmy Bradford. When it came to the death of Mrs Douglas they said that as it was an ongoing enquiry and a suspect awaited interview they were not prepared to comment on that side of the investigation.

The team all congratulated Mike Lewis on the way he had handled the arrest, but it was tainted by the fact that Mrs Douglas was dead. They knew it was possible she had been murdered as soon as Oates had forced her to let him inside her flat. The weary team did not break until two in the morning, knowing that they would reconvene early the next day to re-question Oates. There was no sense of achievement, more of relief, and it still wasn't over. Anna, like everyone else, went home to recharge for the following days, which would finally lead to closing the investigation.

As tired as she was, Anna was unable to sleep. The haunting picture of Mrs Douglas kept returning to her in flashes. It made her angry that the officers sent to question Bradford had not done their job properly. Oates had been inside that flat all that time, most probably in the bathroom, and she wondered if this might even have been when he killed Mrs Douglas in fear she'd cry out for help. Anna tossed and turned. Had he actually killed her as soon as she had let him in? Something didn't add up, but she was too exhausted to put it together. She got up to make herself a cup of hot milk and brought it back to her bed. Sitting up with her hands cupped around it, having taken two aspirins and a sleeping pill, still she couldn't stop her mind churning over all the facts and trying to figure out what was wrong – what was stored in the recess of her mind? The jigsaw pieces that linked one case to the other had all appeared to be in place, but the more restless she became the more fractured the pattern became. Adding a big slug of Scotch to the now tepid milk didn't help. But it made her groggy enough to lie back and close her eyes. She sighed. Maybe it would fall into place in the morning.

Chapter Twenty

Oates was still being held in the cells, apparently having accepted that his bolt for freedom had failed. He was showing no visible signs of stress – on the contrary, he was eating and sleeping well. He looked very odd, as part of his hair was a bright orange colour where he had attempted to dye it.

Anna told Mike that she had arranged to go over to the mortuary to discuss the four bodies recovered from the woods with the pathologist and to get an estimate of how long Mrs Douglas had been dead. She asked Mike what he thought.

Mike shrugged and said that he reckoned that Oates had probably killed her after a few hours. He further suggested that Oates, with Kumar's advice, might try to claim that he left her standing on the stool and she must have slipped and accidently hanged herself.

'See you later then.'

'We got good news about Barolli. It's not as bad as we first thought; he should be on his feet in a week or two,' Mike added.

'That's great. How long do they think before he'll be back at work?'

414

'Good few months – he'll have rehab treatment at the police home in Goring, but at the moment his condition is stable and he's been visited by Barbara and Joan.'

Anna felt a little guilty that she hadn't really given Barolli much thought so she went over to Barbara.

'When you see Paul, give him my best.'

'Will do. Joan's been to see him and took him in some home-cooked meals her mother prepared.'

'That's nice.'

'Yeah. Well you know Joan, she's got nothing else to do with her spare time and it gives her mother something to do.'

'Well, thanks.' Anna paused. 'The girls recovered from the woods, can you do me copies of their "Misper" files?'

'Now?'

'Yes please, I need to take them to the pathologist, might help with how long they have been dead. Never know, evil bastard Oates could have kept them alive for a while before killing them.'

Anna crossed to the incident board and studied the photographs. It was strange: Kelly Mathews, Mary Suffolk, Alicia Jones, Angela Thornton, Rebekka Jordan, Justine Marks and Fidelis Julia Flynn all looked as if a light had been turned off in their eyes, as if it was finally over. Even Mrs Douglas looked distant in the picture most recently attached to the board.

When Anna arrived at Lambeth the mortuary assistant told her that the pathologist, Professor Hall, was currently working on the body of Mrs Douglas in the main examination room. Anna told the assistant that if possible she'd first like to see the remains of the bodies they had recovered from the quarry. He took her into the cold room where dead bodies were kept in metal fridges with four in each compartment stacked on sliding removable trays. The assistant had already removed the bodies, the remains of which were now in new zipped body bags. Each bag was laid out on a trolley along with a copy of the post mortem paperwork attached to a clipboard.

It would be chilling to go from one body to the next unzipping each bag to see how much remained of each victim. Anna stood for a while looking at the first body, the tiny figure of what was left of Rebekka Jordan. She looked through the report; amongst the paperwork was a request for burial and the release of the remains to her parents. It had not yet been signed. As the lab assistant came over, Anna jumped in surprise.

'You see these, and you think at one time they were all young and vibrant with their whole life ahead of them, and one crazy sick bastard is responsible and took it all away. You ever think about why evil is punished? I'm not talking about hang them high, I'm not talking about capital punishment, it's something else and I don't understand it . . .'

Anna turned to face the young man, he was no more than mid-twenties and had a quiet authority. He was so calm, almost dispassionate.

'What don't you understand?' she asked.

'That it doesn't hurt, that he could take these lives in a brutal way, one after the other, and keep walking around, keep living as if there was to be no punishment.'

'Well, the punishment will be meted out at his trial.'

'Going to jail isn't punishment enough, it should be an eye for an eye, a tooth for a tooth.'

She shook her head.

'I don't think I want to get into this, I'm sorry. I've not got a lot of time.'

Anna moved on from one body to the next, glancing through the reports. Kelly Mathews, Mary Suffolk and Alicia Jones's identities had all been confirmed through their dental records. The assistant told her that Kelly and Alicia had broken hyoid bones, which were ante mortem, and so it looked like they had been strangled.

'It's the decomposition, makes it hard. Mary there and the other one at the end, well Prof Hall's got to do more work on them yet.'

'Her name's Angela Thornton,' Anna said, picking up the report.

'No, there's no Angela Thornton here. That one's a UI.'

Anna picked up the report and, sure enough, clearly marked on the front in large red marker pen were the letters 'UI' for unidentified. She looked at the dental records in the report; there was a copy of Angela Thornton's with 'no match' across them, again written in red marker pen.

'The dental records don't fit. We had her listed as possibly being . . .'

'Angela Thornton,' Anna said quietly.

'Yes, but so far we don't have a Scooby Doo who she is. Her body was caked in mud so we didn't really see the hair wasn't a match until we washed her down . . .'

Anna unzipped the bag and this time the smell that hit her from the rotting flesh made her gag, as it was much stronger than the other bodies. The corpse, she noticed, was also the least decomposed of all the recovered victims.

'You're right, Angela had thick blonde curly hair, but this is braided,' Anna remarked as she touched one of the tightly woven braids that was laid out around the skull, which still had a few braids attached to it. It was impossible to tell what colour skin she had or what she originally looked like; her skull with its empty sockets gave no indication of the colour of her eyes, or the shape of her lips.

'Where is the clothing that was removed from her?'

'Wasn't any, not even any fragments. She was the only one in her birthday suit, but with so much on we've not been able to do much more on her yet. Could be a West Indian with hair like that.'

'Thank you.'

Anna went into the examination room where the pathologist was working on Mrs Douglas and gestured at him to see if he could spare her a moment. He was masked and gowned up and not happy with the intrusion.

'Detective Travis, I am working as fast as I can, this has been bordering on the farcical. Detective Chief Superintendent Langton has been bombarding me not only with so many bodies that I've almost lost count, but he's continually on the phone. I've got a forensic anthropologist coming later this afternoon to look at the remains of all the bodies from the quarry and help with how long they have been dead. There is no way I will complete the post mortem on Mrs Douglas today.'

Anna interrupted.

'I'm sorry, Professor Hall, for disturbing you; I have no intention of putting any more pressure on you and your dedicated team.'

'Well that is very civil of you, I am sure.' He was a very old hand and near to retirement age, a tall hooked-nosed man who wore half-moon glasses. He loosened his face mask, revealing his rugged features.

'What is it exactly you want from me?'

'The unidentified remains – we sent you the dental records of a possible victim called Angela Thornton . . .'

'I unfortunately can't recall names, but I am aware the

odontologist did not get a match from one of the bodies' dental records.'

'Yes, I know, and we have been very grateful for your immediate attention with regard to all the victims that were brought in. It's just there is one big favour . . .'

'I knew there had to be something, and you are fortunate that you happen to be a sweet-faced young woman. What is it?

Anna asked if he could give her an estimated time of death for the one unidentified victim.

He sighed and said that after he had finished with Mrs Douglas he would get her brought back in and examine the body with the anthropologist, but it wouldn't be until later that afternoon.

'Would it be possible for me to take a sample of her hair for a DNA test?'

'Yes of course, but you don't need me to be there for that – get my assistant to do it for you.'

He turned away, and Anna hesitated.

'Professor, I just wondered, with regard to Mrs Douglas, how long you think she might have been dead.'

He sighed and glared at her over the top of his glasses and gestured to the examination table.

'A rough estimate based on the skin coloration and the fact that there was no longer any rigor mortis in her body would be at least forty-eight hours. Also the hypostasis is somewhat strange.'

'Sorry, what do you mean strange?'

'About six hours after death the blood in the body will settle in direct response to gravity. After a period of time the staining becomes permanent. In Mrs Douglas's case her blood had settled in her back and legs so she'd clearly been lying flat on a hard surface for some time.'

'You mean she was already dead before she was left hanging from the pulley ring?'

'Ten out of ten, DCI Travis.'

'How did she die then?'

'Can't say until I've completed a full internal examination. I'm not happy with the marks on her neck either so I need to dissect the throat and tongue as well. Now I really do need to get on and, please, no more interruptions, especially from DCS Langton.'

Anna had obtained one of the braids from their unidentified victim and took it to Pete Jenkins' office in the forensic science department. As she entered the room Pete gave her a warm welcoming smile.

'Hi, Anna. Is there a dead body left in London that you haven't unearthed?'

'Don't go there, Pete. How's the forensic work going?'

'I've got more fragments of clothes, but trying to ascertain what they were before they rotted to shreds is very difficult. I'm using the labels mostly, but I don't honestly have much for you to go on and I won't for some time.'

'I need a DNA test on the hair taken from one of the bodies brought out of the woods near the quarry.'

Pete mock-slapped his head and then offered her a coffee as he'd just made a fresh pot.

'I don't have the time, Pete, and if you could do this a.s.a.p. for me, here's the sample. I need to know ethnicity and have it checked for a match if possible.'

'Well, you know hair samples take a lot longer and this one will be pretty degraded due to the decomposition. It'll be at least twenty-four hours, but I'll get it first in line. Anything else?'

She smiled and asked if she could have one more look at the evidence brought from Henry Oates's basement. He raised his eyebrows and said that it had been bagged, tagged and moved into one of the secure rooms.

'Truth was, we couldn't wait to get the stuff out of the lab, it stunk the place out. I doubt most of it is of any use to your case and we're waiting to get it cleared and off our hands – all the vitals have been sent over to the station. Is it anything particular?'

'Yes, it's the women's clothing. I remember there were a number of items and there's now a chance some of it may have belonged to one of his victims.'

Pete led Anna into the ante-room, where the bagged items were stacked in large plastic boxes on long wide shelves.

'Help yourself. With all the work you've been bringing in I don't have the time or inclination to dig around in here with you, but my offer of coffee still stands, so come back to my office if you want to join me.'

'Thank you.'

He turned to go and paused. 'How's Paul Barolli?'

'Recovering very well.'

'That's good.'

'How's Matilda?'

'She is the light of my life, and I don't get much light, been here for night after night, but I read you've got the guy under arrest.'

'Yes. We have.'

He smiled and closed the door, leaving her in the musty-smelling room. There were strip lights overhead and the neon shed a bluish light on the rows of tagged plastic bags. She moved along the shelf until she got to a bag marked women's clothes, then she carried it to a small side table and opened it. There was some rather unpleasant dirty underwear, a pair of drainpipe jeans and some sweaters. She took her time sorting them and then checked the labels, putting a couple of items aside. She then replaced the bag on the shelf and listed the items she had removed. Next she found a smaller bag containing ladies' shoes and opened it. There was one high-heeled shoe and a pair of patent leather knee-high boots. They were all very worn and the shoe was a different size to the boots. She made a note of the sizes and replaced them.

Anna didn't take Pete up on his offer of a coffee. Instead she went back to her flat as it was just across the river from the Lambeth laboratories. There she made herself a sandwich and a cup of tea and skimmed through the Angela Thornton file. She had disappeared after a night out with girlfriends in the Mile End area of London. She had to all intents and purposes been a pleasant young woman, well dressed and still living at home with her parents. The inscribed bracelet that had led eventually to her missing person file was, of all the items removed from Henry Oates's stinking basement, the odd one out because of its value. The fact that the clasp was broken and it was missing some stones, which her parents had said were garnets, also made it different. Nothing else they had recovered had been of anything like the same value.

As soon as Anna got back to the station she rang Glasgow. McBride gave her the contact number of the rehab facility that Corinna Oates had, as a condition of her sentence for drugs offences, been ordered to attend. Frustratingly she was switched from one department to another and no one appeared to know what she was talking about. She tried McBride again, apologizing for bothering him, but explaining she urgently needed to contact either Eileen Oates direct or whoever had been dealing with her daughter absconding from the rehab centre. After yet another series of time-wasting calls she found no one able to give her any assistance, but then McBride called her to say that Eileen was at the hospital with her youngest daughter who was about to give birth.

Everyone had noticed that Anna was obviously caught up on some business or other as she had been on the telephone most of the afternoon. As the team were all working on the charges against Oates, everyone was equally busy. Oates was still being held in the cells at the station, and Mike as the DCI on the investigation had been closeted with the Area Commander and Langton as they reviewed the mass of new evidence. Preparing to re-interview and then charge Oates with the murder of Mrs Douglas along with the other victims was a lengthy process, and they were still waiting on the post mortem reports to finalize the papers, whilst at the same time evidence was still being brought from Mrs Douglas's flat. It was hard to even contemplate that number of man-hours.

Anna had turned her attention to the tapes of Henry Oates's interviews. She was focusing in particular on the moment when Oates placed the bracelet on top of the photograph of Angela Thornton, playing it over and over. She would then rewind to the bit when he had dismissed various other photographs of missing girls until he had selected the ones he claimed to have murdered then taken to the quarry. He was abusive and rude about some of the missing girls' looks, but he had clearly picked out the picture of Angela Thornton and he had placed the gold bracelet on it. Although he did not know their names, he could identify the items he had removed from each body. Backwards and forwards she rewound, replayed, half unsure of what she was looking for, until Barbara interrupted her.

'I've got the name and contact number of a girl who shared a room with Corinna Oates at the rehab centre. She left there just after Corinna absconded. I've not managed to talk to anyone at the centre as they blank me with invasion of privacy, and without having permission from Christ knows who they just clam up, but this girl is clean and doing community work as part of her sentence. Her name is Morag Kelly, she'll be at that number after ten this evening.'

'Terrific, thank you.'

'I've been onto BT and they are getting back to me, but I've been a bit caught up.'

Anna pursed her lips.

'This is very important, Barbara. Leave it with me, I'll do it myself.'

'Mrs Douglas's flat is a crime scene – I mean, surely Mike can get this information within seconds?' Barbara suggested.

'He's busy right now; as I said, I'll check it out. Besides, right now it's just a theory, so don't bother him with it.'

Barbara gave a small shrug of her shoulders and went back to her desk. Bursting with irritation, she turned to Joan.

'She's off on some theory of her own! But she's got me running around for her as if we've not got enough on our plates.'

'Well, she's not the DCI on the case, Mike is, and she's sort of got the Rebekka Jordan charges to deal with.'

'But it's too much. She's constantly interrupting me to check on things that aren't part of our work.' Sighing, Barbara looked across to Mike Lewis's office, where the blinds were drawn down. She checked her watch – it would be time for another round of coffees in there any minute now.

Meanwhile Anna had got onto BT. They were very accommodating and she now had a printout of all the calls made from Mrs Douglas's flat from a month prior to Oates's original arrest. Unfortunately tech support said that because Mrs Douglas's phone was an oldstyle, it did not record details of who had called in during the same period. Anna noticed however that two reverse charge calls had been made to the flat on the day after Oates escaped. Underlining all the numbers of interest in pink highlighter, she carried the pages over to Joan, and asked her to find out who those numbers belonged to. Almost as an after-thought, she also asked Joan to double-check the races held at the Wimbledon dog track on the night Henry Oates escaped from the quarry.

Anna truthfully could not have given her reasons for what she was doing, but knew it was like her father used to say: a gut reaction based on copper's instinct with no rational explanation. She didn't even think about sharing her concerns, as it was very obvious the entire team were inundated. Although time and time again Langton had reprimanded her for not being a team player, she genuinely didn't consider that this was the right time to voice her suspicions.

As tray after tray of coffee disappeared into Mike's office, Anna had the first hint that she might be on the right track. Joan presented her with the traced numbers of the calls made from Mrs Douglas's flat. On the day prior to Oates's escape there had been a call to the NatWest Bank in New Malden and also one the following day. The two reverse charge calls were from pay phones – and they were in the early morning after Oates had escaped from the quarry. Adding to her mounting suspicions was the news that Timmy Bradford had lied about being at the dog racing in Wimbledon on the night Henry Oates had taken his mother hostage. There was no racing as the track was under refurbishment and was not re-opened until the weekend. Annoyingly the bank had already closed for the day, but Joan was given the task of getting hold of the manager and making an appointment for Anna to see him. Fortunately the ten thousand pounds was still retained by the police as evidence.

A second hit came from Professor Hall at the mortuary, who was very loud and pompous when he rang. Anna had to hold the receiver at arm's length.

'DCI Travis?'

'Speaking.'

'The marks on Mrs Douglas's neck are as I quite rightly suspected post mortem. She was hanged with the cord after death.'

'Was she strangled with it first?'

'No, and this is strictly off the record for now, as a neurologist needs to examine her brain before I can give you a definitive cause of death.'

'I really appreciate this, Professor Hall.'

'So you should, dear. Right, I've confirmed the victim did not die from the cord noose: although it was drawn very tightly she was dead before it was wound round her neck. My approximate time of death is, again subject to further tests, but I'd say at least two days ago and no more than three. No signs of defence wounds, but there is a large bruise to the back of her head and also one on her chest and it's possible your victim died of natural causes.'

'What?'

'I can't confirm it just yet, but although there is some swelling to the brain from the head injury, Mrs Douglas may have died of a heart attack. Also, whoever was with her re-dressed her as her nightdress was on back to front, unless of course she put it on back to front herself.' He gave a snorting laugh.

Anna was too impatient to be amused by his joke, but as she listened further she could feel her heart start pumping.

'The anthropologist has looked at the unidentified remains and believes, from the cranial features, that our victim is white European, aged between eighteen and twenty-five, and from the decomposition she has been dead for less than six months.'

'She's not black then?'

'This is more or less an observation and not a certain fact – further tests will need to be done on the bones, soil particles, the clay and the chalk effects to give a much clearer time frame. At this stage I couldn't even begin to give you a cause of death.'

'I really appreciate you contacting me.'

'So you should, and kindly inform those concerned that I am doing everything within my power to ensure they get results as soon as possible, but it will take considerable time thanks to the decomposition of—'

'Yes, yes,' she interrupted, wanting to get him off the phone, and finally managed to get rid of him.

She sat back and closed her eyes. If she was correct she would still have to get more evidence.

'Joan, have you arranged a meeting for me with the bank manager yet?'

'Not yet, but you know I have some priority files to get in order and—'

'Just do it now. Contact him at home if necessary!' Anna snapped and got up from her desk, so tense she needed to go to the Ladies'. She banged out of the incident room as Joan angrily snatched up her phone.

Sitting in the cubicle Anna leaned forwards, trying to ease her stomach, which was cramping from her being so wound up. Now, thinking about what she had learnt, she made the decision that she wouldn't go it alone, but tell Mike and Langton what she had uncovered, even though the picture was far from complete because she still had to make further enquiries in Glasgow. By the time she had washed her hands and combed her hair she was calmer, and almost relieved that she was going to get it off her chest.

Anna tapped on Mike's office door, opened it and entered.

'Ah, we wanted some sandwiches – oh, it's you, Travis, where have you been . . .?'

She interrupted Langton before he could get started.

'The mortuary and then making some urgent enquiries. I need to have a talk with you and Mike.'

'You are the other DCI on this investigation. You should have been here when we began. I'm not going to repeat everything we have discussed over the last few hours so—'

'It's important.' She clutched her notebook tightly.

Mike was sitting behind his desk, with Langton on one of the chairs in front of him. There were stacks of files everywhere and the room felt overheated and claustrophobic.

'Floor's yours,' Langton said.

Anna was flushed as she stood in front of them.

'Firstly I have to say I have not confirmed everything, and I have been acting on a sort of gut instinct that we might have been—'

'Never mind the bloody instinct, Travis, get on with it – we've still got a lot of work to plough through,' Langton cut in.

She was hesitant at first and shifted her weight from foot to foot, but forgot her nerves as her conviction grew.

'Angela Thornton's is not one of those bodies at the mortuary, the dental records didn't match. We've got an unidentified white female, aged eighteen to twenty-five, who's been dead for less than six months.'

'So Oates made a mistake with the "Misper" photographs and killed someone else.'

'I'm not sure about that, but I took a hair sample to the lab to try and identify her by DNA. The other thing is, Timmy Bradford lied to me when I first interviewed him with regard to how well he knew Henry Oates. When he was brought into the station for further questioning he gave us more details about when he had actually met with him, and he admitted taking him to the quarry.'

'We know all this, Travis,' Langton said irritably.

She opened her notebook.

'After Henry Oates escaped from the quarry, we spent a long time trying to trace his whereabouts, only to discover he was holding Mrs Douglas hostage, and we believed—'

Langton leaned towards her.

'Believed? What are you talking about?'

She kept it as brief as possible: she now suspected that Henry Oates made prior contact with Timmy Bradford because the same night he escaped there were two reverse charge calls from public pay phones to Mrs Douglas's flat in the early hours of the morning. One made from Hammersmith and the other from Soho. It was likely that Oates had some very big hold over him. At the present time she was unable to determine what exactly it was, but she thought that Bradford had agreed to help hide him and give him the ten thousand pounds to aid his escape.

Langton got up and pulled at his tie, shaking his head. He couldn't fathom out where the hell she was going with this.

'I think that Timmy Bradford's mother was already dead,' Anna went on. 'It is not yet confirmed, but it's a possibility the time of death does tie in with when Bradford told us Henry Oates broke into the flat.'

Langton sat back down in his chair, as Anna explained that Bradford's claim that he was at the dog track was a lie, and furthermore she had been checking the phone calls from the flat and it appeared that Bradford was possibly making arrangements at the NatWest to get his mother's money before Oates was even there.

'Jesus Christ,' muttered Langton.

Mike Lewis stared down at his hands and then looked at the stunned face of Langton. He was red-faced with anger and clenched his fists.

'Is this all confirmed by the pathologist's report?'

'Not one hundred per cent, yet! But if Bradford gets a call from Oates asking for help, it would have been a perfect set-up to frame him for his mother's murder – he might even have intended to kill him. There was immediate media coverage and it was plastered over every newspaper, Oates was on the run and—'

'Hold it right there,' Langton said. Mike and Anna fell silent as he yanked at his tie.

'This is all conjecture right now, and you're running on empty as far as Bradford's concerned; you'll need a lot more evidence, but if this is true we'd better clear it up and fast. We go pressing charges against Oates for the old girl's murder and his legal team prove we've screwed up, we could lose the whole fucking case in court.'

'Exactly, which is why I felt it was necessary to give you as much detail as I have been able to acquire.'

It was decided that they would call it quits for the night as everyone was tired out. Tomorrow morning they would bring in Timmy Bradford for questioning, tease him out with the carrot of the ten thousand and see if they could break him down. By that time they would have made contact with the bank manager and hopefully had Mrs Douglas's time of death confirmed.

As Anna packed up ready to leave for the night, Langton came and perched on the edge of her desk.

'What's the hold you reckon Oates has over Bradford?'

'I don't know.'

He cocked his head to one side.

'You have an idea though?'

'I've not thought it through yet, but as I said I'm trying to get more information on the unidentified victim.'

'Like what?'

'Well obviously, who she is for starters. I've not got anything confirmed and then there's also Angela Thornton.
Although we haven't found her body I do think Oates
murdered her as well.'

Langton walked over to the incident board and stared at
the girls' photographs. He realized what Anna was thinking.

'Why did he put that bracelet on her picture, claim that
she was one of his victims,' he wondered, tapping the photograph.

Anna stood beside him, arms folded.

'That's what bothers me. I've looked at the footage from
his interview and he carefully places her bracelet over her
picture, just as he did with all the other victims' posses-
sions.'

'But she wasn't brought back from the quarry.'

'No, so that leaves us with either another body up there
in the woods, or wherever, and the unidentified remains
in the morgue.'

'Shit, this case is like a nightmare, it never ends.'

He eased his tie back up and pressed down the edge of
his collar.

'Well, tomorrow is another day and I'm going home.'

He gave the small of her back an affectionate pat and
smiled.

'Good work. I think you gave Mike heart failure, but if
you're correct, thank Christ for you. Like it or not, now
the press are all over the investigation and due to the fuck-
ups so far we now have to run everything by Commander
Leigh — you know, protocol, big brother, et cetera.'

The night staff were beginning to take their desks as he
strolled out. Barbara and Joan had already left, but Anna

felt restless and sat at her desk. She saw the lights go off in Mike's office and kept her head down as if reading her notes as he walked past.

He paused in the doorway, turning back to her.

'Are we to expect any further surprises from you?'

'Depends on how tomorrow pans out. But if it all tallies up it could be the reason Oates has behaved himself since we re-arrested him.'

'Goodnight, Anna,' he said quietly.

'Goodnight, Mike,' she replied.

Chapter Twenty-One

The first thing Anna did when she got home was to ring Morag Kelly's mobile phone. It was after ten so she hoped the young woman would pick up. It rang and rang, and she was impatiently about to end the call when someone answered.

'Is this Morag Kelly?'

'Aye.'

'I wondered if you could help me. I am trying to trace Corinna Oates and I know you were in rehab with her.'

There was an intake of breath and Anna quickly tried to keep the girl calm, explaining that Morag was not in any kind of trouble whatsoever, but the call was very important as Anna was part of a police investigation attempting to find Corinna's whereabouts.

'Well I cannae help ye. I've not seen her since she ran off, and we wasnae that friendly anyway.'

'But you knew her?'

'Aye, but she's nae friend of mine. When she left she nicked some of ma stuff, so even if I did meet up with her, I'd slap her face.'

'I just need to ask if you remember maybe Corinna saying anything about where she might go.'

'Nae, we've all been asked about her, but she never told

nobody – she did a runner when we was supposed tae be workin'.'

'You are being really helpful, and just one more thing: can you recall any of her clothes, what she might have been wearing?'

'Nae, we hadda wear smocks cos we was doin' the kitchen cleanin'; she could've worn somethin' under the smock, but she wasnae wearin' them then or I'd have noticed cos they were mine.'

'What did she take of yours, Morag?'

'Ma patent leather boots.'

'Could you describe them to me? And maybe give me a better idea of what Corinna looked like?'

Anna spent a few more moments talking to Morag about Corinna. Eventually the young woman grew less suspicious and told Anna what she needed to know. Anna thanked her profusely for her help before hanging up. There was no way she could do anything about the information until morning, but it was another connection and one that might be another piece of the jigsaw.

Professor Hall, for all his pomposity, had evidently pulled out all the stops, as the following morning they received the official post mortem report on Mrs Douglas. Neither Anna nor Langton was at the station when it arrived, making Mike even more impatient than usual.

'Where is she? We're bringing in Timmy Bradford!'

Joan called her mobile, but it was turned off.

'She's not answering.'

'It's bloody ten-thirty, for God's sake – what does she think she's playing at!'

Barbara whispered aside to Joan that perhaps she was

solving the case, but shut up quickly as Mike turned on her.

'What did you say?'

'Just had a call from Barolli, guv, wanting to know if we've solved the case, we've been giving him an update,' Barbara improvised swiftly.

'Good, how's he doing?'

'Oh he's fine, up and out of bed and—'

Mike didn't wait to hear any more as Langton walked in, signalling for Mike to join him in his office, which he treated like his own.

'Barbara spoke with Paul Barolli earlier. He's doing well and has managed to get out of bed,' Mike informed Langton.

'That's good news,' Langton replied.

'Yeah well, the bad news is I can't track Travis down and her mobile is turned off.'

'She called me and said she was going to the NatWest at New Malden to speak with the bank manager and then coming back here,' Langton informed Mike.

'Doesn't she want to speak to me?' Mike asked.

'She knows how busy you are so she asked me to tell you, which I just have. Now what's happening with Timmy Bradford?'

'He's been at a bed and breakfast until we've cleared all the forensic work at his flat; he was allowed back to get some clothes,' Mike told him.

'How's he holding up?'

'Seems fine, asked about when he could arrange a funeral for his mother. Did you see the post mortem report?'

Langton hadn't, so Mike showed him a copy, which he read at once, and then let it drop onto the desk.

'Shit, a bloody heart attack!'

'But it could have been caused by fear – there are bruises to her head and chest. She was hung up by the cord after she was dead.'

Langton wafted his hand.

'Okay, let's go over how we handle the interview.'

'What about Travis?'

Langton gave him a direct look.

'Your enquiry, Mike, never mind what she's doing.' He tapped the report with his finger and suggested they interview Bradford as a witness first before arresting him and having a solicitor present.

Anna's immediate task that day had been to visit the bank manager, who told her that Bradford had called the bank twice a couple of days before he came in to collect the money. The original calls were taken by a cashier; Bradford had enquired about what he would have to do to withdraw money on his mother's behalf and his mother, Mrs Douglas, had even spoken with the cashier, giving her password and approving withdrawal by her son. The call on the day he picked up the money was, as Anna already knew, thanks to the wiretap, to arrange for the time of collection.

Anna's next stop was to see Pete Jenkins. He was, as she had requested, examining the pair of patent leather knee-high boots. The size and description fitted the ones mentioned by Morag Kelly; they were also in good condition unlike the other shoes found at the basement. Anna asked for them to be bagged up.

'What about the DNA test? Did you get anything for me?'

Pete nodded and they headed into the lab. She was

buzzing, her adrenalin pumping, and she couldn't resist asking him for the result.

'Am I right?'

'Aren't you always?'

'Is that a yes, Pete, is that a YES?'

'Not quite yet, the hair was too degraded to get a full DNA result, but I did get a mitochondrial DNA profile, which is inherited from the mother's side. I'll need a sample from the mother to make the comparison and access to the Scottish DNA database.'

'Leave it with me, and thanks, Pete.'

Anna rang Glasgow on her drive back to the station, asking to speak to DCI McBride, who came onto the phone with obvious irritation. She thanked him for helping her trace Morag Kelly, but she now needed another favour, and one that was connected to Eileen Oates. When she explained the importance of it, he agreed to set the wheels in motion.

Just after twelve-fifteen, Timmy Bradford was brought to the station in a patrol car. He was a little over-bright, joking about how he hoped none of his friends saw him as they'd think he'd been arrested. He was led into the interview-room corridor and asked if he would like coffee or a tea, but he said he'd stick to water as he didn't drink either. When he was shown into the room, Langton and Mike were sitting side by side waiting.

'Morning, Mr Bradford,' Langton said, smiling.

'Morning.'

Bradford took a seat opposite them.

'Thank you for agreeing to come in to see us, we just need to clear up a few things. You can have a solicitor present, if you want.'

'Why should I want a solicitor – am I under arrest?'

'No. Just standard procedure to ask in cases like this.'

'I don't want one.'

Langton rested his elbows on the table and waited.

'Listen, I come in because it's about that ten grand belonging to my mother. By rights that money is mine, right? So I'm here and I'd like to know when I can get it back, cos I've got to arrange and pay for her funeral. I mean, everyone's been very nice to me, I'll give you all that, but I have things I've got to organize, understand me?'

'Do you go to the dog tracks on a regular basis?' Mike asked.

Bradford nodded but seemed surprised by Mike's sudden line of questioning.

'Yeah I do, dogs, horses, I like a flutter.'

'On the night you say Henry Oates broke into your flat . . .'

'Me mother let him in.'

'Sorry, yes of course, you have said that the reason you weren't at home until midnight was because you were at Wimbledon dog track,' Mike reminded him.

'Yeah, I'm a regular there, why? It's the truth.'

'Back a few winners, did you?'

'No, I was on a real losing streak, tearing up the betting slips all night, not one winner.'

Langton tapped the table twice with his pen and took over the questioning.

'You're definitely on a losing streak, Mr Bradford, a very big one, because on that specific night the track was closed for refurbishment,' Langton remarked.

Bradford blinked and then gave a half smile, unsure of who would ask the next question.

'No way.'

'Let's not mess around any longer, because you are very close to being arrested on suspicion of assisting an escaped murderer.'

Bradford opened and closed his mouth.

'I don't understand what's going on here.'

Langton began opening a file in front of him.

'Why you got me here? I thought it was about me money.'

'Is it about the money, Mr Bradford? We know you were in touch with the NatWest Bank in New Malden before Mr Oates came to your mother's flat.'

'This isn't right.'

'So do you agree that before Mr Oates stayed at your flat you had already arranged—'

'Listen, my mother wanted me to get ten grand out so we could go on a luxury cruise, that's why I was doing all the arrangements, and it just coincided with Oates turning up.'

Langton leaned back in his chair, smiling.

'You are a very good actor, Mr Bradford, in fact so good I think you could have taken it up as a profession, but right now I am getting very tired of this performance. I believed you and Detective Chief Inspector Lewis here also believed you, that big act in the Kingston Lodge Hotel about how fearful you were for your mother – that was, I suppose, partly due to nerves. I mean, you didn't expect to get picked up, did you? But then you played it to the hilt, didn't you? DIDN'T YOU?'

Langton slapped the table so hard the water bottles jumped.

'She was already dead, wasn't she? WASN'T SHE? All that bullshit about Oates threatening to hang her – what's the matter with you? You think we're so dumb we can't get a time of death for her? That we can't get evidence that she was never hanged? Strung up, yes, but she was already dead, wasn't she?'

'I want a solicitor.' Bradford kept his head down.

'Well now that I'm arresting you for not only harbouring Oates, but also on suspicion of being complicit in your mother's murder, you can have one.'

Mike Lewis then cautioned Bradford and took him to the custody area to be booked in and the duty solicitor Mary Adams was called to represent him.

Anna went into the viewing room to watch as soon as she got back to the station. Barbara got up to leave as Anna sat down.

'No, stay put, I need you to fill me in on what's happened to date.'

'Well, he's denying that he had anything to do with his mother's death, he's admitted lying about going to the dog track, but he said he was forced to do it because Oates had tied his mother up and threatened him. He's also said that his mother had asked him to withdraw ten thousand in cash to pay for a cruise and she had signed the necessary papers. He claims Oates found them and then threatened to kill his mother if he didn't withdraw the lot and give it to him.'

Anna looked at the monitor screen as Langton suggested that they now go from the beginning again as Bradford was plainly lying.

'I'm telling you the truth.'

'Really? Then how do you explain that your mother was already dead before Oates had even escaped from the quarry?'

Anna sipped her coffee, watching Bradford's reaction, which did not give much away. He was drinking from a bottle of water, then turning the cap this way and that.

'What's he got on you?' Langton asked.

'Who?'

'Henry Oates. What's he got on you to make you hide him and then get the money out?'

Bradford shook his head and mumbled something inaudible.

'Listen to me, Timmy, we know someone called you from payphones reverse charge, you knew he was coming to your mother's flat, so why didn't you call the police?'

No reaction.

'You are an intelligent man, Timmy. If you are protecting him . . .'

'I'm fucking not.'

'So what made you let him into your flat? Why did you help him?'

There was no reaction, and then Anna leaned forwards as Langton searched through a file and whispered something to Mike. Mike reached for a separate file on the trolley and passed it to Langton.

'Have you ever seen any of these girls, Timmy?'

Out came the photographs of their victims, each one laid flat in front of Bradford, but he shook his head over and over again.

'I've never seen any of them, I swear before God.'

Langton quietly told Bradford that they were the young women that his friend Oates had admitted to killing.

'Jesus Christ, I had nothin' to do with them. I've never seen any of them before in my life.'

Langton gathered up the photographs and stacked them on the edge of the table like a pack of cards.

'It's hard for me to believe that. You see, I can't understand why you would let him hide out in your flat, unless you were involved. You were the one who originally took him to the quarry, you—'

'I had nothing to do with any of them.' Bradford was becoming very agitated and starting to sweat.

'You expect me to believe you? You've lied about your mother. She was eighty-two years old, wasn't she? You think she deserved to end up dead, strung up on a pulley over her bath?'

'No,' Bradford replied quietly.

'What happened, Timmy, did she find out you were trying to steal her money, caught you red-handed faking her signature on a cheque and you argued?'

Bradford was beginning to break, his body language indicating that he was finding it hard to control himself. His hands were clasped at his sides and he was still sweating, with stains spreading under the armpits of his denim shirt.

'Let me tell you what I think happened: you had this argument with your mother and you snapped, you didn't mean to hurt her, you couldn't stop yourself, you needed that money and . . .'

'She wouldn't give it to me.' Bradford blurted it out.

Anna stood up and looked to Barbara.

'Got him, he's going to spill the beans.'

'You want a coffee?'

'Nope, I need to make some urgent calls,' Anna said as she left the room.

The next time Anna saw Barbara was when she hurried into the incident room an hour later.

'DCS Langton wants the gold bracelet from the evidence locker room.'

'How's it going in there?' Anna asked.

'Well it's not really, they still haven't broken him.'

Anna raced down into the basement to unlock the evidence cage with Barbara hurrying alongside her.

'He's opened the floodgates, we've had tears and at one point he even tried to get on his knees to beg forgiveness. Bradford's got a lot of debts from his gambling and there's some heavy guys onto him so he needed to get some cash to pay them off.'

Anna began to dig around for the bag containing the gold bracelet. 'Did he explain why he helped Oates?'

'No,' said Barbara as Anna handed her the little bag. 'He won't say it.' She held up the bag. 'Maybe this is connected?' Then she hurried back to the interview-room corridor to hand over the bracelet.

Anna slipped back into the viewing room a few moments later and Barbara rejoined her. Bradford now looked in bad shape – his hair was sodden and his face was shiny from sweat. He was hunched in his seat, his hands clasped tightly together.

'Sorry for the delay, Mr Bradford,' smiled Langton, 'but I now need to take you right back to when you first heard from Henry Oates on the night he escaped . . .'

'I've told you, I've told you, he just turned up.'

'But we have these two calls, Timmy, one at 3 a.m. from Hammersmith where he dumped the police car after he escaped, and the other at 5 a.m. from Soho, which is about a two-hour walk from Hammersmith.'

Joan tapped on the door of the viewing room and told Anna that DCI Alex McBride was on the phone, urgently wanting to talk to her. By the time Anna had taken the call and returned to her seat Mike and Langton had still made no headway. Mike was now asking the same questions. All they got for an answer was that Bradford was scared not to help Oates, but he had admitted he had slapped his mother during an argument.

'Did Langton show him the bracelet?' Anna asked Barbara.

She shook her head. 'It's amazing, isn't it? They kind of go round and round in circles.'

'It's called wearing the suspect down,' Anna said drily.

'Well I know that, but one minute he does look worn down through his lies, and then the next he claims that he's telling the truth. One minute he admits to pushing or slapping his mother, the next he denies it, and yet we have the time of death that makes it impossible for Oates to have killed her.'

Anna focused on the screen as Langton laid out the plastic evidence bag containing the gold bracelet. He gently flattened the air out of it with his hand.

'Have you ever seen this before, Mr Bradford?'

'No.'

'Let me take it out so you can get a closer look.'

Langton held the bracelet up and then rested it across his wrist.

'Look at it, Timmy, take a good look at it.'

Bradford's chest heaved and he straightened his back, shaking his head.

'Take hold of it, Tim, really, go on, have a good look.'

Anna tensed up, leaning forwards, wondering what Langton's intentions were. But disappointingly Bradford showed little reaction.

'No.'

'Why does it worry you to touch it? Here, take hold of it.'

'I don't want to.'

'It's not your mother's, is it?'

'No.'

Langton looked through the stack of photographs and placed the one of Angela Thornton down in front of Bradford.

'You know this girl, don't you?' he asked as he placed the bracelet beside the photograph.

It was astonishing because Bradford started to cry like a kid. Snot dripped from his nose and he wiped it with the cuff of his shirt, then he put his head in his hands and started sobbing heavily.

An hour later Bradford asked for a bathroom break. Langton had been given a real talking-to by Bradford's solicitor, Miss Adams, as she had no disclosure regarding Angela Thornton and felt that Langton was being, at times, overbearing with her client. They had a very heated discussion and by the time Langton came into the incident room he was in a real temper. He paced in front of Anna's desk, snatching at a sandwich she'd brought in for him.

'I can't bloody break the little sod: every time I think he's going to come clean he backs off and turns the water-works on.'

'I thought you were onto something with the bracelet and the photo of Angela. It did get a big reaction – it was the first time he really broke down.'

'I'd like to break his sodding little neck.' He sighed.

'Do you think there is a connection between him and Angela Thornton?'

'I don't honestly know. I was just trying it on because that's another fucking scenario we need to explore.'

He wiped his fingers on a paper napkin, rolled it up into a tight ball and tossed it into the wastebasket.

'We believe that Oates has some hold over Bradford, right? And it's a big one, so is there any possibility that it was the two of them? That they're both killers, and did all of the murders between them?'

Anna shook her head.

'No, I don't buy that; Oates has admitted to the murders. Why would he protect Timmy if he was an accomplice? It couldn't have been the two of them with Mrs Douglas if she was already dead.'

'Yes, yes, I know that,' he snapped.

Anna found it difficult to know what to say to Langton as he was in such a foul mood.

'Listen, let me dig around and see if I can find any connection between Bradford and Angela Thornton, because of the way he reacted the first time he broke down.'

'The little fucker could get an Oscar nomination for his performances; it's hard to get anything out of him.'

Anna suggested that in the next session they should pull back on the accusation about his mother. They now knew she had died of a heart attack, so maybe if they went softly and encouraged Bradford to talk about the possibility of it being an accident, that he had never intended to hurt her, he would divulge more about his relationship with Oates.

Langton checked his watch and agreed that he would give it a go.

Bradford appeared to be calmer. He'd washed his face and hands, and sat pressing back into his chair, his solicitor beside him. Mike reminded him that he was still under caution, and that anything he said might be used as evidence in court. Before Langton started the interview

Bradford cleared his throat and said that he had been answering all their questions truthfully, and he was still very distressed about what had happened. He then gave a long rambling explanation of how he had been out shopping and when he returned Oates had already been let into the flat by his mother. He said that Oates had tied her up and she was lying on the sofa in her nightdress and had wet herself. He said she had sticky tape wrapped around her face and hands and her feet were tied with the cord from her dressing gown.

'I'd fancied a beer so I just walked round to the off-licence, they're open until late, and I made up that story about the dog track because I didn't want to admit that Oates scared me.'

Anna licked her fingers as she sifted through her pages and pages of notes. In fact she had filled up one notebook and was on to her second. Eventually she found what she was looking for, her interview with Ira Zacks. She had made only sporadic notes, mostly about the last time he said he had seen Oates and his work in the clubs. She closed her eyes, willing herself to remember. She recalled he had said that Oates only worked for him briefly as he was not suitable, but no matter how many times she went backwards and forwards through her jottings she couldn't find what she was looking for, so she snapped her book closed and crossed to stare once more at the incident board. She concentrated on Angela Thornton's missing persons details and then it clicked.

She absolutely had to speak to Ira Zacks. She knew that he hadn't been granted bail and was awaiting trial for drug dealing, so she called Brixton Prison, stressing it was of the utmost importance and involved a murder enquiry. There was a long delay as she hung on waiting before eventually being told that it would take at least half an hour for them to bring Ira Zacks to the governor's office, always supposing he would agree to talk to her. Frustrated, she even suggested that she could make the journey to the prison in person. She insisted it had nothing to do with his drug charges but it was imperative she speak to him and for them to explain who she was and that they had met before.

Anna waited impatiently for nearly an hour, but eventually the call came.

'He's through, Detective Travis.'

'Thank you. Mr Zacks, I don't know if you remember me – I came to your flat to ask you some questions about Henry Oates.'

'Yeah.'

'I am really grateful that you have agreed to talk to me.'

'Yeah.'

'You mentioned to me that you ran a business supplying doormen to a number of clubs in London.'

'Not any more.'

'But you did, and you had a very successful business.'

'Yeah.'

'You started off in the East End, is that right?'

'Yeah, Mile End Road, near the boxing club.'

'Do you recall the names of any of the men you employed?'

'It's not exactly employed – I give 'em the job and they give me a cut; it wasn't like I employed them back then, if you know what I mean, and I didn't have no contracts, it was verbal with me.'

'Yes, I understand, it's just very important if you could remember any of the men that worked for you and I realize it is a long time ago, but perhaps they were ex-boxers ...'

'Yeah.'

'I am talking nearly five years ago, so it might be a test of your memory.'

'You don't say. What's in this for me anyway?'

Anna licked her lips and decided to test Zacks' empathy.

'You remember me showing you a picture of a little girl that was missing? Well, if you could remember – you have children of your own and ...'

'Yeah, yeah, it's to do with Henry Oates, right?'

'Yes.'

'Well I only used him the once and he was no use, didn't have a suit either, but it wasn't in Mile End, that was over in Kilburn.'

'So do you remember anyone working for you in Mile End?'

There was a pause and she could hear his heavy breathing.

'Yeah, okay, Brian Heigh, middleweight, good bloke.'

She waited; he was clicking his tongue against his teeth.

'Tony Jackson, he used to be there, but I don't remember nobody else. Wait a minute, there was one of the guys I knew from York Hall, he worked there a few times, shit, can't remember his name.'

'Describe him to me.'

Ira exhaled and said she was asking a lot and then without hesitation he said, 'Of course, it was Tim Bradford, there you go, shows my grey cells are still working, nice fighter, but bled like a stuck pig. I remember him now, lived up the road in Bromley-by-Bow, but he didn't do more than a few months.'

*

Anna's hand was shaking as she replaced the phone, and she had to take a few deep breaths before she could write down the information. Then she made her way to the interview room, tapped on the door and opened it. 'DCI Travis with a message for DCS Langton,' she said for the benefit of the tape. Langton came out, closing the door behind him.

'I tried the softly-softly and he still won't give it up.'

'Try this.'

Anna explained to him about the Mile End connection, and her idea that the night Angela Thornton had disappeared, Bradford could have been working the doors on the club. He had lived just up the road from there and had never been questioned about her disappearance as they had CCTV footage of her leaving the club and heading for the Tube station. Anna had also checked with the DVLA to confirm that at that time Bradford owned a car. It was a red Ford Fiesta and a witness had claimed to have seen a red car parked close to the Tube station, although the car and driver had never been traced. Langton folded the notes and gave a brief nod of his head, but he took a few moments before he returned to the interview room.

Anna sat in the viewing room, watching as Langton took his seat, intrigued as to how he would handle the new information. First he set aside the files he had been using before the interruption. He then stacked them onto the trolley. He next removed the Angela Thornton file and the exhibit bag with her bracelet, setting them in front of him. He took out his fountain pen, drew his notebook close, wrote something and then replaced the cap.

Bradford looked at his solicitor then back to Langton.

Meanwhile, Mike had been given Anna's latest findings, which he read before returning them to Langton.

'My client has been in custody since midday and it is now 7.30 p.m.,' the solicitor pointed out. 'If you have no further questions to put to him and are not charging him with any offence then I suggest—'

Langton ignored her and cut in.

'Tell me about the time you worked on the Mile End Road, Mr Bradford.'

Bradford's mouth dropped open.

'What is this in reference to?' his solicitor asked.

Langton held up the photograph of Angela Thornton.

'The murder of this girl, Miss Adams.' He turned to Bradford. 'What happened, Tim, you see her dancing around, having a night out with her friends, too good for the likes of you, you try and get a date, did you? She turn you down, did she? Look at her, LOOK AT HER!' He slapped the photograph down on the table. 'Just a washed-up amateur boxer, only jobs you could get were working the doors, and there was this lovely girl, shiny blonde hair, blue eyes, and this lovely bracelet – was it that you were after? Did you want to nick her gold bracelet? You'd never be able to afford anything as nice as this to give to a girl. You were still dependent on your mother and stepfather; he didn't like you, did he? Reckoned you were a big free-loader ...'

As Langton talked it was like watching a tight spring begin to uncoil. Bradford was squirming in his seat, his fists clenched one minute, the next pressing down on his thighs. His body twisted, and he kept moving his head from side to side as if his neck was stiffening up.

'Can I give you a lift, love, can I give you a lift in my red Ford Fiesta?' Langton adopted a singsong voice,

smiling. 'You can trust me, love, I work the doors, I protect people, I don't let in the tough guys, I look out for
the customers, you can trust me, get in the car, I can take
you home . . .'

Langton stopped smiling as he leaned across the table
and raised his voice.

'But you didn't take her home, did you? DID YOU?
How did you break her little gold bracelet? Grab her by
the wrists, did you? Smack her around, did you? Punch
out this lovely little girl, look at her face, look at her face,
Timmy.'

'I want to speak with my solicitor,' Bradford said softly.

'You do that and I hope she advises you that it would be
in your best interests to tell us the truth about everything!'
Langton shouted.

Anna thought that Langton was going to reach over and
grab Bradford by the hair and shove his face down onto
the table. But before he could launch into another likely
scenario of what might have happened that fatal evening,
Bradford began to punch his own chest. His fists smacked
hard into his flesh, ape-like, but far from an animal show
of superiority, it was a pitiful show, his last fight, before he
broke down and the floodgates opened.

Chapter Twenty-Two

The following morning the team gathered in the incident room at 9 a.m. for an update briefing from Mike Lewis and Anna about the previous day's interviews and interesting developments concerning Timmy Bradford working at the nightclub in the Mile End Road. The same club that Angela Thornton had been to the night she was believed to have been abducted and murdered. Langton stayed in Mike's office, listening to the recorded interviews they had already had with Bradford and preparing for the further interview with him that was to take place after the briefing.

The interview of Timmy Bradford, again with his solicitor Mary Adams present, started at just after 10 a.m. Anna, Barbara and Joan were all in the viewing room, eager to see if Langton would finally get Timmy Bradford to tell the truth and confess to his involvement in Angela and his mother's deaths, but more importantly if he would reveal Oates's involvement in the crimes.

'I tell you, I reckon there'll be floods of tears again in that room,' Barbara said with a serious look on her face.

'Bradford looks pretty calm to me,' Joan replied.

'No, not him, bloody Langton if he doesn't get

Bradford to roll over this time!' Barbara retorted amusingly, causing everyone to laugh loudly.

Mike had turned on the recording equipment and Langton was about to start his questioning when Miss Adams interjected.

'As you are aware, Detective Langton, I had a lengthy consultation with my client both last night and this morning. He has informed me that he had not told you the truth previously, as he was afraid of Henry Oates who is clearly a violent and dangerous man. Mr Bradford is now prepared to tell you about both his mother's and Angela Thornton's deaths. He is also willing to give evidence against Oates at trial.'

'Thank you, Miss Adams, for advising your client to assist us,' Langton said before again being interrupted by Miss Adams.

'However, he maintains, and will explain why in detail, that the deaths of both women were not in any way premeditated.'

'Let's start with Angela then, Timmy. Tell me about how you met her and the night she died,' Langton said, and then sat back in his chair, anticipating only partial truths from Bradford.

'I was working at the nightclub in Mile End and I'd seen Angela there a few times and I asked her out once but she said she had a boyfriend. Henry knew who she was as well cos I pointed her out and told him I fancied her.'

'Where was that?' Mike asked.

'The nightclub. I'd got Henry a temporary job there under a false name, cash in hand, while another bloke was off sick. It was to make up for him not getting work at the chalk quarry. I can't remember the exact night, but Henry was with me and we'd finished work and were going back to my flat in Bow in my car.'

'The red Fiesta?' Mike asked.

'Yes. I saw Angela by the Mile End Tube Station; she looked drunk and was staggering about, carrying a bottle of alcopop and her shoes. I stopped and asked her if she was okay. She said she had missed the last Tube home and didn't have enough money for a cab,' Bradford told them in a subdued voice.

'Timmy. I need you to speak up so the recorder picks up everything you are saying,' Mike told him.

'Sorry. It's just so hard because I lied to her. I said I didn't have any insurance and had been drinking so I didn't want to risk driving her all the way out to Epping.'

Langton sat up and leaned towards Bradford, expecting him to say that he and Oates then left Angela in the street and someone else must have picked her up and killed her. He was surprised when Bradford went on to say that he offered Angela a lift home, thinking at first that she lived locally, and she got in the car. Once in the car she said she lived in Epping so he lied about the insurance and drinking. He realized how drunk she was and, wanting to take advantage of this, he told her that he had a spare room at his flat and she could stay there for the night and get the Tube home in the morning.

'So you coaxed her back to your flat with the intention of having sex with her and no doubt you then plied her with more drink,' Langton stated and Bradford nodded.

'She got so drunk she fell asleep on the settee and I carried her through to my bedroom and had sex with her.

She didn't resist though,' Bradford said in a feeble attempt to excuse his actions.

'Did Henry have sex with her as well?' Mike asked, deliberately avoiding the fact that it was rape for fear of upsetting the flow of Bradford's account of what happened to Angela.

'No, he slept in the spare room and he was still there in the morning when I was panicking and asking him what to do cos I couldn't wake her up.'

'So how did you kill her?' Langton asked, confused by what Bradford had just said.

'That's it – I didn't. Henry came and looked at her and said she must have choked on her own vomit and died. Henry laughed, he thought it was funny, but I wanted to call an ambulance. He said no way because they would call the police then we'd be arrested for rape and murder.'

Anna and the others were still in the viewing room and it seemed to them that Bradford, although visibly distraught, was holding himself together and probably now telling the truth, and his further account of what happened explained why Oates had such a strong hold over him.

Bradford went on to say that he had found himself in an unreal place, terrified of being arrested and consumed by guilt about Angela's death. Oates had told him that he shouldn't worry as he would get rid of the body for him but he needed to use his car to do this. Oates had said that by disposing of the body it made them partners and Timmy owed him. Bradford never knew or asked where the body had been taken and he thought that Oates had since sold the car or burnt it.

*

Bradford went on to say that after Angela's death Oates had contacted him five or six times demanding money. He gave him what he could but about two years ago he told Oates that he had had enough and if Henry didn't leave him alone he would go and tell the police what had happened to Angela. After reading about Oates's arrest in the paper, Bradford was sure it was all going to come out but he figured Oates hadn't said anything about it as he was never arrested and was not asked about Angela when DCI Travis came to see him or when he was asked about the quarry incident at the police station.

Langton decided that it was time to move on to the death of Bradford's mother, Mrs Douglas.

'Thank you, Timmy, for telling us about what happened to Angela Thornton, but I now want to move on to the death of your mother. Do you want to continue or would you like a short break to compose yourself?' Langton asked.

'No, thanks. I had been running up gambling debts and I was two grand in debt to a loan shark so I asked my mum if I could borrow some money to pay him off but she refused to help me.'

'When was this?' Langton asked.

'A day or so before Henry escaped and came to the flat. I was desperate, so while Mum was out I phoned the bank and said that she wanted me to make a withdrawal on her behalf and I asked what they needed for me to do this.'

'The cashier said she spoke with your mum for her password and approval,' Mike informed Bradford.

'That was me pretending to be her. She kept her bank stuff and password in her bedside table. She obviously guessed I was up to something cos that night she searched my room and found the letter of authority that I had made up and signed in her name.'

'Did this lead to an argument?' Langton asked, wanting to cut to the chase.

'Yes, in the living room. She was shouting and swearing at me and telling me to get out. I pleaded with her and said I was sorry and she came right up to me, face to face, and said that as long as she lived she never wanted to see me again and she slapped me.' Bradford went silent and started to cry.

'What happened then, Timmy?' Mike asked.

'I gently pushed her away; she tripped over the rug and fell backwards. Her head hit the window ledge and then she just slumped onto the floor. There was no blood coming from her head. I thought she had passed out. I tried but I couldn't wake her up.'

'Why didn't you call an ambulance?' Langton asked.

'She was just lying there like Angela. I knew she was dead so I put her in her nightdress and then in her bed. I was going to call her doctor in the morning and say she must have died in her sleep,' Bradford replied, staring at the floor with more tears streaming down his cheeks.

'So if she was already dead before Oates escaped and you let him into your mum's flat, you must have agreed to help him when he rang you at 3 a.m.,' Mike said.

'Not at first. Henry was hysterical and said he was on the run and needed a place to stay. I lied and told him my mother was in hospital after a heart attack but he phoned again and made threats about Angela, saying that he had kept her gold bracelet and the police had found it, so I went and picked him up in Soho,' Bradford told them.

'I have to say, Timmy, as unbelievable as it all sounds I

doubt you'd be capable of making it up. What I'd like to know is how the hell your already dead mother was found hanging in the bathroom?' Langton asked, trying to keep up with Bradford's astonishing account of what had happened.

Bradford told Langton and Mike that he hadn't wanted Oates to see his mother's body, because he would yet again have another hold over him, so he removed the bath panel and laid her on a dressing gown behind the panel before borrowing a friend's car and picking Oates up in Soho. Then on the way back to the flat he told Oates that while his mother was ill in hospital he had made an arrangement with the bank to withdraw ten grand and he would give Henry half of it to help him get out of the country.

'What on earth were you going to do with your mother after Oates left?' Langton asked incredulously and looked at Mike, who seemed as confused as he was.

'Well, it was all happening so fast I wasn't sure. At first, if Henry took the money and left, I was going to call the police and say that he had tied me up but I escaped and then found my mother hanging from the pulley and you would think he had killed her.'

'You said "at first", so the second option was . . .?'

'Kind of forced upon me when you lot nabbed me after I got the money from the bank.'

Both Langton and Mike noticed the change in Bradford's demeanour. He had stopped crying and was smiling as he went on to explain how, even after they had apprehended him at the Kingston Lodge Hotel, he still tried to turn the tables on Oates and frame him for his mother's murder. Langton and Mike were initially confused about the telephone call Bradford had with Oates from the hotel, but all was revealed as Bradford explained that although Oates had said he was edgy, the clock was ticking, and he might kill someone, Henry wasn't referring to Timmy's mother as he thought she was in hospital, and the same thing when Timmy said at the flat that he wanted to see his mother. Langton was annoyed with himself as it dawned on him that it was after Oates had put the phone down that Bradford started pleading for him not to kill his mother. Langton realized that Timmy Bradford, like Oates, was not as stupid as he looked – they were both streetwise quick thinkers.

Insult was added to injury for Langton as Bradford explained that Oates had never threatened him, other than about Angela's death, and when Henry was taking his time counting out the money he had gone to the bathroom and removed his mother's body from behind the bath panel and hung her from the pulley with her dressing-gown cord. He took the stepping stool from the kitchen and put it beside his mother. Bradford went on to say that he knew the police would soon burst in as he saw the camera drill start to come through the wall, so he went back into the living room, knowing that Oates had already said he would tie him up and leave after he had dyed his hair. He had figured that even if Oates denied murdering his mother the police would never believe him and not only would he be rid of Oates for ever but he would get his mother's money as well. He said that he had even considered stabbing and killing Oates at one time and saying it was self-defence, but he didn't have the bottle to physically murder someone.

At the conclusion of the interview Langton informed

Bradford that he would be charged with the murders of Angela Thornton and his mother, and also with perverting the course of justice and harbouring Henry Oates.

'I swear I didn't mean to kill them, it was accidental.'

'Well it won't be accidental if a jury convicts you of murder, Mr Bradford!' Langton said as he got up and left the room.

It had been yet another exhausting day full of surprises. Langton, although irate that Timmy Bradford had had him over, more than once, was nevertheless pleased that he and Mike Lewis had finally got out of him what seemed, as amazing as it was, to be the truth. Certainly the post mortem results confirmed to a large extent that his account of his mother's death was true, and where Angela was concerned he did not appear to be a cold-blooded killer, and ironically this might be something that Oates could confirm.

Now it was time for the final onslaught: the last interview with Henry Oates, before having him formally charged with all the other murders they had uncovered as well as perverting the course of justice by disposing of Angela Thornton's body. Armed with the new information from Bradford, the team began to prepare for the final interview.

The full and detailed post mortem reports on the victims' remains would take a number of weeks, as there were many scientific tests that still needed to be carried out, so the team would not know how long the women had been dead or exactly how, if they would ever know at all, some of the victims had died until those examinations were completed. For now, discovering how Oates had abducted, murdered and eventually buried them was heavily dependent on what he said during further interviews. Only Rebekka Jordan's file was complete. Enquiries into where Oates had buried Angela Thornton and the identity of the unknown body recovered from the woods were still ongoing.

Still the team hoped that with the pressure of having been recaptured and the recovery of the bodies while he was on the run, Oates would make a full confession and confirm Timmy Bradford's admissions.

Henry Oates had remained well behaved since his re-arrest at the flat and was quite content sitting in the police cell reading about himself in the papers. There were no signs of depression – more of elation and arrogance that he had escaped at the quarry. He even boasted to his guard about being shot with the Taser gun and how the officers who entered the flat were scared to take him on in a fight. Kumar had been to visit him and to explain that the police had recovered the bodies from the woods and were making further enquiries before they would interview him again. Oates had laughed and told Kumar that he wasn't going anywhere, so the police could take as much time as they wanted.

Oates was reserved and polite when he was led into the interview room. He still bore the remains of red hair dye, which gave him an almost clownish appearance, but he didn't act the fool. Langton and Mike were sitting waiting. Much as Anna would have liked to have been part of the interview, she was not the senior DCI and Langton was still intent on Mike getting as much kudos as possible, so she took her seat in the viewing room. As she did so, her mobile rang. It was Pete Jenkins saying that he had received the DNA swab and access to the Scottish database from DCI McBride and should therefore have a result later that morning. Eileen Oates's saliva sample was being tested and he would get back to her as soon as he could; he knew the importance of it, so was dealing with it personally.

Anna turned her attention back to the interview. She could tell by how slowly it was going that it could be hours before they got to Mrs Douglas. The only good thing about it was the way Oates appeared to be being helpful and answered clearly as they took him through one victim at a time. Since he had already admitted to the murder of Justine Marks and Fidelis Julia Flynn, they had moved on to Kelly Mathews, Mary Suffolk and Alicia Jones, asking where he had abducted and murdered them before taking their bodies to the woods and burying them. He had difficulty recalling the exact dates and places so Mike used the 'Misper' files to help jog Oates's memory as to where they had last been seen and what they were wearing.

Anna broke off to drop into the incident room and ask Barbara if she'd taken a call from Pete Jenkins, but she hadn't.

'How's it all going?'

'Slowly, but he's behaving himself.'

Anna checked her mobile for a text message from Pete but there wasn't one, so she headed back to the viewing room, where the tension had gone up a notch. Langton and Mike were revisiting the case of Rebekka Jordan as they were not happy with Oates's account of how he had killed her and that he had not sexually abused her. Oates continued to repeat that he had never intended to hurt her, that it was an accident. Anna watched Langton move off on a tangent, asking about the Jeep and how he had stolen it – anything to keep him calm and pliable. Oates liked to talk about how clever he was, and even discussed how he'd slipped up by not watching the Jeep blow up rather than just catch fire.

Langton put down the photograph of Angela Thornton.

'Tell me about this girl.'

'I had her gold bracelet, that's about as much as I can remember about her. I prised out the red stones – they was garnets, not worth much.'

'Where did you meet her?'

'Don't remember.'

'You sure about that? Only we have a problem, Henry: none of the bodies we've brought back from the woods matches her dental records – do you understand what I mean by that?'

'I took her up there, that's all I know.'

'I am going to come clean with you, Henry: Angela Thornton went missing in June 2007 and the unidentified body we recovered has been dead less than six months. I think you murdered both of them and what I need to know is where you buried Angela and who the unidentified girl is.'

'I don't know what you are talking about.'

'Yes you do, you're lying.'

'Why would I lie?'

'You didn't kill Angela, you just want us to think you

did. The more the merrier, is that it, Henry? Another one for the front page in the papers?'

'You are such a bunch of fucking wankers – why are you wasting my time? I killed that bitch like all the others. I took off her bracelet and I kept it with the rest of my gear, so go on, charge me.'

He pushed back his chair and Mike ordered him to sit down.

'You got a mouth, have you? I was beginning to think you was dumb.'

He turned on Kumar and prodded him.

'Get me out of here.'

Kumar shrank away from him. Oates's rage was starting to surface.

'What are you fuckers waiting for? I done all those, right? RIGHT?'

He shoved his hand towards the stack of victims' photographs.

'I dunno their names, I don't give a fucking shit about a single one of them. Who cares what time I met them, where I fucked them? I am sick of this, I killed them, I buried them and you dug them up, right? RIGHT?'

Kumar told his client to calm down and Oates raised his hands.

'For Chrissake, what more do you want from me?'

'Timmy Bradford, did he kill Angela Thornton?' asked Langton.

Oates's mood suddenly changed and he began to laugh out loud, shaking his head and smiling.

Anna felt her phone vibrate and dashed out of the viewing room as she couldn't get good reception in there. It was Pete Jenkins. The results were in. She waited a few moments, listening to Oates, who was still laughing in the interview room. She knocked on the door and looked in on him; he was flushed and gesturing wildly and refusing to answer any further questions. It was Mike and not Langton who came out.

'Give me ten minutes with Oates,' she said, before he could ask her what she wanted. She watched, holding her breath, as Mike spoke to Langton, who gestured to her to go in.

Langton spoke into the tape recorder, stating the time and that Detective Chief Inspector Travis had now replaced DCI Lewis. She was flushed and very tense as she quietly put down her briefcase. Langton didn't say anything, but from the look on his face she knew he was thinking that it had better be good, especially as she had interrupted the interview at such a vital moment.

'You're aware, Mr Oates, that we recovered a body from the wood close to the quarry,' she began, knowing that she had to play her hand carefully.

'Yeah, you dug up four, didn't you?'

'Please don't interrupt me. Angela Thornton is not one of those four bodies as her dental records don't match any of them. So this leaves us with one unknown female, which as I'm sure you understand we need to identify so we can inform her family.'

Anna passed across a photograph of the black patent leather knee-high boots.

'Do you recall ever seeing these boots, Mr Oates?'

'No.'

'The boots belonged to a girl called Morag Kelly; she was in a rehab clinic with your daughter Corinna. Are you sure you have never seen them before?'

'Yes, I'm sure.'

'These boots were found in the basement where you lived, Mr Oates.'

'So, I get stuff from charity shops and car boot sales.'

Anna brought out more photographs, of cheap under-wear, and tapped them with her pencil.

'What about these items, would you say you got these from a charity shop?'

'What the fuck is this? I've never seen none of this shit before.'

Langton sat with his hands folded in front of him, with no idea where Anna was going with this line of question-ing, yet he couldn't ask her to divulge anything in front of Oates and his solicitor. Kumar seemed equally nonplussed, as Oates pushed the photographs away.

'You were accused of molesting Corinna—'

Oates interrupted her, angrily saying that only his wife had accused him, that he hadn't and would never have interfered with his own daughter. The next photograph Anna put down was the mortuary shot of the decomposed and as yet unidentified victim. She used the same pencil to indicate the hair.

'As you can see, most of the hair is no longer attached to the skull. It doesn't matter as through toxicology tests the scientists can still say the victim was a heroin addict.'

The next photograph was from the burial site, red markers indicating each grave's location. The pictures were taken at various stages of the exhumations. Anna kept her voice low as she pointed out the graves of Kelly Mathews, Mary Suffolk, Alicia Jones and the grave with the uniden-tified body.

'The boots were stolen from a rehab centre by this victim. The underwear belonged to her and I can now tell you that a comparison with your ex-wife Eileen's

DNA has identified the body as that of her daughter.'

Oates drew back in his chair. Kumar muttered to Anna that this information should have been disclosed to him, and she replied that it had only just been verified to her.

'You killed your own daughter, didn't you, Mr Oates? Whether or not you also sexually abused her–'

'I never fucking touched her!' he screeched.

'Yes you did, YES YOU DID – what happened? Did she come to you after she'd run away from the rehab centre, come to ask for your help, and you—'

'I never touched her, I swear before God I never touched her.'

Langton warned Oates to sit still as he had started kicking at the table leg.

'If you didn't kill her, why did you take her to the woods and bury her alongside your other victims?' Anna said.

'Someone else did that, not me, I didn't do that.'

'Your own daughter couldn't be allowed to get away from you, was it that your wife had taken your children away from you before you could molest them and so when she turns up you couldn't keep your hands off her?'

'NO, NO.'

'YES. Your own flesh and blood, you stripped her naked – look at how we found her.'

Oates stopped kicking the table, and asked for water. He drank the entire bottle, screwed the cap back on and crushed it in his hand.

'I'm no pervert, and I'm gonna come clean with you, about the Angela girl as well.'

Langton gave an open-handed gesture; making eye contact with Anna he took over.

'Well that's really very impressive, but you see, Mr

Oates, we have already charged Tim Bradford with her murder.'

'No, that's not right.'

Kumar looked nonplussed, as he was not privy to the fact that Timmy Bradford had admitted his part in the death of Angela Thornton. For the first time Oates looked bewildered, and Langton leaned across and snatched the crushed plastic bottle out of his hand.

Mike Lewis was in the viewing room, Barbara standing by his chair.

'I don't understand why he's claiming ...' Her voice trailed off.

Mike agreed with her that it didn't make sense. Either Oates wanted to claim he murdered Angela out of some sick need for attention, or he was trying to make out he was mad by admitting to anything so he could be deemed unfit to plead and his admissions would be held as unreliable. He nodded to the monitor screen.

'He's a clever bastard, or he's been so well briefed by that bastard Kumar that he knows his way around the law.'

'Why would Kumar do such a thing?'

'This gets to trial and it'll be the focus of media attention on a par with Fred and Rosemary West, never mind the Yorkshire Ripper.'

'Beats me.'

'What beats you, Barbara?'

'These games. It starts not to be about the victims, doesn't it?'

Mike stood up.

'It's always about the victims for us, that's the big difference, and if that scum killed his own daughter and shows hardly any reaction he's got to be—'

Mike just managed to stop himself blurting out the word psychopath. But there on the screen was Oates, head bowed, crying like a baby, blowing his nose and wiping his eyes.

'I never done another one after her.'

They took a break so that Oates could be fed while they disclosed to Kumar the admissions that Bradford had made about Angela Thornton and how he had caused the death of his own mother and then intended to frame Oates with her murder. Kumar reported that Oates had told him that Mrs Douglas was not at the flat when he'd gone there and that Bradford had said she was in hospital after a heart attack. Furthermore, Oates was adamant that he, not Bradford, had killed Angela Thornton but had not told him how or why. Langton told Kumar to stop trying to pull a fast one for a psychologist's nut and gut decision that Oates was not fit to plead. Kumar was insistent that no matter what Langton thought, he had not instructed his client to make false confessions; he certainly didn't want to upset Langton again after the incident at the quarry and he hoped the matter of the press helicopter had been forgotten.

After Oates had had some food, Langton and Mike continued interviewing him for another two hours. Oates claimed that Corinna had turned up late one night at his basement in the late spring. She had been very strung out and in need of a fix as she had started using heroin again as soon as she had run away from the rehab centre. She had gone out and turned a few tricks to get money and he insisted that he had told her that he didn't want her around. She had come back in an even worse state, fallen asleep, and when he went to wake her she was dead. He had described undressing her, wrapping her body up, stealing a car and driving her to the woods. Langton didn't believe his account of the way Corinna had died, but there was not as yet any forensic evidence to prove he was lying and he doubted Oates would ever admit to what he really did to her, his own daughter.

Lastly, Oates explained how Angela Thornton had really died. He said that everything happened as Timmy Bradford had told them, up to a point. They'd seen Angela alone and drunk by the Tube station, persuaded her into the car and to go to Bradford's flat, then to have more alcohol with them both. Timmy got drunk and had sex with her in the bedroom. Oates said that he had carried on drinking a bottle of brandy, and the more drunk he got the more he thought she was a cheap slut – in fact she reminded him of what his mother was like. When he went into the bedroom, Timmy and Angela were both out of it in a drunken stupor. The bombshell came when Oates said that he had felt like a child again seeing his mother in bed with yet another man. He wanted to end the misery so he put a pillow over her face and suffocated her. To him it wasn't Angela he had killed but his mother. The next morning he realized what he had done and thought it was funny. He told Timmy that the police would think he had raped and killed Angela. Timmy thought it was all his fault, and started to panic and cry. Oates realized that by getting rid of the body he would have a hold over Timmy that he could call upon whenever he wanted something from him. He used Bradford's car to take the body to the quarry. The pathway along the side of the woods was so wet and muddy he didn't dare risk driving down it, not after the incident with the Jeep, so he carried her to the first part of the woods and dug a shallow grave with his hands as he didn't have a spade or anything he could use to bury her properly, and covered her over with old logs and leaves. Afterwards he cleaned the car and sold it to a dealer at a car auction close to Wandsworth Bridge. He had kept her bracelet as he knew he could always use it against Timmy Bradford.

Oates confirmed that over the last five years he had obtained sums of money from Bradford, threatening that if he didn't give him what he wanted he would go to the police and tell them about Angela. He knew Bradford would have to help him after his escape because of the hold he had over him. Oates admitted he was surprised that Bradford had intended to fit him up with his mother's murder, and the coolness of this statement left Mike and Langton stunned.

After the interviews were over Oates was formally charged with four further murders: Rebekka Jordan, Kelly Mathews, Mary Suffolk and Alicia Jones. Langton had contacted the CPS, who had said that they would want to read the files on Angela Thornton and Corinna Oates before they decided whether to have him charged with their murders as well. This was not only due to the fact that Angela's body had not as yet been recovered but also because there was a possibility that Oates might be lying and Bradford had killed her after all, or they had both done it together. As for Corinna, Oates had denied murdering her and said she died of an overdose, so the CPS decided to wait for the forensic and pathology work to be done on the body, before reaching a decision on whether or not to charge him with her murder.

Langton had asked for a crate of wine to be brought into the incident room, and they had a surprise visitor, Paul Barolli, on crutches, looking a lot thinner and very pale-faced, who was given a round of applause. It wasn't exactly a celebration, but there was a sense of incredible relief. Meanwhile, the work would continue for months in prepa-ration for the trials, and the pathology department would have their work cut out for them as they continued the detailed examination of the victims' remains to try and establish the likely dates when each victim had been buried.

Members of the team would also be present at the funeral of not only Rebekka Jordan but those of all the victims. Grieving parents and other members of their families might then manage to reach some kind of peace, but they would all have to face the trial and learn the horrific details of what happened to their daughters.

Anna did not call Eileen Oates personally, but informed McBride that they had found Corinna Oates's body. It would be left to a family liaison officer to tell Eileen.

Anna was sipping the last drop of her wine, watching the party begin to break up, when Langton approached to say he would like a word with her in private. She saw him asking Mike if he could use his office. Mike glanced over, and then turned away, back to his conversation with Barolli, who was sitting down. Joan and Barbara had fussed over him and he'd told them he was going on extended leave for while.

Anna closed the office door. Langton was sitting behind the desk, flipping a pack of cigarettes up on its end and back flat down again.

'You wanted to see me?'

'Too damned right I do. You walk in on an interrogation, having, I believe, not mentioned to a single member of the team the fucking mind-blowing information regarding the fate of the suspect's bloody daughter.'

'Hang on a second, it was all just supposition until I got the DNA result from Pete Jenkins.'

'What do you take me for, take us all for? You have photographs of boots, underwear, you'd got a toxicology report . . .'

'It wasn't finalized, it still isn't, I said there was heroin found in her hair to unnerve him.'

'Lying to a suspect can get interviews thrown out in court, you know that.'

'Yes, but I'd received a phone call about it and besides you're always pulling tricks in inter—'

'This is not about me! What about the DNA? How long were you working solo on this line of enquiry, Travis?'

She felt her legs begin to shake.

'Again it was just supposition on my part, knowing that Corinna had run away from the rehab centre.'

'Is that on the board?' he snapped.

'I think it might be, but I was just piecing together bits of information that I'd picked up.'

'That you declined to share with anyone else.'

'That is not quite true – I didn't get to speak to the contact from the rehab until late at night, the girl Morag Kelly.'

'This on the board, is it?'

475

'No it isn't, I didn't have the time.'

'So go on, you got in contact with – who was it?'

'Morag Kelly, she had been in rehab with Corinna Oates, and the reason I wanted to talk to her was to try and find out what clothes Corinna might have been wearing and a description of her hairstyle.'

'Why was that? Did you happen to mention this to anyone?'

'Joan or Barbara – I can't remember – one of them got me Morag's number.'

'But they didn't know why you wanted it.'

'No. I knew that Mike and you were busy with Timmy Bradford's interview and I went to the forensic lab. This was after Morag had mentioned that she thought Corinna had stolen her boots. I found the boots described by her in the bundles of clothes removed from Oates's basement.'

'But you didn't mention this to anyone?'

'No, because I couldn't be certain they were the same boots until I'd seen them for myself.'

'So when did you start this DNA enquiry?'

Anna had to gasp for breath, and her legs were shaking even more as she tried hard to control her temper.

'When I saw the body of the unidentified victim.'

'I see. So while we were interrogating Bradford you were running around the mortuary . . .'

'I wasn't running around. I went there out of interest, and I told you when I got back that we had not recovered Angela Thornton and therefore had an unidentified victim. Also I—'

'Yes, yes. I know this – so you go on your own accord out of interest to check the remains, am I right?'

'Yes, and I noticed that her hair was braided and very

dark. Eileen Oates said Corinna used to wear it in braids like Jamaican girls do. I wasn't sure about her ethnic origin.'

Langton flicked at the cigarette box; it was really irritating.

'Tell me why the ethnic origin was of such interest?'

'Well it's bloody obvious we didn't have the remains identified, so I suspected from the hair that it could also possibly be a black girl—'

'Yes, yes, you are missing the point. Why did you request DNA samples from the victim to be matched with Oates?'

'The forensic anthropologist wasn't sure but said the unidentified victim could be white European.'

'Oh, so now the body is not black but white.'

'The age range fitted Corinna, as did the decomposition to the time frame from when she absconded from rehab. Do you mind if I sit down?'

'Be my guest.'

She sat down.

'I had interviewed Bradford and Ira Zacks and they had told me that Eileen Oates had maybe forced Oates into marrying her because she was pregnant.'

He did a mock look around the room.

'I never had a report about this. You inform anyone else about this shotgun wedding?'

'No I did not,' she snapped. 'At the time it did not appear to be of any consequence.'

'Oh I see, so when did it, in your opinion, become of consequence?'

She had to clear her throat before she could continue.

'Bradford told me that when the baby was born, Oates flew into a rage and claimed it could not be his child because it was dark-skinned and Ira Zacks made a similar comment.'

Langton waved at her with his hand.

'All this is in your notes, yes?'

'Yes, but I didn't think at that time it was of importance to the case so I didn't add it to the incident board, as it was eighteen years ago.'

'When did it become important then?'

'Bits of information just all suddenly seemed to fit together. Corinna missing, the boots, the hair colour and hairstyle of the body.'

Langton ran his fingers along the edge of the desk, clicking them, and then looked up.

'Well go on, I'm listening.'

'I began to wonder if the unidentified girl was Corinna. Eileen Oates had been adamant that she was Henry's daughter so I asked for her hair to be tested, and knowing we had Oates's DNA on record I wanted to determine from familial DNA if it was his daughter. I still only had the boots to really make the connection, the hair was just a possibility.'

'And?'

She felt as if she was on trial, and it was almost impossibly hard for her to keep her temper in check.

'It was negative, the hair was no longer suitable for a full DNA profile, only mitochondrial inherited from the mother.'

He leaned forwards.

'Negative, negative?'

'Yes.'

'Jesus Christ, are you now telling me it wasn't his daughter?'

'If you would just let me finish: it was obviously

disappointing, and one of the reasons why I didn't put all this out to the team because I still wasn't sure—'

'Corinna Oates is not his fucking daughter?'

'NO, but I then had sent from Glasgow a swab from Eileen Oates, and a blood sample which she agreed to give. Corinna is her daughter, but Oates is not her biological father, even though he is named on her birth certificate.'

Langton jerked at the knot of his tie so hard it came loose.

'But that still doesn't prove it's Corinna. Eileen Oates could have a hundred daughters for all we know. I can't believe you didn't see fit not to divulge any of this to the team, to me, to DCI Lewis.'

'The Scottish DNA database sent a copy of Corinna's DNA profile to Pete Jenkins and he's still working on a bone sample from the body for a direct comparison and match.'

'This just gets better and better, Travis! So you made Oates think in interview that Corinna was his daughter without a full DNA match?'

'No, I said that a comparison with his ex-wife Eileen's DNA has identified the body as his daughter.'

'You lured him into a confession with a lie. If Kumar picks up on this that whole interview will be out the window, case over.'

'I didn't lie to him. Yes, I took a calculated gamble, but it paid off.'

'You seem to have forgotten that I was blind in that interview. I had no idea what you knew or where you were going. You accused him of murdering his own flesh and blood when she wasn't. The defence will call it oppression and ask for the interview to be thrown out!'

She stood up to face him. She sensed her control was on the verge of slipping.

'I only got the result ten minutes before I came into the interview room. Yes I had the photographs of the boots, yes I had the photographs of the underwear, yes I had her identified when nobody else bloody had, and I can't understand why you are interrogating me as if I have acted or conducted myself in an unprofessional way. Everything I requested from the lab was logged and listed, everything I wanted from forensics was logged and listed — do you want to see the reports?'

'Sit down.'

'No I won't. You know maybe, just maybe, you should be giving me a fucking pat on the shoulder. The connection between Oates and the murder of his daughter was what opened him up: after he was accused of having sex with her, abusing her, he hated it! I DIDN'T DO THAT! From then on he started telling the truth. Now you maybe don't like the fact that it was me and not you that brought the evidence to the table, but facts are facts.'

'Sit down, Travis, don't you dare yell at me.'

'I am not yelling!' She was. 'I am telling you the facts. You brought me onto this team because of Rebekka Jordan, a case from five years ago that you headed up. Do I hear "Congratulations, Travis"? I have been out there working my arse off, so EXCUSE me if I have not marked up a couple of items on the board.'

Still refusing to sit, she faced him across the desk.

'Maybe, sir, I should also have added to the incident board that the victim Rebekka Jordan's doll's house was discovered in your flat! Not on the incident board, why not? Oh, it wouldn't look very good, would it? WOULD IT?'

She leaned across the desk, pushing her face towards him, spittle forming at the edge of her mouth in her rage.

'If it hadn't been for me, Chief Superintendent, we'd never have got the Cherokee Jeep connection. You want me to list how much I have brought to this case, do you? DO YOU?'

The slap was so hard it sent her reeling sideways, but she managed to stay upright, her fists clenched. She lunged at him across the desk, swinging a punch; he was so shocked he stepped back, away from her. She picked up the telephone and threw it at him, then anything she could lay her hands on she hurled with as much strength as she could. He dodged sideways and the next moment she was round the desk and fighting like a wildcat, kicking and punching. He didn't defend himself, just tried to catch hold of her arms.

He was amazed at her strength, and it took all of his to grip hold of her and lift her off her feet. Then her right foot kicked him viciously in his injured kneecap, and he was forced to let go of her as he crunched over in agony.

She paced up and down, wrapping her arms around herself, muttering almost inaudibly that if it wasn't for her they would never have gone to the quarry, if it wasn't for her they would not have uncovered the fact that Bradford's mother was already dead. He leaned with one hand on the desk, the other rubbing at his knee as she opened her briefcase and began ripping up pages from her notebook, hurling them into the air as she continued, 'Did anyone else bring up the excavation of the Jordans' property? NO! Here's my notes, want to read my notes about the way I pieced together that the Jordans' house extension had to be a lead? What about Andrew Markham? He only employed Oates to work for him, who got that lead? ME. All on the board, sir, everything written down.'

One of her high-heeled shoes had fallen off, her hair had come loose from its band, and two buttons on her blouse had come undone. She was panting, her chest heaving, and there was a pitiful pain-wracked expression in her eyes. Slowly the rage calmed and she gave a helpless look around the office as if only just aware of what she had done.

'It's okay,' he said softly.

He gently took her in his arms, her heart was beating so rapidly he could feel it against his chest.

'It's okay,' he repeated.

'Why wasn't I able to stop it? I didn't do enough.'

Her voice was muffled and he couldn't quite make out what she said.

'Why did he have to die? I didn't do the work, it was my fault, I should have been more aware that it might happen.'

Then he understood. What he had just witnessed was the rage he had long suspected lay hidden, and had finally erupted, all this time after the trauma of losing her fiancé. Anna blamed herself for not being more aware of the danger Ken Hudson had been in, as a crazed prisoner who'd had a fixation on her had murdered him. Her obsession with the Oates murder case had really been fuelled by her guilt, and her refusal to grieve.

He stroked her hair as she calmed.

'I want you to take a couple of weeks off, while we get ready for the trial, are you listening to me?'

She nodded.

'Then you get back to work.'

She nodded again.

'Now I think we'd better clear up Mike's office.'

She moved away from him, picked up her shoe, and watched him bending and wincing as he collected all her torn scraps of paper from her notebook.

'Now we have to be singing off the same hymn sheet, Travis. What happened here is over and done with. I guarantee that crew out there were all ears, so I will tell them we just had a bit of an argument and you accidentally threw the telephone at the wall!'

She laughed then went to him and held him, resting her head on his shoulder.

'Thank you.'

'Think nothing of it, button up your blouse, and what went on we put to bed, I mean it . . . it's over. That said, it was a very low blow, kicking an injured man where you knew it would hurt.'

'I wasn't aiming for your knee.' She gave him a wonderful smile.

'Don't push your luck with me, Travis, I'll be limping out of here now.'

He didn't; they both went back into the incident room and behaved as if nothing had happened. Langton quietly joked with Barolli about Joan bringing him her mother's home-cooked meals in hospital. He noticed Anna walking out, briefcase in her hand and back straight; she didn't say goodnight to anyone.

'Everything all right, guv?' Mike asked.

'Everything's fine, but you might need to order a new desk phone – tripped on the wire and hit my bloody knee.'

'Travis has gone, has she?'

Langton gave him a cool dismissive glance and helped himself to a glass of wine.

'Well, she certainly did her homework,' Mike observed.

'Yes she did, Mike.'

He held up his glass.

'Cheers.'

He turned towards the incident board as he sipped his rather tepid white wine. The faces of the victims all appeared in shadows – it was late, the main lights turned low. He walked slowly from section to section, victim to victim. Lastly he paused in front of the photographs of little Rebekka Jordan. He more than anyone knew the toll this enquiry had taken on them all, especially Travis. She was a loner, like himself, and he knew that she was probably one of the best detectives he had ever worked with. He turned to the room and raised his glass.

'To DCI Anna Travis.'

'Thank you very much, sir.' He turned in surprise. She had combed her hair and put fresh make-up on, showing no sign of what had taken place just minutes before. He watched her move from one member of the team to another, sipping her wine and smiling, until she came to stand beside him.

'How's your knee, sir?'

'Aching.'

'Like my heart. But I want you to know that I will take on board everything we discussed. I promise. Goodnight.'

For the second time he watched her leaving. The double doors swung closed behind her. His admiration for the way she handled herself went up another notch. DCI Anna Travis was a class act.

PRIME SUSPECT

Available in Paperback and e-Book

Detective Chief Inspector Jane Tennison is determined to catch the madman stalking women in the shadows of London, and after identifying a prime suspect, she'll do anything to make the charges against him stick. But perhaps most terrifying is her obsession with cracking the case, which threatens to destroy her life.

PRIME SUSPECT 2
A Face in the Crowd
Available in Paperback and e-Book

In one of London's poorest communities, filled with racial strife, the murder of a young black woman threatens to tear apart the already divided city. But Jane Tennison won't let anything get in the way of her passion for justice. As long as a killer is at large, stalking her prime suspect is Tennison's prime fixation.

PRIME SUSPECT 3
Silent Victims
Available in Paperback and e-Book

A sex-for-hire street kid is found dead in the apartment of a drag queen. But even more intriguing is the prime suspect—an influential do-gooder who is tied in to the secret lives of politicians, judges, and cops. Detective Jane Tennison has been told whom to arrest—and whom to back off of—but she can't follow orders knowing a destroyer of children is out there.

BOOKS BY LYNDA LA PLANTE

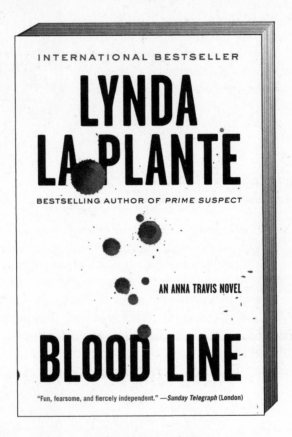

BLOOD LINE
An Anna Travis Novel
Available in Paperback and e-Book

Still reeling from the death of her fiancé, Detective Anna Travis has thrown herself into her new role as the chief inspector for London's murder squad. When Scotland Yard's Missing Persons Bureau is unable to locate the son of a court employee, the superintendent—James Langton, Anna's former lover—urges her to take on the suspicious assignment.